JUSTIC… UNLIMITED

GALACTIC JUSTICE

BEN CALDWELL collection cover artist

SUPERMAN created by **JERRY SIEGEL** and **JOE SHUSTER**
By special arrangement with the **Jerry Siegel** family

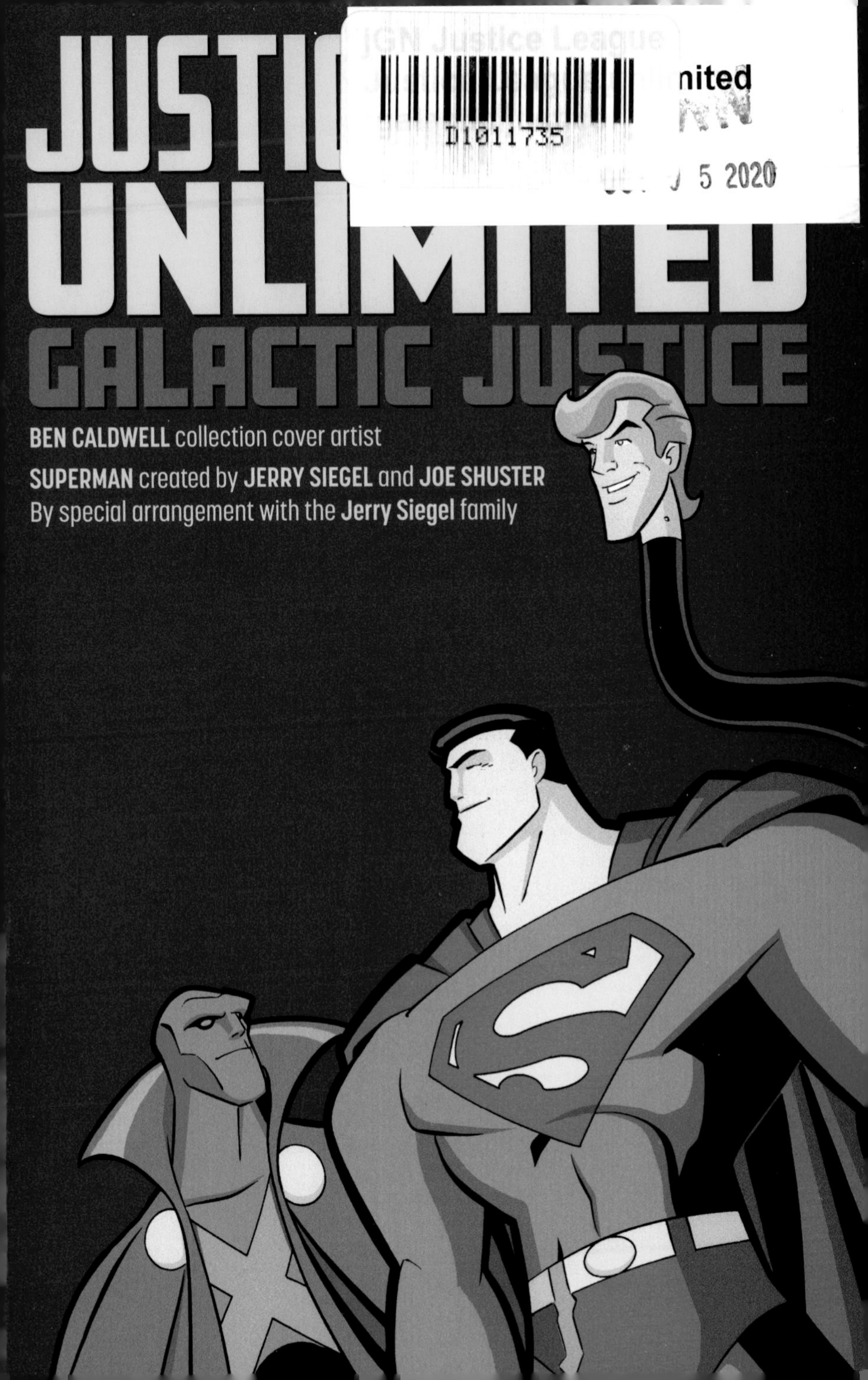

TOM PALMER JR.
MICHAEL WRIGHT
RACHEL GLUCKSTERN
Editors - Original Series

JEANINE SCHAEFER
Assistant Editor - Original Series

JEB WOODARD
Group Editor - Collected Editions

REZA LOKMAN
Editor - Collected Edition

STEVE COOK
Design Director - Books

AMIE BROCKWAY-METCALF
Publication Design

KATE DURRÉ
Publication Production

BOB HARRAS
Senior VP - Editor-in-Chief, DC Comics

JIM LEE
Publisher & Chief Creative Officer

BOBBIE CHASE
VP - Global Publishing Initiatives & Digital Strategy

DON FALLETTI
VP - Manufacturing Operations & Workflow Management

LAWRENCE GANEM
VP - Talent Services

ALISON GILL
Senior VP - Manufacturing & Operations

HANK KANALZ
Senior VP - Publishing Strategy & Support Services

DAN MIRON
VP - Publishing Operations

NICK J. NAPOLITANO
VP - Manufacturing Administration & Design

NANCY SPEARS
VP - Sales

JONAH WEILAND
VP - Marketing & Creative Services

MICHELE R. WELLS
VP & Executive Editor, Young Reader

DC Comics, 2900 West Alameda Ave., Burbank, CA 91505
Printed by LSC Communications, Crawfordsville, IN, USA. 7/17/20. First Printing.
ISBN: 978-1-77950-673-3
Library of Congress Cataloging-in-Publication Data is available.

PEFC Certified

This product is from sustainably managed forests and controlled sources

PEFC/29-31-337   www.pefc.org

CONTENTS

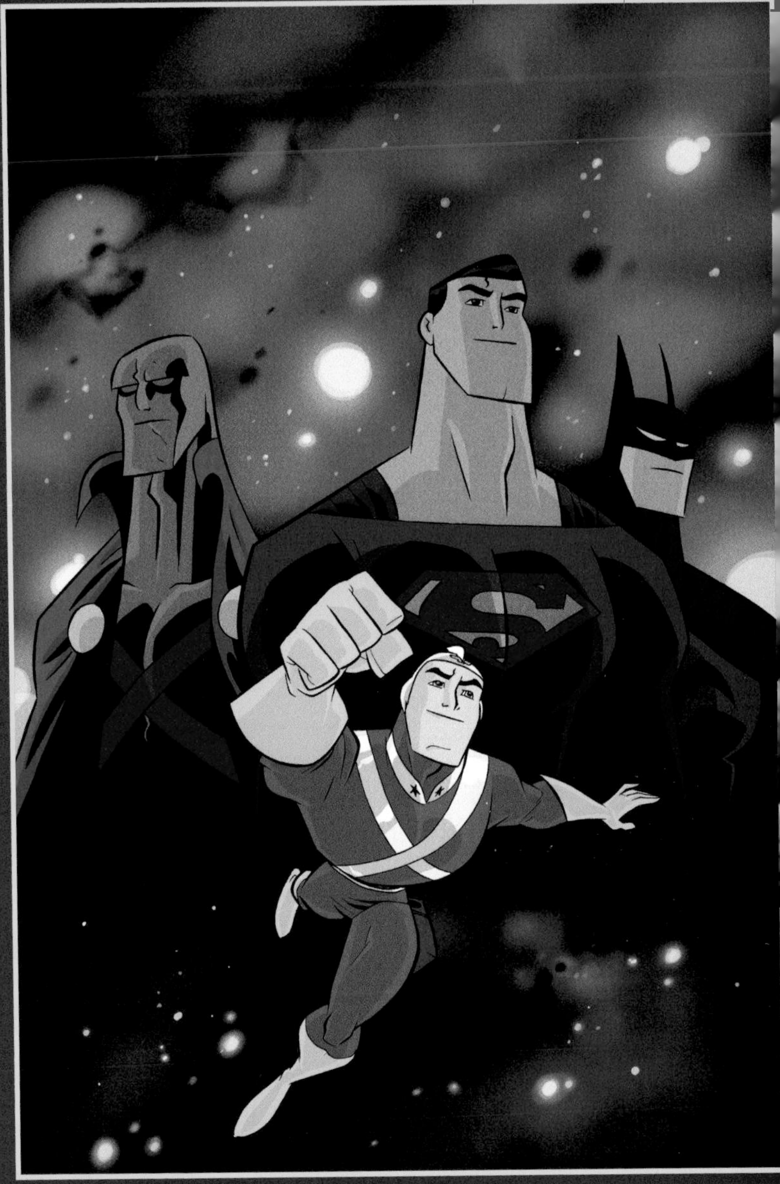

CHAPTER 1: LOCAL HERO

JUSTICE LEAGUE UNLIMITED

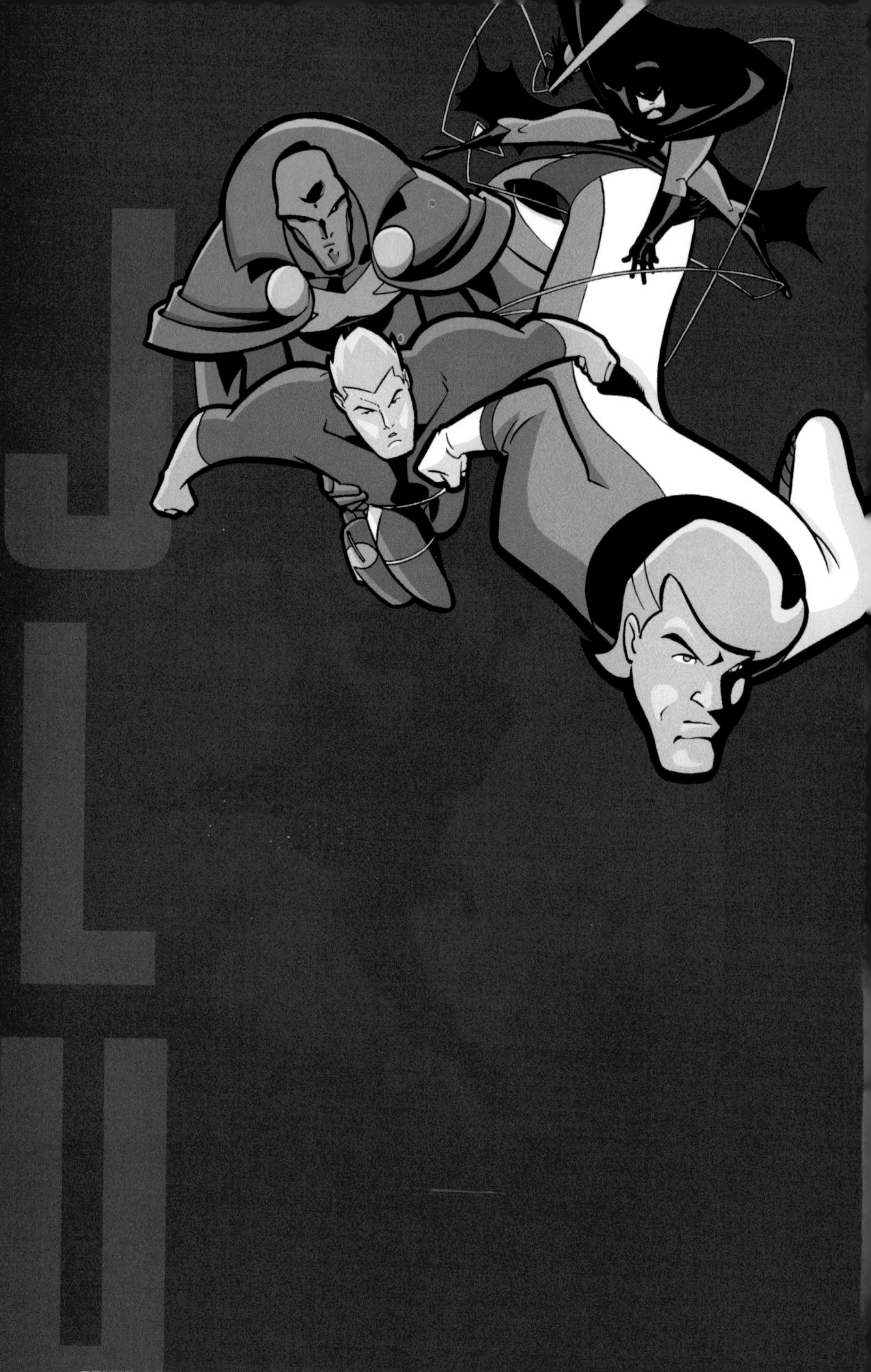
JLU

COVER ART BY BEN CALDWELL

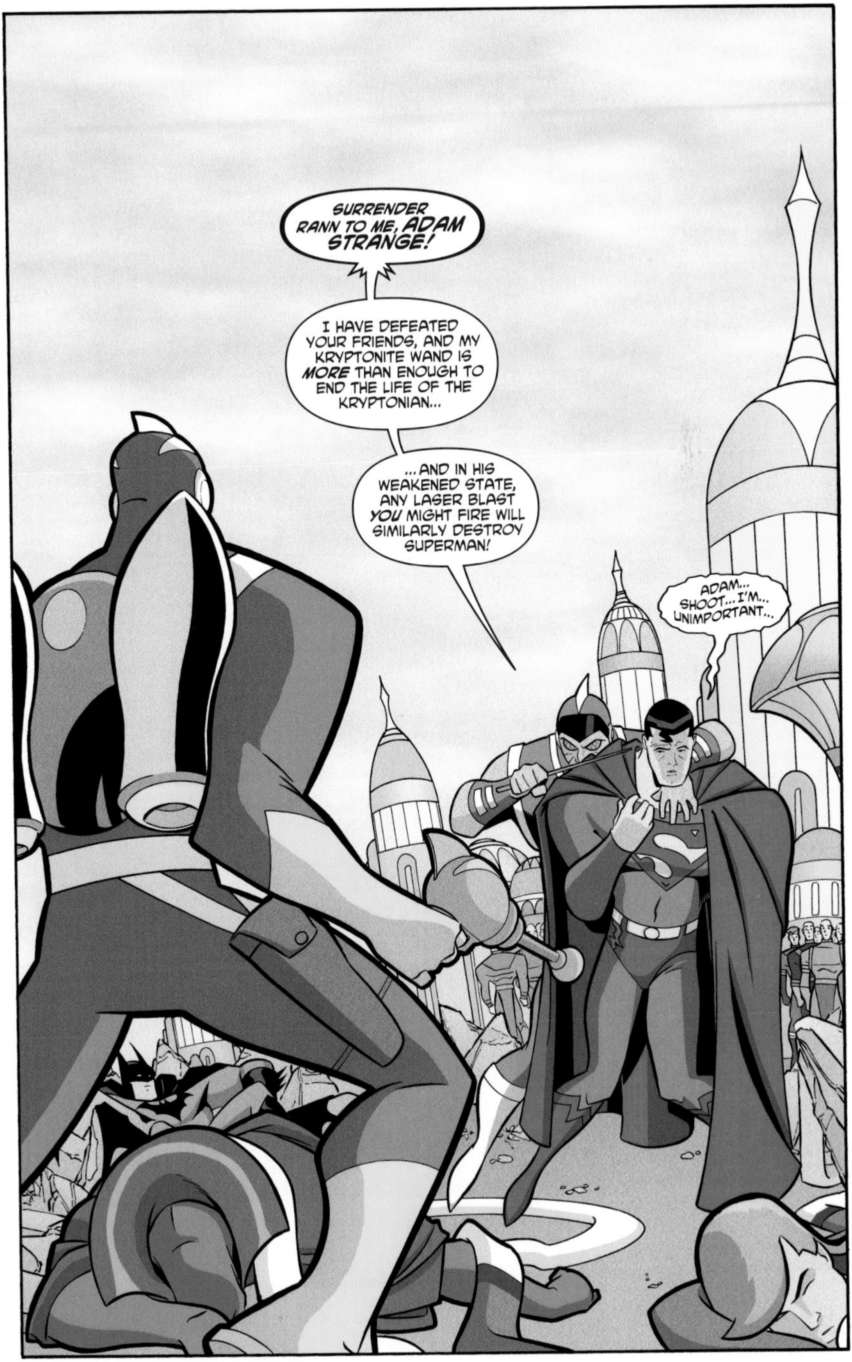
SURRENDER RANN TO ME, ADAM STRANGE!
I HAVE DEFEATED YOUR FRIENDS, AND MY KRYPTONITE WAND IS MORE THAN ENOUGH TO END THE LIFE OF THE KRYPTONIAN...
...AND IN HIS WEAKENED STATE, ANY LASER BLAST YOU MIGHT FIRE WILL SIMILARLY DESTROY SUPERMAN!
ADAM... SHOOT... I'M... UNIMPORTANT...

DON'T KNOW WHO YOU THINK YOU'RE TALKING TO, *KANJAR RO*...

...BUT I DIDN'T JUST FALL OFF THE *ZETA BEAM.*

I'VE BEEN PROTECTING THIS PLANET FOR A LONG TIME NOW...

I'VE KICKED YOUR ALIEN BUTT MORE TIMES THAN I CAN COUNT, *WITH* HELP FROM MY FRIENDS IN THE *JUSTICE LEAGUE* AND *WITHOUT...*

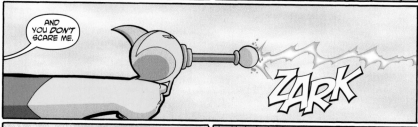

AND YOU *DON'T* SCARE ME.

ZARK

EH?

PING

SUPERMAN...

...HE'S ALL YOURS.

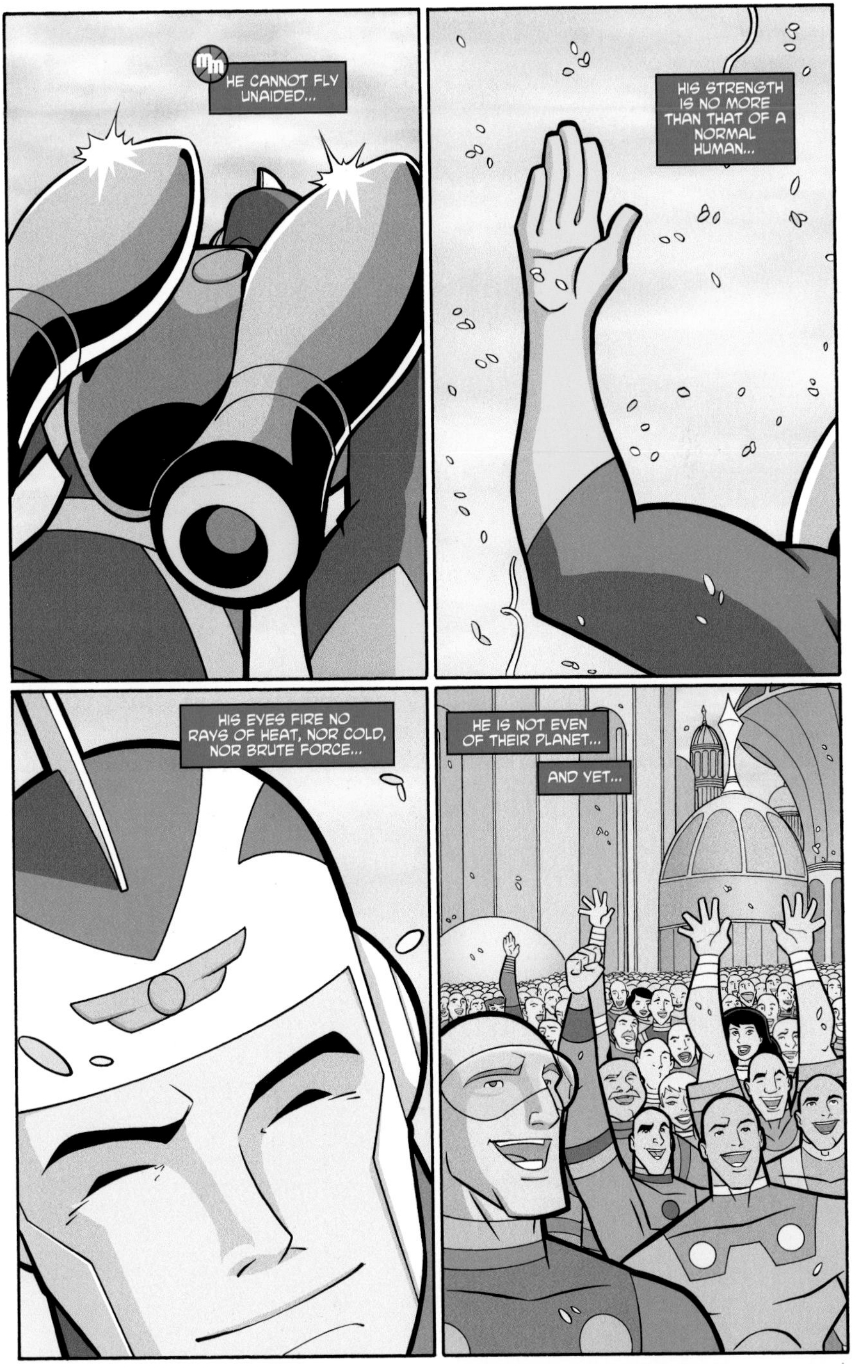
HE CANNOT FLY UNAIDED...
HIS STRENGTH IS NO MORE THAN THAT OF A NORMAL HUMAN...
HIS EYES FIRE NO RAYS OF HEAT, NOR COLD, NOR BRUTE FORCE...
HE IS NOT EVEN OF THEIR PLANET...
AND YET...

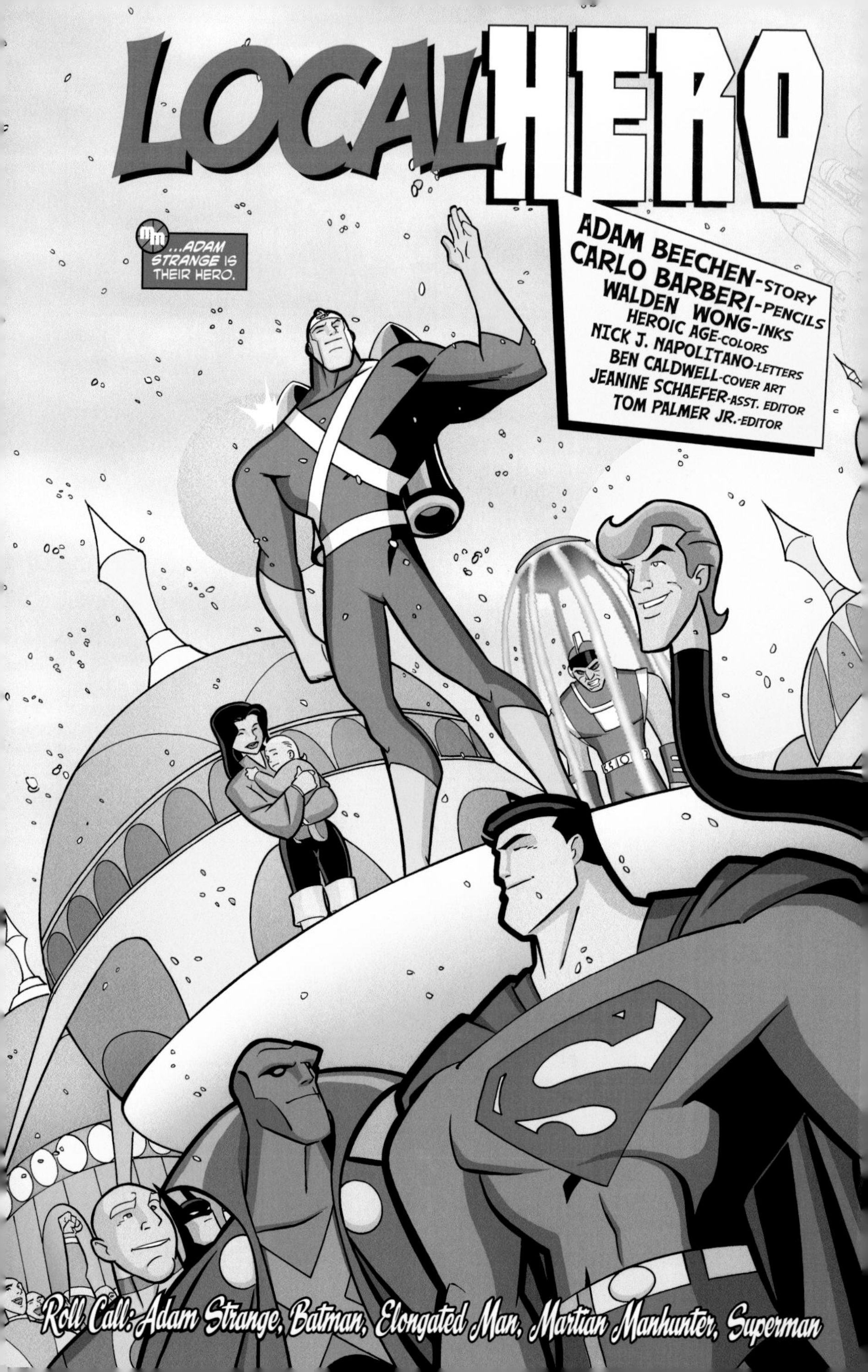
LOCAL HERO
...ADAM STRANGE IS THEIR HERO.
ADAM BEECHEN-STORY
CARLO BARBERI-PENCILS
WALDEN WONG-INKS
HEROIC AGE-COLORS
NICK J. NAPOLITANO-LETTERS
BEN CALDWELL-COVER ART
JEANINE SCHAEFER-ASST. EDITOR
TOM PALMER JR.-EDITOR
Roll Call: Adam Strange, Batman, Elongated Man, Martian Manhunter, Superman

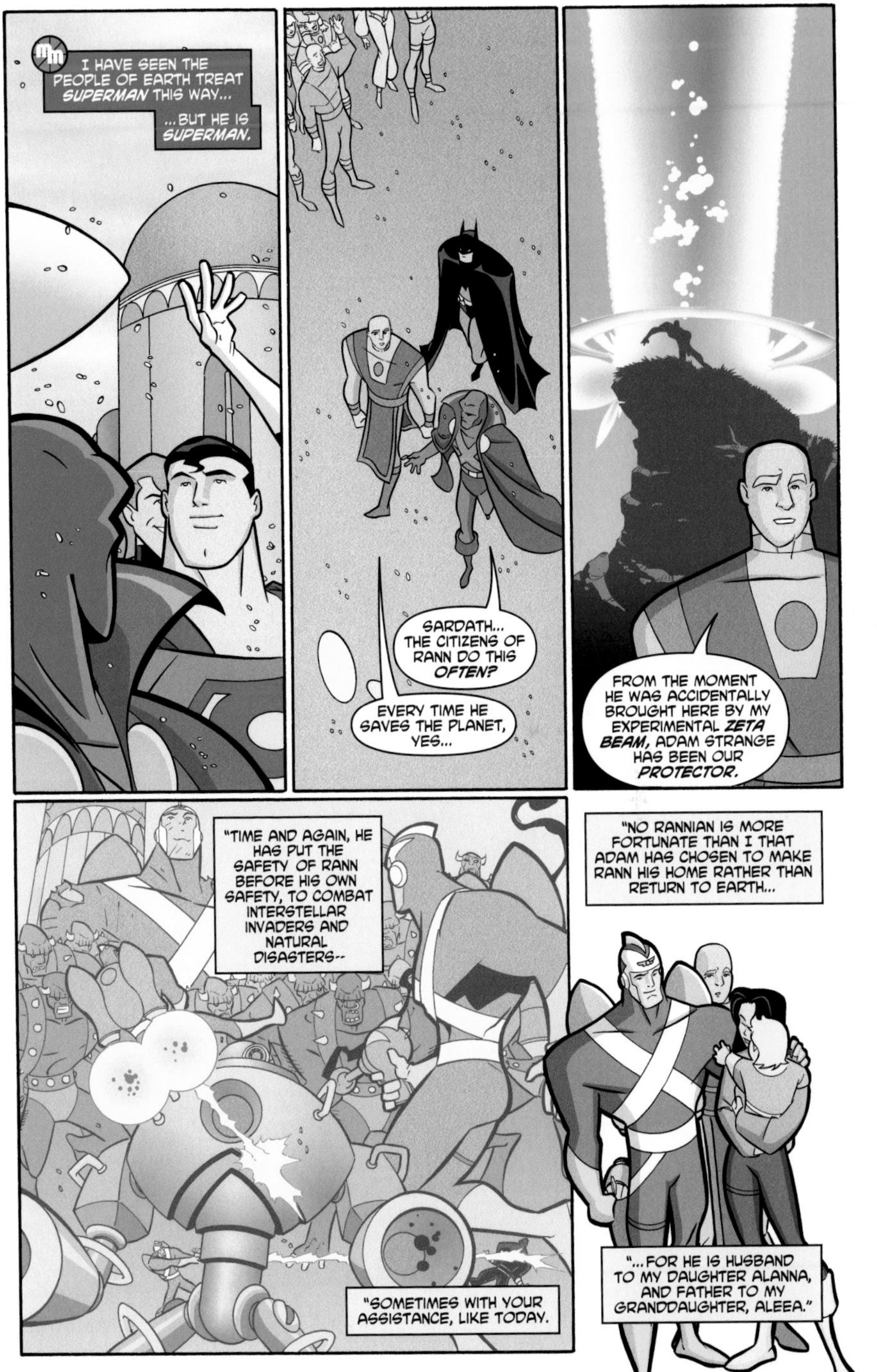
I HAVE SEEN THE PEOPLE OF EARTH TREAT SUPERMAN THIS WAY...
...BUT HE IS SUPERMAN.
SARDATH... THE CITIZENS OF RANN DO THIS OFTEN?
EVERY TIME HE SAVES THE PLANET, YES...
FROM THE MOMENT HE WAS ACCIDENTALLY BROUGHT HERE BY MY EXPERIMENTAL ZETA BEAM, ADAM STRANGE HAS BEEN OUR PROTECTOR.
"TIME AND AGAIN, HE HAS PUT THE SAFETY OF RANN BEFORE HIS OWN SAFETY, TO COMBAT INTERSTELLAR INVADERS AND NATURAL DISASTERS--
"SOMETIMES WITH YOUR ASSISTANCE, LIKE TODAY.
"NO RANNIAN IS MORE FORTUNATE THAN I THAT ADAM HAS CHOSEN TO MAKE RANN HIS HOME RATHER THAN RETURN TO EARTH...
"...FOR HE IS HUSBAND TO MY DAUGHTER ALANNA, AND FATHER TO MY GRANDDAUGHTER, ALEEA."

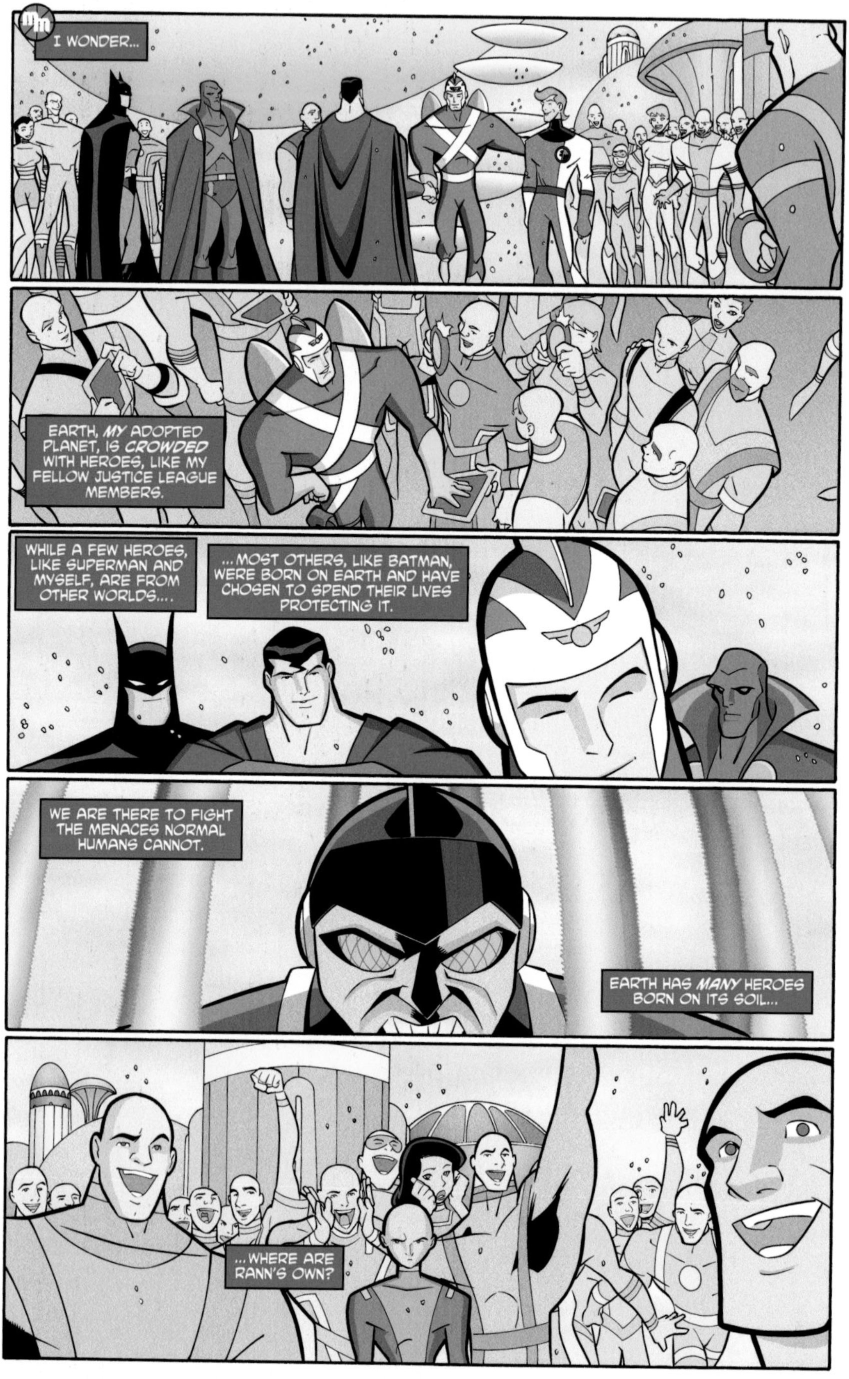
I WONDER...
EARTH, MY ADOPTED PLANET, IS CROWDED WITH HEROES, LIKE MY FELLOW JUSTICE LEAGUE MEMBERS.
WHILE A FEW HEROES, LIKE SUPERMAN AND MYSELF, ARE FROM OTHER WORLDS....
...MOST OTHERS, LIKE BATMAN, WERE BORN ON EARTH AND HAVE CHOSEN TO SPEND THEIR LIVES PROTECTING IT.
WE ARE THERE TO FIGHT THE MENACES NORMAL HUMANS CANNOT.
EARTH HAS MANY HEROES BORN ON ITS SOIL...
...WHERE ARE RANN'S OWN?

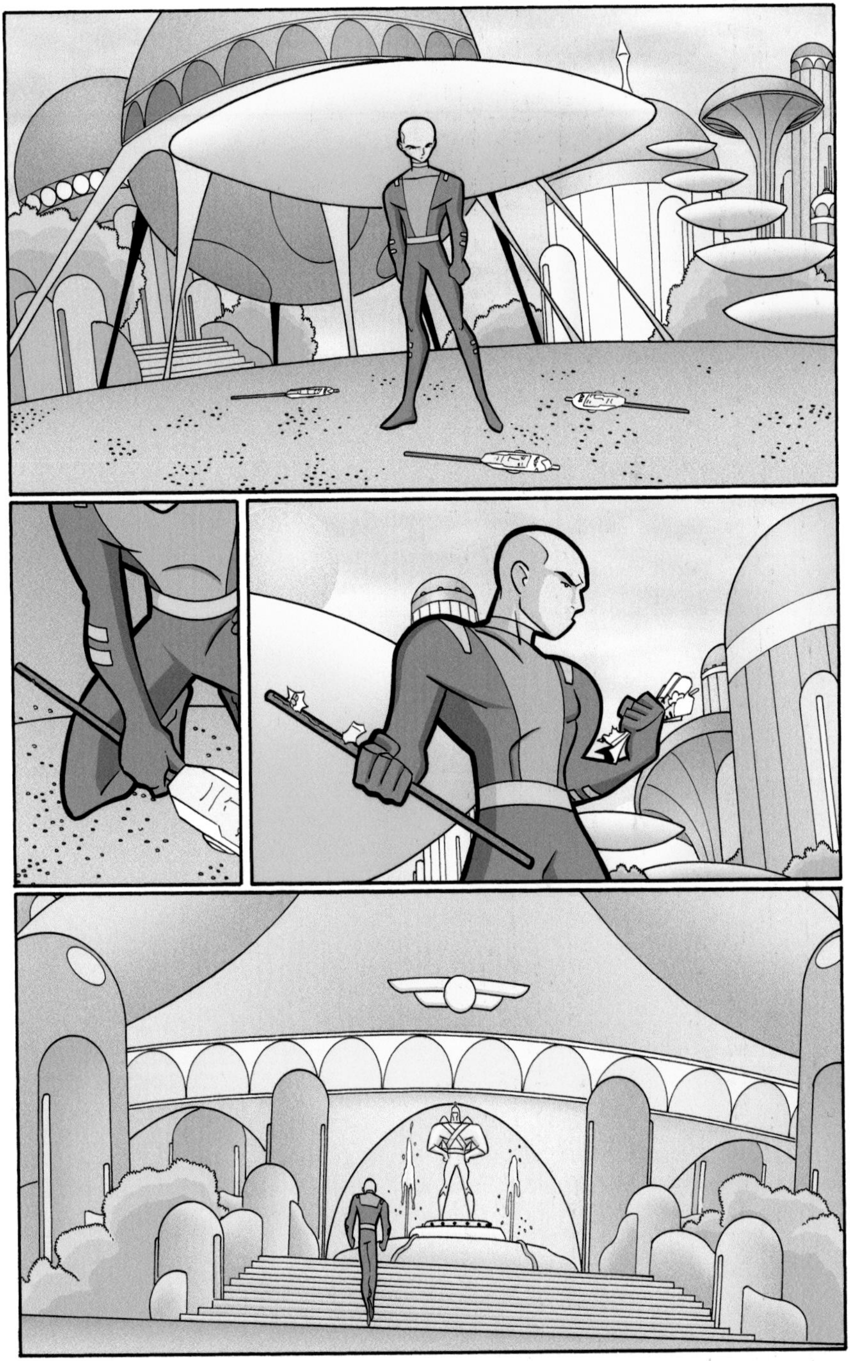

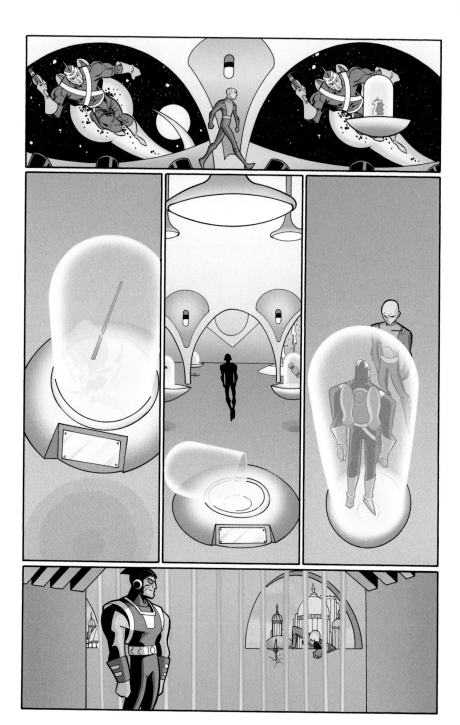

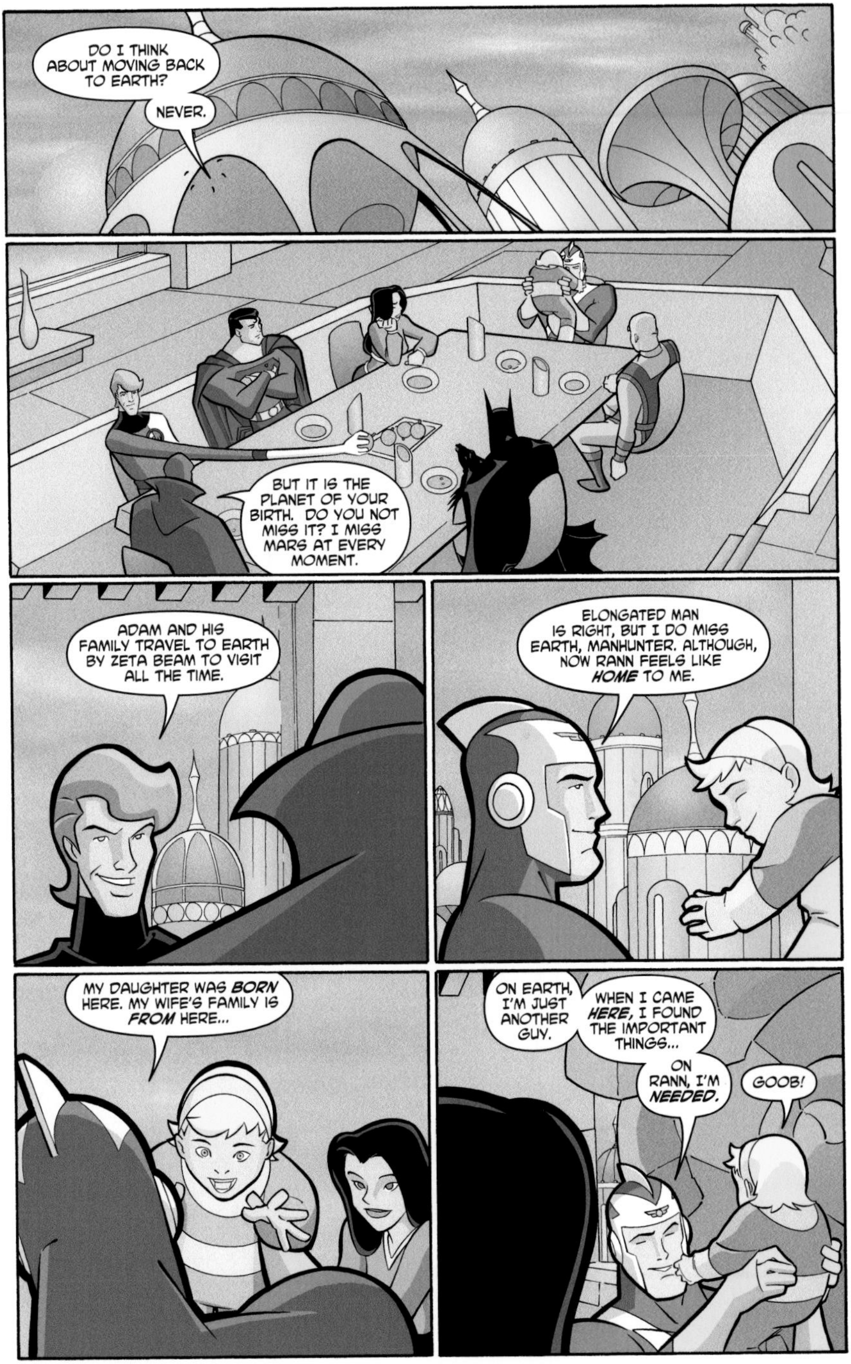
DO I THINK ABOUT MOVING BACK TO EARTH?
NEVER.
BUT IT IS THE PLANET OF YOUR BIRTH. DO YOU NOT MISS IT? I MISS MARS AT EVERY MOMENT.
ADAM AND HIS FAMILY TRAVEL TO EARTH BY ZETA BEAM TO VISIT ALL THE TIME.
ELONGATED MAN IS RIGHT, BUT I DO MISS EARTH, MANHUNTER. ALTHOUGH, NOW RANN FEELS LIKE *HOME* TO ME.
MY DAUGHTER WAS *BORN* HERE. MY WIFE'S FAMILY IS *FROM* HERE...
ON EARTH, I'M JUST ANOTHER GUY.
WHEN I CAME *HERE,* I FOUND THE IMPORTANT THINGS...
ON RANN, I'M *NEEDED.*
GOOB!

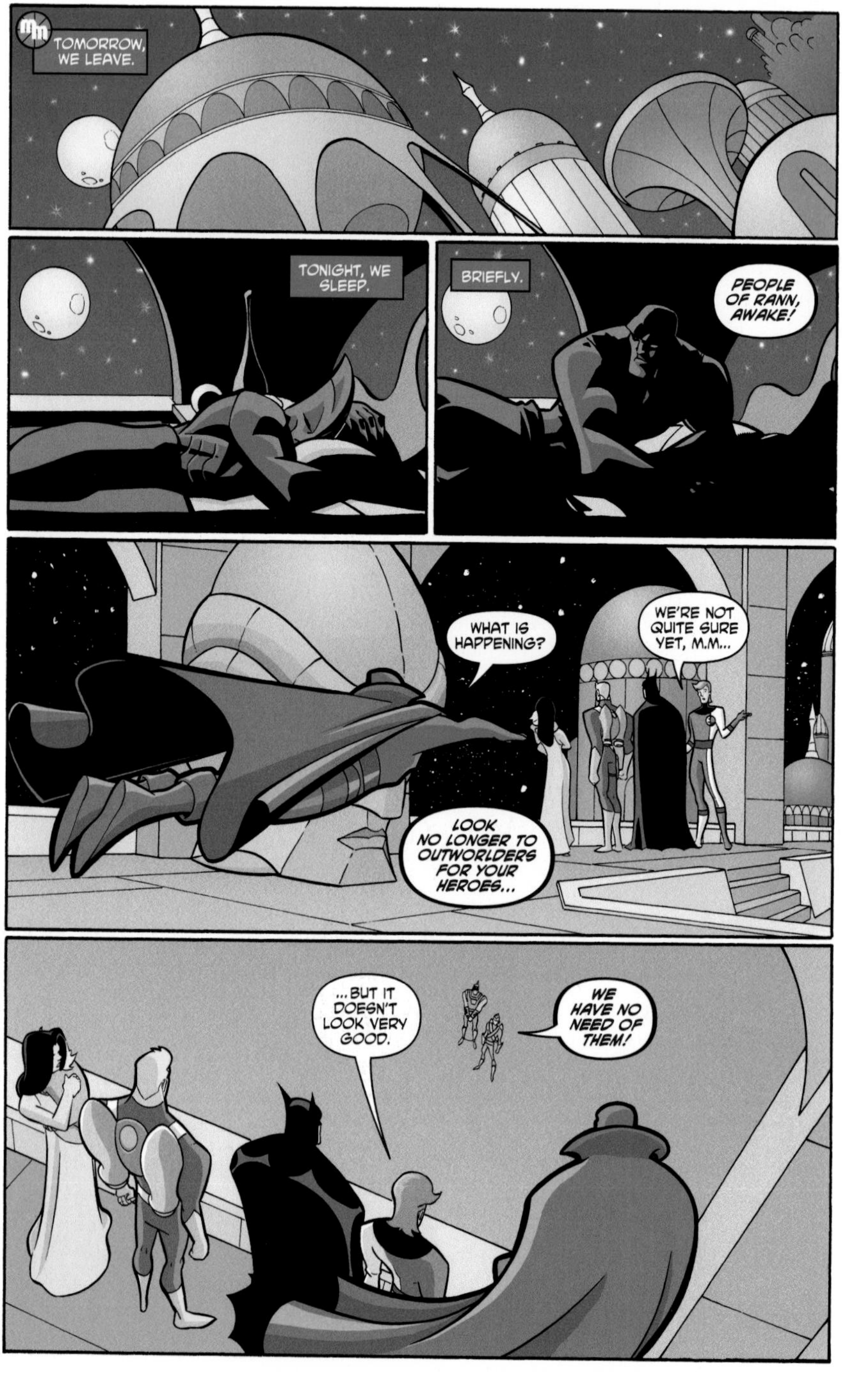
TOMORROW, WE LEAVE.
TONIGHT, WE SLEEP.
BRIEFLY.
PEOPLE OF RANN, AWAKE!
WHAT IS HAPPENING?
WE'RE NOT QUITE SURE YET, M.M...
LOOK NO LONGER TO OUTWORLDERS FOR YOUR HEROES...
...BUT IT DOESN'T LOOK VERY GOOD.
WE HAVE NO NEED OF THEM!

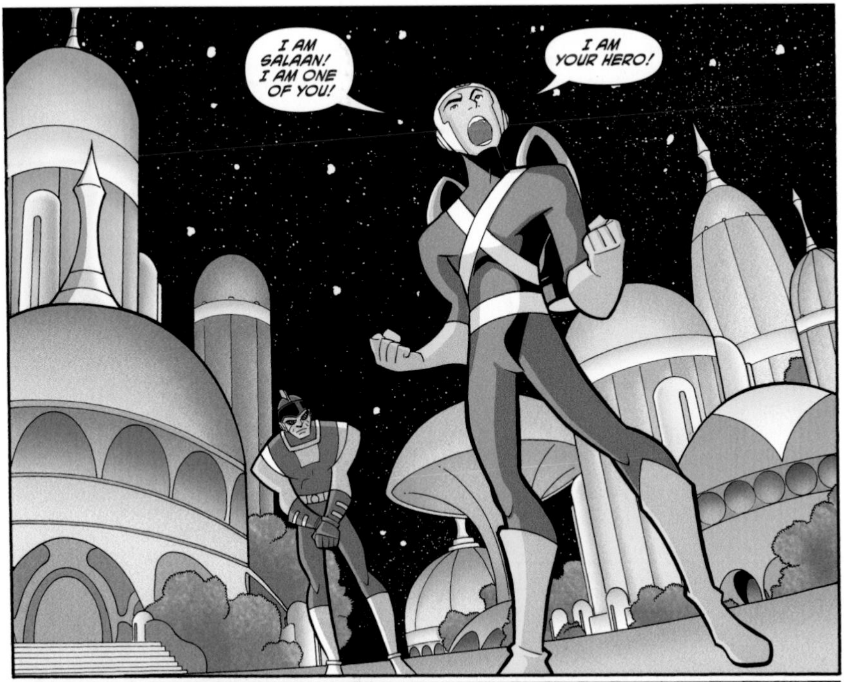
I AM SALAAN! I AM ONE OF YOU!
I AM YOUR HERO!

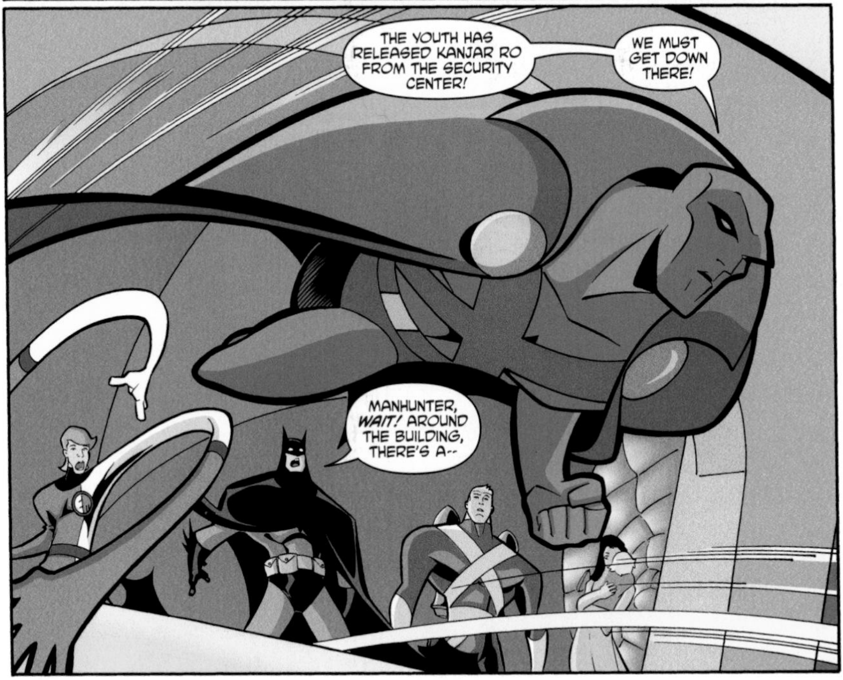
THE YOUTH HAS RELEASED KANJAR RO FROM THE SECURITY CENTER!
WE MUST GET DOWN THERE!
MANHUNTER, WAIT! AROUND THE BUILDING, THERE'S A--

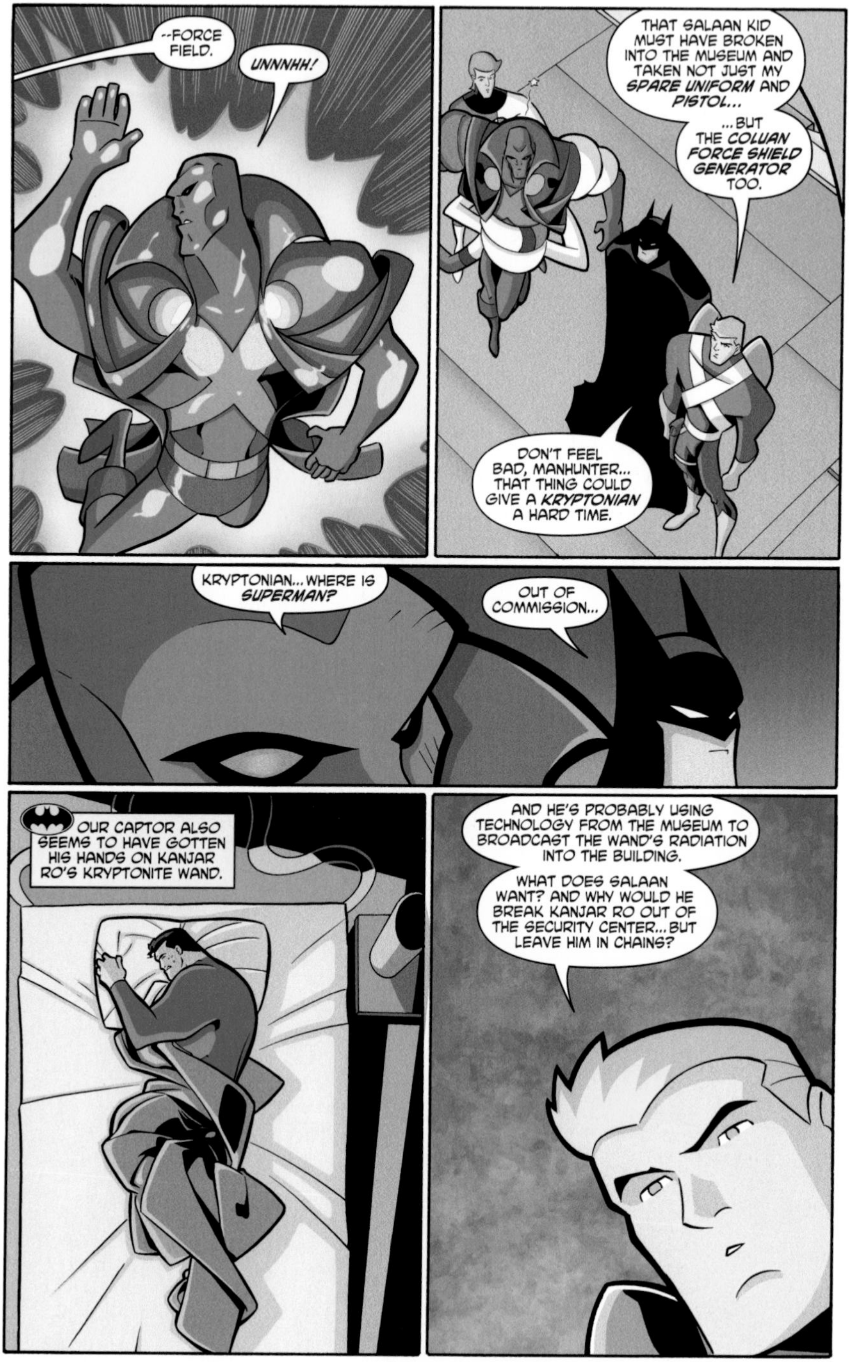
--FORCE FIELD.
UNNNHH!
THAT SALAAN KID MUST HAVE BROKEN INTO THE MUSEUM AND TAKEN NOT JUST MY SPARE UNIFORM AND PISTOL...
...BUT THE COLUAN FORCE SHIELD GENERATOR TOO.
DON'T FEEL BAD, MANHUNTER... THAT THING COULD GIVE A KRYPTONIAN A HARD TIME.
KRYPTONIAN... WHERE IS SUPERMAN?
OUT OF COMMISSION...
OUR CAPTOR ALSO SEEMS TO HAVE GOTTEN HIS HANDS ON KANJAR RO'S KRYPTONITE WAND.
AND HE'S PROBABLY USING TECHNOLOGY FROM THE MUSEUM TO BROADCAST THE WAND'S RADIATION INTO THE BUILDING.
WHAT DOES SALAAN WANT? AND WHY WOULD HE BREAK KANJAR RO OUT OF THE SECURITY CENTER... BUT LEAVE HIM IN CHAINS?

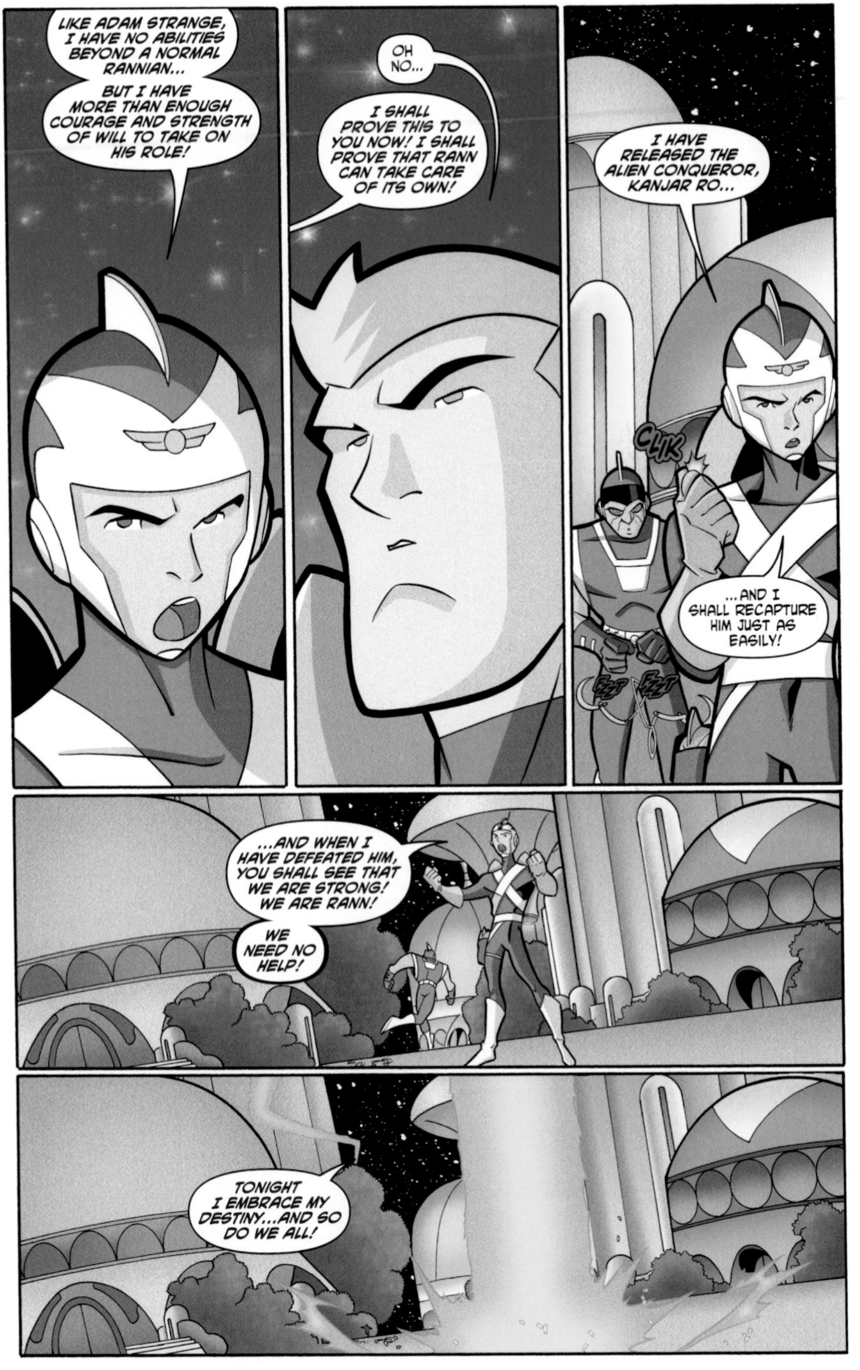
LIKE ADAM STRANGE, I HAVE NO ABILITIES BEYOND A NORMAL RANNIAN...
BUT I HAVE MORE THAN ENOUGH COURAGE AND STRENGTH OF WILL TO TAKE ON HIS ROLE!
OH NO...
I SHALL PROVE THIS TO YOU NOW! I SHALL PROVE THAT RANN CAN TAKE CARE OF ITS OWN!
I HAVE RELEASED THE ALIEN CONQUEROR, KANJAR RO...
CLIK
...AND I SHALL RECAPTURE HIM JUST AS EASILY!
FZZT
FZZT
...AND WHEN I HAVE DEFEATED HIM, YOU SHALL SEE THAT WE ARE STRONG! WE ARE RANN!
WE NEED NO HELP!
TONIGHT I EMBRACE MY DESTINY...AND SO DO WE ALL!

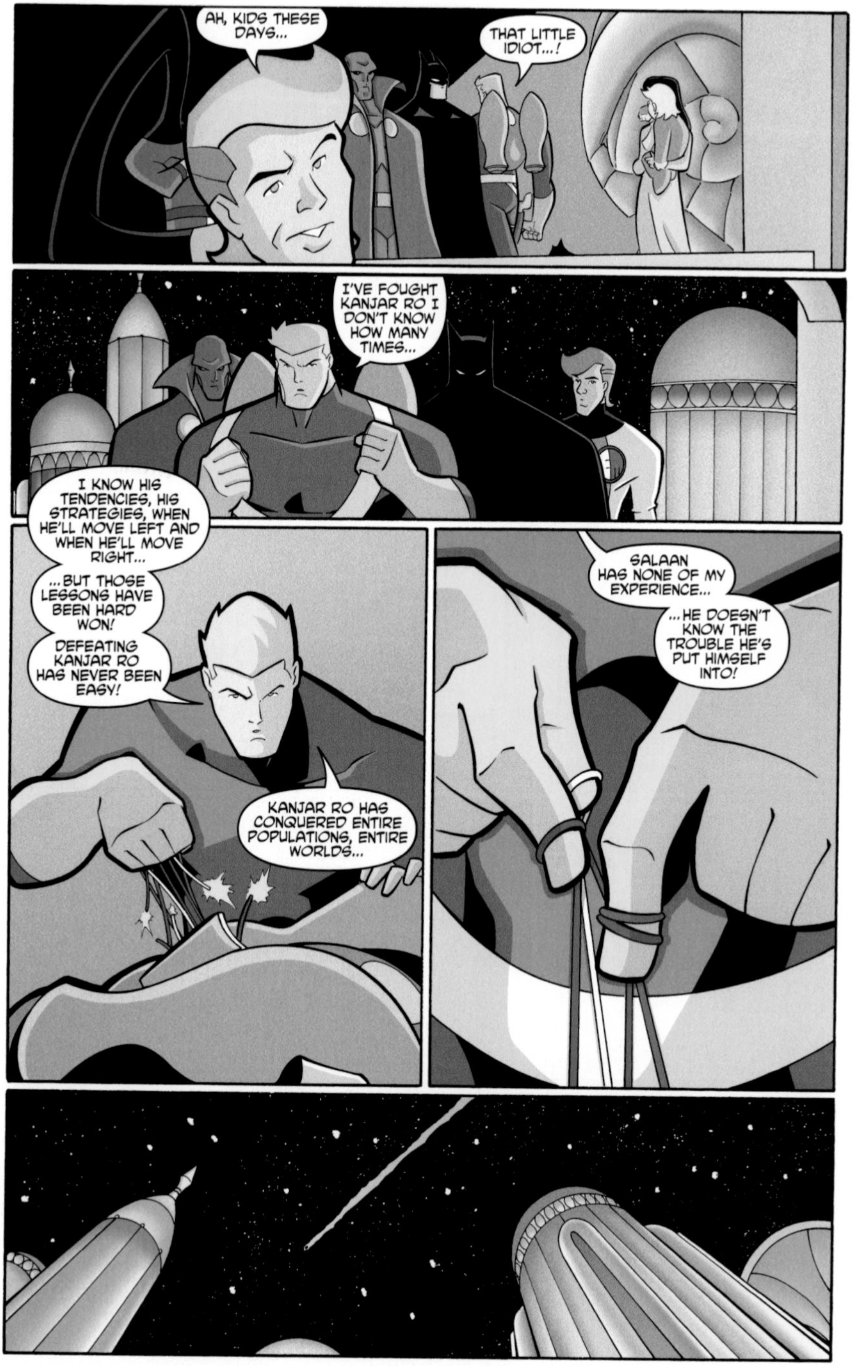
AH, KIDS THESE DAYS...
THAT LITTLE IDIOT...!
I'VE FOUGHT KANJAR RO I DON'T KNOW HOW MANY TIMES...
I KNOW HIS TENDENCIES, HIS STRATEGIES, WHEN HE'LL MOVE LEFT AND WHEN HE'LL MOVE RIGHT...
...BUT THOSE LESSONS HAVE BEEN HARD WON!
DEFEATING KANJAR RO HAS NEVER BEEN EASY!
KANJAR RO HAS CONQUERED ENTIRE POPULATIONS, ENTIRE WORLDS...
SALAAN HAS NONE OF MY EXPERIENCE...
...HE DOESN'T KNOW THE TROUBLE HE'S PUT HIMSELF INTO!

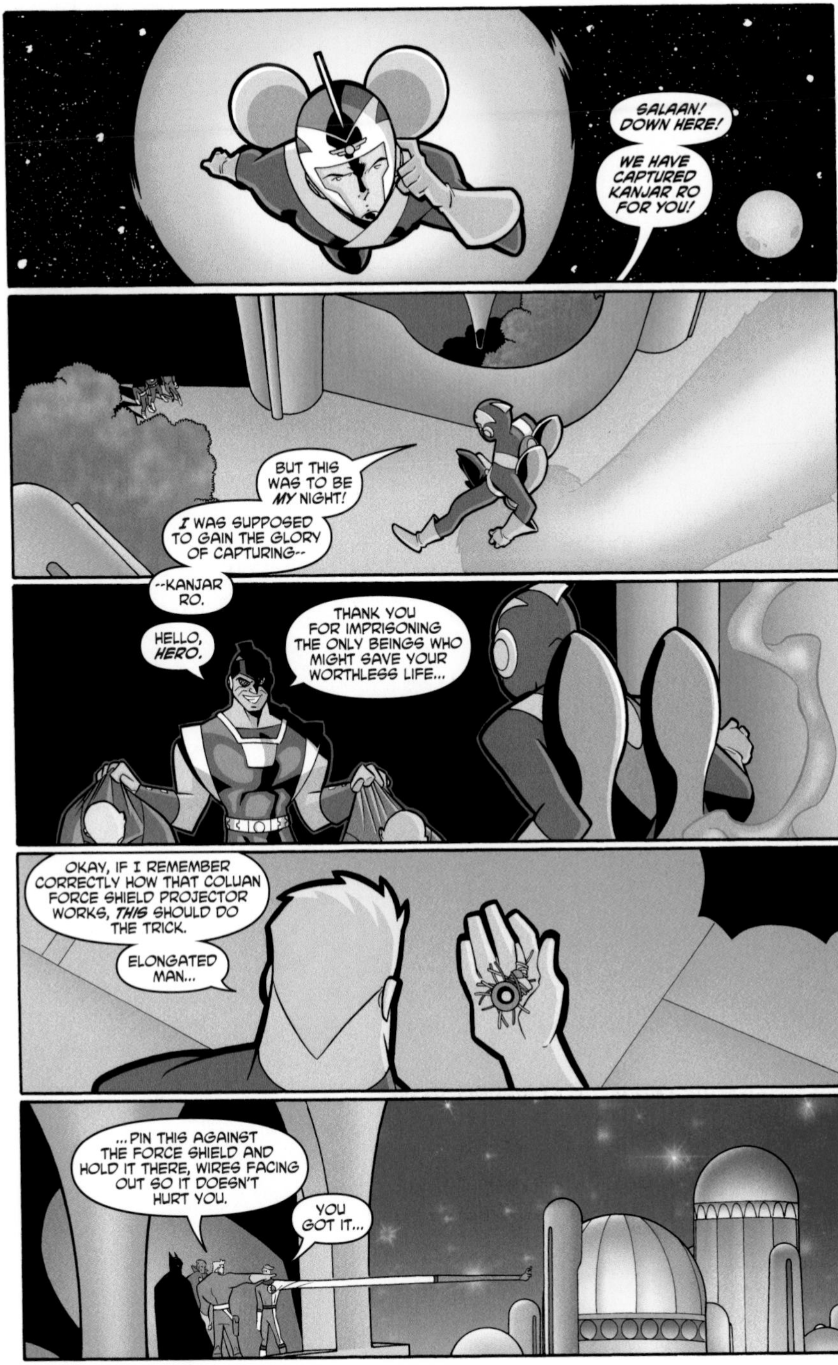
SALAAN! DOWN HERE!
WE HAVE CAPTURED KANJAR RO FOR YOU!
BUT THIS WAS TO BE MY NIGHT!
I WAS SUPPOSED TO GAIN THE GLORY OF CAPTURING--
--KANJAR RO.
HELLO, HERO.
THANK YOU FOR IMPRISONING THE ONLY BEINGS WHO MIGHT SAVE YOUR WORTHLESS LIFE...
OKAY, IF I REMEMBER CORRECTLY HOW THAT COLUAN FORCE SHIELD PROJECTOR WORKS, THIS SHOULD DO THE TRICK.
ELONGATED MAN...
...PIN THIS AGAINST THE FORCE SHIELD AND HOLD IT THERE, WIRES FACING OUT SO IT DOESN'T HURT YOU.
YOU GOT IT...

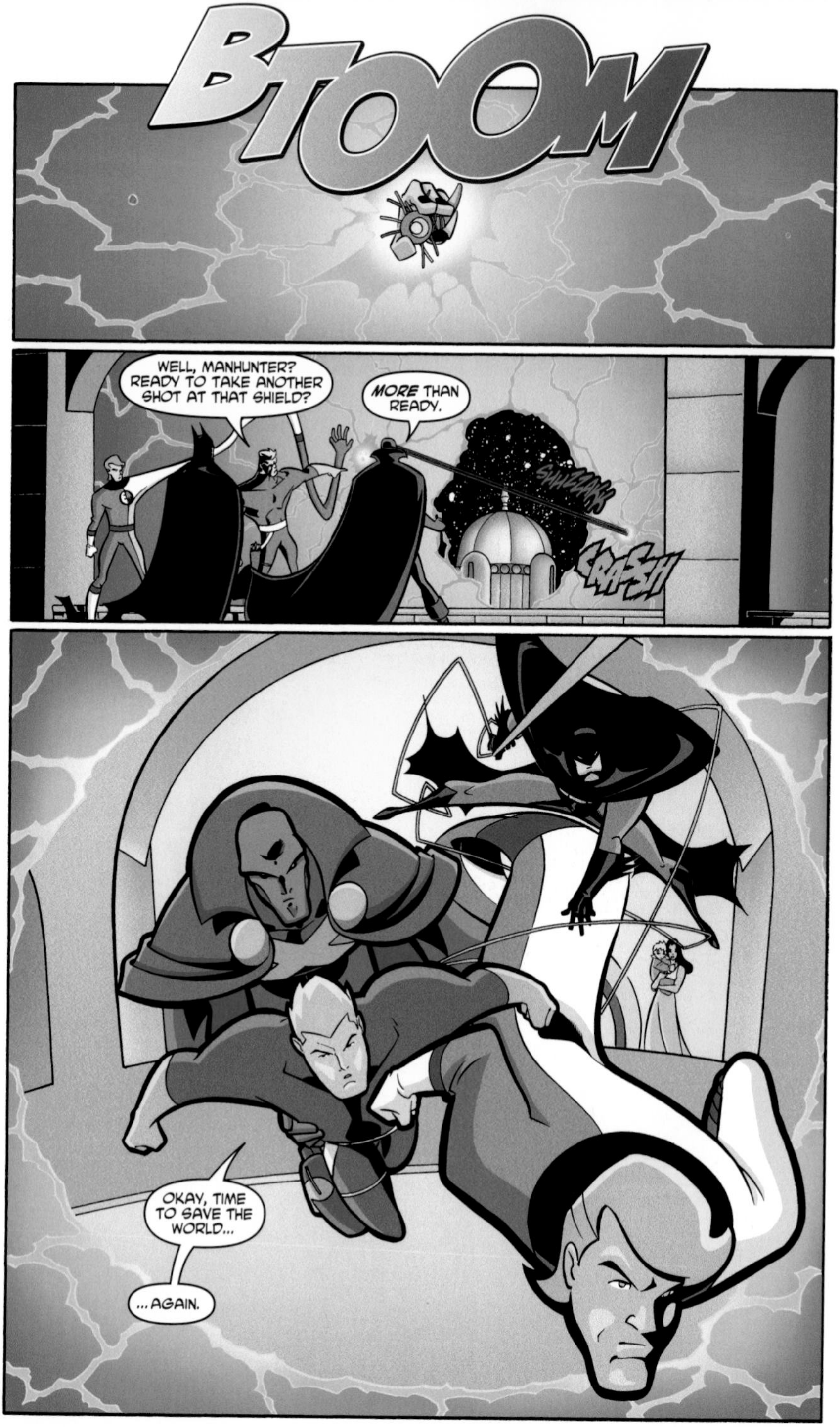
BTOOM
WELL, MANHUNTER? READY TO TAKE ANOTHER SHOT AT THAT SHIELD?
MORE THAN READY.
SHAZZAK
CRASH
OKAY, TIME TO SAVE THE WORLD...
...AGAIN.

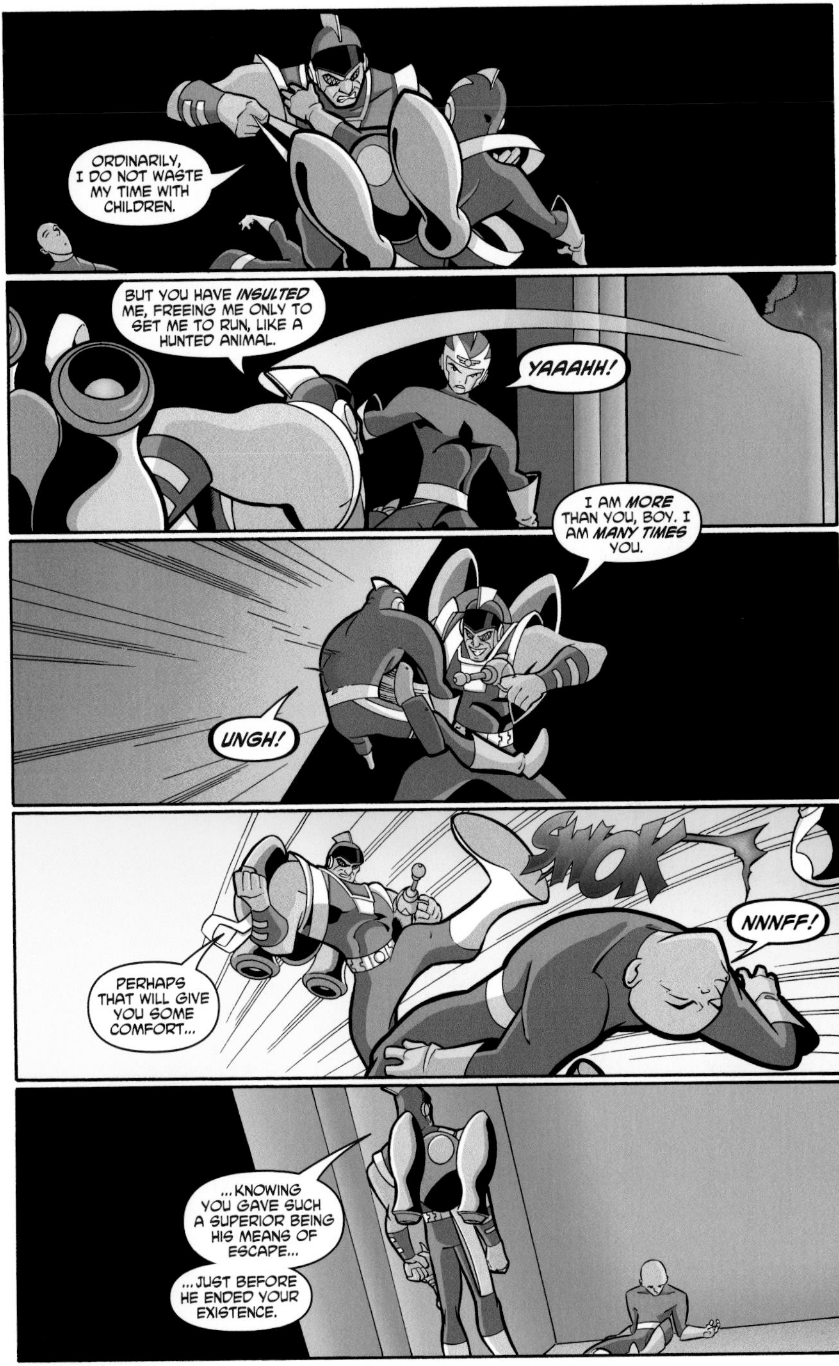
ORDINARILY, I DO NOT WASTE MY TIME WITH CHILDREN.
BUT YOU HAVE INSULTED ME, FREEING ME ONLY TO SET ME TO RUN, LIKE A HUNTED ANIMAL.
YAAAHH!
I AM MORE THAN YOU, BOY. I AM MANY TIMES YOU.
UNGH!
SWOK
NNNFF!
PERHAPS THAT WILL GIVE YOU SOME COMFORT...
...KNOWING YOU GAVE SUCH A SUPERIOR BEING HIS MEANS OF ESCAPE...
...JUST BEFORE HE ENDED YOUR EXISTENCE.

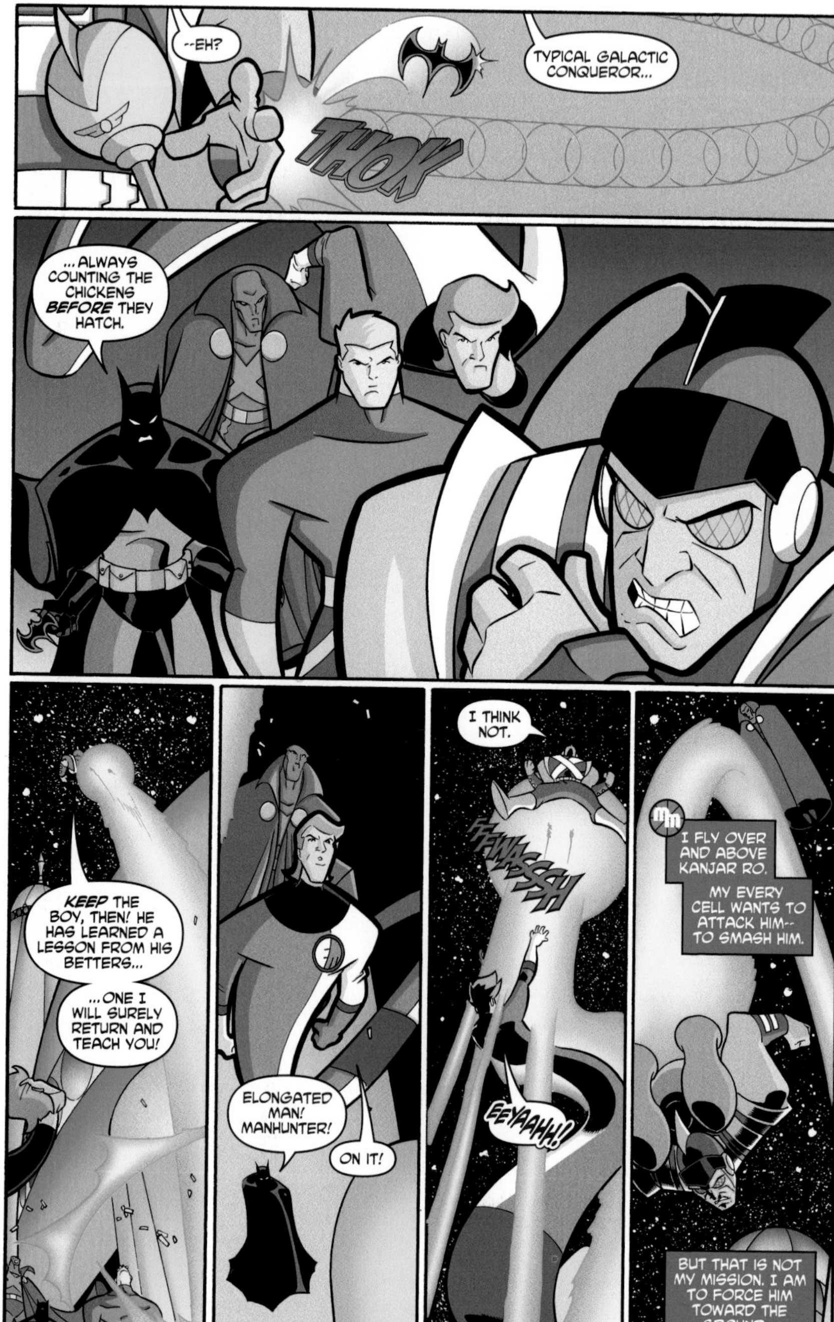
--EH?
TYPICAL GALACTIC CONQUEROR...
THOK
...ALWAYS COUNTING THE CHICKENS BEFORE THEY HATCH.
KEEP THE BOY, THEN! HE HAS LEARNED A LESSON FROM HIS BETTERS...
...ONE I WILL SURELY RETURN AND TEACH YOU!
ELONGATED MAN! MANHUNTER!
ON IT!
I THINK NOT.
FFFWASSSH
EEYAAHH!
I FLY OVER AND ABOVE KANJAR RO.
MY EVERY CELL WANTS TO ATTACK HIM-- TO SMASH HIM.
BUT THAT IS NOT MY MISSION. I AM TO FORCE HIM TOWARD THE GROUND...

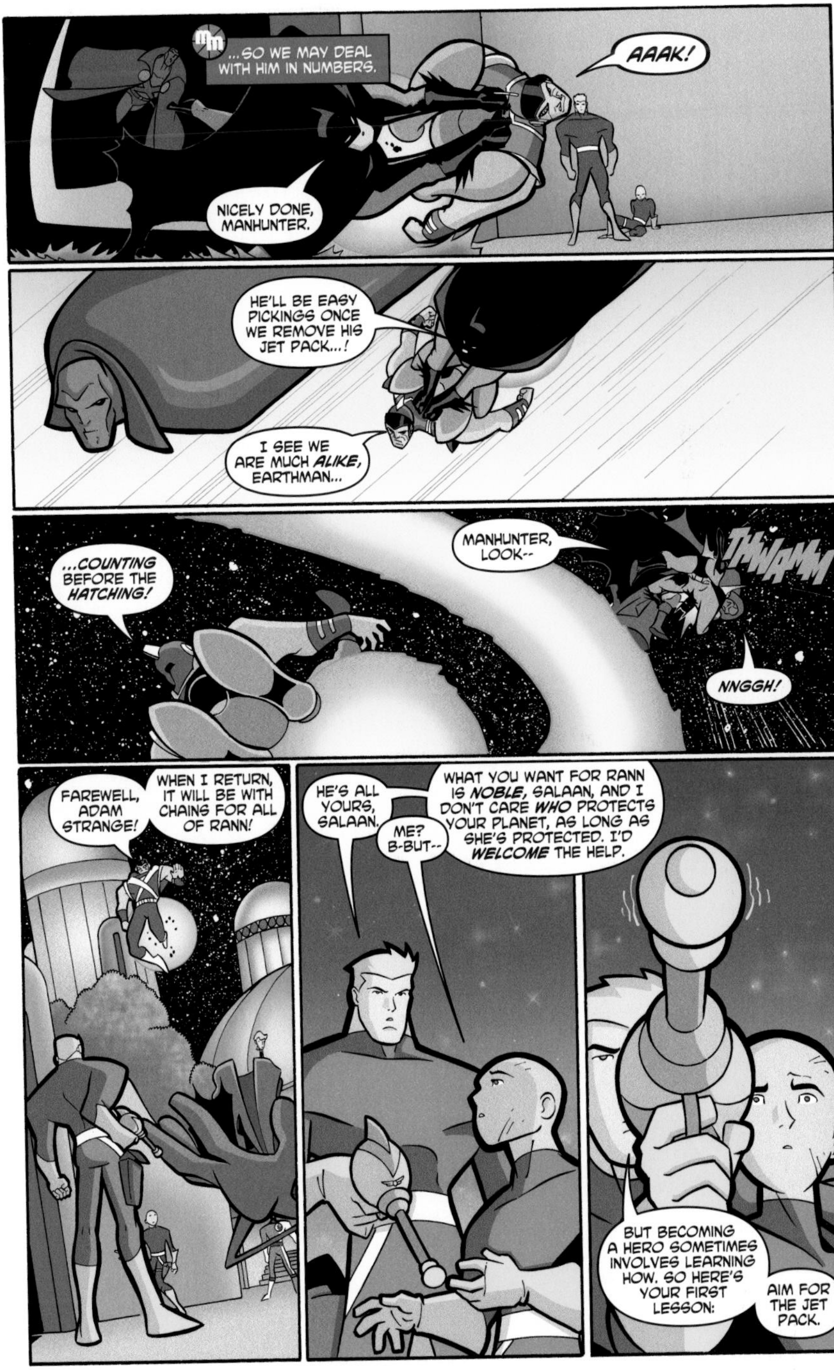
...SO WE MAY DEAL WITH HIM IN NUMBERS.
AAAK!
NICELY DONE, MANHUNTER.
HE'LL BE EASY PICKINGS ONCE WE REMOVE HIS JET PACK...!
I SEE WE ARE MUCH ALIKE, EARTHMAN...
...COUNTING BEFORE THE HATCHING!
MANHUNTER, LOOK--
THWAMM
NNGGH!
FAREWELL, ADAM STRANGE!
WHEN I RETURN, IT WILL BE WITH CHAINS FOR ALL OF RANN!
HE'S ALL YOURS, SALAAN.
ME? B-BUT--
WHAT YOU WANT FOR RANN IS NOBLE, SALAAN, AND I DON'T CARE WHO PROTECTS YOUR PLANET, AS LONG AS SHE'S PROTECTED. I'D WELCOME THE HELP.
BUT BECOMING A HERO SOMETIMES INVOLVES LEARNING HOW. SO HERE'S YOUR FIRST LESSON:
AIM FOR THE JET PACK.

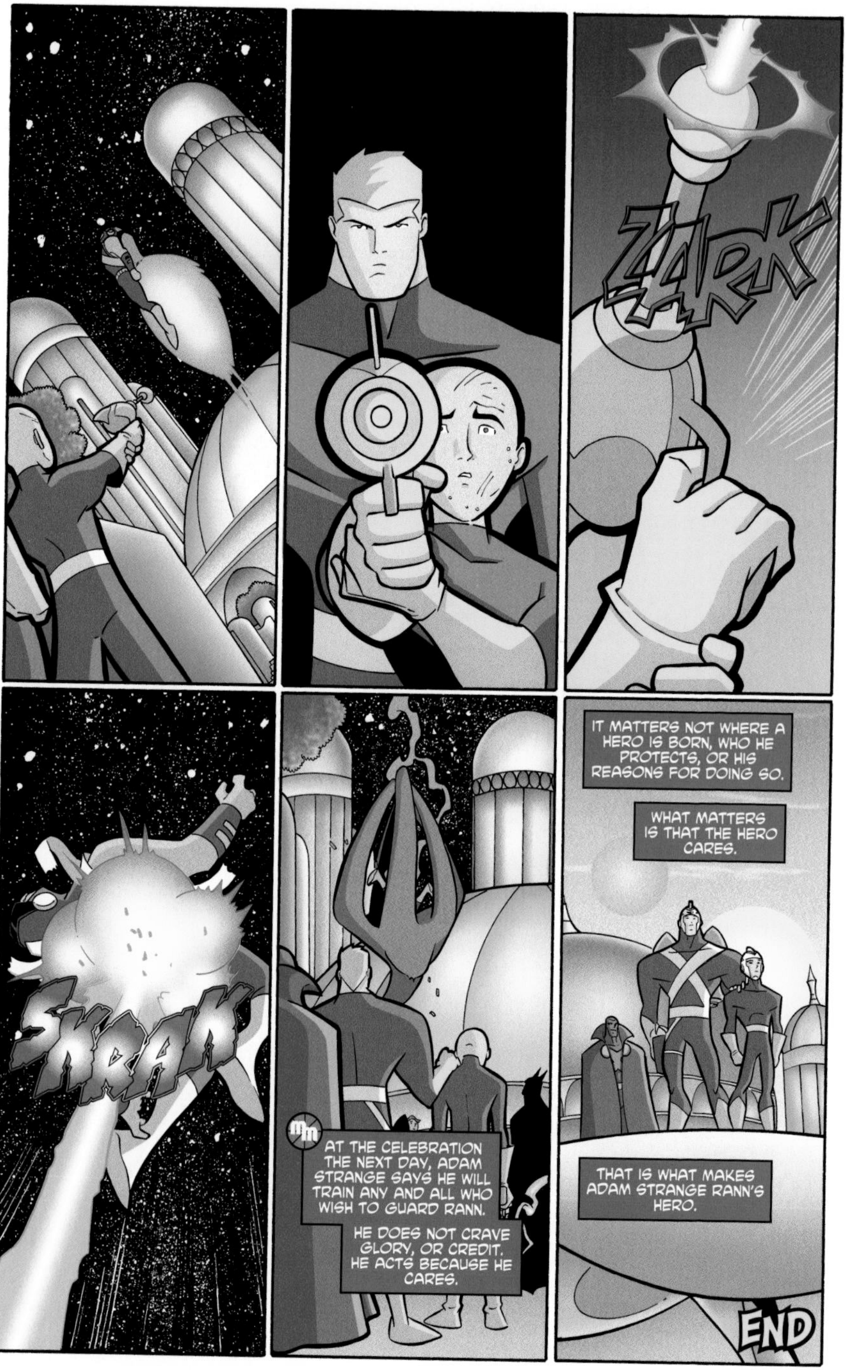
ZZARK
SKRAK
IT MATTERS NOT WHERE A HERO IS BORN, WHO HE PROTECTS, OR HIS REASONS FOR DOING SO.
WHAT MATTERS IS THAT THE HERO CARES.
AT THE CELEBRATION THE NEXT DAY, ADAM STRANGE SAYS HE WILL TRAIN ANY AND ALL WHO WISH TO GUARD RANN.
HE DOES NOT CRAVE GLORY, OR CREDIT. HE ACTS BECAUSE HE CARES.
THAT IS WHAT MAKES ADAM STRANGE RANN'S HERO.
END

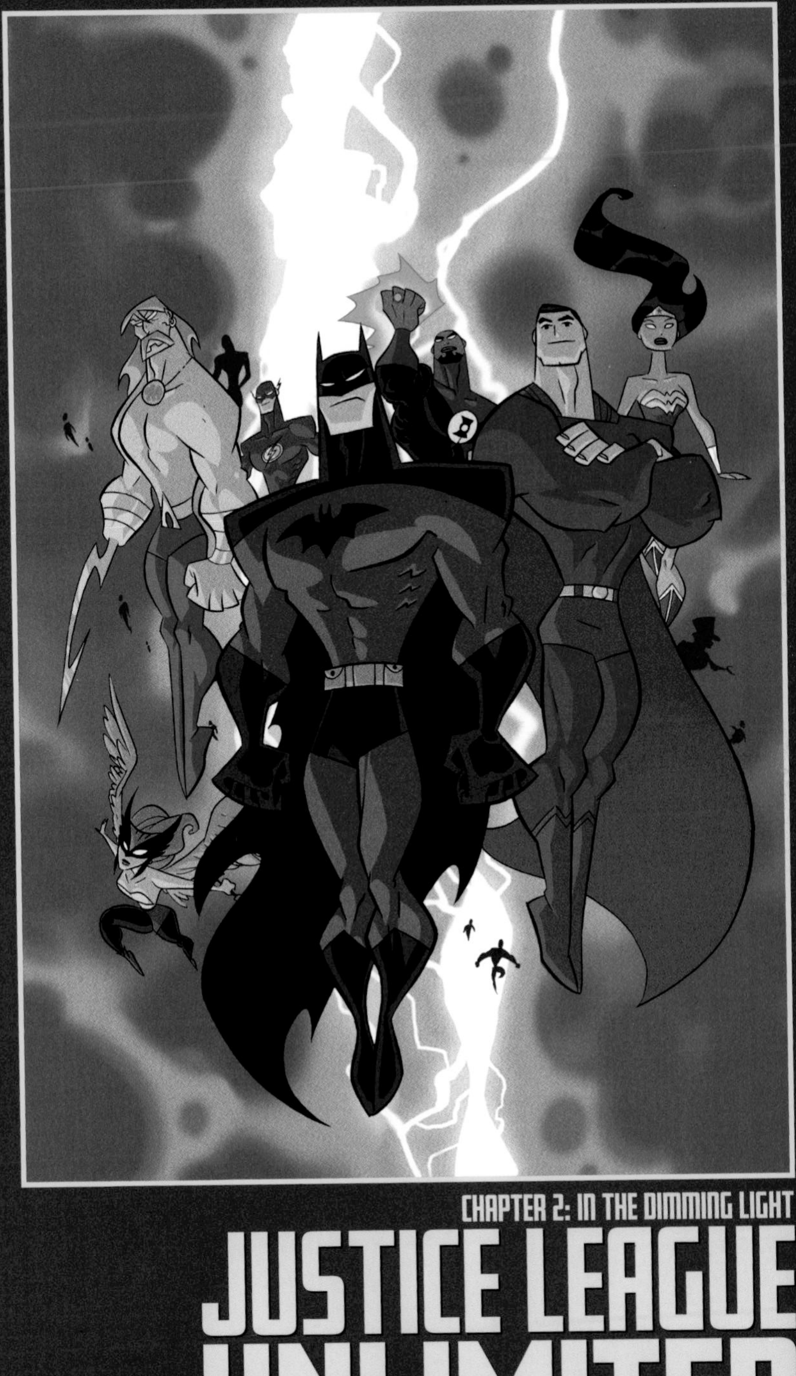

CHAPTER 2: IN THE DIMMING LIGHT

JUSTICE LEAGUE UNLIMITED

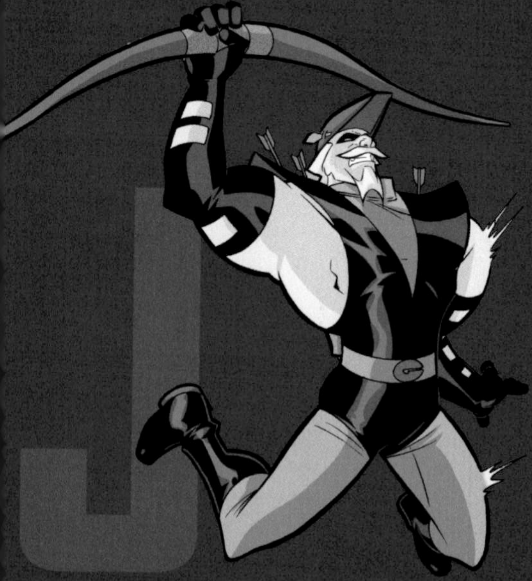

COVER ART BY BEN CALDWELL

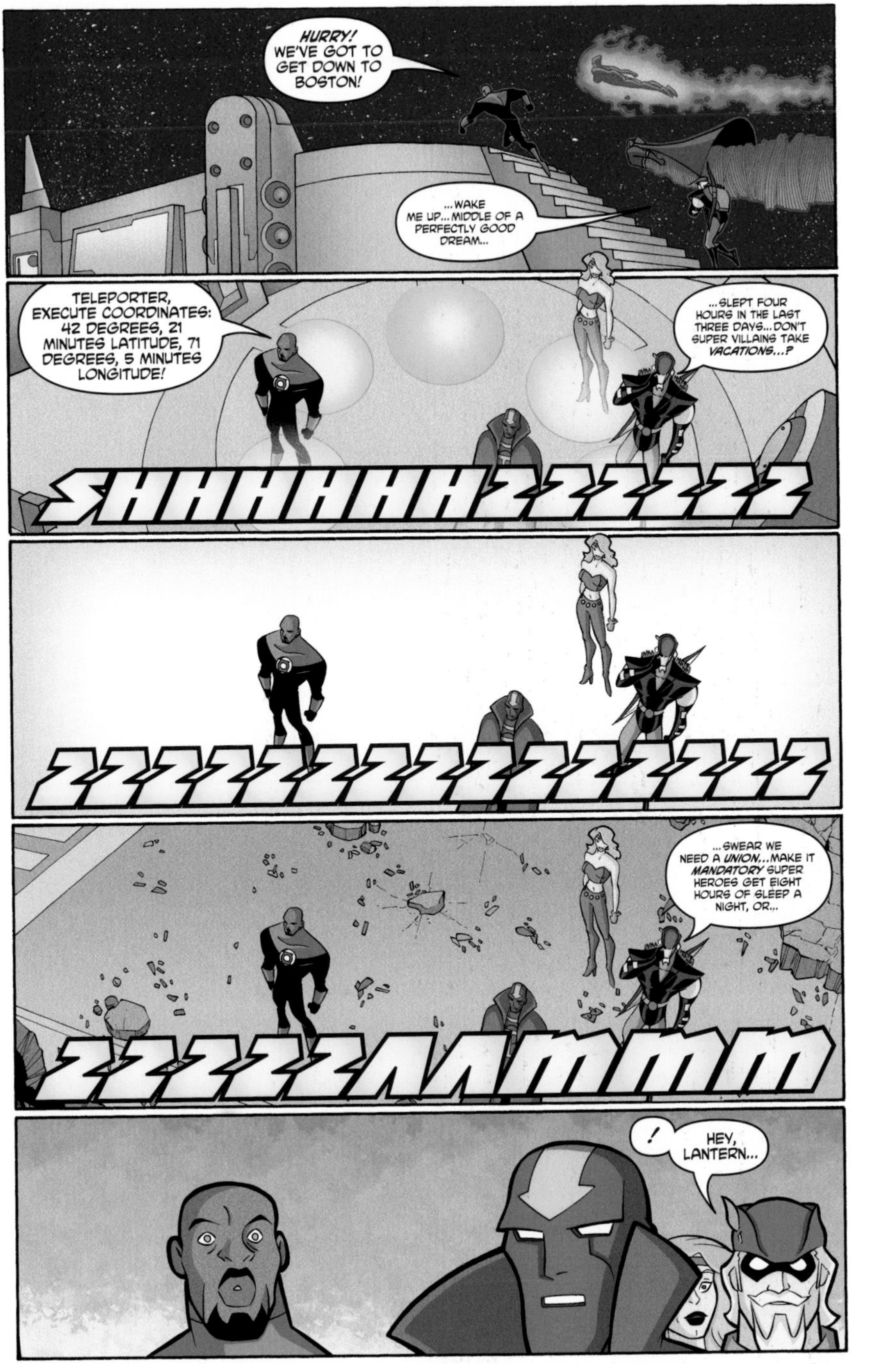
HURRY! WE'VE GOT TO GET DOWN TO BOSTON!
...WAKE ME UP...MIDDLE OF A PERFECTLY GOOD DREAM...
TELEPORTER, EXECUTE COORDINATES: 42 DEGREES, 21 MINUTES LATITUDE, 71 DEGREES, 5 MINUTES LONGITUDE!
...SLEPT FOUR HOURS IN THE LAST THREE DAYS...DON'T SUPER VILLAINS TAKE VACATIONS...?
SHHHHHHZZZZZZ
ZZZZZZZZZZZZZZZZZ
...SWEAR WE NEED A UNION...MAKE IT MANDATORY SUPER HEROES GET EIGHT HOURS OF SLEEP A NIGHT, OR...
ZZZZZZAAMMMM
!
HEY, LANTERN...

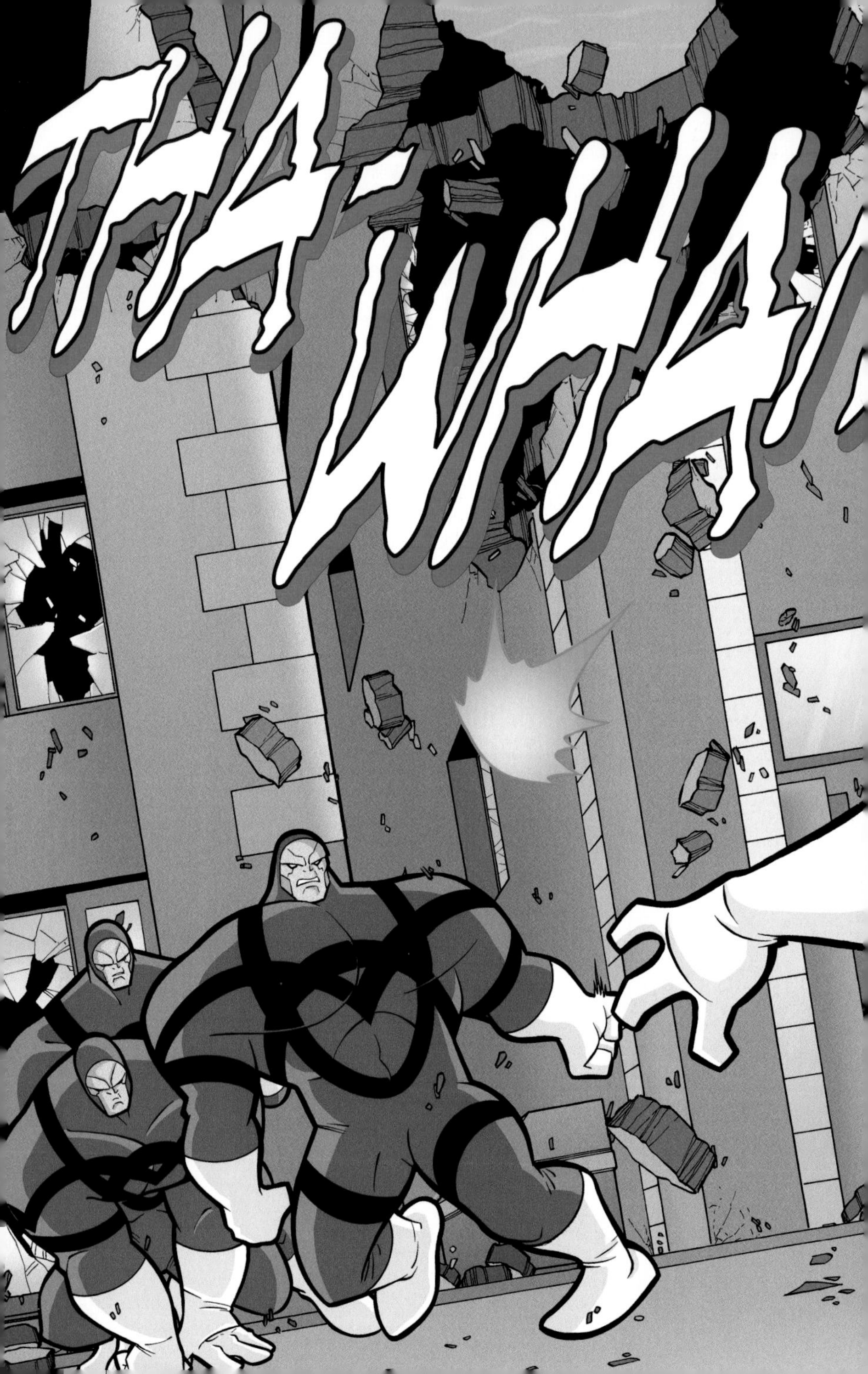
THA-WHA

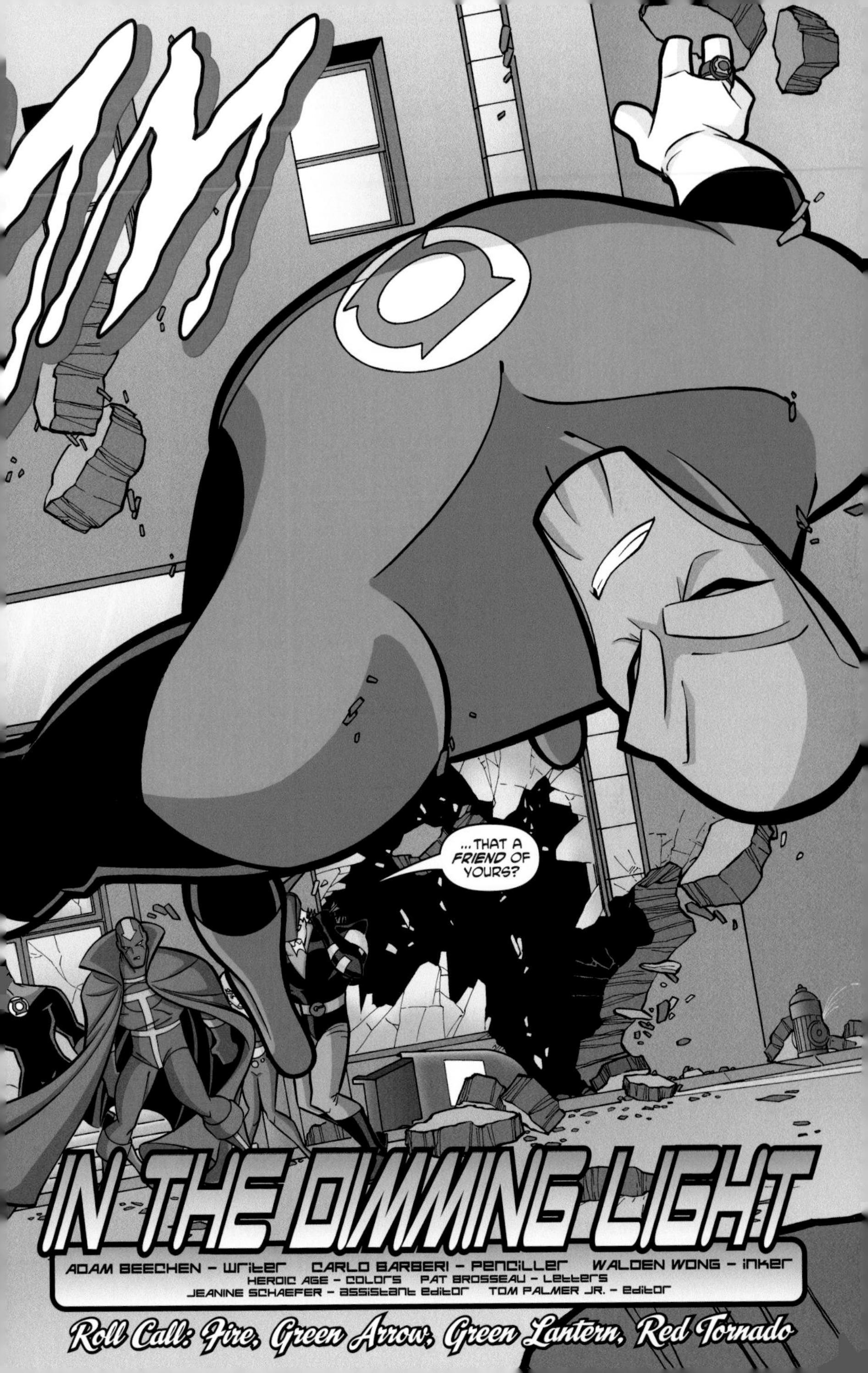
...THAT A FRIEND OF YOURS?
IN THE DIMMING LIGHT
ADAM BEECHEN - WRITER CARLO BARBERI - PENCILLER WALDEN WONG - INKER
HEROIC AGE - COLORS PAT BROSSEAU - LETTERS
JEANINE SCHAEFER - ASSISTANT EDITOR TOM PALMER JR. - EDITOR
Roll Call: Fire, Green Arrow, Green Lantern, Red Tornado

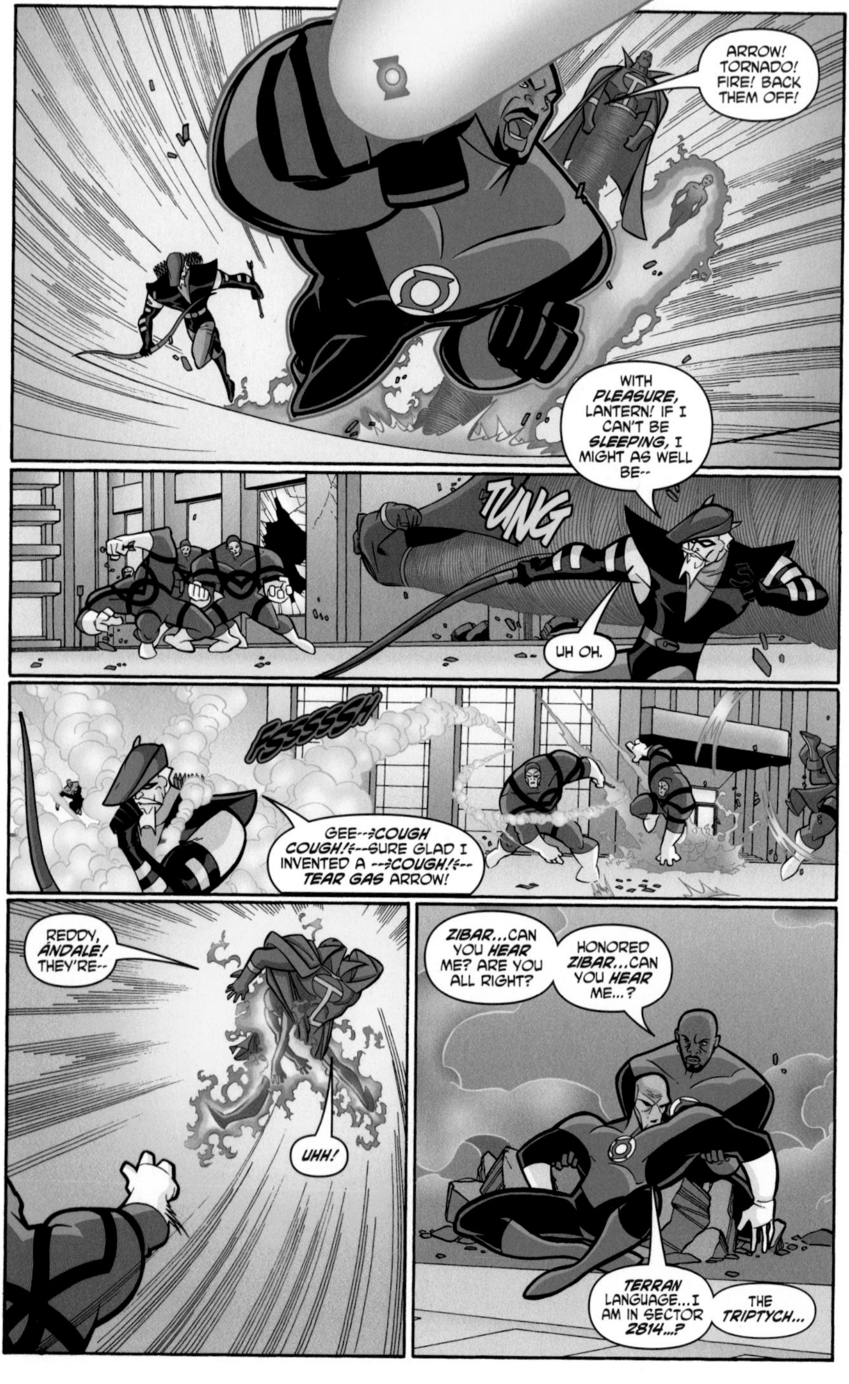

ARROW! TORNADO! FIRE! BACK THEM OFF!
WITH PLEASURE, LANTERN! IF I CAN'T BE SLEEPING, I MIGHT AS WELL BE--
TUNG
UH OH.
FSSSSSSH
GEE--COUGH COUGH!--SURE GLAD I INVENTED A --COUGH!-- TEAR GAS ARROW!
REDDY, ÁNDALE! THEY'RE--
UHH!
ZIBAR...CAN YOU HEAR ME? ARE YOU ALL RIGHT?
HONORED ZIBAR...CAN YOU HEAR ME...?
TERRAN LANGUAGE...I AM IN SECTOR 2814...?
THE TRIPTYCH...

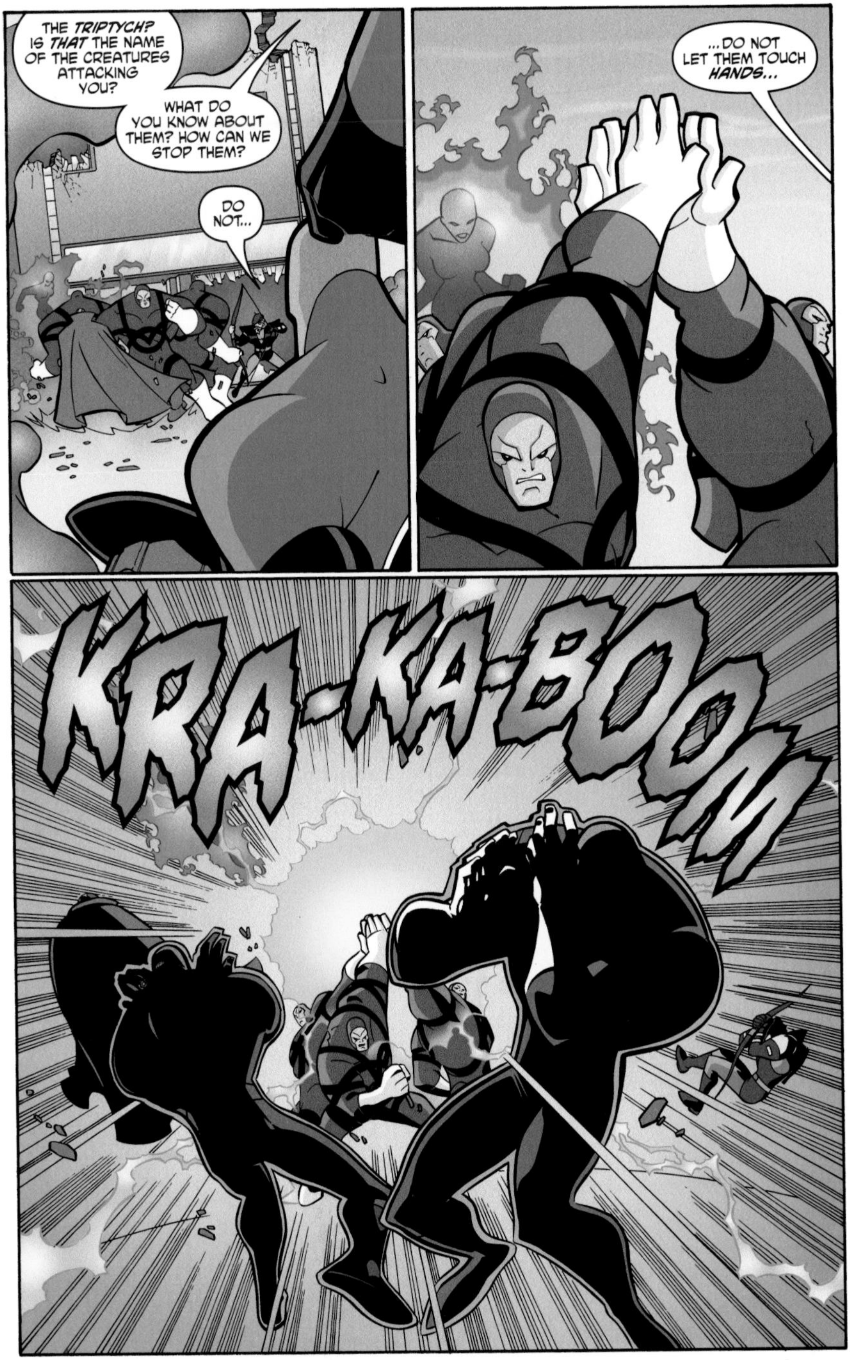
THE *TRIPTYCH?* IS *THAT* THE NAME OF THE CREATURES ATTACKING YOU?
WHAT DO YOU KNOW ABOUT THEM? HOW CAN WE STOP THEM?
DO NOT...
...DO NOT LET THEM TOUCH *HANDS*...
KRA-KA-BOOM

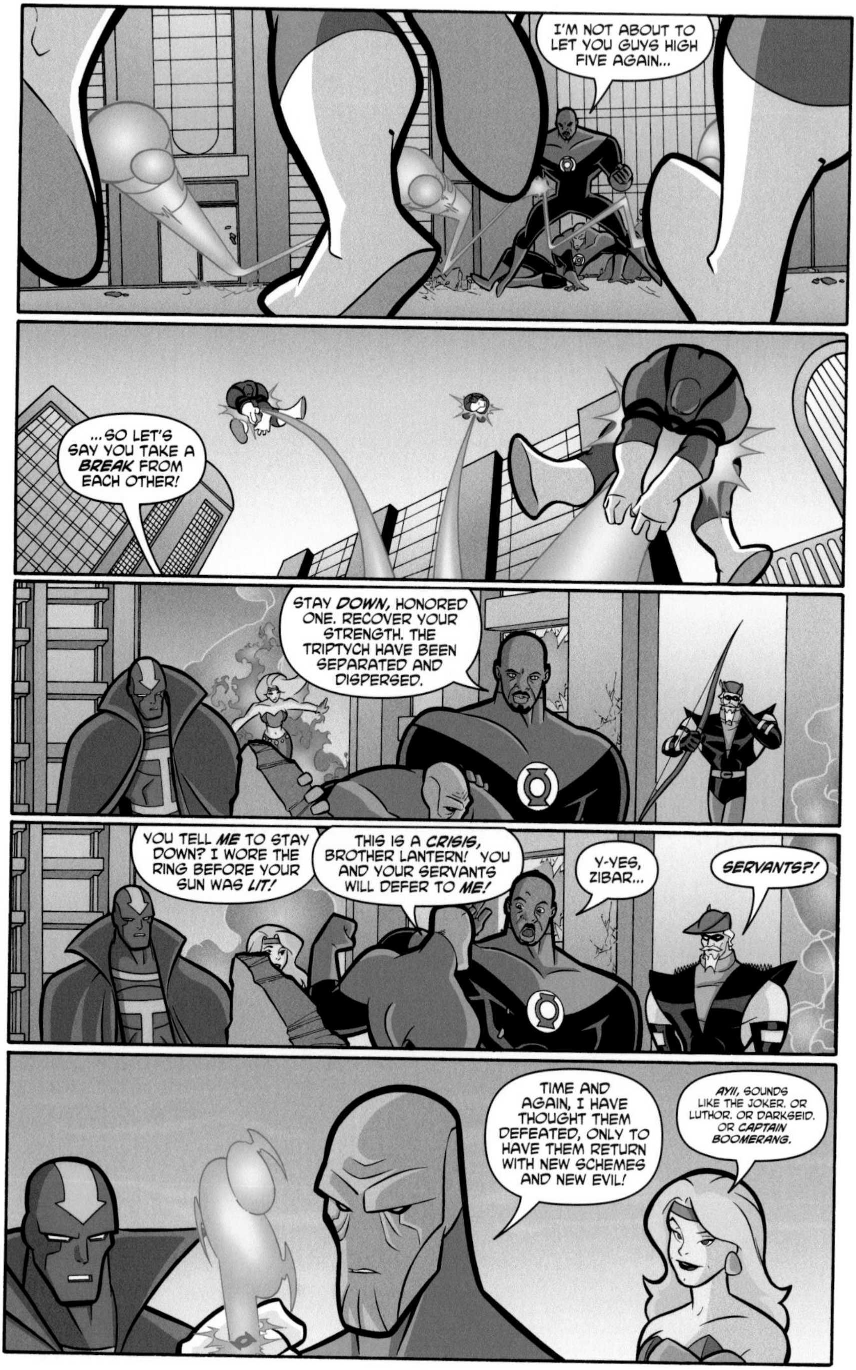
I'M NOT ABOUT TO LET YOU GUYS HIGH FIVE AGAIN...
...SO LET'S SAY YOU TAKE A BREAK FROM EACH OTHER!
STAY DOWN, HONORED ONE. RECOVER YOUR STRENGTH. THE TRIPTYCH HAVE BEEN SEPARATED AND DISPERSED.
YOU TELL ME TO STAY DOWN? I WORE THE RING BEFORE YOUR SUN WAS LIT!
THIS IS A CRISIS, BROTHER LANTERN! YOU AND YOUR SERVANTS WILL DEFER TO ME!
Y-YES, ZIBAR...
SERVANTS?!
TIME AND AGAIN, I HAVE THOUGHT THEM DEFEATED, ONLY TO HAVE THEM RETURN WITH NEW SCHEMES AND NEW EVIL!
AYII, SOUNDS LIKE THE JOKER. OR LUTHOR. OR DARKSEID. OR CAPTAIN BOOMERANG.

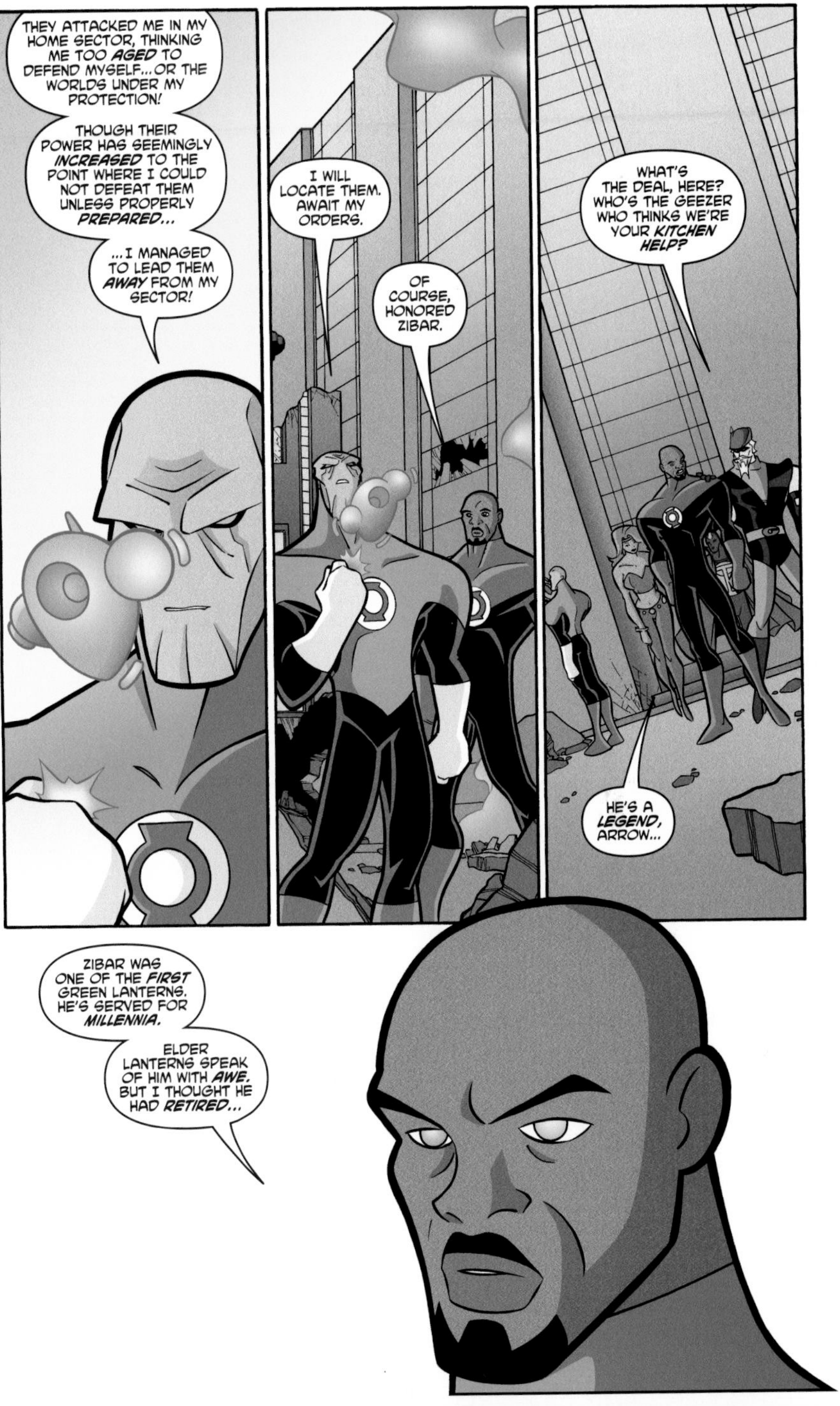
THEY ATTACKED ME IN MY HOME SECTOR, THINKING ME TOO AGED TO DEFEND MYSELF...OR THE WORLDS UNDER MY PROTECTION!
THOUGH THEIR POWER HAS SEEMINGLY INCREASED TO THE POINT WHERE I COULD NOT DEFEAT THEM UNLESS PROPERLY PREPARED...
...I MANAGED TO LEAD THEM AWAY FROM MY SECTOR!
I WILL LOCATE THEM. AWAIT MY ORDERS.
OF COURSE, HONORED ZIBAR.
WHAT'S THE DEAL, HERE? WHO'S THE GEEZER WHO THINKS WE'RE YOUR KITCHEN HELP?
HE'S A LEGEND, ARROW...
ZIBAR WAS ONE OF THE FIRST GREEN LANTERNS. HE'S SERVED FOR MILLENNIA.
ELDER LANTERNS SPEAK OF HIM WITH AWE. BUT I THOUGHT HE HAD RETIRED...

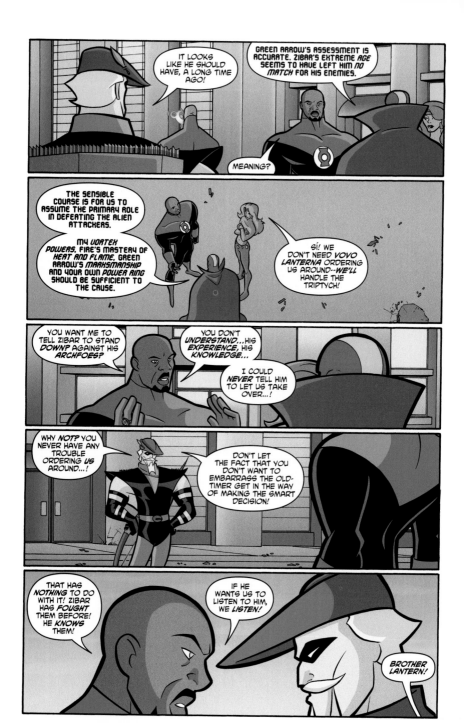

IT LOOKS LIKE HE SHOULD HAVE, A LONG TIME AGO!

GREEN ARROW'S ASSESSMENT IS ACCURATE. ZIBAR'S EXTREME *AGE* SEEMS TO HAVE LEFT HIM *NO MATCH* FOR HIS ENEMIES.

MEANING?

THE SENSIBLE COURSE IS FOR US TO ASSUME THE PRIMARY ROLE IN DEFEATING THE ALIEN ATTACKERS.

MY *VORTEX POWERS*, FIRE'S MASTERY OF *HEAT AND FLAME*, GREEN ARROW'S *MARKSMANSHIP* AND YOUR OWN *POWER RING* SHOULD BE SUFFICIENT TO THE CAUSE.

SÍ! WE DON'T NEED *VOVO LANTERNA* ORDERING US AROUND--*WE'LL* HANDLE THE *TRIPTYCH!*

YOU WANT ME TO TELL ZIBAR TO STAND *DOWN?* AGAINST HIS *ARCHFOES?*

YOU DON'T *UNDERSTAND...*HIS *EXPERIENCE*, HIS *KNOWLEDGE...*

I COULD *NEVER* TELL HIM TO LET US TAKE OVER...!

WHY *NOT?* YOU NEVER HAVE ANY TROUBLE ORDERING *US* AROUND...!

DON'T LET THE FACT THAT YOU DON'T WANT TO EMBARRASS THE OLD-TIMER GET IN THE WAY OF MAKING THE SMART DECISION!

THAT HAS *NOTHING* TO DO WITH IT! ZIBAR HAS *FOUGHT* THEM BEFORE! HE *KNOWS* THEM!

IF HE WANTS US TO LISTEN TO HIM, WE *LISTEN!*

BROTHER LANTERN!

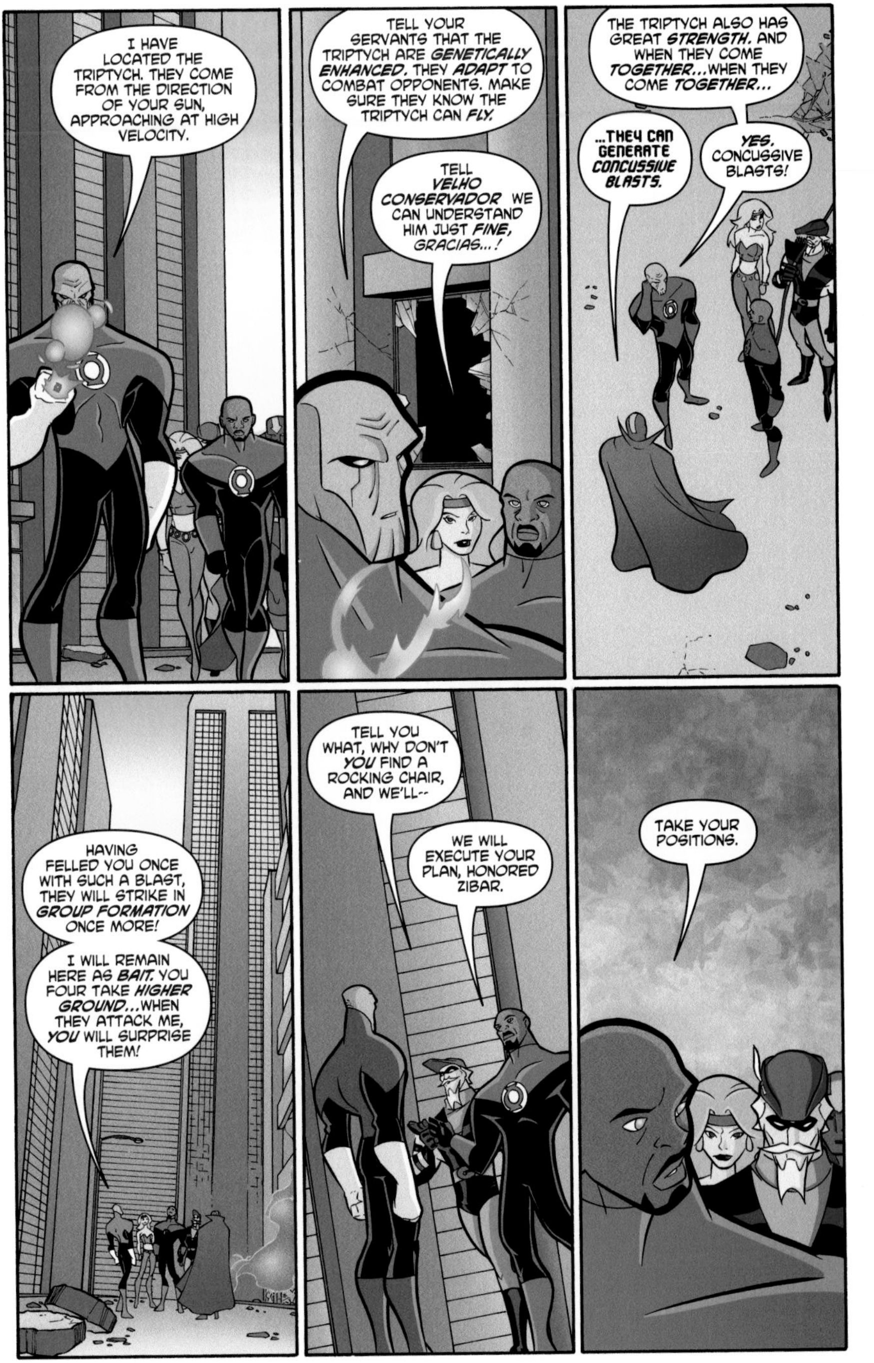
I HAVE LOCATED THE TRIPTYCH. THEY COME FROM THE DIRECTION OF YOUR SUN, APPROACHING AT HIGH VELOCITY.
TELL YOUR SERVANTS THAT THE TRIPTYCH ARE GENETICALLY ENHANCED. THEY ADAPT TO COMBAT OPPONENTS. MAKE SURE THEY KNOW THE TRIPTYCH CAN FLY.
TELL VELHO CONSERVADOR WE CAN UNDERSTAND HIM JUST FINE, GRACIAS...!
THE TRIPTYCH ALSO HAS GREAT STRENGTH. AND WHEN THEY COME TOGETHER...WHEN THEY COME TOGETHER...
...THEY CAN GENERATE CONCUSSIVE BLASTS.
YES. CONCUSSIVE BLASTS!
HAVING FELLED YOU ONCE WITH SUCH A BLAST, THEY WILL STRIKE IN GROUP FORMATION ONCE MORE!
I WILL REMAIN HERE AS BAIT. YOU FOUR TAKE HIGHER GROUND...WHEN THEY ATTACK ME, YOU WILL SURPRISE THEM!
TELL YOU WHAT, WHY DON'T YOU FIND A ROCKING CHAIR, AND WE'LL--
WE WILL EXECUTE YOUR PLAN, HONORED ZIBAR.
TAKE YOUR POSITIONS.

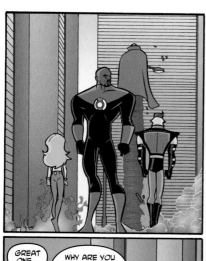

GREAT ONE...

WHY ARE YOU NOT ON *HIGHER GROUND*, AS I ORDERED? THE *TRIPTYCH* WILL BE HERE SOON...

ZIBAR, I HAD HEARD YOU'D AGREED TO *RELINQUISH* YOUR RING, TO FIND A WORTHY *SUCCESSOR* FROM YOUR SECTOR...

I HEARD YOUR SERVANTS, BROTHER LANTERN. THEY THINK I AM *OLD* AND *INCAPABLE.* I HAVE HEARD MANY *OTHERS* WHISPER THE SAME THINGS. THEY SEE ONLY MY *BODY,* NOT MY *WILL.*

AND MY *WILL,* WHICH POWERS MY RING, IS *NOT* OLD. I SHALL SERVE THE GUARDIANS AS LONG AS I AM ABLE. *NONE* SHALL TELL ME WHEN IT IS MY TIME TO STOP!

NOW FIND HIGHER GROUND. THE TRIPTYCH APPROACHES.

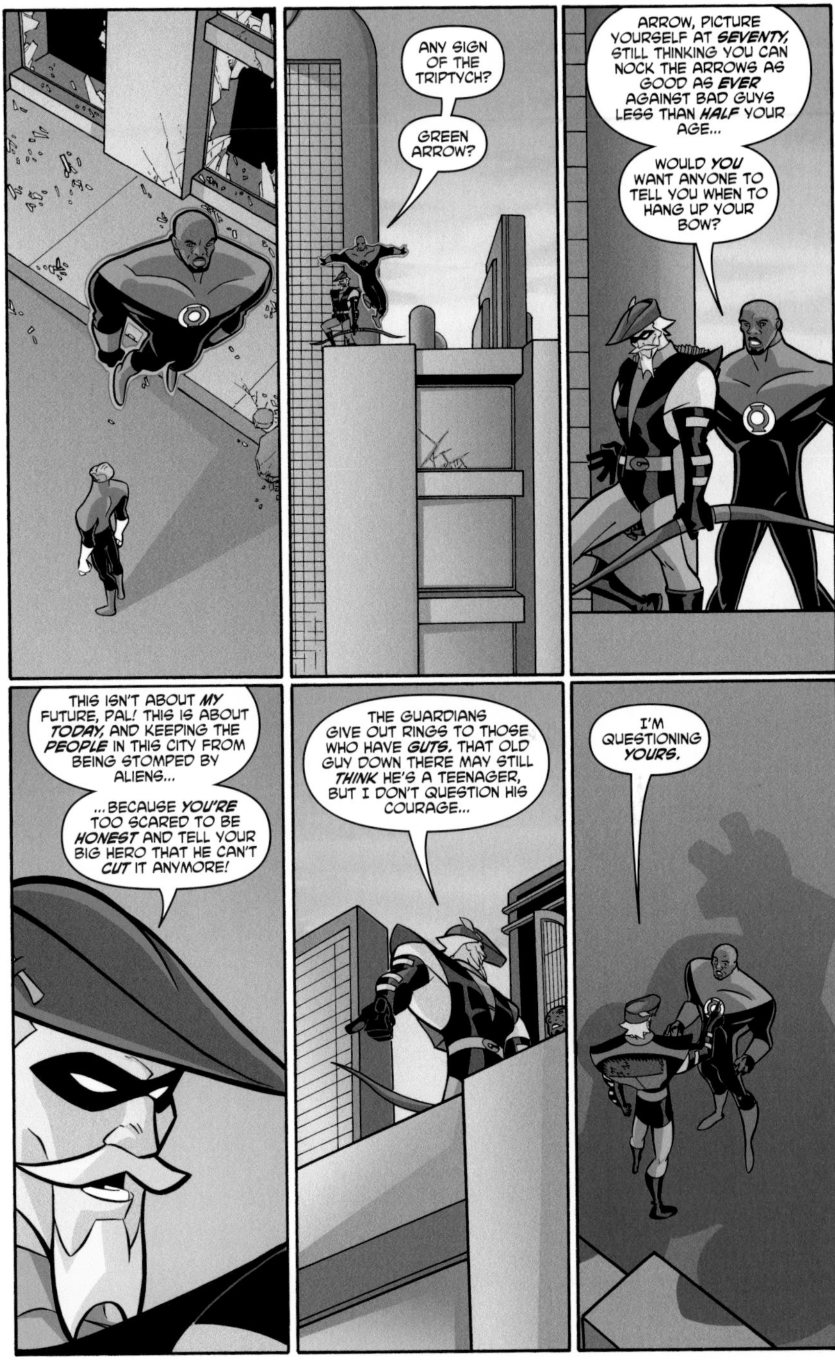
ANY SIGN OF THE TRIPTYCH?
GREEN ARROW?
ARROW, PICTURE YOURSELF AT SEVENTY, STILL THINKING YOU CAN NOCK THE ARROWS AS GOOD AS EVER AGAINST BAD GUYS LESS THAN HALF YOUR AGE...
WOULD YOU WANT ANYONE TO TELL YOU WHEN TO HANG UP YOUR BOW?
THIS ISN'T ABOUT MY FUTURE, PAL! THIS IS ABOUT TODAY, AND KEEPING THE PEOPLE IN THIS CITY FROM BEING STOMPED BY ALIENS...
...BECAUSE YOU'RE TOO SCARED TO BE HONEST AND TELL YOUR BIG HERO THAT HE CAN'T CUT IT ANYMORE!
THE GUARDIANS GIVE OUT RINGS TO THOSE WHO HAVE GUTS. THAT OLD GUY DOWN THERE MAY STILL THINK HE'S A TEENAGER, BUT I DON'T QUESTION HIS COURAGE...
I'M QUESTIONING YOURS.

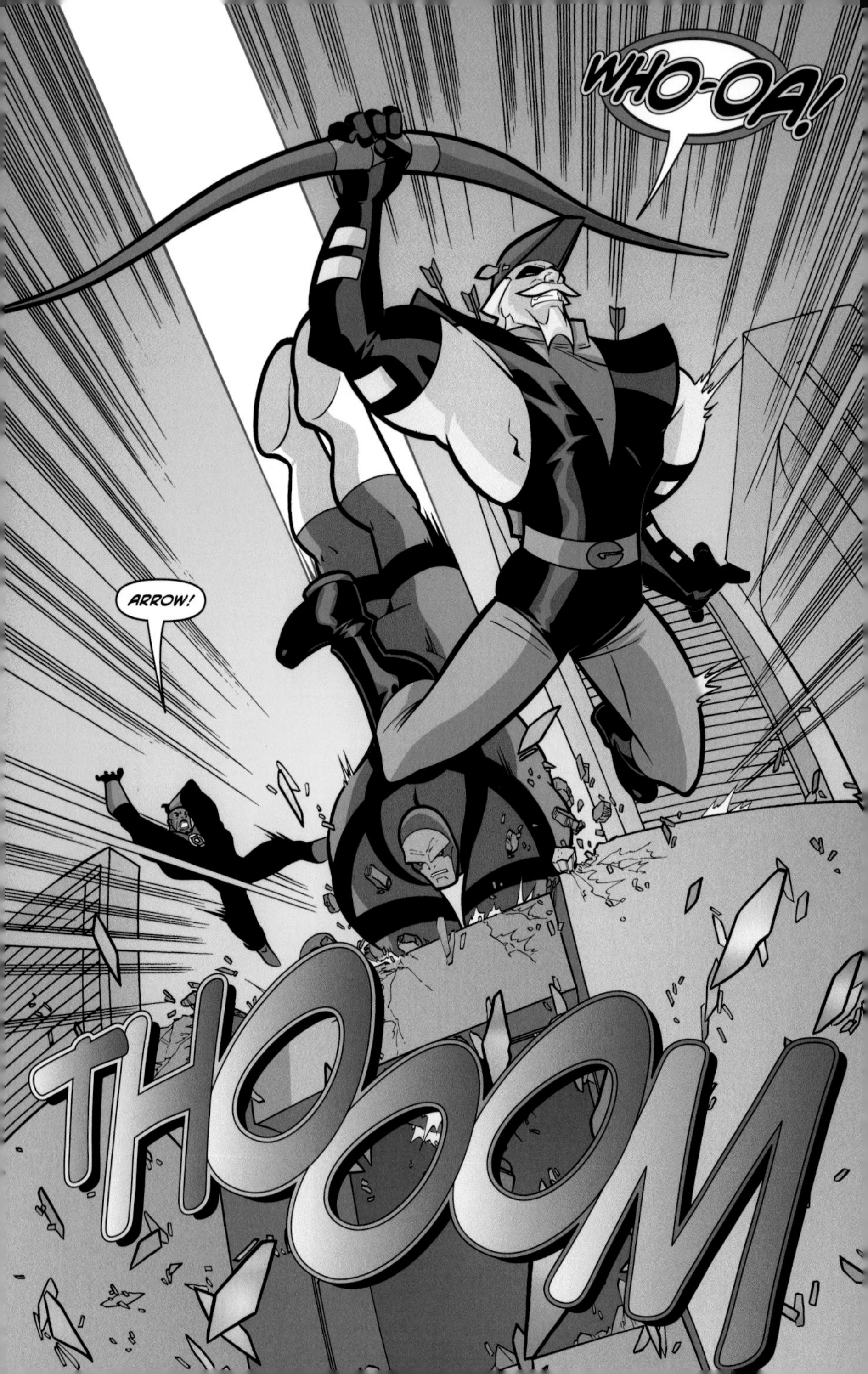
WHO-OA!
ARROW!
THOOOM

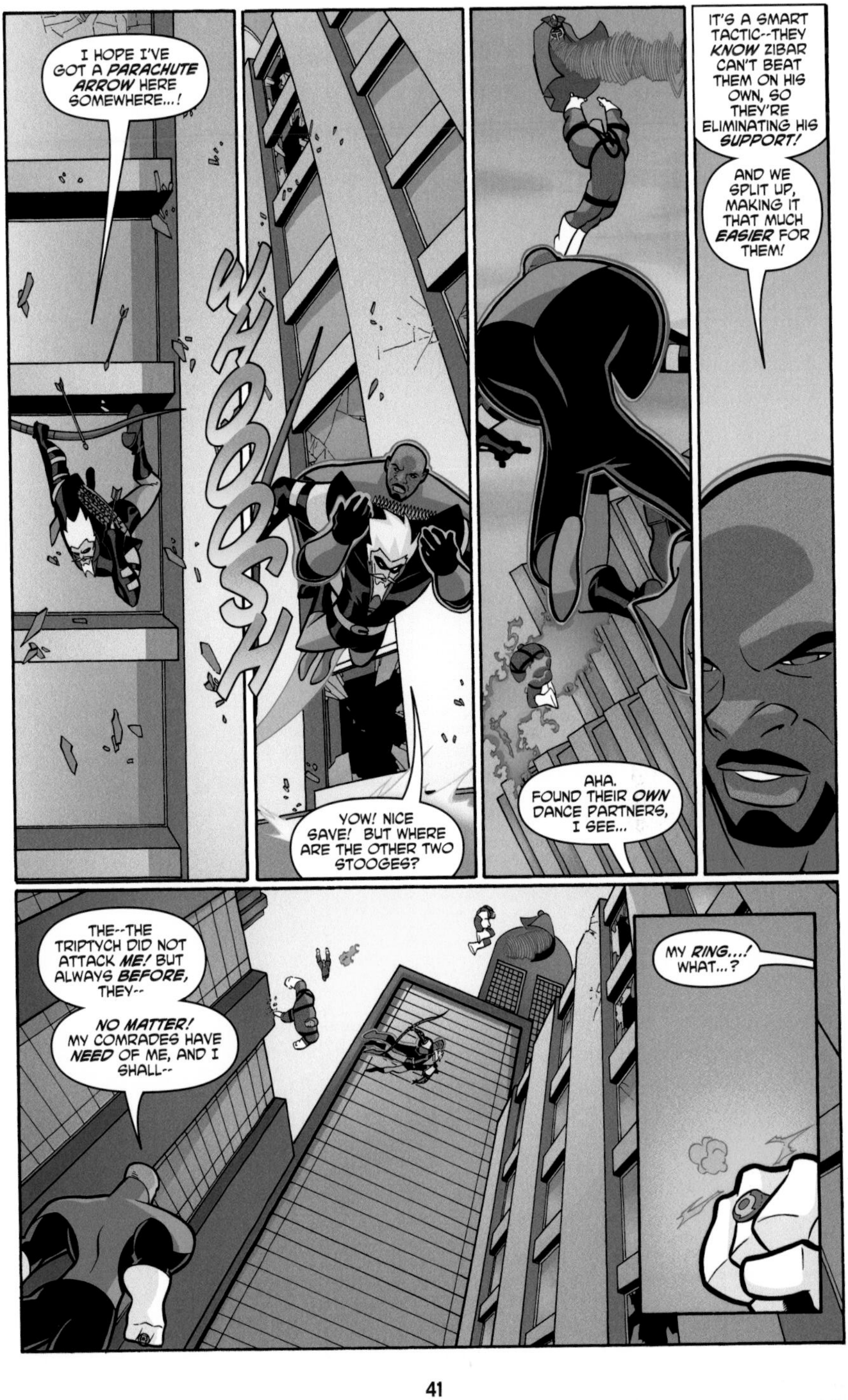
I HOPE I'VE GOT A *PARACHUTE ARROW* HERE SOMEWHERE...!
WHOOOSH
YOW! NICE SAVE! BUT WHERE ARE THE OTHER TWO STOOGES?
AHA. FOUND THEIR *OWN* DANCE PARTNERS, I SEE...
IT'S A SMART TACTIC--THEY *KNOW* ZIBAR CAN'T BEAT THEM ON HIS OWN, SO THEY'RE ELIMINATING HIS *SUPPORT!*
AND WE SPLIT UP, MAKING IT THAT MUCH *EASIER* FOR THEM!
THE--THE TRIPTYCH DID NOT ATTACK *ME!* BUT ALWAYS *BEFORE,* THEY--
NO MATTER! MY COMRADES HAVE *NEED* OF ME, AND I SHALL--
MY *RING...!* WHAT...?

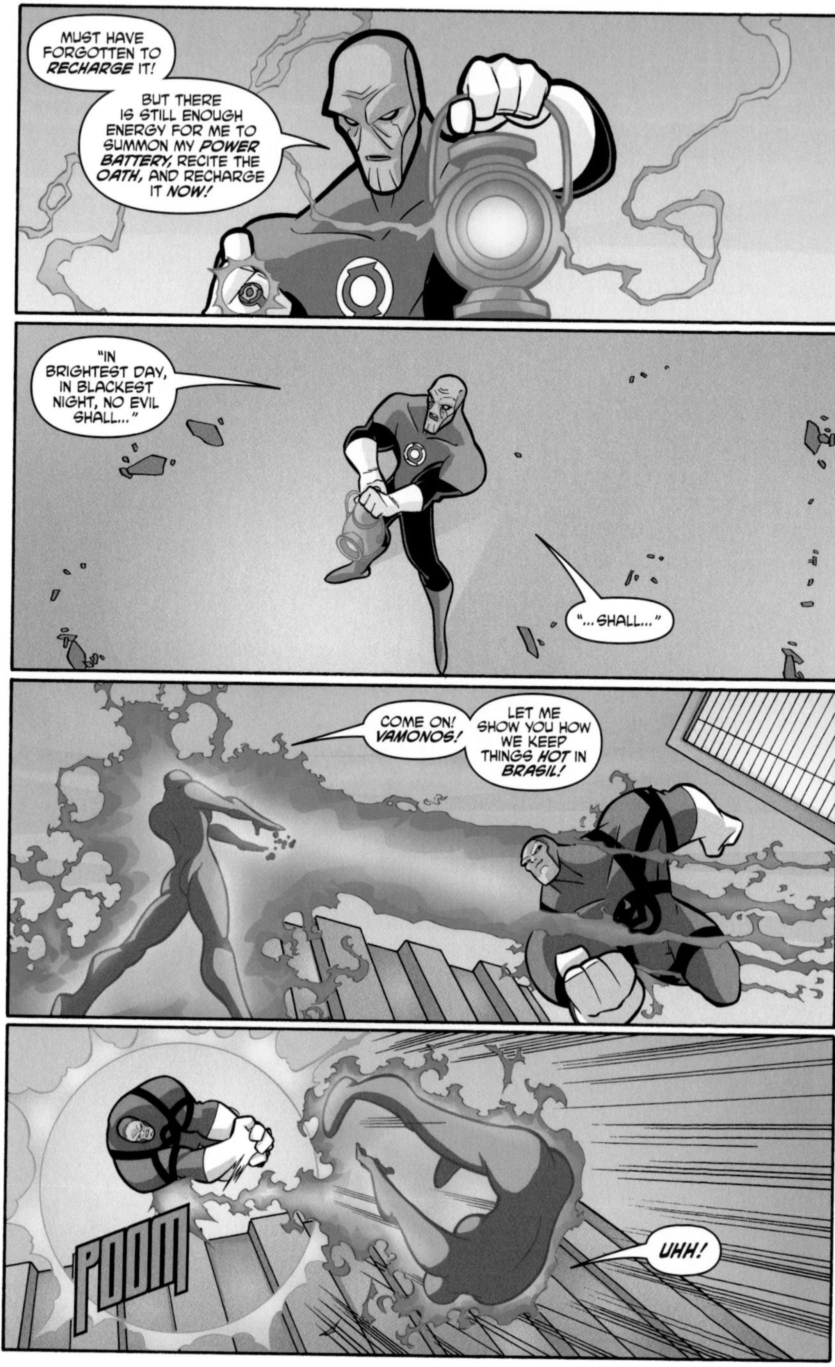
MUST HAVE FORGOTTEN TO RECHARGE IT!
BUT THERE IS STILL ENOUGH ENERGY FOR ME TO SUMMON MY POWER BATTERY, RECITE THE OATH, AND RECHARGE IT NOW!
"IN BRIGHTEST DAY, IN BLACKEST NIGHT, NO EVIL SHALL..."
"...SHALL..."
COME ON! VAMONOS!
LET ME SHOW YOU HOW WE KEEP THINGS HOT IN BRASIL!
POOM
UHH!

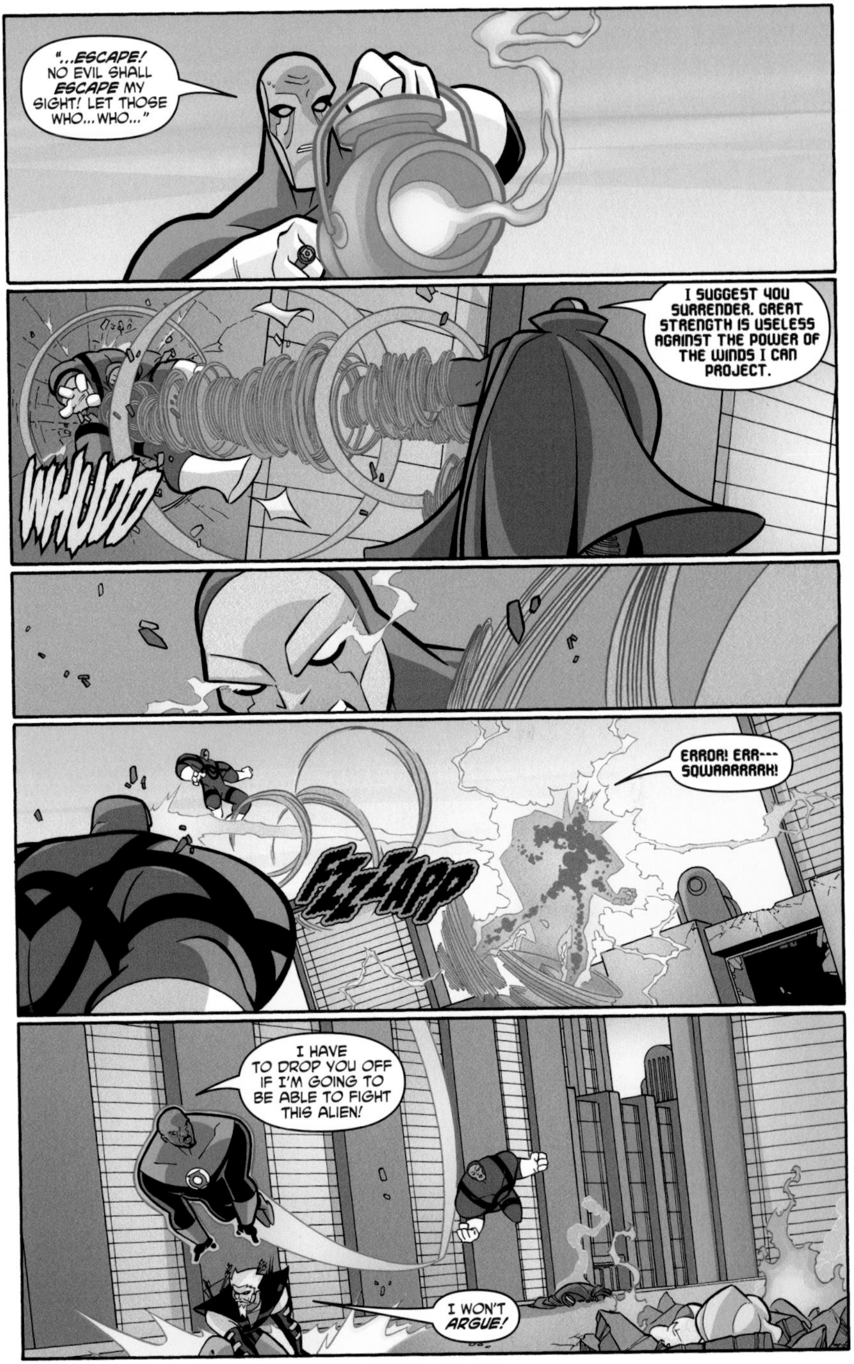
"...ESCAPE! NO EVIL SHALL ESCAPE MY SIGHT! LET THOSE WHO...WHO..."
I SUGGEST YOU SURRENDER. GREAT STRENGTH IS USELESS AGAINST THE POWER OF THE WINDS I CAN PROJECT.
WHUDD
ERROR! ERR---SQWAARRRRK!
FZ-ZAPP
I HAVE TO DROP YOU OFF IF I'M GOING TO BE ABLE TO FIGHT THIS ALIEN!
I WON'T ARGUE!

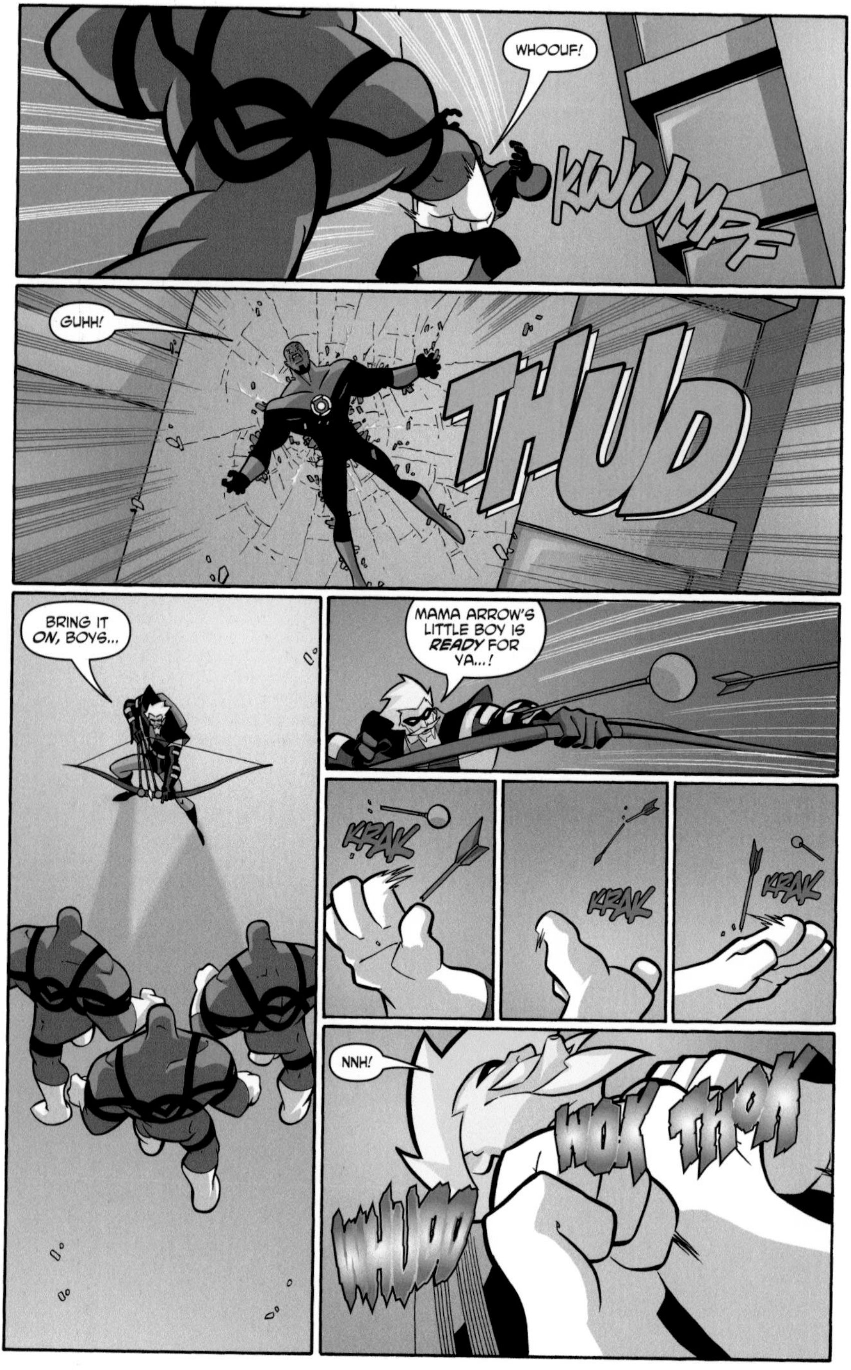
WHOOUF!
KWUMPF
GUHH!
THUD
BRING IT ON, BOYS...
MAMA ARROW'S LITTLE BOY IS READY FOR YA...!
KRAK
KRAK
KRAK
NNH!
WOK
THOK
WHUDD

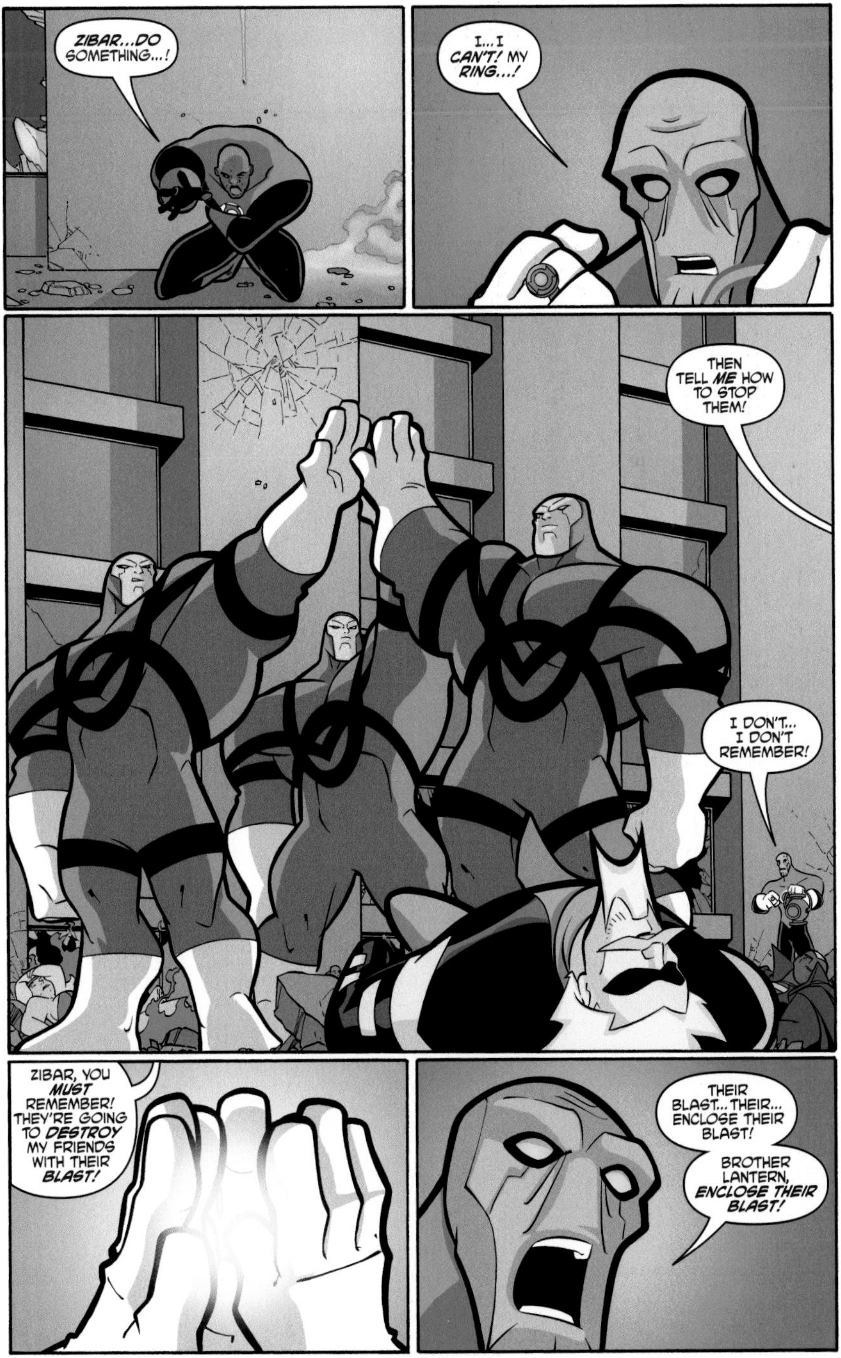
ZIBAR...DO SOMETHING...!
I...I CAN'T! MY RING...!
THEN TELL ME HOW TO STOP THEM!
I DON'T... I DON'T REMEMBER!
ZIBAR, YOU MUST REMEMBER! THEY'RE GOING TO DESTROY MY FRIENDS WITH THEIR BLAST!
THEIR BLAST... THEIR... ENCLOSE THEIR BLAST!
BROTHER LANTERN, ENCLOSE THEIR BLAST!

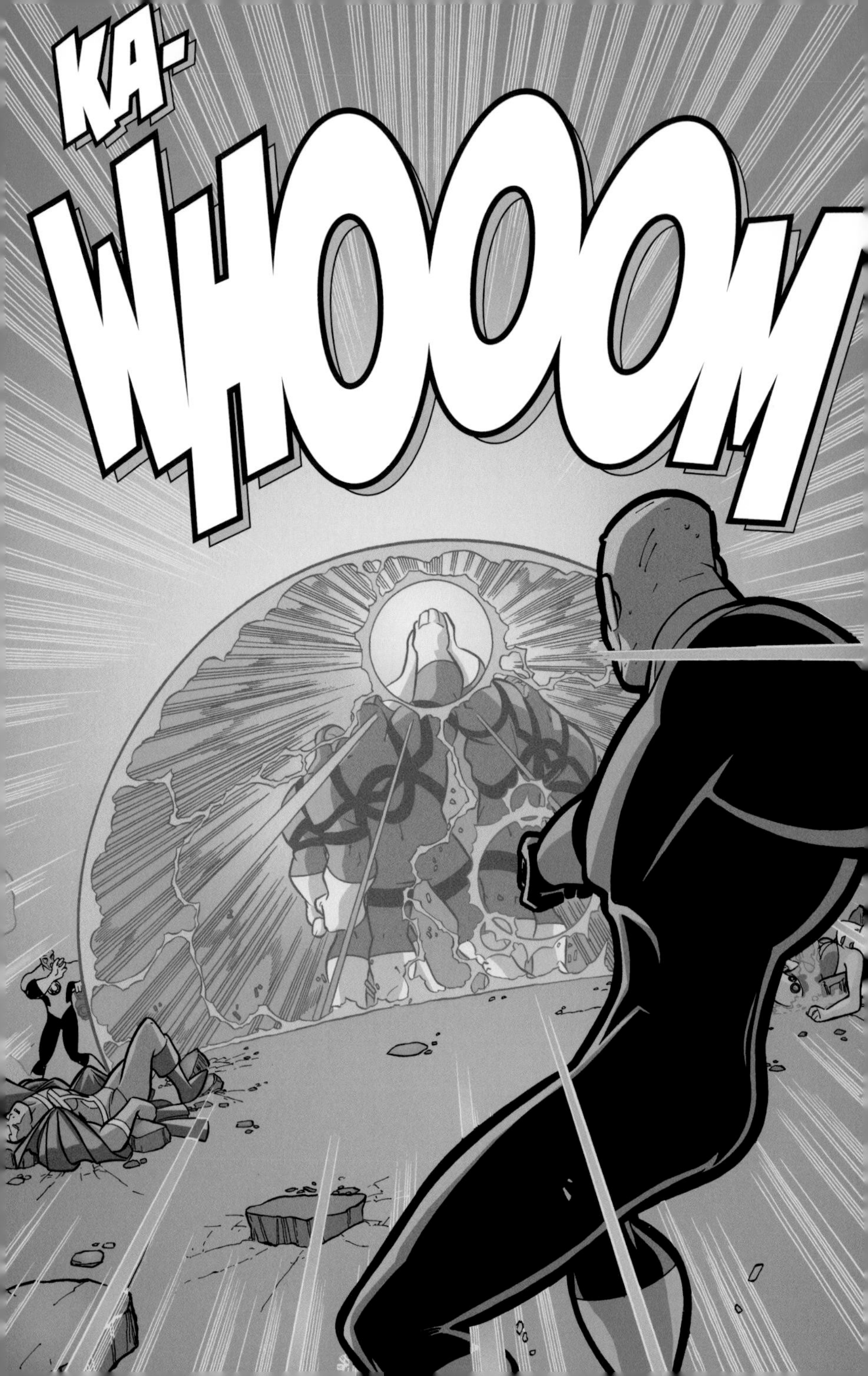
KA-
WHOOOM

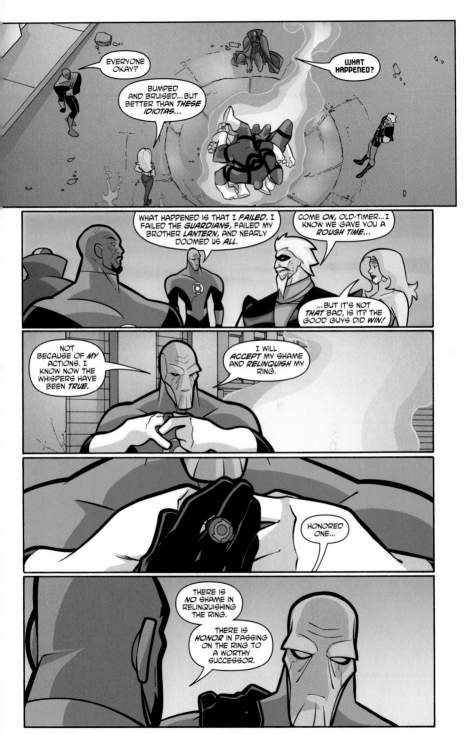

EVERYONE OKAY?

BUMPED AND BRUISED...BUT BETTER THAN *THESE IDIOTAS*...

WHAT HAPPENED?

WHAT HAPPENED IS THAT I *FAILED*. I FAILED THE *GUARDIANS*, FAILED MY BROTHER *LANTERN*, AND NEARLY DOOMED US *ALL*.

COME *ON*, OLD-TIMER...I KNOW WE GAVE YOU A *ROUGH TIME*...

...BUT IT'S NOT *THAT* BAD, IS IT? THE GOOD GUYS DID *WIN!*

NOT BECAUSE OF *MY* ACTIONS. I KNOW NOW THE WHISPERS HAVE BEEN *TRUE.*

I WILL *ACCEPT* MY SHAME AND *RELINQUISH* MY RING.

HONORED ONE...

THERE IS *NO SHAME* IN RELINQUISHING THE RING.

THERE IS *HONOR* IN PASSING ON THE RING TO A WORTHY SUCCESSOR.

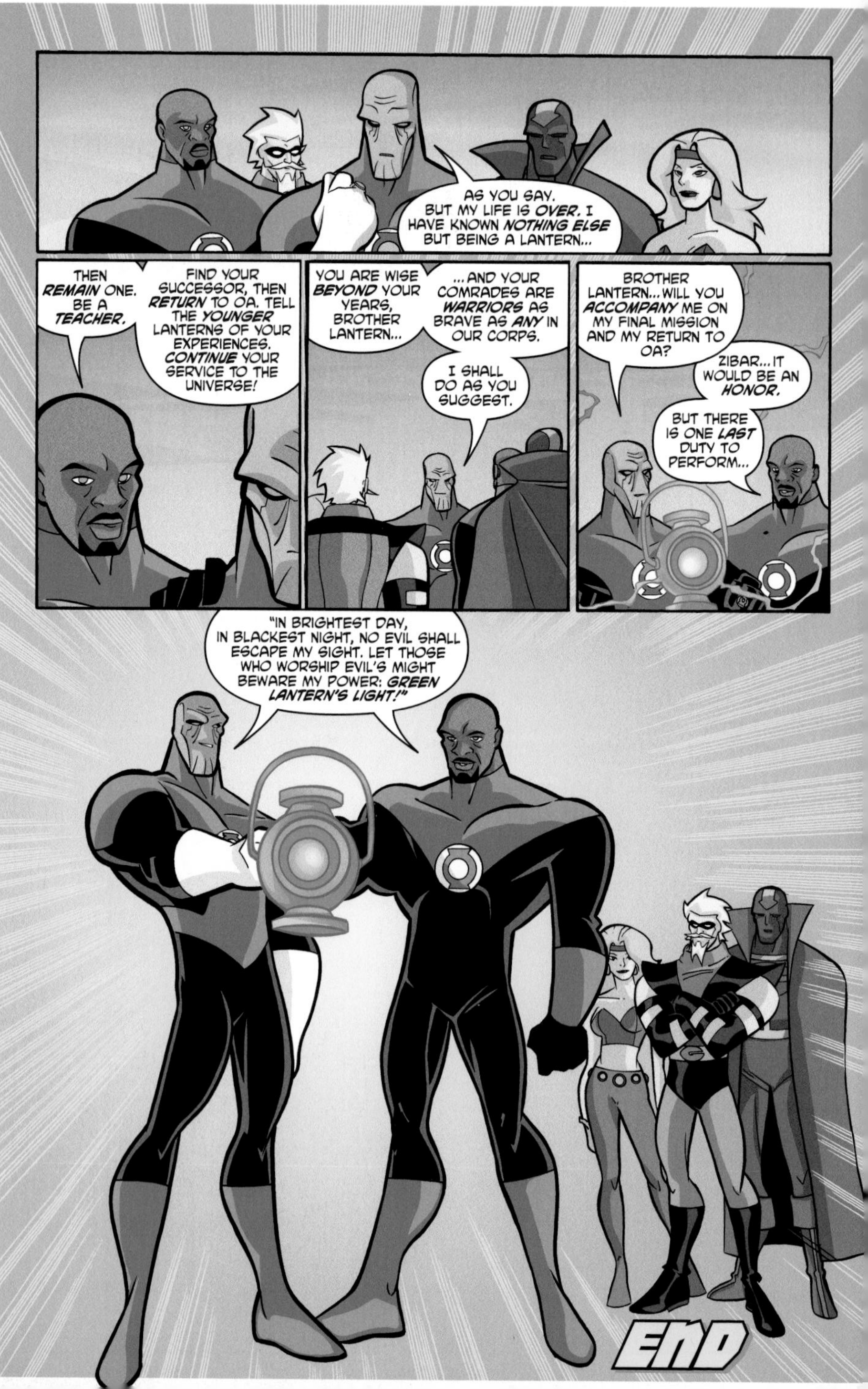

AS YOU SAY. BUT MY LIFE IS OVER. I HAVE KNOWN NOTHING ELSE BUT BEING A LANTERN...
THEN REMAIN ONE. BE A TEACHER.
FIND YOUR SUCCESSOR, THEN RETURN TO OA. TELL THE YOUNGER LANTERNS OF YOUR EXPERIENCES. CONTINUE YOUR SERVICE TO THE UNIVERSE!
YOU ARE WISE BEYOND YOUR YEARS, BROTHER LANTERN...
...AND YOUR COMRADES ARE WARRIORS AS BRAVE AS ANY IN OUR CORPS.
I SHALL DO AS YOU SUGGEST.
BROTHER LANTERN... WILL YOU ACCOMPANY ME ON MY FINAL MISSION AND MY RETURN TO OA?
ZIBAR... IT WOULD BE AN HONOR.
BUT THERE IS ONE LAST DUTY TO PERFORM...
"IN BRIGHTEST DAY, IN BLACKEST NIGHT, NO EVIL SHALL ESCAPE MY SIGHT. LET THOSE WHO WORSHIP EVIL'S MIGHT BEWARE MY POWER: GREEN LANTERN'S LIGHT!"
END

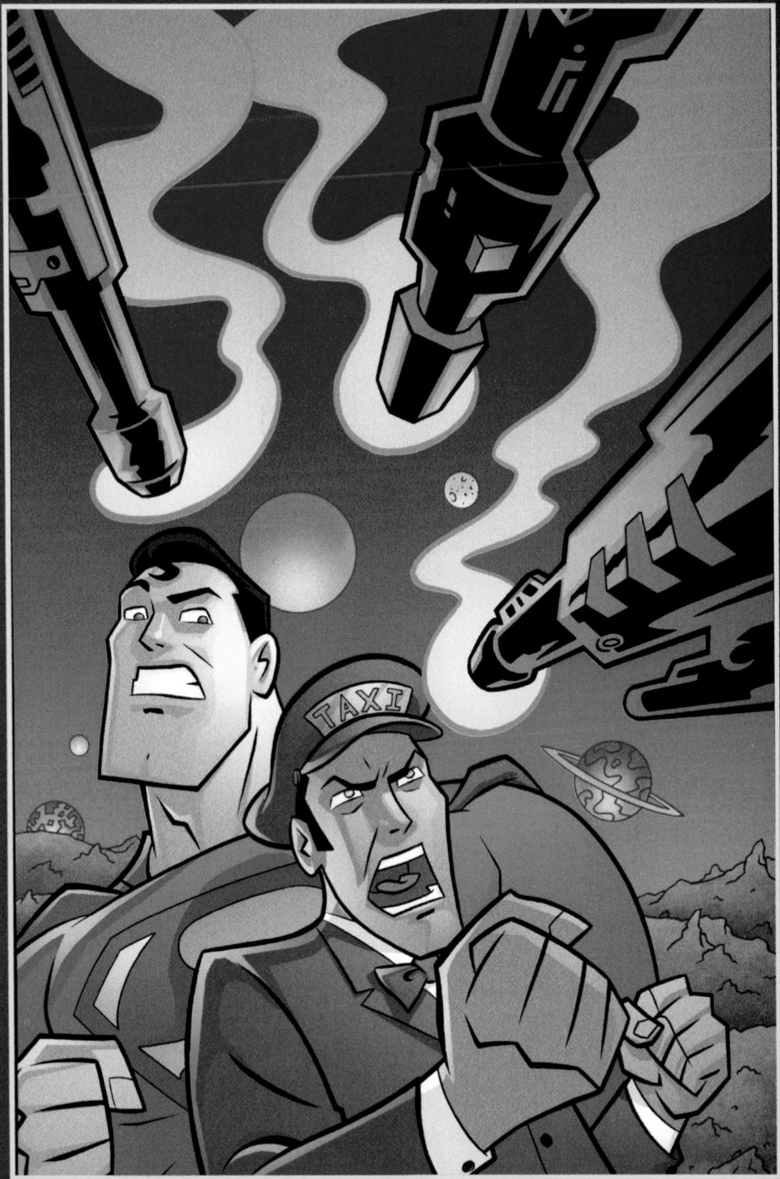
TAXI

CHAPTER 3: FARE 48

JUSTICE LEAGUE UNLIMITED

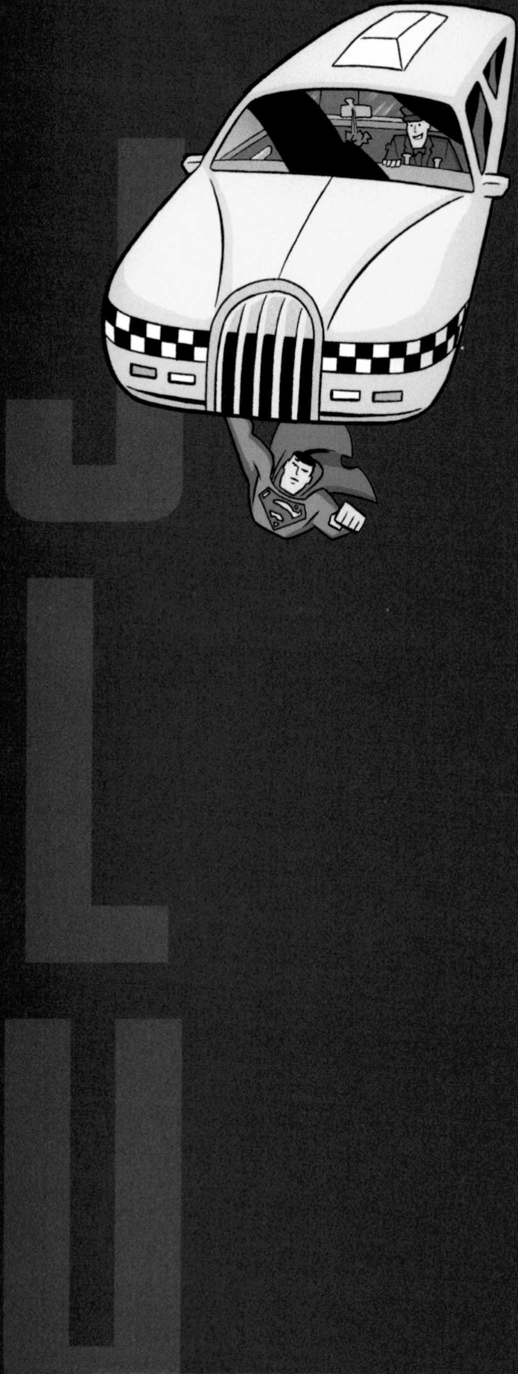
JLU

COVER ART BY ETHAN BEAVERS AND KANILA TRIPP

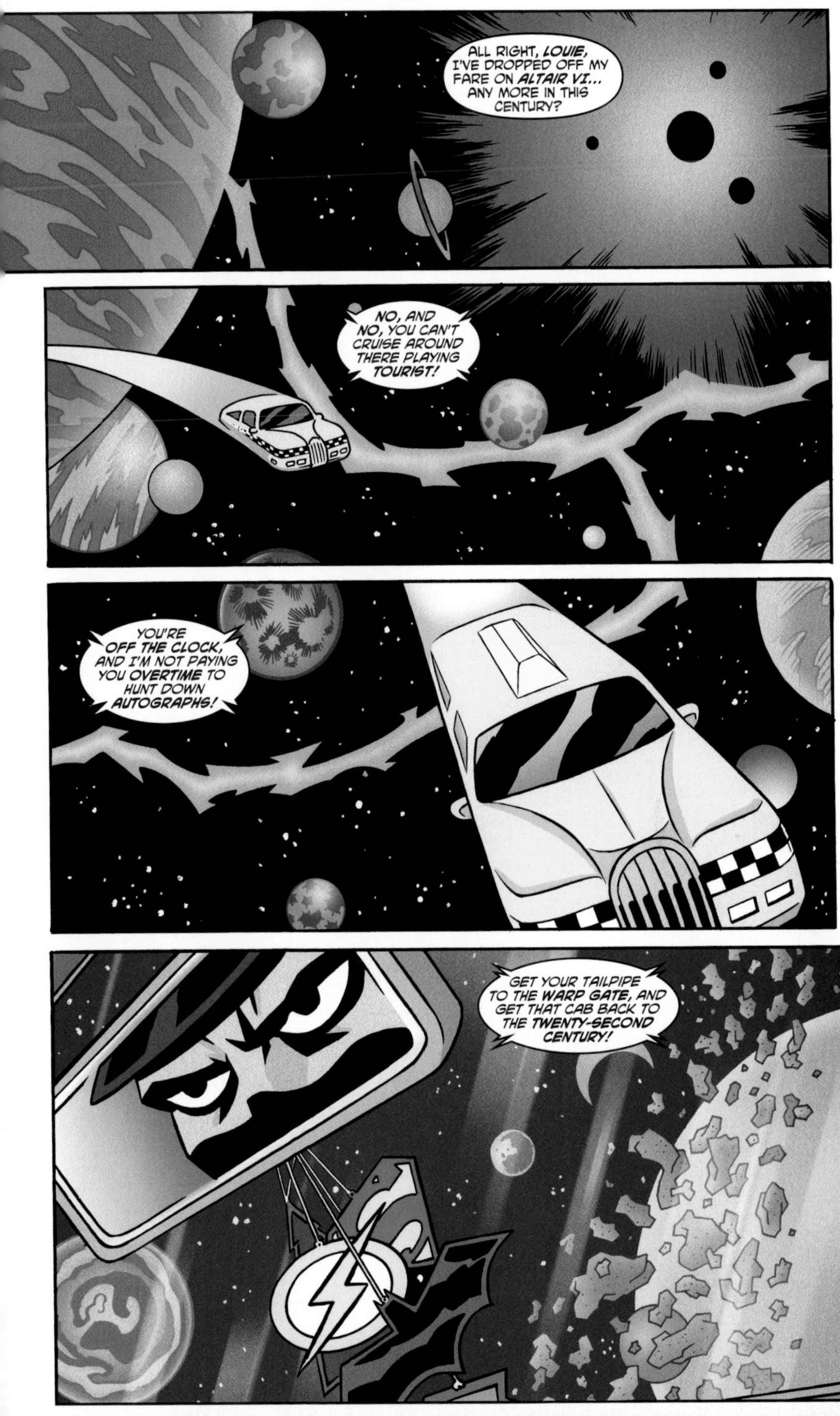
ALL RIGHT, LOUIE, I'VE DROPPED OFF MY FARE ON ALTAIR VI... ANY MORE IN THIS CENTURY?
NO, AND NO, YOU CAN'T CRUISE AROUND THERE PLAYING TOURIST!
YOU'RE OFF THE CLOCK, AND I'M NOT PAYING YOU OVERTIME TO HUNT DOWN AUTOGRAPHS!
GET YOUR TAILPIPE TO THE WARP GATE, AND GET THAT CAB BACK TO THE TWENTY-SECOND CENTURY!

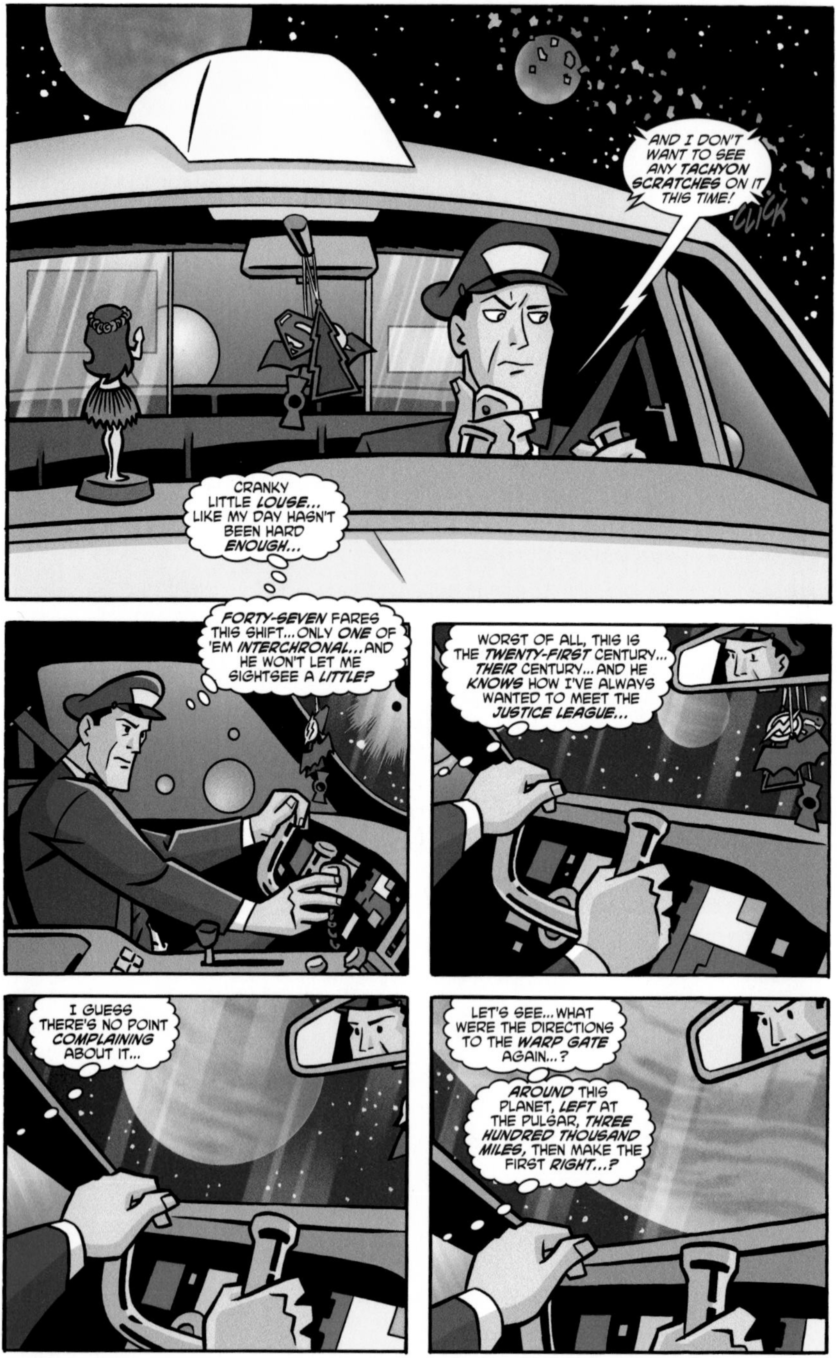
AND I DON'T WANT TO SEE ANY TACHYON SCRATCHES ON IT THIS TIME!
CLICK
CRANKY LITTLE LOUSE... LIKE MY DAY HASN'T BEEN HARD ENOUGH...
FORTY-SEVEN FARES THIS SHIFT... ONLY ONE OF 'EM INTERCHRONAL... AND HE WON'T LET ME SIGHTSEE A LITTLE?
WORST OF ALL, THIS IS THE TWENTY-FIRST CENTURY... THEIR CENTURY... AND HE KNOWS HOW I'VE ALWAYS WANTED TO MEET THE JUSTICE LEAGUE...
I GUESS THERE'S NO POINT COMPLAINING ABOUT IT...
LET'S SEE... WHAT WERE THE DIRECTIONS TO THE WARP GATE AGAIN...?
AROUND THIS PLANET, LEFT AT THE PULSAR, THREE HUNDRED THOUSAND MILES, THEN MAKE THE FIRST RIGHT...?

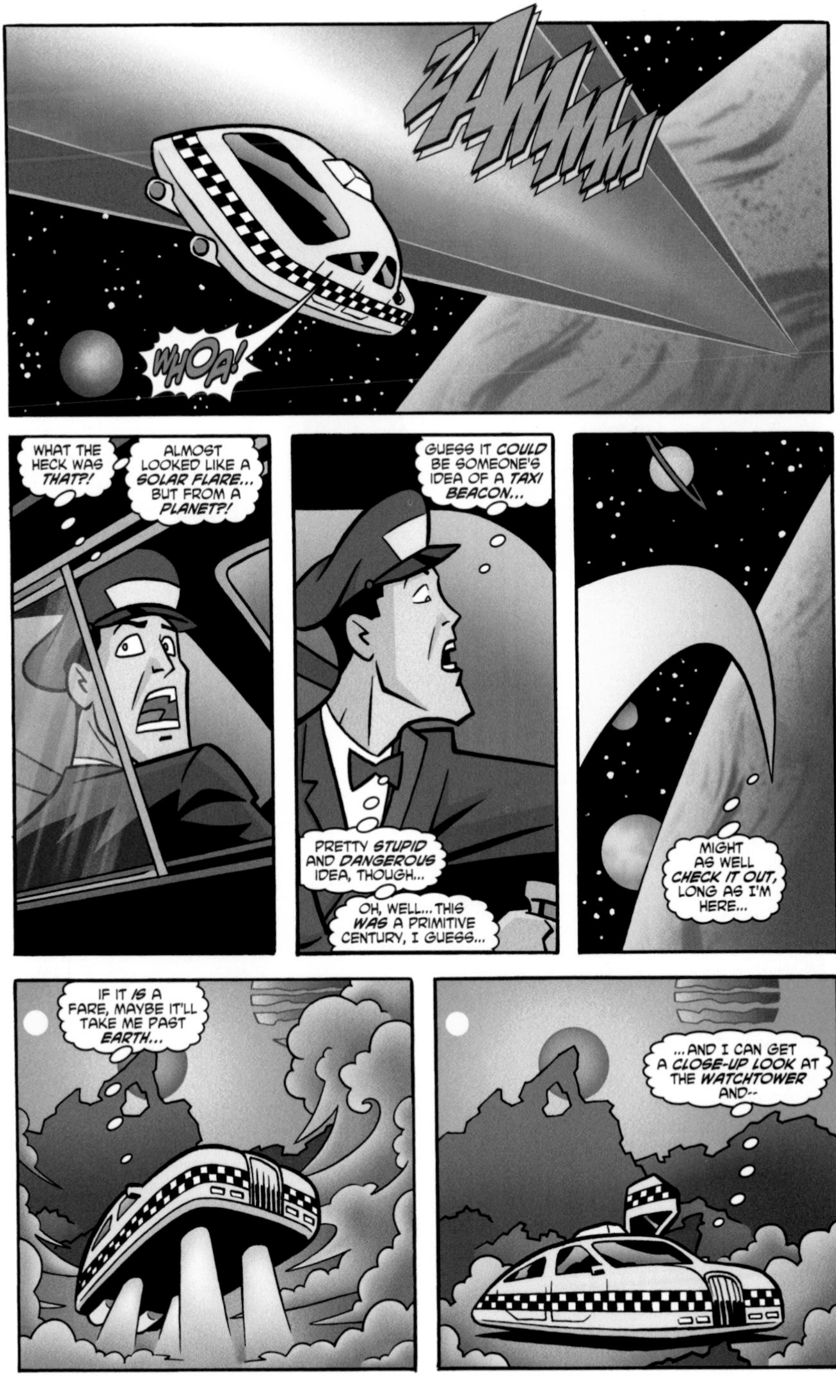
ZAMMMM
WHOA!
WHAT THE HECK WAS THAT?!
ALMOST LOOKED LIKE A SOLAR FLARE... BUT FROM A PLANET?!
GUESS IT COULD BE SOMEONE'S IDEA OF A TAXI BEACON...
PRETTY STUPID AND DANGEROUS IDEA, THOUGH...
OH, WELL...THIS WAS A PRIMITIVE CENTURY, I GUESS...
MIGHT AS WELL CHECK IT OUT, LONG AS I'M HERE...
IF IT IS A FARE, MAYBE IT'LL TAKE ME PAST EARTH...
...AND I CAN GET A CLOSE-UP LOOK AT THE WATCHTOWER AND--

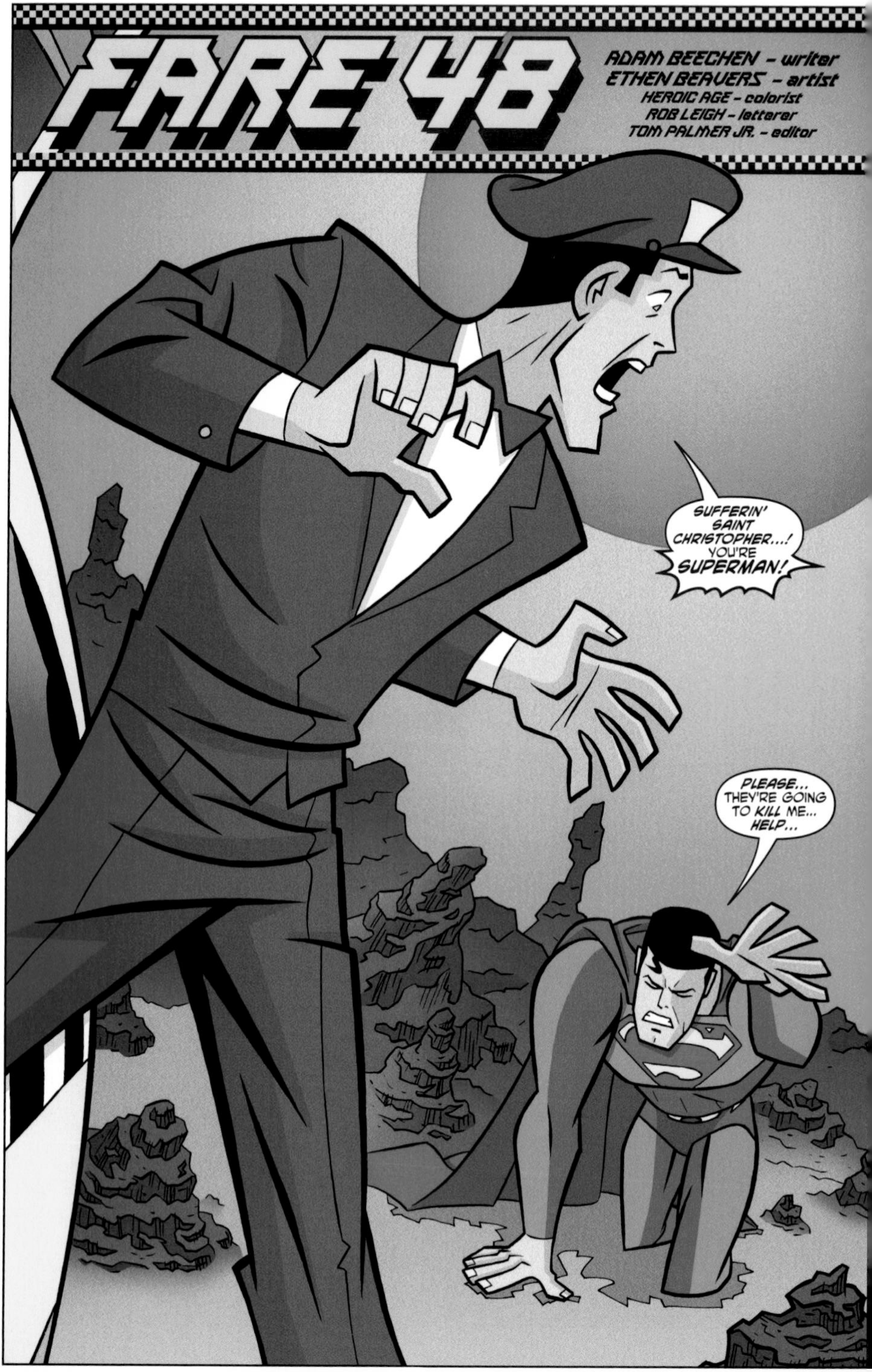
FARE 48
ADAM BEECHEN - writer
ETHEN BEAVERS - artist
HEROIC AGE - colorist
ROB LEIGH - letterer
TOM PALMER JR. - editor
SUFFERIN' SAINT CHRISTOPHER...! YOU'RE SUPERMAN!
PLEASE... THEY'RE GOING TO KILL ME... HELP...

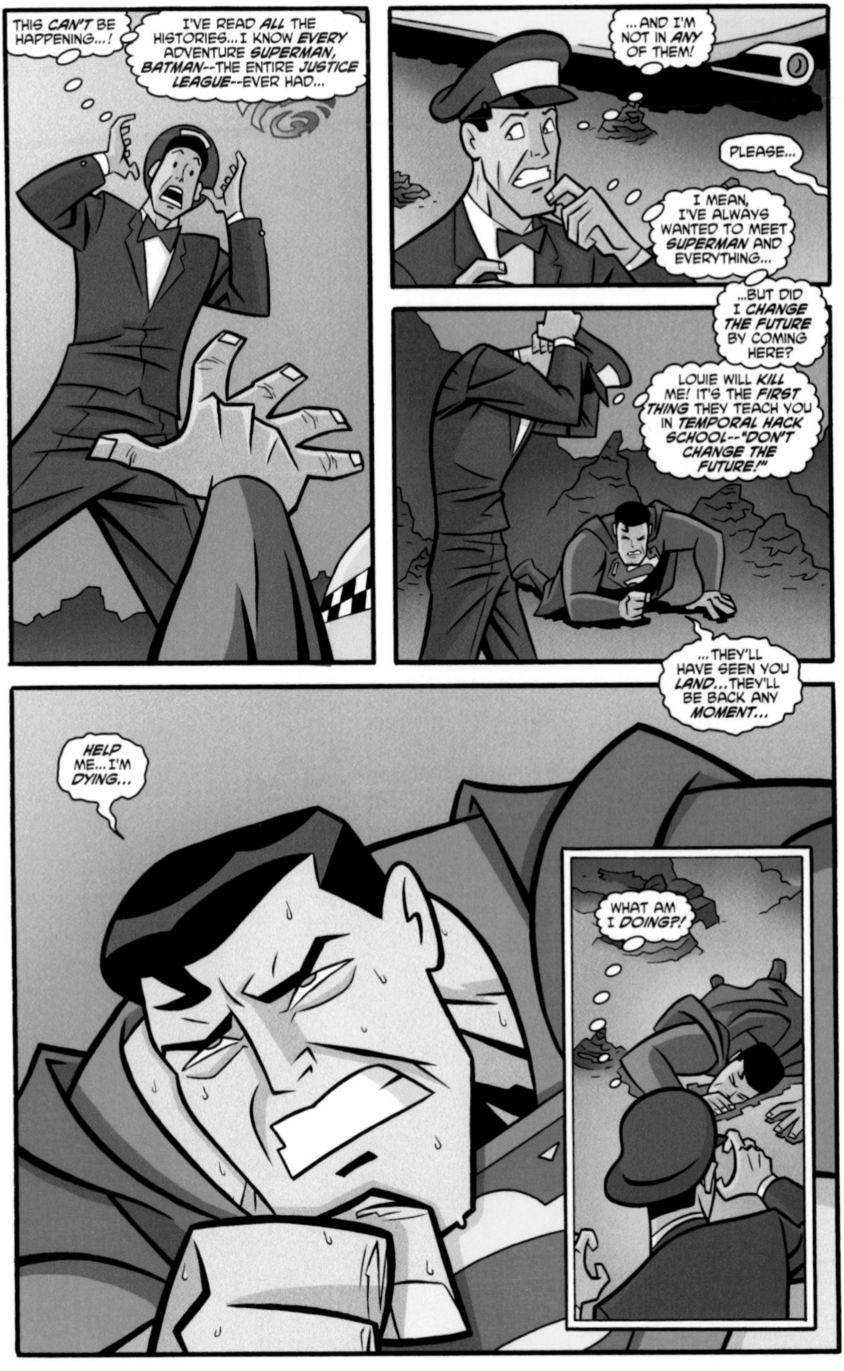
THIS CAN'T BE HAPPENING...!
I'VE READ ALL THE HISTORIES...I KNOW EVERY ADVENTURE SUPERMAN, BATMAN--THE ENTIRE JUSTICE LEAGUE--EVER HAD...
...AND I'M NOT IN ANY OF THEM!
PLEASE...
I MEAN, I'VE ALWAYS WANTED TO MEET SUPERMAN AND EVERYTHING...
...BUT DID I CHANGE THE FUTURE BY COMING HERE?
LOUIE WILL KILL ME! IT'S THE FIRST THING THEY TEACH YOU IN TEMPORAL HACK SCHOOL--"DON'T CHANGE THE FUTURE!"
...THEY'LL HAVE SEEN YOU LAND...THEY'LL BE BACK ANY MOMENT...
HELP ME...I'M DYING...
WHAT AM I DOING?!

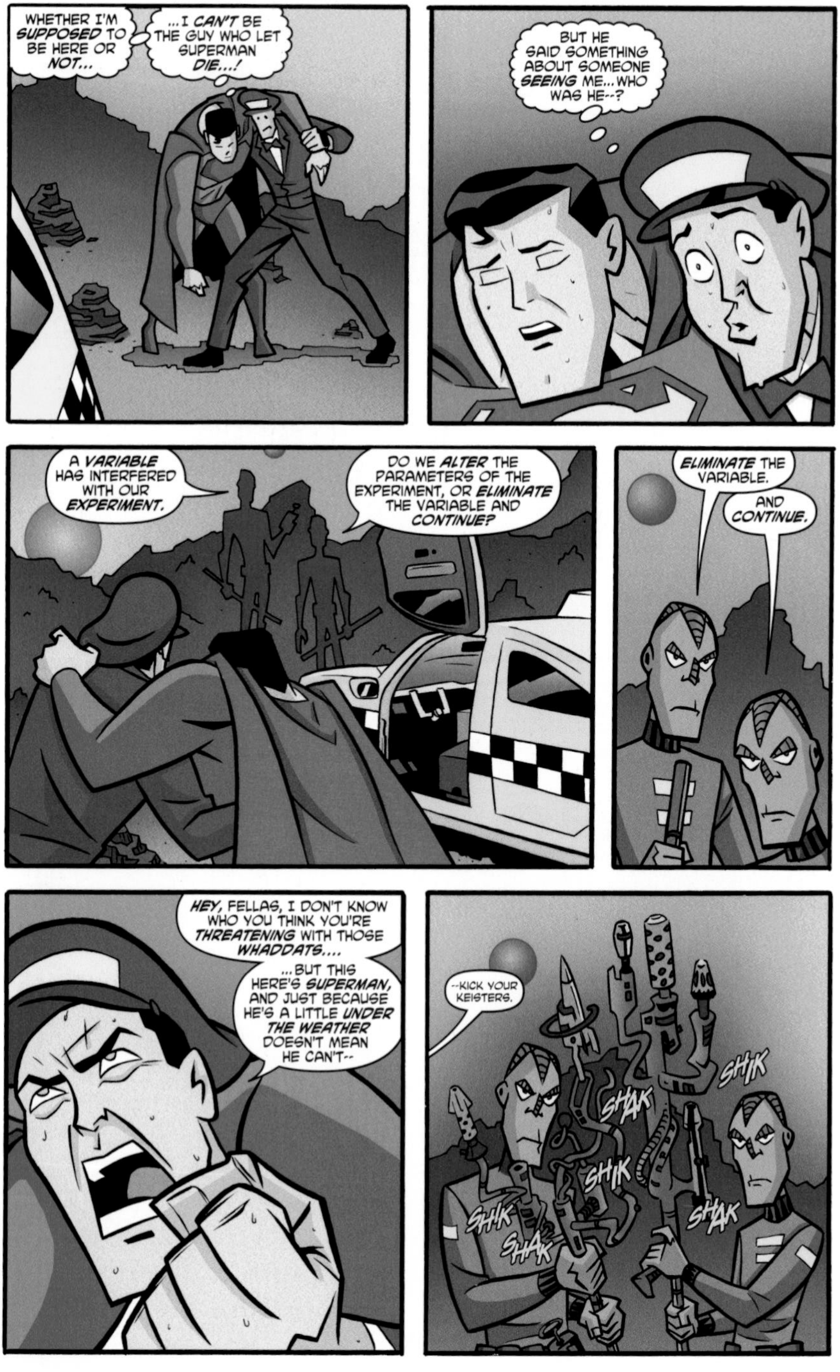

WHETHER I'M SUPPOSED TO BE HERE OR NOT...
...I CAN'T BE THE GUY WHO LET SUPERMAN DIE...!
BUT HE SAID SOMETHING ABOUT SOMEONE SEEING ME...WHO WAS HE--?
A VARIABLE HAS INTERFERED WITH OUR EXPERIMENT.
DO WE ALTER THE PARAMETERS OF THE EXPERIMENT, OR ELIMINATE THE VARIABLE AND CONTINUE?
ELIMINATE THE VARIABLE.
AND CONTINUE.
HEY, FELLAS, I DON'T KNOW WHO YOU THINK YOU'RE THREATENING WITH THOSE WHADDATS....
...BUT THIS HERE'S SUPERMAN, AND JUST BECAUSE HE'S A LITTLE UNDER THE WEATHER DOESN'T MEAN HE CAN'T--
--KICK YOUR KEISTERS.
SHIK
SHAK
SHIK
SHIK
SHAK
SHAK

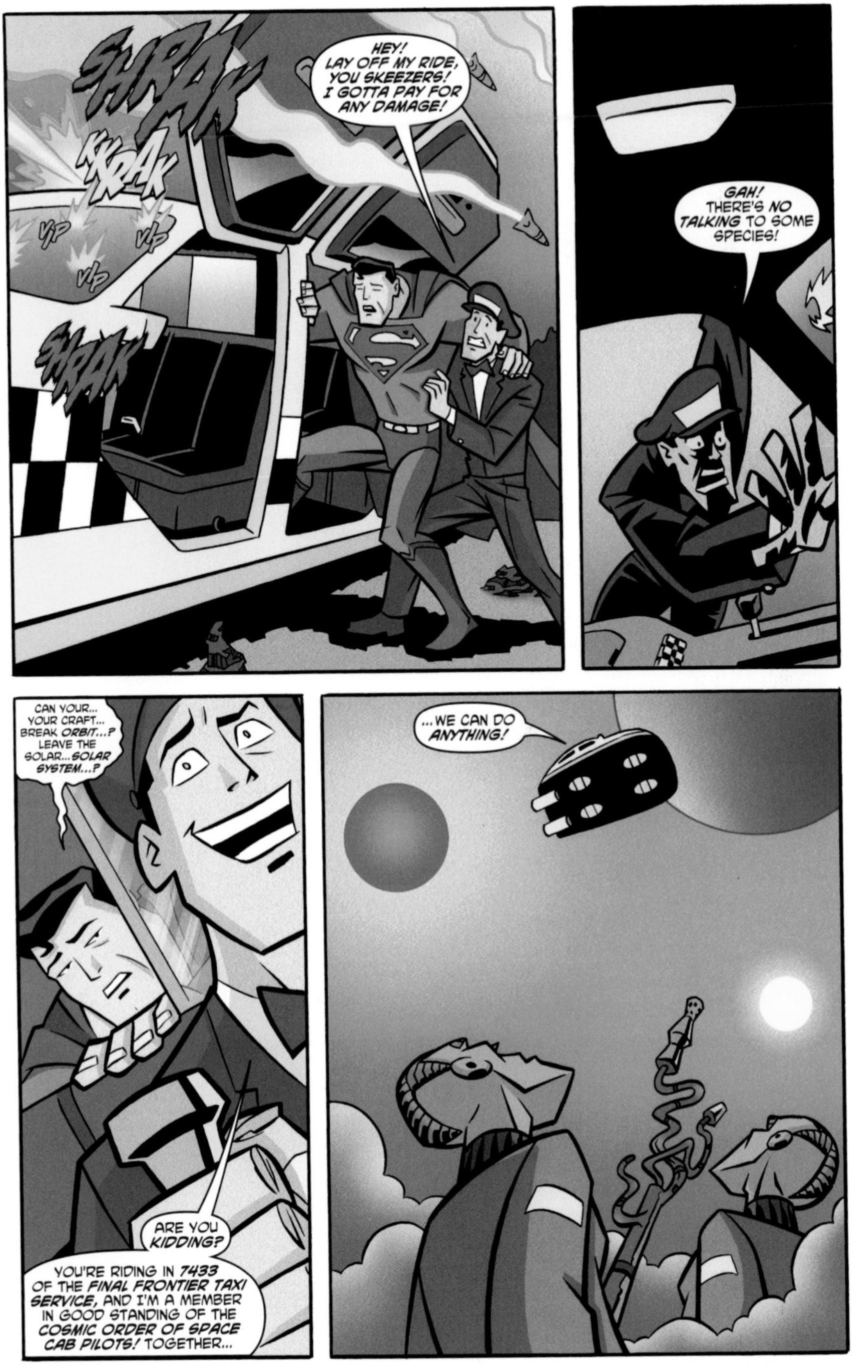
SHRAK
HEY! LAY OFF MY RIDE, YOU SKEEZERS! I GOTTA PAY FOR ANY DAMAGE!
KKRAK
VIP
VIP
VIP
SHRAK
GAH! THERE'S NO TALKING TO SOME SPECIES!
CAN YOUR... YOUR CRAFT... BREAK ORBIT...? LEAVE THE SOLAR... SOLAR SYSTEM...?
ARE YOU KIDDING?
YOU'RE RIDING IN 7433 OF THE FINAL FRONTIER TAXI SERVICE, AND I'M A MEMBER IN GOOD STANDING OF THE COSMIC ORDER OF SPACE CAB PILOTS! TOGETHER...
...WE CAN DO ANYTHING!

IF OUR SUBJECT *ESCAPES*, AND NEWS OF OUR EXPERIMENT REACHES OUR *INSTRUCTORS*, IT COULD HAVE *NEGATIVE CONSEQUENCES* ON OUR GRADES.

ACCURATE, HOWEVER...

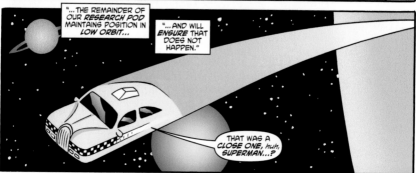

"...THE REMAINDER OF OUR *RESEARCH POD* MAINTAINS POSITION IN *LOW ORBIT*..."

"...AND WILL *ENSURE* THAT DOES NOT HAPPEN."

THAT WAS A *CLOSE ONE*, *huh*, *SUPERMAN*...?

BUT YOU GOT *NOTHIN'* TO WORRY ABOUT *NOW*, NO SIR! YOU ARE MOST DEFINITELY *HOME*--

--FRE-*eep!*

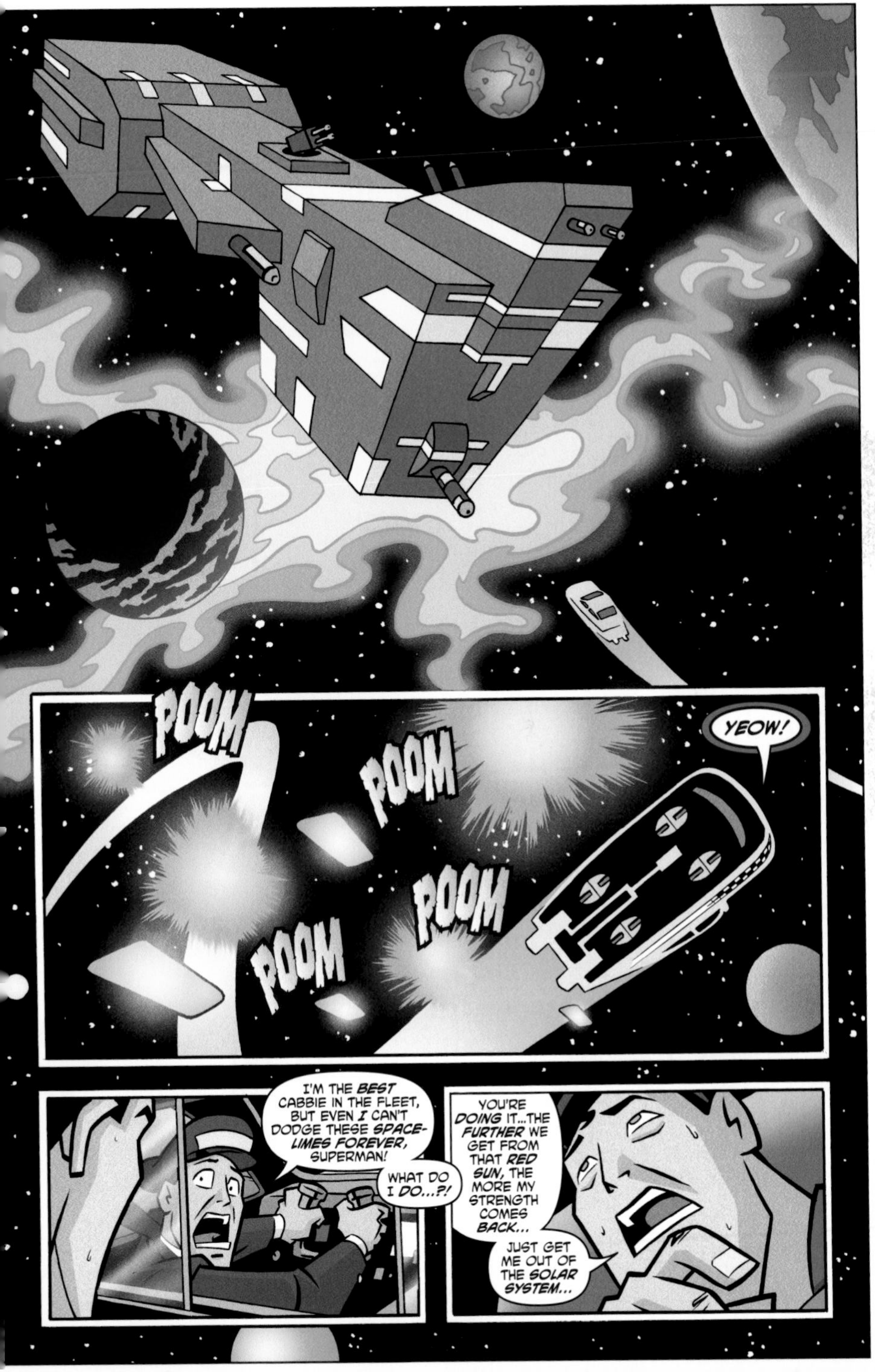
POOM
POOM
POOM
POOM
YEOW!
I'M THE BEST CABBIE IN THE FLEET, BUT EVEN I CAN'T DODGE THESE SPACE-LIMES FOREVER, SUPERMAN!
WHAT DO I DO...?!
YOU'RE DOING IT...THE FURTHER WE GET FROM THAT RED SUN, THE MORE MY STRENGTH COMES BACK...
JUST GET ME OUT OF THE SOLAR SYSTEM...

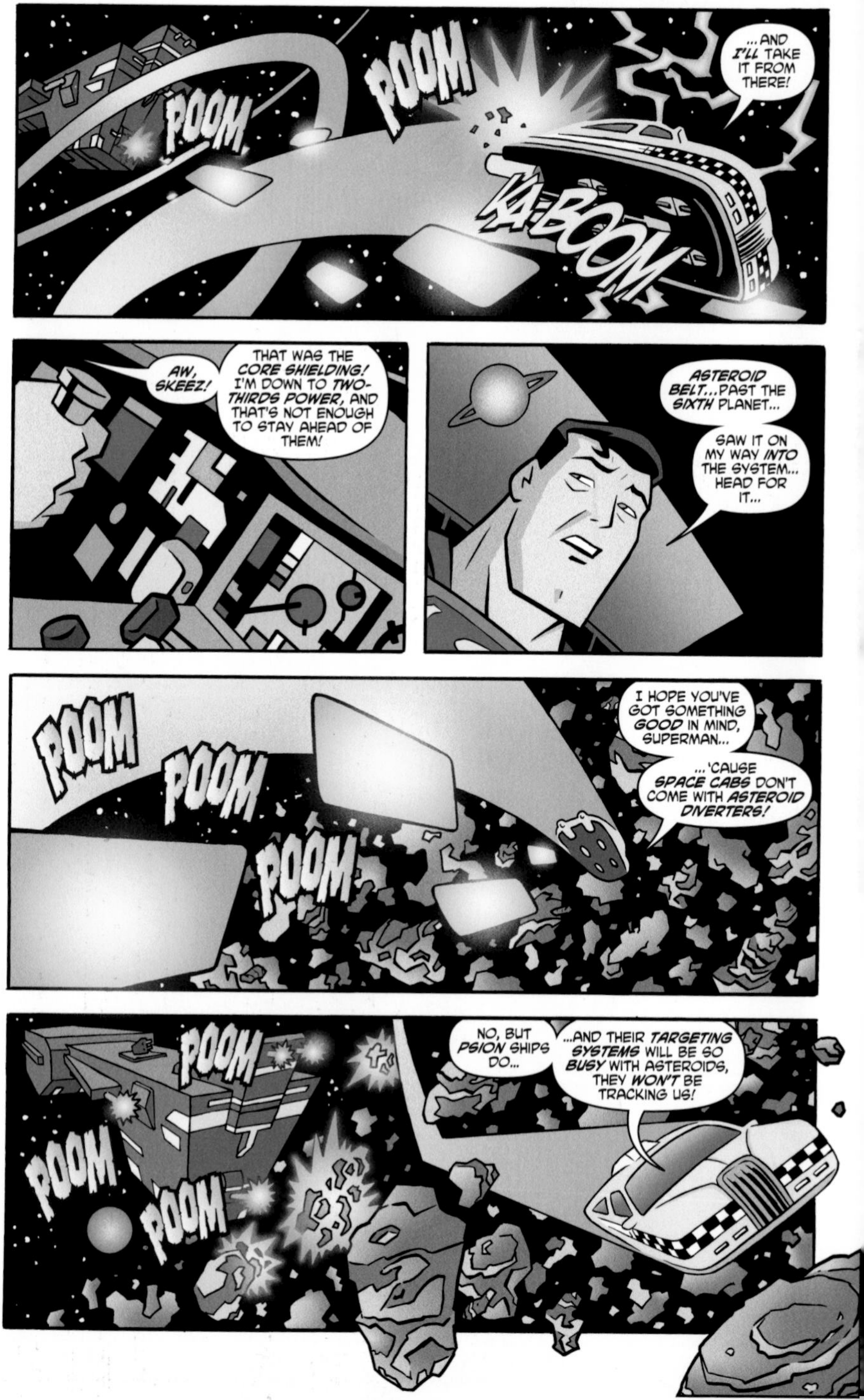
POOM
POOM
...AND I'LL TAKE IT FROM THERE!
KA-BOOM
AW, SKEEZ!
THAT WAS THE CORE SHIELDING! I'M DOWN TO TWO-THIRDS POWER, AND THAT'S NOT ENOUGH TO STAY AHEAD OF THEM!
ASTEROID BELT...PAST THE SIXTH PLANET...
SAW IT ON MY WAY INTO THE SYSTEM... HEAD FOR IT...
POOM
POOM
POOM
I HOPE YOU'VE GOT SOMETHING GOOD IN MIND, SUPERMAN...
...'CAUSE SPACE CABS DON'T COME WITH ASTEROID DIVERTERS!
POOM
POOM
POOM
NO, BUT PSION SHIPS DO...
...AND THEIR TARGETING SYSTEMS WILL BE SO BUSY WITH ASTEROIDS, THEY WON'T BE TRACKING US!

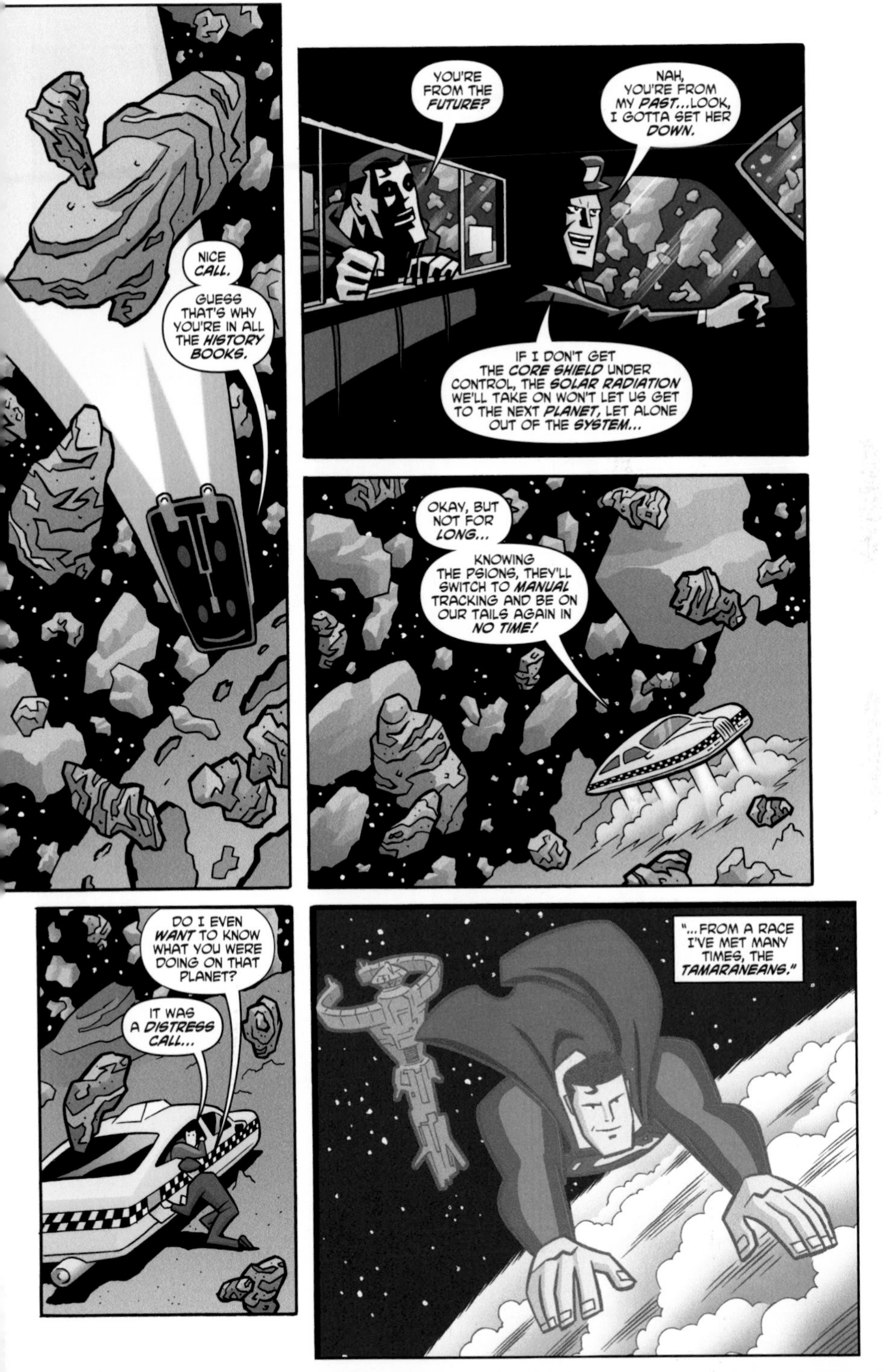
NICE CALL.
GUESS THAT'S WHY YOU'RE IN ALL THE HISTORY BOOKS.
YOU'RE FROM THE FUTURE?
NAH, YOU'RE FROM MY PAST...LOOK, I GOTTA SET HER DOWN.
IF I DON'T GET THE CORE SHIELD UNDER CONTROL, THE SOLAR RADIATION WE'LL TAKE ON WON'T LET US GET TO THE NEXT PLANET, LET ALONE OUT OF THE SYSTEM...
OKAY, BUT NOT FOR LONG...
KNOWING THE PSIONS, THEY'LL SWITCH TO MANUAL TRACKING AND BE ON OUR TAILS AGAIN IN NO TIME!
DO I EVEN WANT TO KNOW WHAT YOU WERE DOING ON THAT PLANET?
IT WAS A DISTRESS CALL...
"...FROM A RACE I'VE MET MANY TIMES, THE TAMARANEANS."

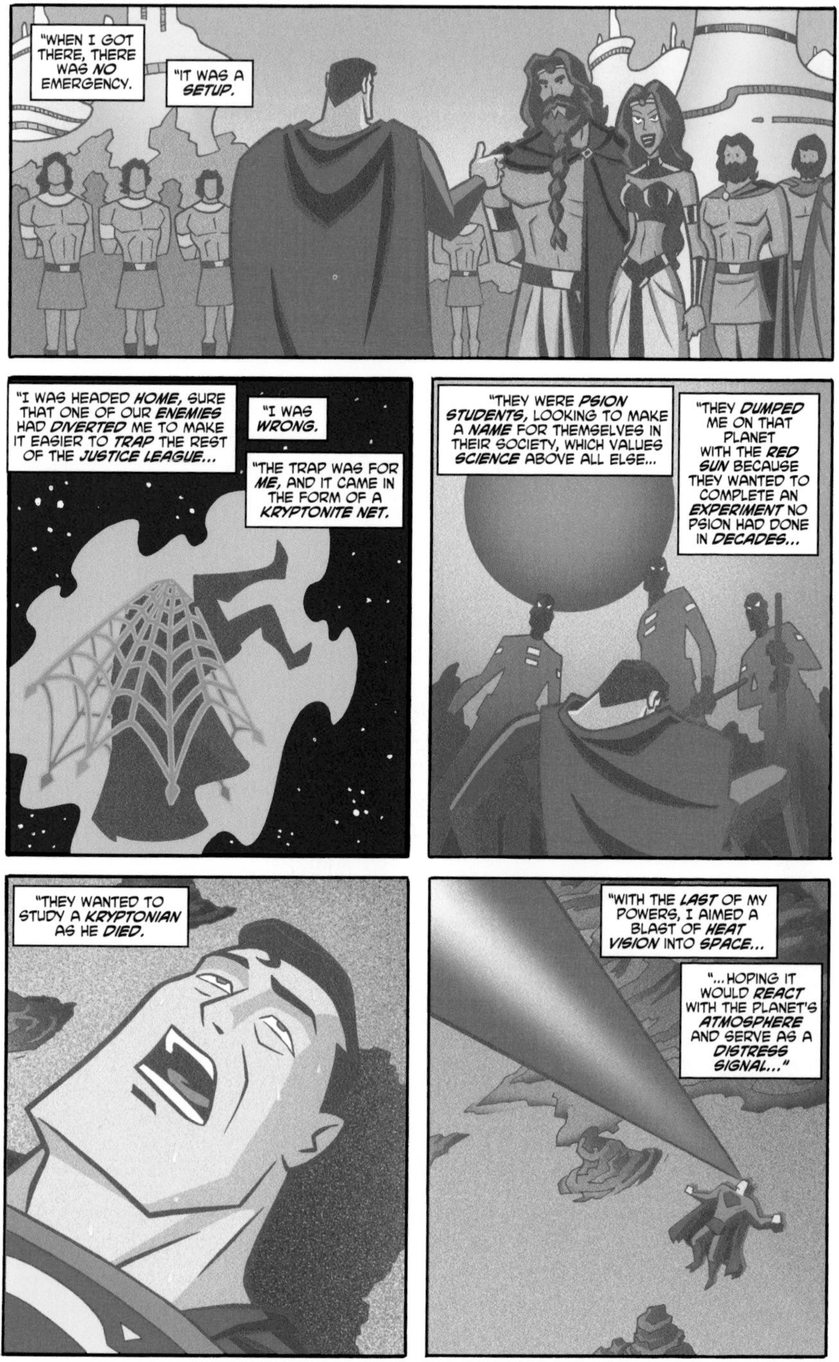
"WHEN I GOT THERE, THERE WAS NO EMERGENCY.
"IT WAS A SETUP.
"I WAS HEADED HOME, SURE THAT ONE OF OUR ENEMIES HAD DIVERTED ME TO MAKE IT EASIER TO TRAP THE REST OF THE JUSTICE LEAGUE...
"I WAS WRONG.
"THE TRAP WAS FOR ME, AND IT CAME IN THE FORM OF A KRYPTONITE NET.
"THEY WERE PSION STUDENTS, LOOKING TO MAKE A NAME FOR THEMSELVES IN THEIR SOCIETY, WHICH VALUES SCIENCE ABOVE ALL ELSE...
"THEY DUMPED ME ON THAT PLANET WITH THE RED SUN BECAUSE THEY WANTED TO COMPLETE AN EXPERIMENT NO PSION HAD DONE IN DECADES...
"THEY WANTED TO STUDY A KRYPTONIAN AS HE DIED.
"WITH THE LAST OF MY POWERS, I AIMED A BLAST OF HEAT VISION INTO SPACE...
"...HOPING IT WOULD REACT WITH THE PLANET'S ATMOSPHERE AND SERVE AS A DISTRESS SIGNAL..."

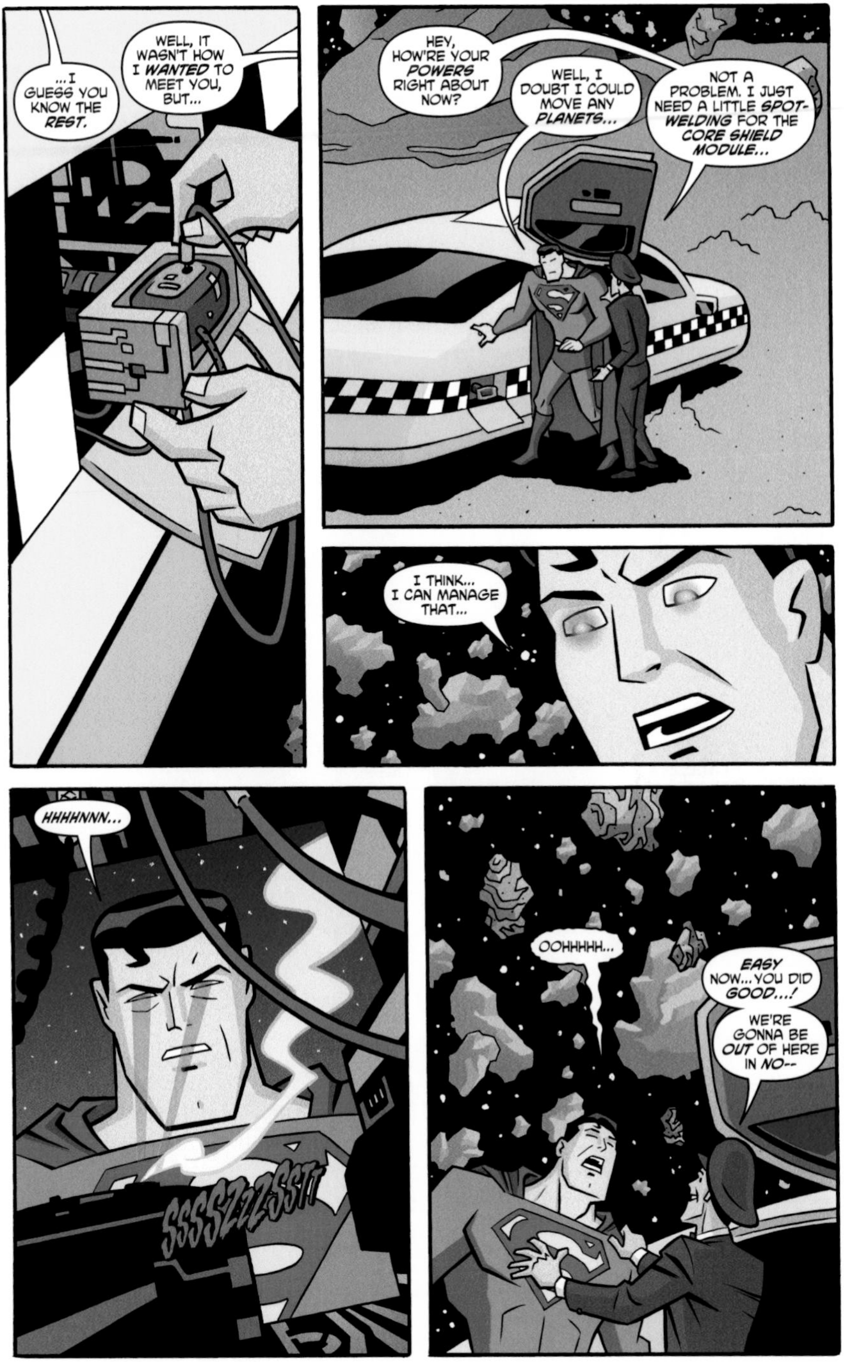
WELL, IT WASN'T HOW I WANTED TO MEET YOU, BUT...
...I GUESS YOU KNOW THE REST.
HEY, HOW'RE YOUR POWERS RIGHT ABOUT NOW?
WELL, I DOUBT I COULD MOVE ANY PLANETS...
NOT A PROBLEM. I JUST NEED A LITTLE SPOT-WELDING FOR THE CORE SHIELD MODULE...
I THINK... I CAN MANAGE THAT...
HHHHNNN...
SSSSZZZSSTT
OOHHHHH...
EASY NOW...YOU DID GOOD...!
WE'RE GONNA BE OUT OF HERE IN NO--

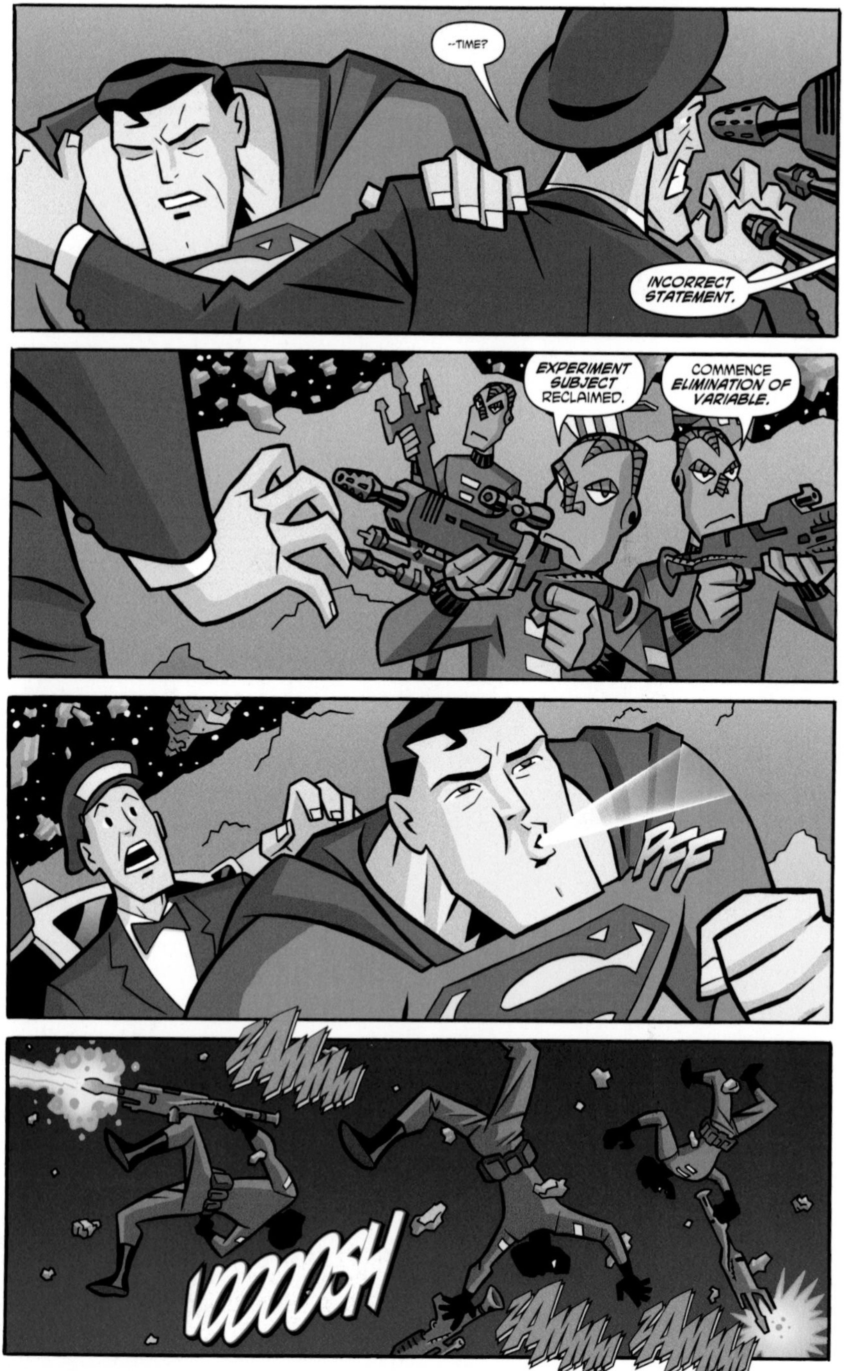
--TIME?
INCORRECT STATEMENT.
EXPERIMENT SUBJECT RECLAIMED.
COMMENCE ELIMINATION OF VARIABLE.
PFF
ZAMMM
VOOOOSH
ZAMMM
ZAMMM

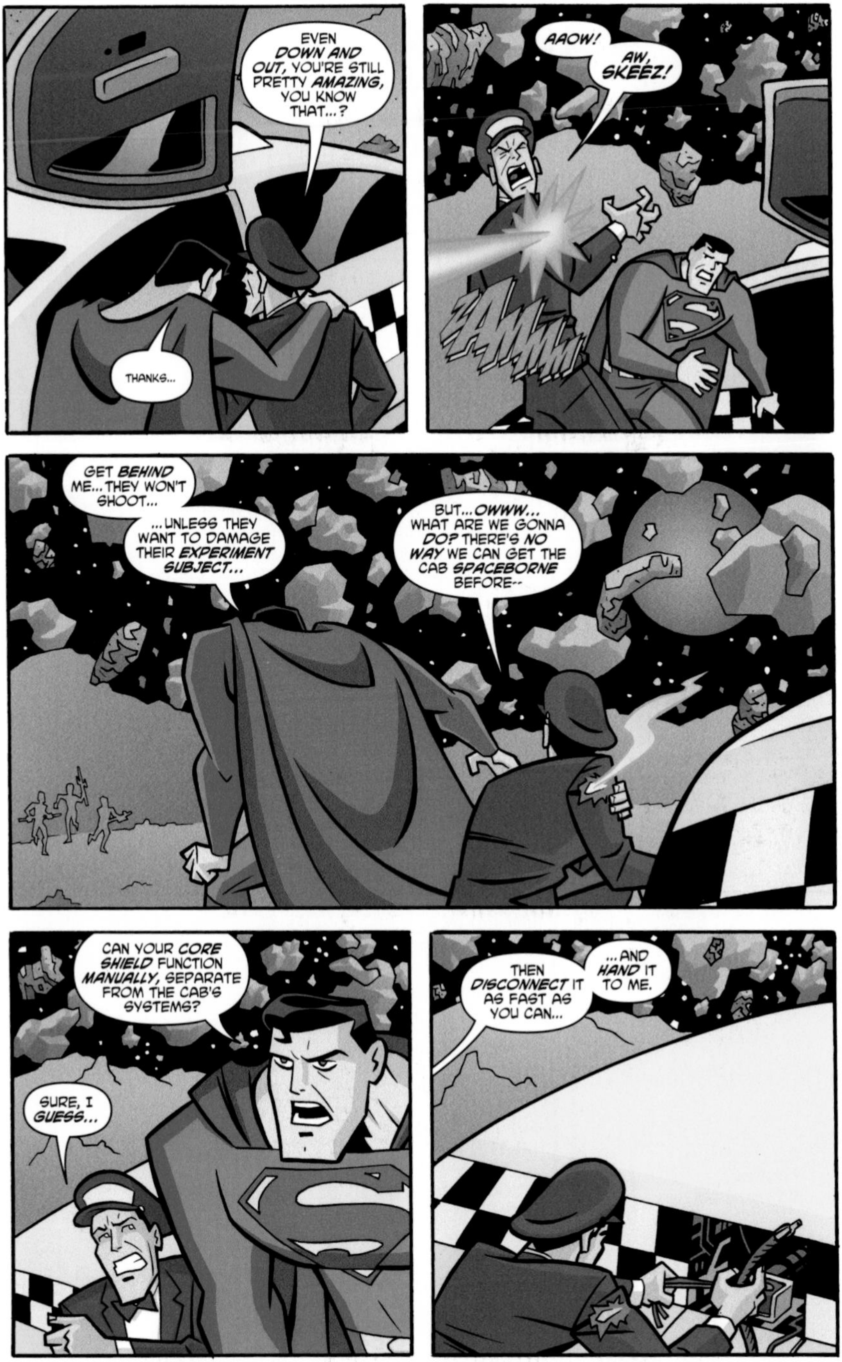
EVEN DOWN AND OUT, YOU'RE STILL PRETTY AMAZING, YOU KNOW THAT...?
THANKS...
AAOW!
AW, SKEEZ!
ZAMMM
GET BEHIND ME... THEY WON'T SHOOT...
...UNLESS THEY WANT TO DAMAGE THEIR EXPERIMENT SUBJECT...
BUT... OWWW... WHAT ARE WE GONNA DO? THERE'S NO WAY WE CAN GET THE CAB SPACEBORNE BEFORE--
CAN YOUR CORE SHIELD FUNCTION MANUALLY, SEPARATE FROM THE CAB'S SYSTEMS?
SURE, I GUESS...
THEN DISCONNECT IT AS FAST AS YOU CAN...
...AND HAND IT TO ME.

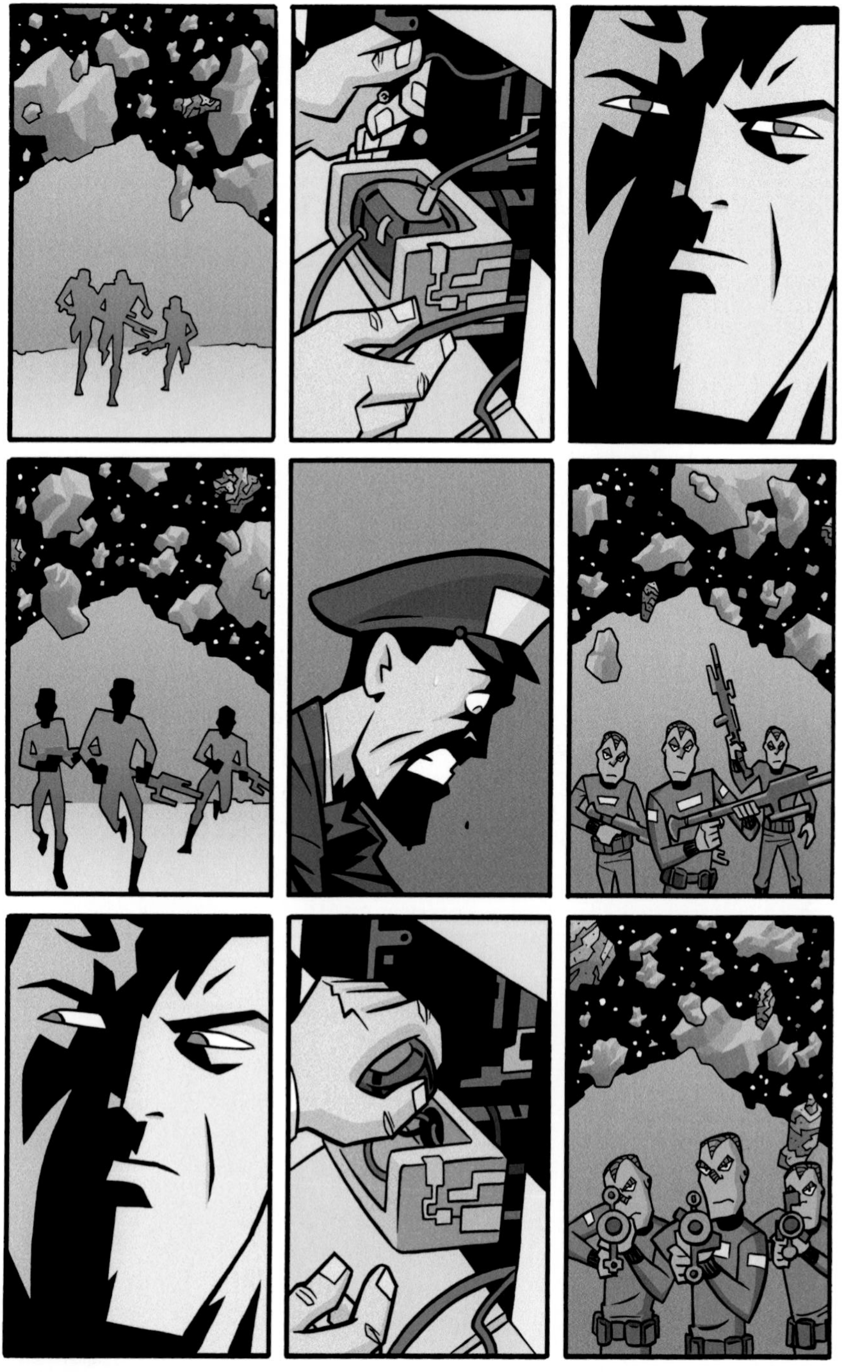

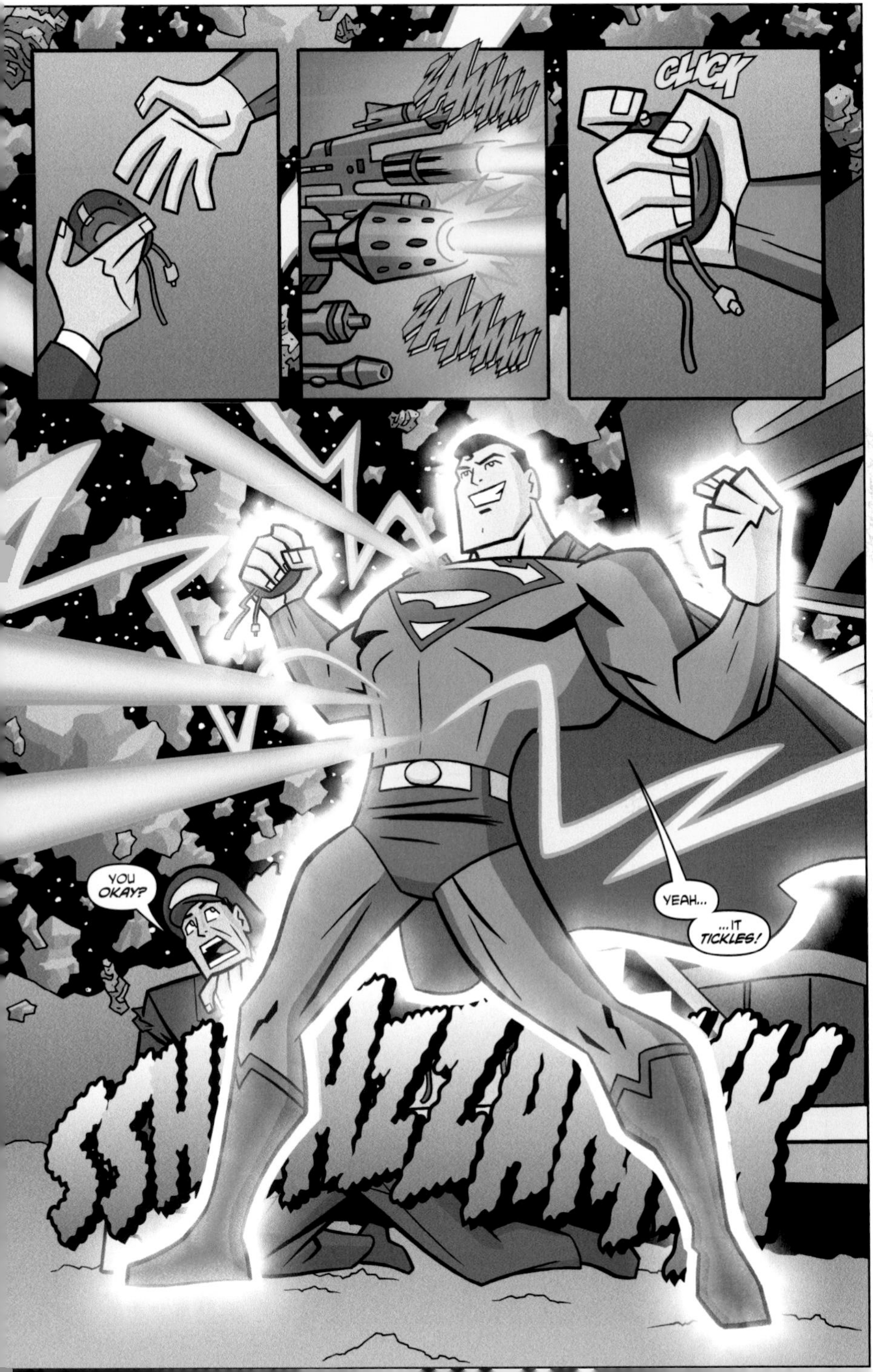
CLICK
YOU OKAY?
YEAH...
...IT TICKLES!

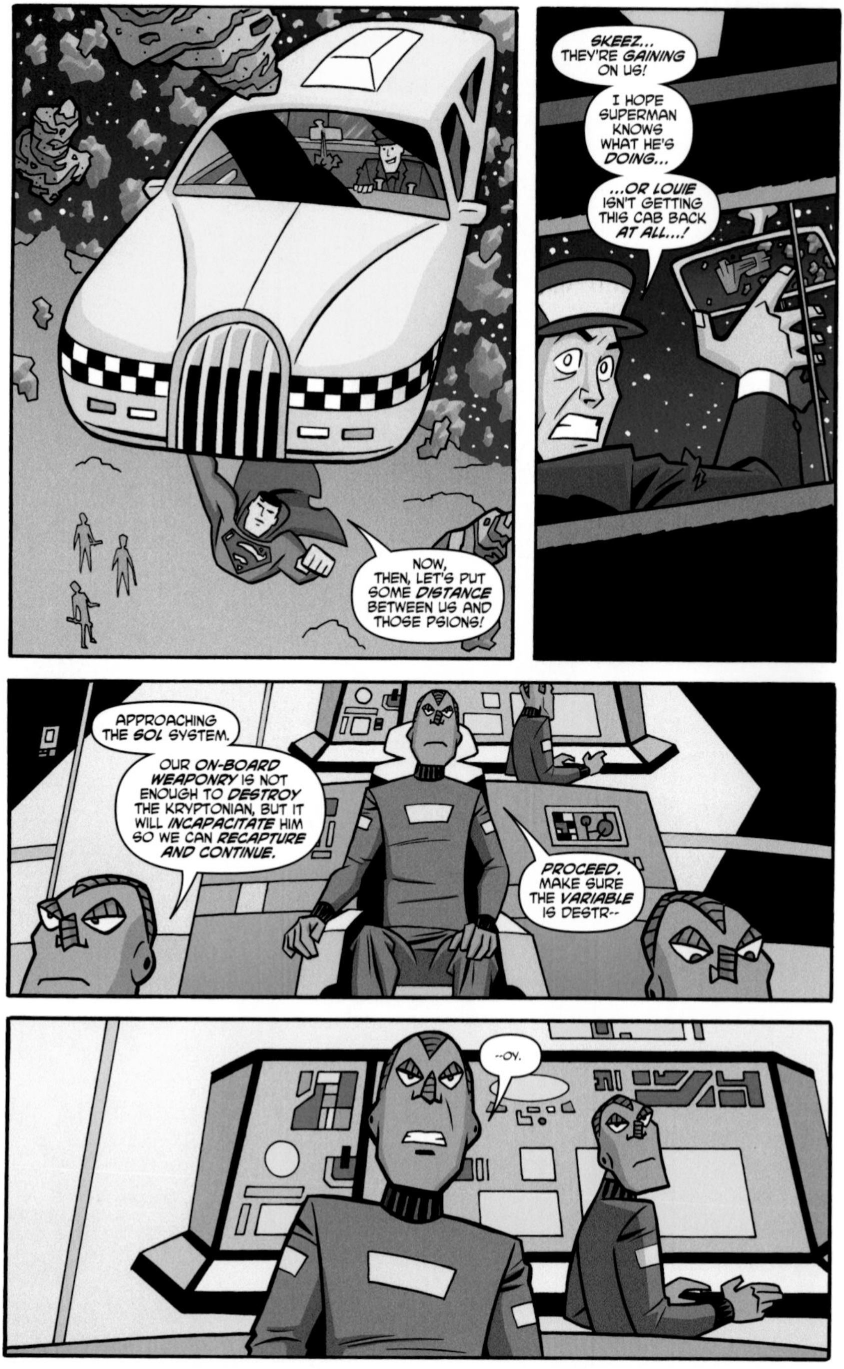
NOW, THEN, LET'S PUT SOME DISTANCE BETWEEN US AND THOSE PSIONS!
SKEEZ... THEY'RE GAINING ON US!
I HOPE SUPERMAN KNOWS WHAT HE'S DOING...
...OR LOUIE ISN'T GETTING THIS CAB BACK AT ALL...!
APPROACHING THE SOL SYSTEM.
OUR ON-BOARD WEAPONRY IS NOT ENOUGH TO DESTROY THE KRYPTONIAN, BUT IT WILL INCAPACITATE HIM SO WE CAN RECAPTURE AND CONTINUE.
PROCEED. MAKE SURE THE VARIABLE IS DESTR--
--OY.

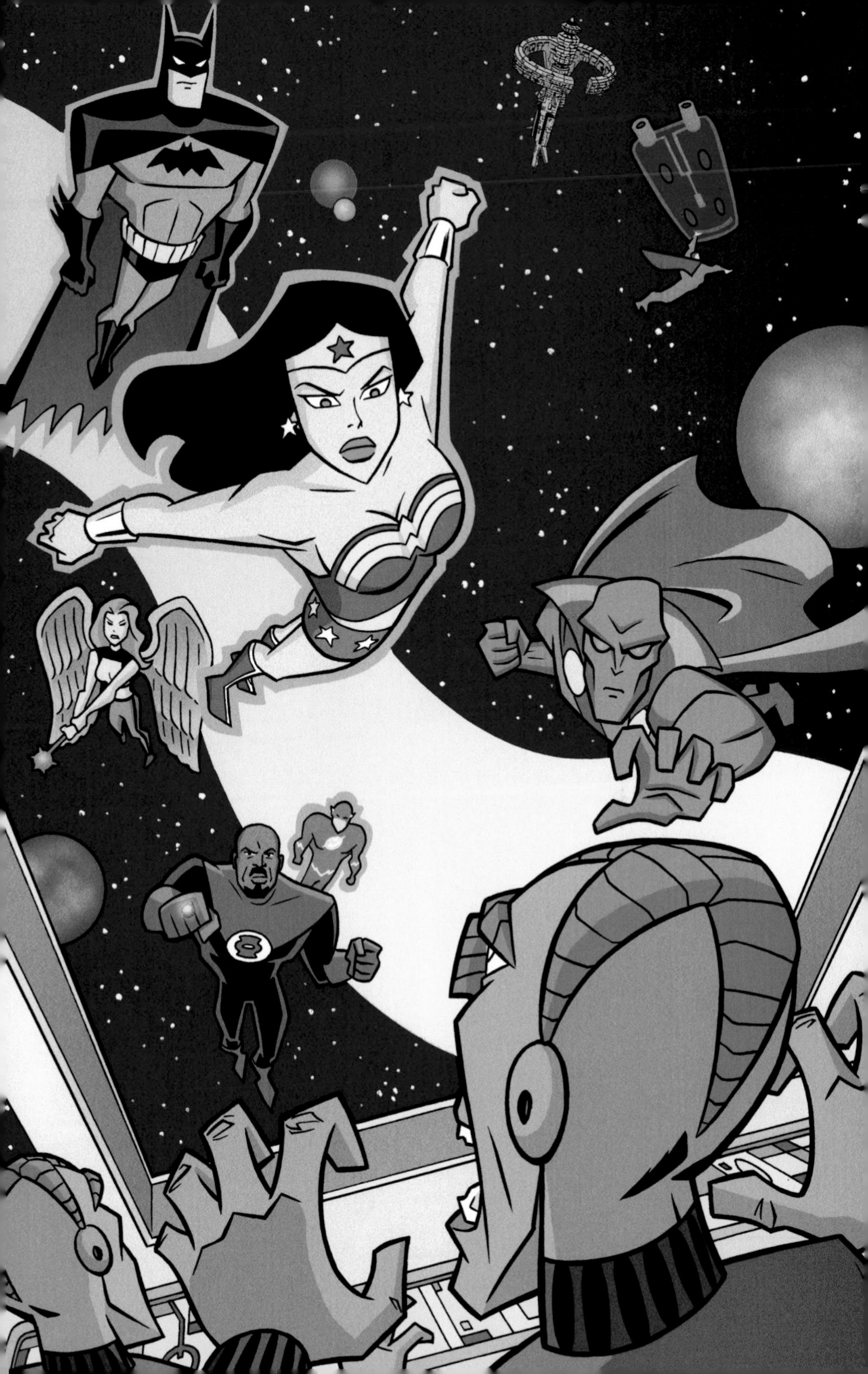

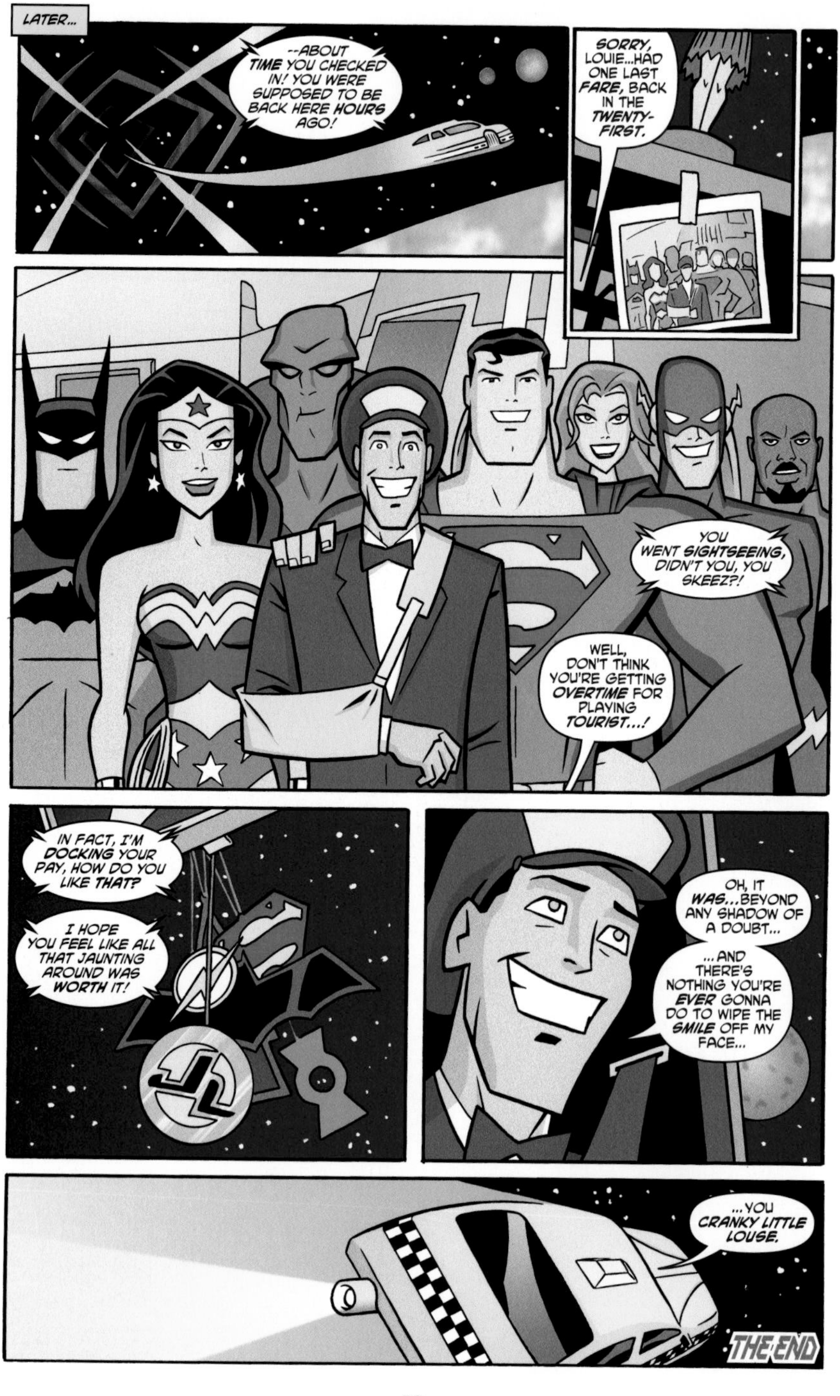
LATER...
--ABOUT TIME YOU CHECKED IN! YOU WERE SUPPOSED TO BE BACK HERE HOURS AGO!
SORRY, LOUIE...HAD ONE LAST FARE, BACK IN THE TWENTY-FIRST.
YOU WENT SIGHTSEEING, DIDN'T YOU, YOU SKEEZ?!
WELL, DON'T THINK YOU'RE GETTING OVERTIME FOR PLAYING TOURIST...!
IN FACT, I'M DOCKING YOUR PAY, HOW DO YOU LIKE THAT?
I HOPE YOU FEEL LIKE ALL THAT JAUNTING AROUND WAS WORTH IT!
OH, IT WAS...BEYOND ANY SHADOW OF A DOUBT...
...AND THERE'S NOTHING YOU'RE EVER GONNA DO TO WIPE THE SMILE OFF MY FACE...
...YOU CRANKY LITTLE LOUSE.
THE END

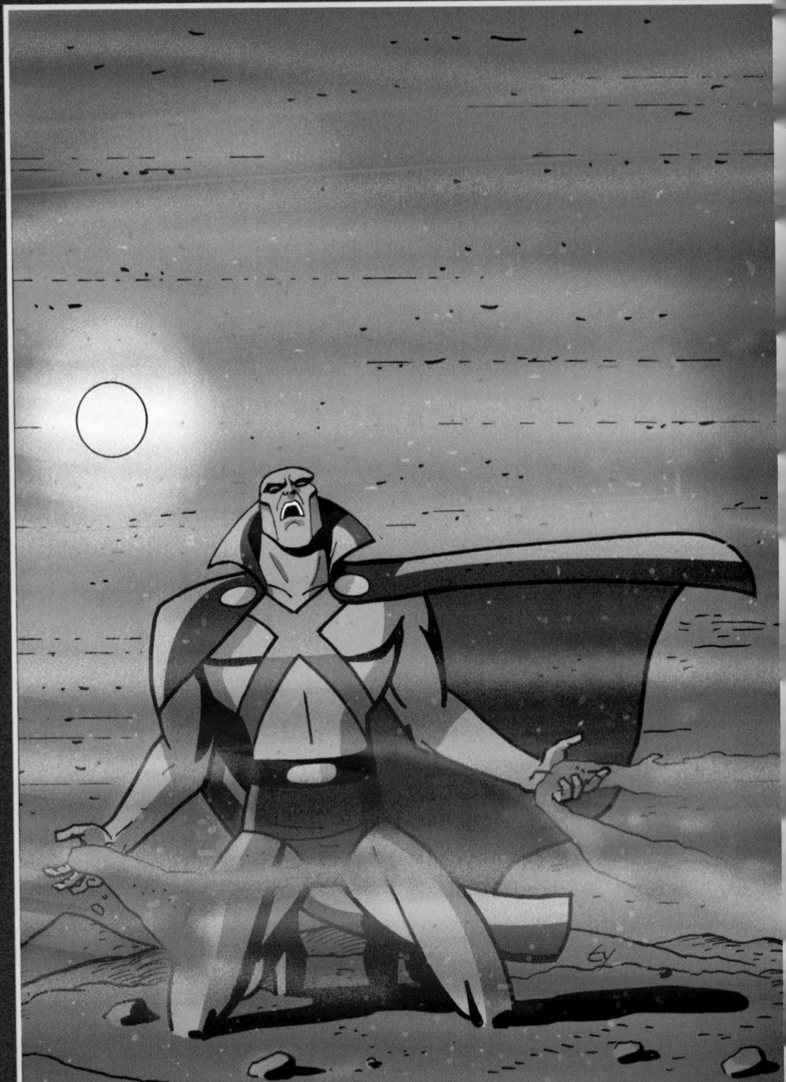

CHAPTER 4: ALONE AMONG THE STARS

JUSTICE LEAGUE UNLIMITED

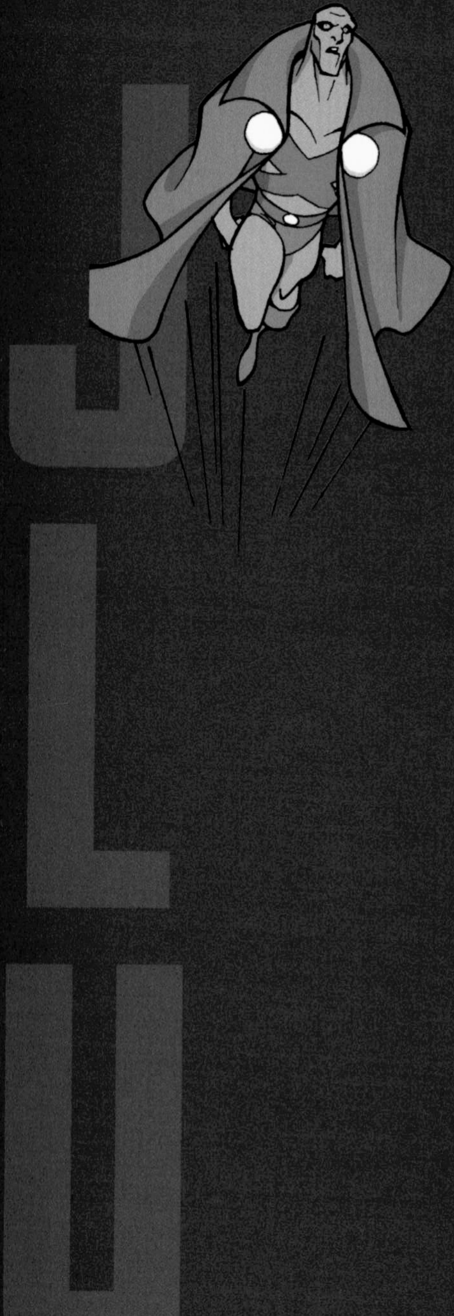
JLU

COVER ART BY TY TEMPLETON

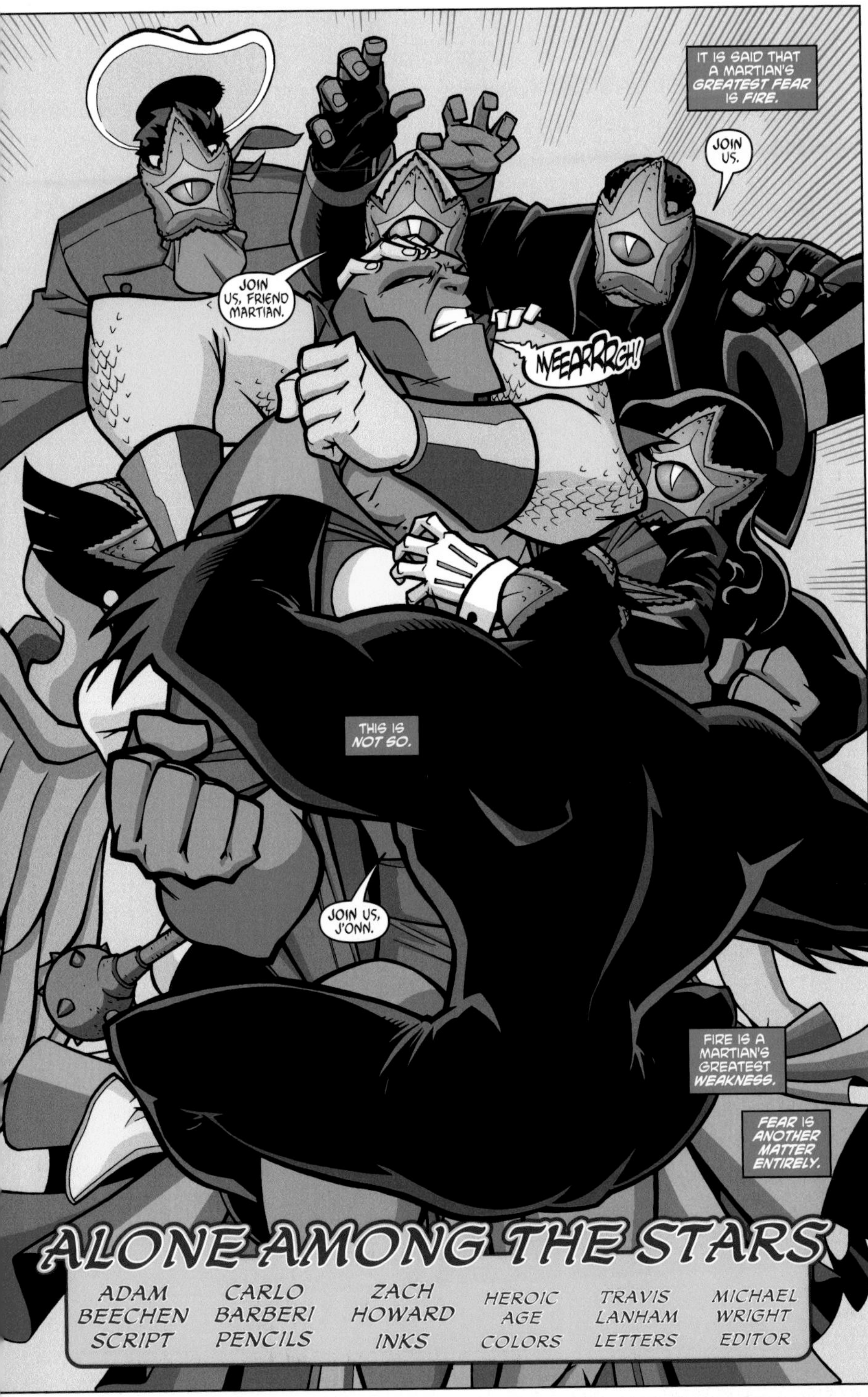

IT IS SAID THAT A MARTIAN'S GREATEST FEAR IS FIRE.
JOIN US.
JOIN US, FRIEND MARTIAN.
MVEEARRRGH!
THIS IS NOT SO.
JOIN US, J'ONN.
FIRE IS A MARTIAN'S GREATEST WEAKNESS.
FEAR IS ANOTHER MATTER ENTIRELY.
ALONE AMONG THE STARS
ADAM BEECHEN SCRIPT
CARLO BARBERI PENCILS
ZACH HOWARD INKS
HEROIC AGE COLORS
TRAVIS LANHAM LETTERS
MICHAEL WRIGHT EDITOR

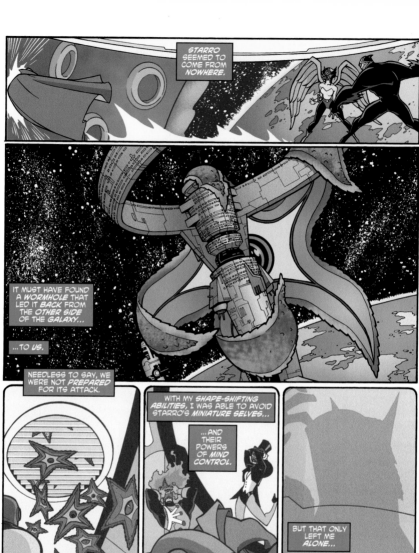

STARRO SEEMED TO COME FROM *NOWHERE.*

IT MUST HAVE FOUND A *WORMHOLE* THAT LED IT *BACK* FROM THE *OTHER SIDE* OF THE *GALAXY...*

...TO *US.*

NEEDLESS TO SAY, WE WERE NOT *PREPARED* FOR ITS ATTACK.

WITH MY *SHAPE-SHIFTING ABILITIES,* I WAS ABLE TO AVOID STARRO'S *MINIATURE SELVES...*

...AND THEIR POWERS OF *MIND CONTROL.*

BUT THAT ONLY LEFT ME *ALONE...*

...AGAINST *ALL* OF MY *HYPNOTIZED* TEAMMATES.

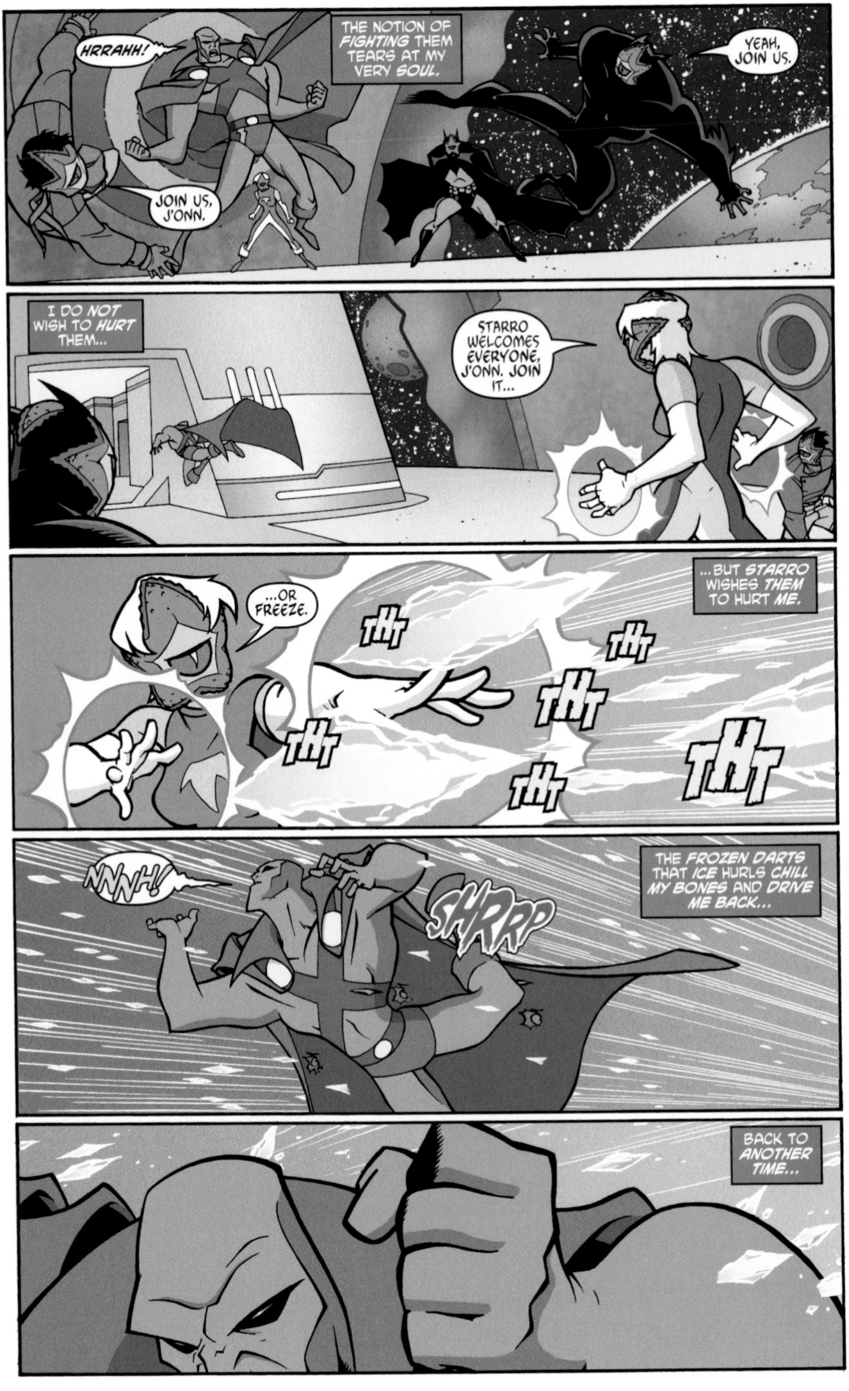
HRRAHH!
THE NOTION OF *FIGHTING* THEM TEARS AT MY VERY *SOUL.*
YEAH, JOIN US.
JOIN US, J'ONN.
I DO *NOT* WISH TO *HURT* THEM...
STARRO WELCOMES EVERYONE, J'ONN. JOIN IT...
...OR FREEZE.
...BUT *STARRO* WISHES *THEM* TO HURT *ME.*
THT
THT
THT
THT
THT
THT
NNNH!
SHRRP
THE *FROZEN DARTS* THAT *ICE* HURLS *CHILL MY BONES* AND *DRIVE ME BACK...*
BACK TO *ANOTHER TIME...*

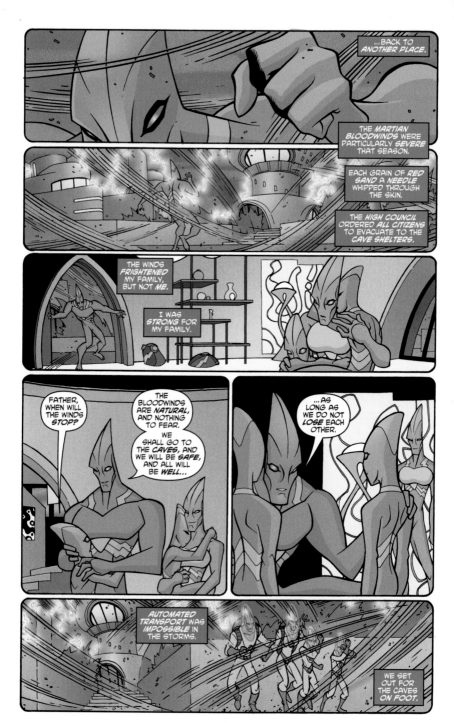

...BACK TO *ANOTHER PLACE.*

THE *MARTIAN BLOODWINDS* WERE PARTICULARLY *SEVERE* THAT SEASON.

EACH GRAIN OF *RED SAND* A *NEEDLE* WHIPPED THROUGH THE SKIN.

THE *HIGH COUNCIL* ORDERED *ALL* CITIZENS TO EVACUATE TO THE *CAVE SHELTERS.*

THE WINDS *FRIGHTENED* MY FAMILY, BUT NOT *ME.*

I WAS *STRONG* FOR MY FAMILY.

FATHER, WHEN WILL THE WINDS *STOP?*

THE BLOODWINDS ARE *NATURAL,* AND NOTHING TO FEAR.

WE SHALL GO TO THE *CAVES,* AND WE WILL BE *SAFE,* AND ALL WILL BE *WELL...*

...AS LONG AS WE DO NOT *LOSE* EACH OTHER.

AUTOMATED *TRANSPORT* WAS IMPOSSIBLE IN THE STORMS.

WE SET OUT FOR THE CAVES ON FOOT.

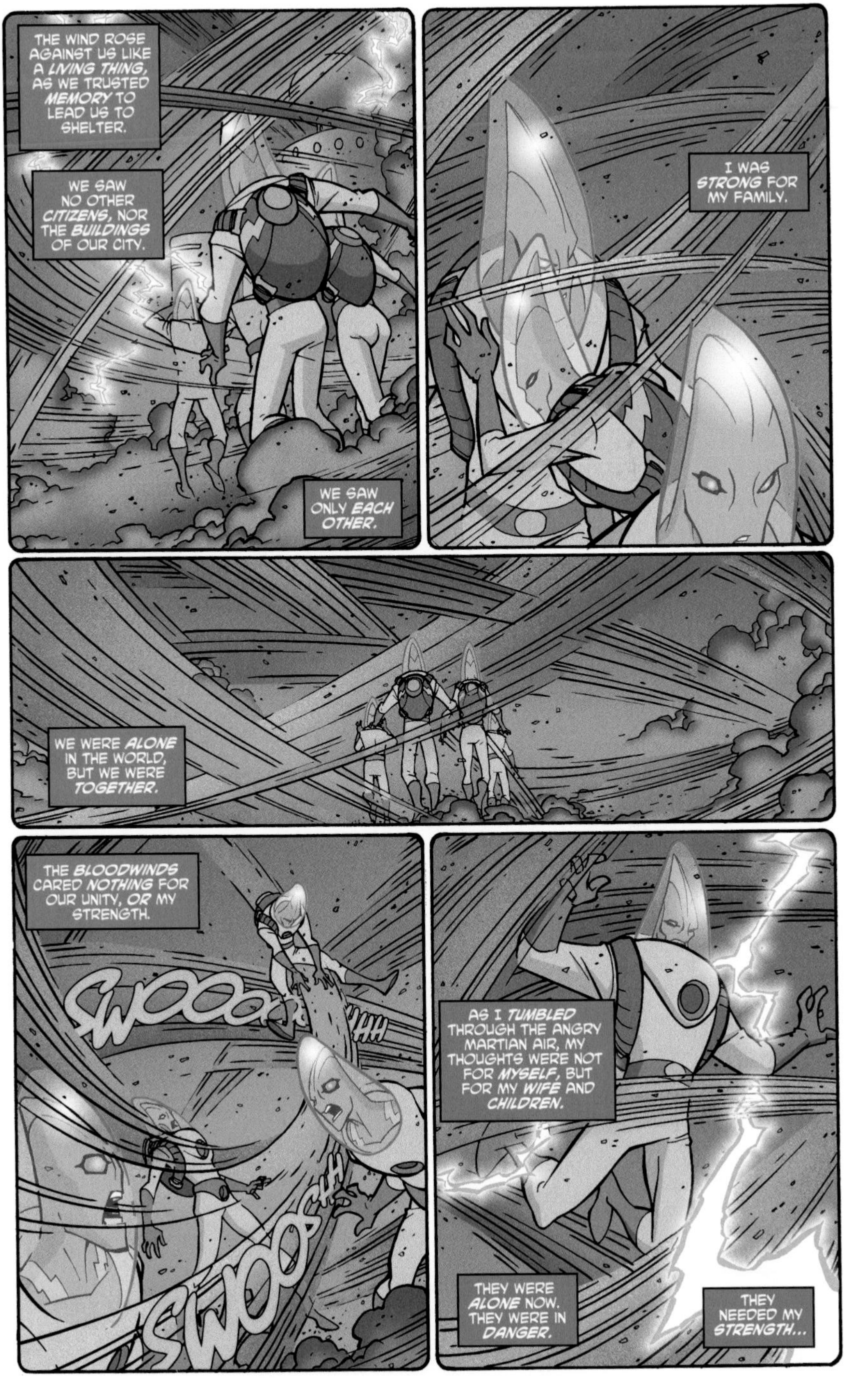
THE WIND ROSE AGAINST US LIKE A *LIVING THING*, AS WE TRUSTED *MEMORY* TO LEAD US TO SHELTER.
WE SAW NO OTHER *CITIZENS*, NOR THE *BUILDINGS* OF OUR CITY.
WE SAW ONLY *EACH OTHER*.
I WAS *STRONG* FOR MY FAMILY.
WE WERE *ALONE* IN THE WORLD, BUT WE WERE *TOGETHER*.
THE *BLOODWINDS* CARED *NOTHING* FOR OUR UNITY, *OR* MY STRENGTH.
SWOOOOSHHH
SWOOSH
AS I *TUMBLED* THROUGH THE ANGRY MARTIAN AIR, MY THOUGHTS WERE NOT FOR *MYSELF*, BUT FOR MY *WIFE* AND *CHILDREN*.
THEY WERE *ALONE* NOW. THEY WERE IN *DANGER*.
THEY NEEDED MY *STRENGTH*...

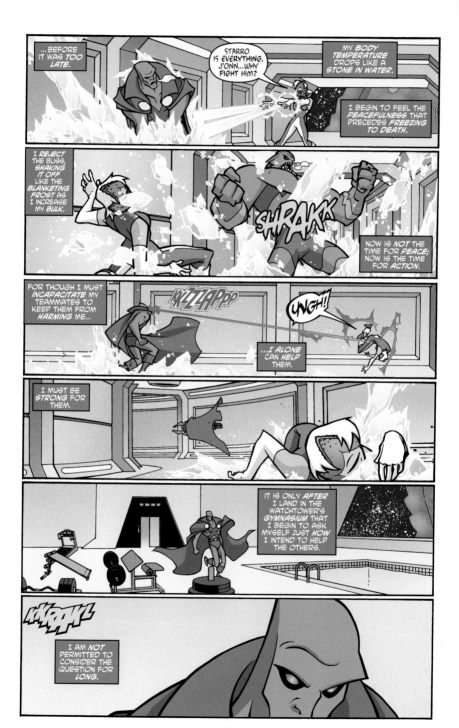

...BEFORE IT WAS *TOO* LATE.

STARRO IS EVERYTHING, J'ONN...WHY FIGHT HIM?

MY *BODY TEMPERATURE* DROPS LIKE A *STONE IN WATER*.

I BEGIN TO FEEL THE *PEACEFULNESS* THAT PRECEDES *FREEZING TO DEATH*.

I *REJECT* THE BLISS, *SHAKING* IT OFF LIKE THE *BLANKETING FROST* AS I INCREASE MY *BULK*.

SHRAKK

NOW IS *NOT* THE TIME FOR *PEACE*; NOW IS THE TIME FOR *ACTION*.

FOR THOUGH I MUST *INCAPACITATE* MY TEAMMATES TO KEEP THEM FROM *HARMING ME*...

KZZZAPPP

UNGH!

...I ALONE CAN *HELP* THEM.

I MUST BE *STRONG* FOR THEM.

IT IS ONLY *AFTER* I LAND IN THE WATCHTOWER'S *GYMNASIUM* THAT I BEGIN TO ASK MYSELF JUST *HOW* I INTEND TO HELP THE OTHERS.

K'KRAKL

I AM *NOT* PERMITTED TO CONSIDER THE QUESTION FOR *LONG*.

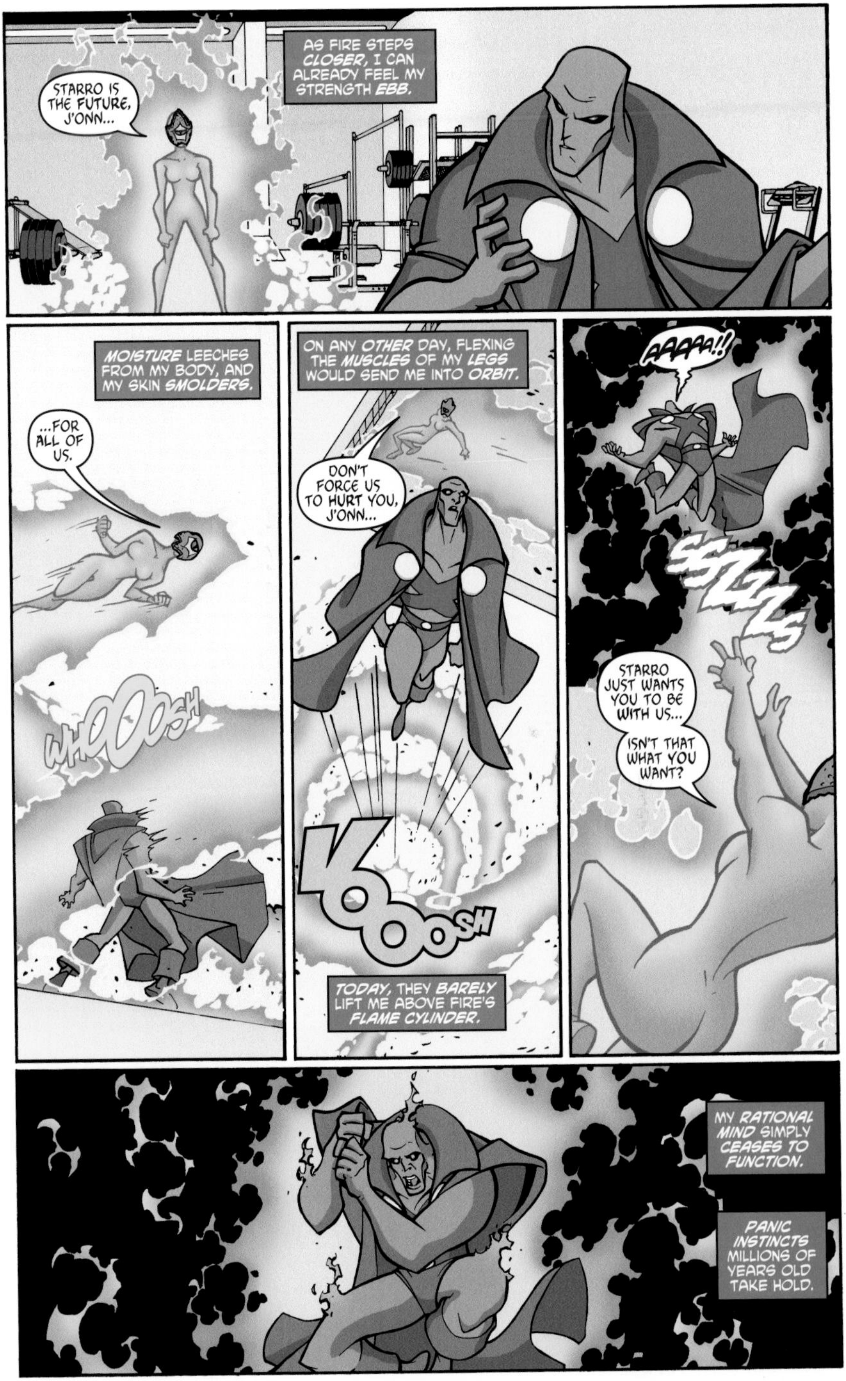

STARRO IS THE FUTURE, J'ONN...
AS FIRE STEPS CLOSER, I CAN ALREADY FEEL MY STRENGTH EBB.
MOISTURE LEECHES FROM MY BODY, AND MY SKIN SMOLDERS.
...FOR ALL OF US.
WHOOOSH
ON ANY OTHER DAY, FLEXING THE MUSCLES OF MY LEGS WOULD SEND ME INTO ORBIT.
DON'T FORCE US TO HURT YOU, J'ONN...
KOOOOSH
TODAY, THEY BARELY LIFT ME ABOVE FIRE'S FLAME CYLINDER.
AAAAA!!
SSZZZZS
STARRO JUST WANTS YOU TO BE WITH US...
ISN'T THAT WHAT YOU WANT?
MY RATIONAL MIND SIMPLY CEASES TO FUNCTION.
PANIC INSTINCTS MILLIONS OF YEARS OLD TAKE HOLD.

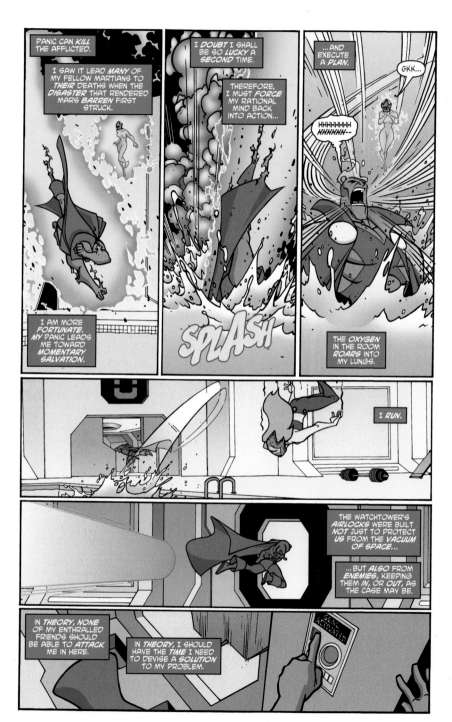

PANIC CAN *KILL* THE AFFLICTED.

I SAW IT LEAD *MANY* OF MY FELLOW MARTIANS TO *THEIR* DEATHS WHEN THE *DISASTER* THAT RENDERED MARS *BARREN* FIRST STRUCK.

I AM MORE *FORTUNATE.* MY PANIC LEADS ME TOWARD *MOMENTARY* SALVATION.

I *DOUBT* I SHALL BE SO *LUCKY* A *SECOND* TIME.

THEREFORE, I MUST *FORCE* MY RATIONAL MIND BACK INTO ACTION...

SPLASH

...AND *EXECUTE* A *PLAN.*

GKK...

HHHHHHHH HHHHHH--

THE *OXYGEN* IN THE ROOM *ROARS* INTO MY LUNGS.

I *RUN.*

THE *WATCHTOWER'S* *AIRLOCKS* WERE BUILT *NOT* JUST TO PROTECT *US* FROM THE *VACUUM* OF *SPACE...*

...BUT *ALSO* FROM *ENEMIES,* KEEPING THEM *IN,* OR *OUT,* AS THE CASE MAY BE.

IN *THEORY, NONE* OF MY *ENTHRALLED* FRIENDS SHOULD BE ABLE TO *ATTACK* ME IN HERE.

IN *THEORY,* I SHOULD HAVE THE *TIME* I NEED TO DEVISE A *SOLUTION* TO MY PROBLEM.

SEAL ACTIVATED

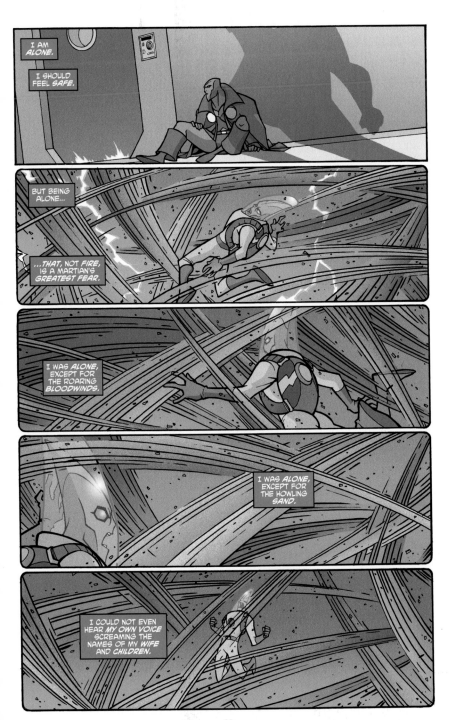

I AM *ALONE*.

I SHOULD FEEL *SAFE*.

BUT BEING *ALONE*...

...*THAT*, NOT *FIRE*, IS A MARTIAN'S *GREATEST FEAR*.

I WAS *ALONE*, EXCEPT FOR THE ROARING *BLOODWINDS*.

I WAS *ALONE*, EXCEPT FOR THE HOWLING *SAND*.

I COULD NOT EVEN HEAR *MY OWN VOICE* SCREAMING THE NAMES OF MY *WIFE* AND *CHILDREN*.

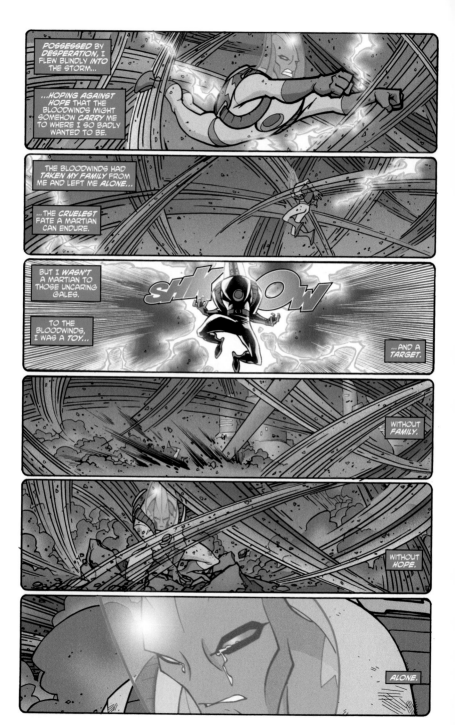

POSSESSED BY *DESPERATION*, I FLEW BLINDLY *INTO* THE STORM...

...HOPING AGAINST *HOPE* THAT THE BLOODWINDS MIGHT SOMEHOW *CARRY* ME TO WHERE I SO BADLY WANTED TO BE.

THE BLOODWINDS HAD *TAKEN MY FAMILY* FROM ME AND LEFT ME *ALONE*...

...THE *CRUELEST* FATE A MARTIAN CAN ENDURE.

BUT I *WASN'T* A MARTIAN TO THOSE UNCARING GALES.

TO THE BLOODWINDS, I WAS A *TOY*...

...AND A *TARGET*.

SHK*OW*

WITHOUT *FAMILY*.

WITHOUT *HOPE*.

ALONE.

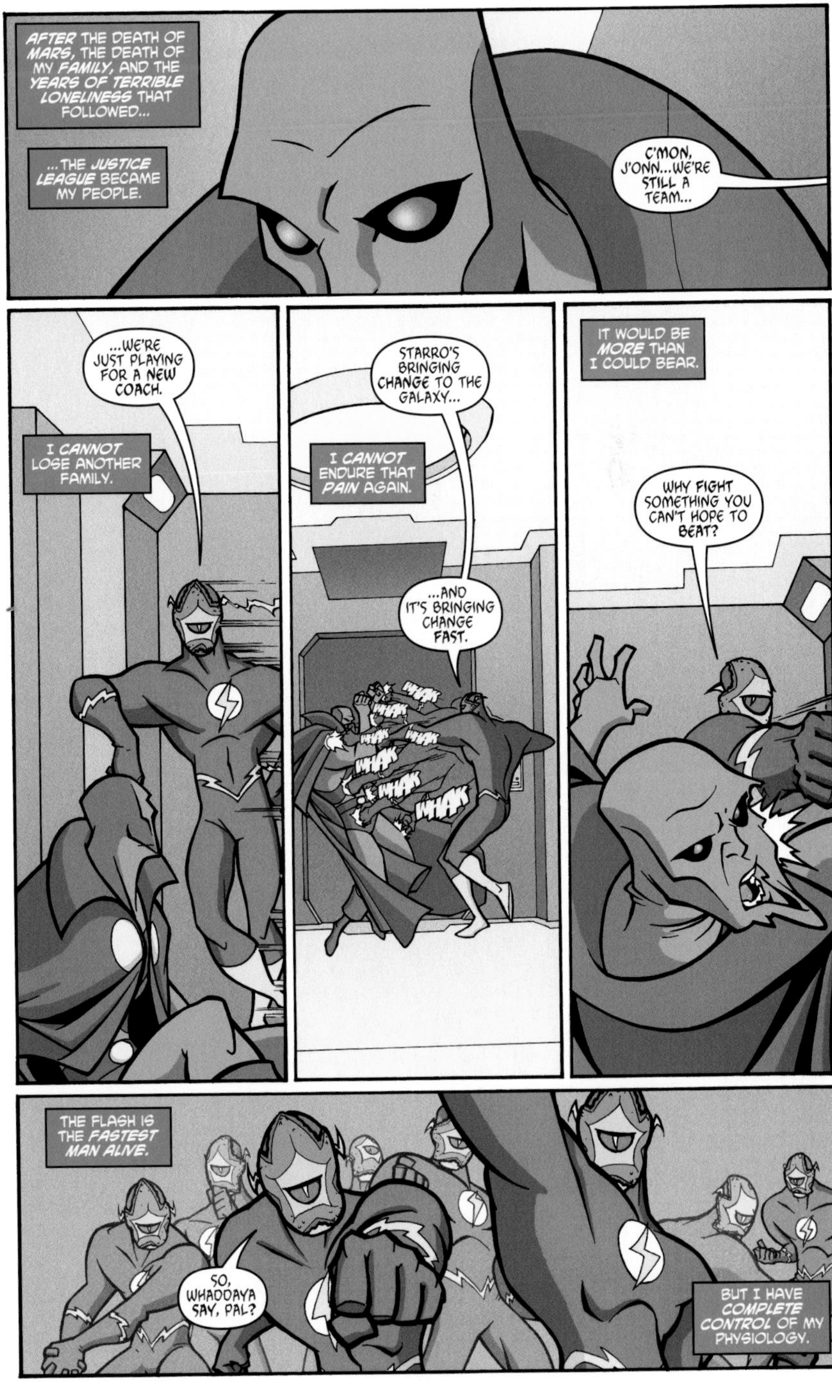
AFTER THE DEATH OF MARS, THE DEATH OF MY FAMILY, AND THE YEARS OF TERRIBLE LONELINESS THAT FOLLOWED...
...THE JUSTICE LEAGUE BECAME MY PEOPLE.
C'MON, J'ONN...WE'RE STILL A TEAM...
...WE'RE JUST PLAYING FOR A NEW COACH.
I CANNOT LOSE ANOTHER FAMILY.
STARRO'S BRINGING CHANGE TO THE GALAXY...
I CANNOT ENDURE THAT PAIN AGAIN.
...AND IT'S BRINGING CHANGE FAST.
WHAK
WHAK
WHAK
WHAK
WHAK
WHAK
WHAK
IT WOULD BE MORE THAN I COULD BEAR.
WHY FIGHT SOMETHING YOU CAN'T HOPE TO BEAT?
THE FLASH IS THE FASTEST MAN ALIVE.
SO, WHADDAYA SAY, PAL?
BUT I HAVE COMPLETE CONTROL OF MY PHYSIOLOGY.

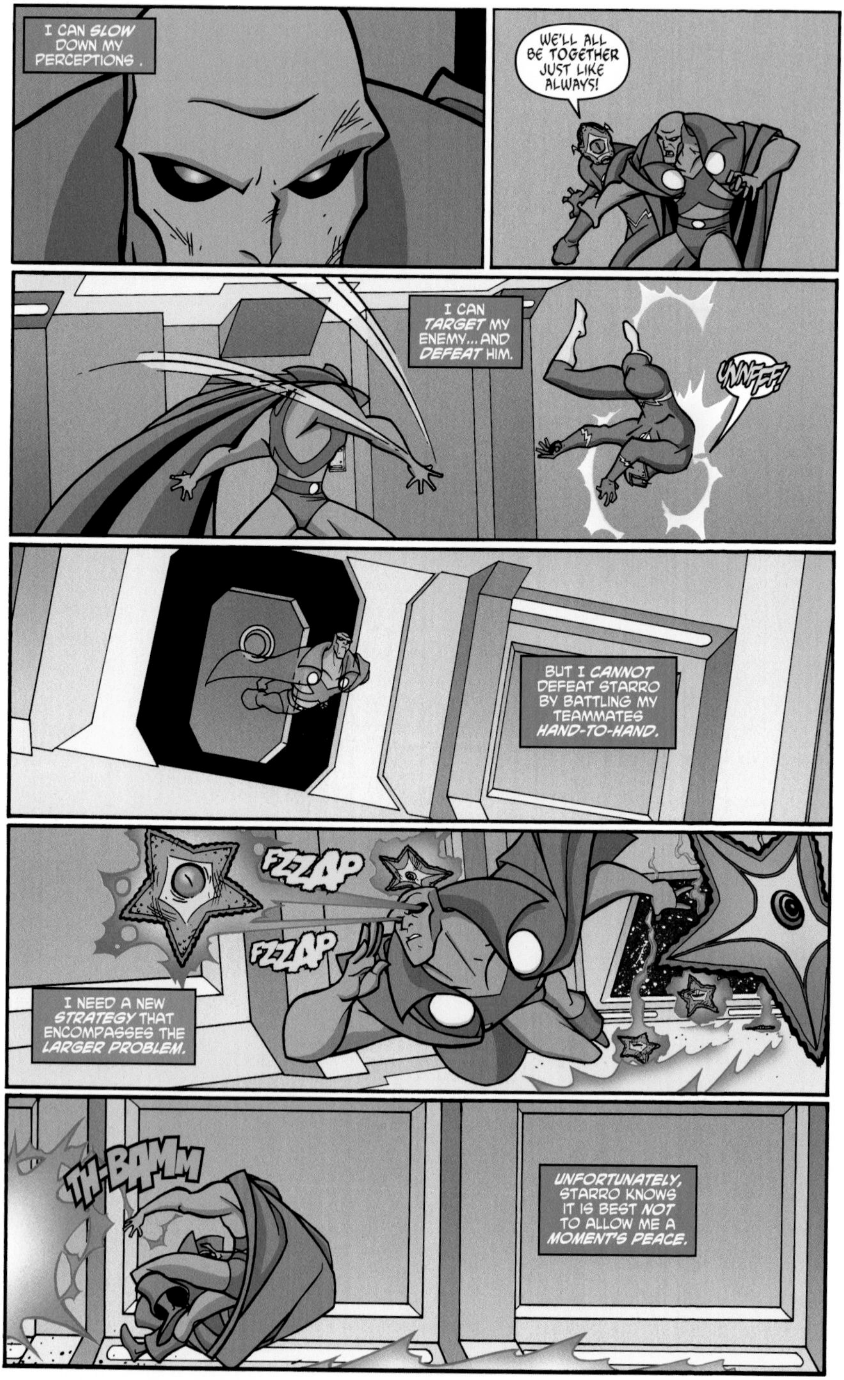
I CAN SLOW DOWN MY PERCEPTIONS .
WE'LL ALL BE TOGETHER JUST LIKE ALWAYS!
I CAN TARGET MY ENEMY... AND DEFEAT HIM.
UNNFFF!
BUT I CANNOT DEFEAT STARRO BY BATTLING MY TEAMMATES HAND-TO-HAND.
FZZAP
FZZAP
I NEED A NEW STRATEGY THAT ENCOMPASSES THE LARGER PROBLEM.
TH-BAMM
UNFORTUNATELY, STARRO KNOWS IT IS BEST NOT TO ALLOW ME A MOMENT'S PEACE.

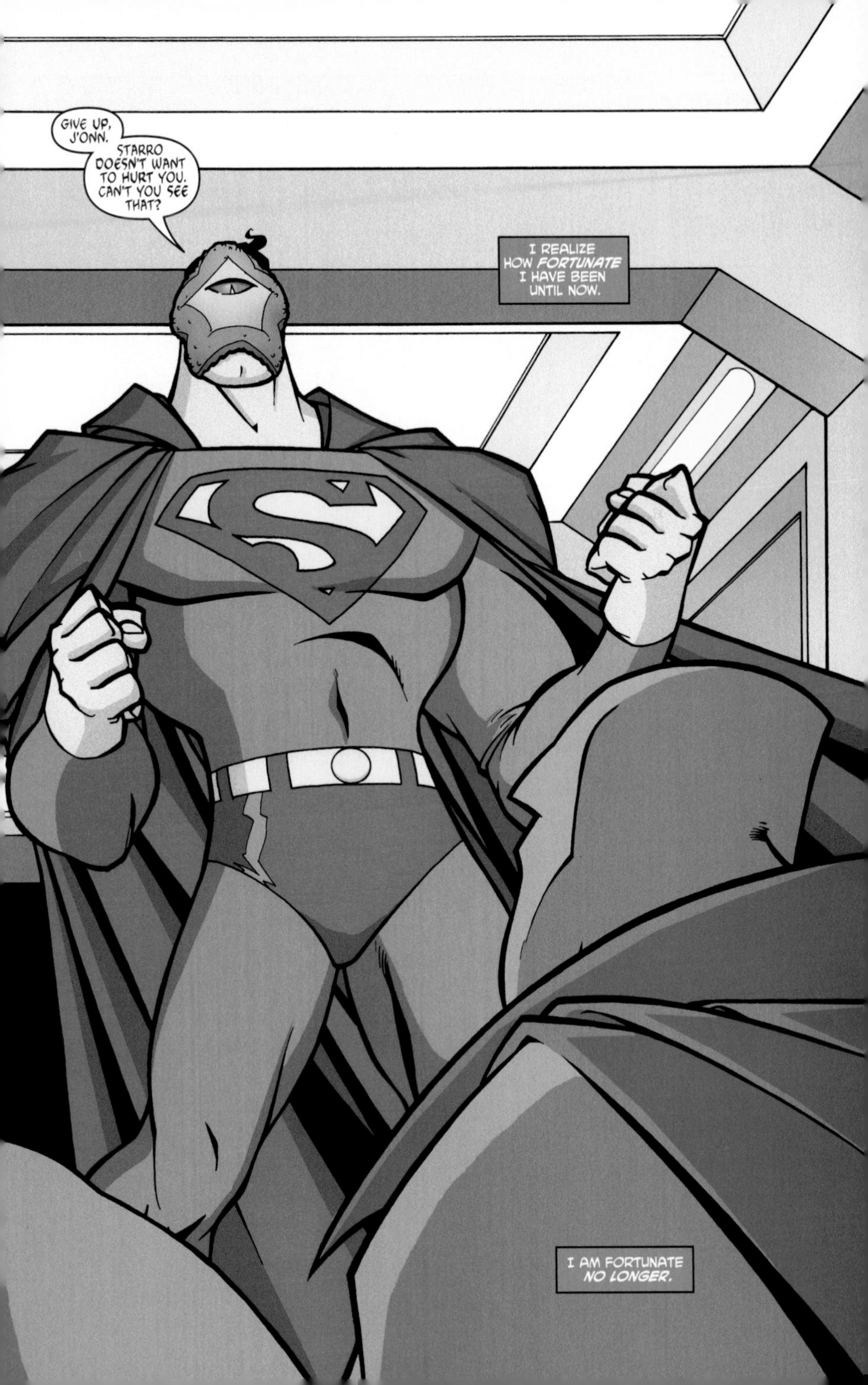

GIVE UP, J'ONN. STARRO DOESN'T WANT TO HURT YOU. CAN'T YOU SEE THAT?
I REALIZE HOW *FORTUNATE* I HAVE BEEN UNTIL NOW.
I AM FORTUNATE *NO LONGER.*

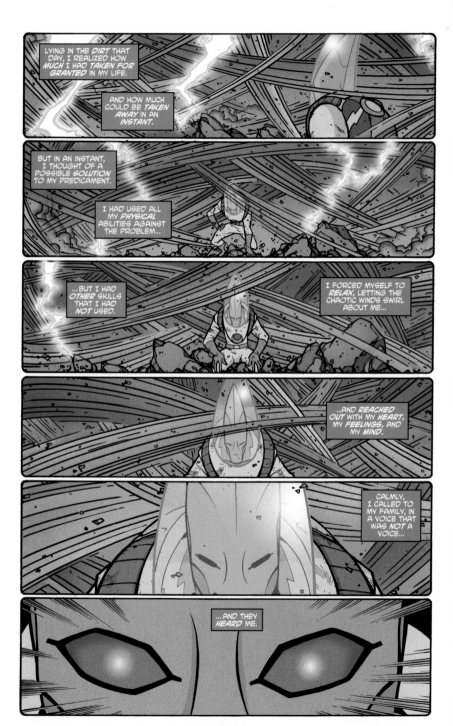

LYING IN THE *DIRT* THAT DAY, I REALIZED HOW MUCH I HAD *TAKEN FOR GRANTED* IN MY LIFE.

AND HOW MUCH COULD BE *TAKEN AWAY* IN AN *INSTANT.*

BUT IN AN INSTANT, I THOUGHT OF A POSSIBLE *SOLUTION* TO MY PREDICAMENT.

I HAD USED ALL MY *PHYSICAL* ABILITIES AGAINST THE PROBLEM...

...BUT I HAD *OTHER* SKILLS THAT I HAD *NOT USED.*

I FORCED MYSELF TO *RELAX,* LETTING THE CHAOTIC WINDS SWIRL ABOUT ME...

...AND *REACHED OUT* WITH MY *HEART,* MY *FEELINGS,* AND MY *MIND*.

CALMLY, I CALLED TO MY FAMILY, IN A VOICE THAT WAS *NOT* A VOICE...

...AND THEY *HEARD* ME.

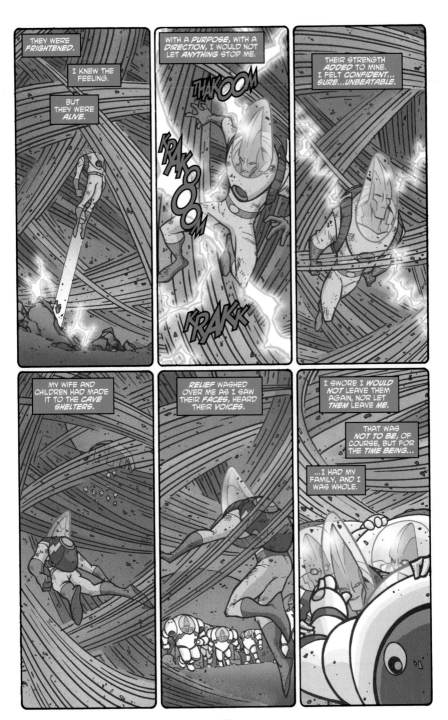

THEY WERE *FRIGHTENED.*

I KNEW THE FEELING.

BUT THEY WERE *ALIVE.*

WITH A *PURPOSE,* WITH A *DIRECTION,* I WOULD NOT LET *ANYTHING* STOP ME.

THAKOOM

KRAKOOM

KRAKK

THEIR STRENGTH *ADDED* TO MINE. I FELT *CONFIDENT... SURE...UNBEATABLE.*

MY WIFE AND CHILDREN HAD MADE IT TO THE *CAVE SHELTERS.*

RELIEF WASHED OVER ME AS I SAW THEIR *FACES,* HEARD THEIR *VOICES.*

I SWORE I *WOULD NOT* LEAVE THEM AGAIN, NOR LET *THEM* LEAVE *ME.*

THAT WAS *NOT TO BE,* OF COURSE, BUT FOR THE *TIME BEING...*

...I HAD MY FAMILY, AND I WAS WHOLE.

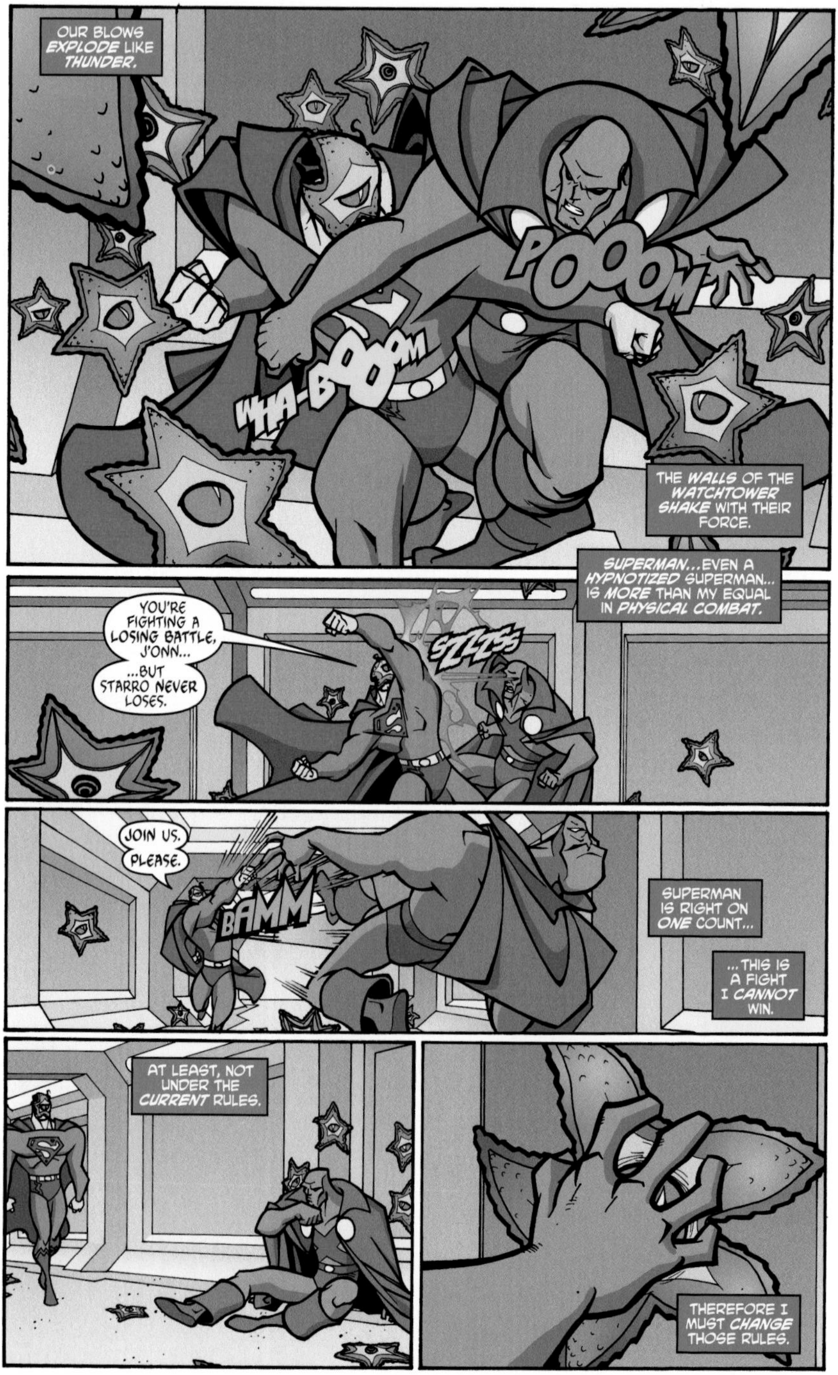
OUR BLOWS EXPLODE LIKE THUNDER.
POOOOM
WHA-BOOOOM
THE WALLS OF THE WATCHTOWER SHAKE WITH THEIR FORCE.
SUPERMAN...EVEN A HYPNOTIZED SUPERMAN... IS MORE THAN MY EQUAL IN PHYSICAL COMBAT.
YOU'RE FIGHTING A LOSING BATTLE, J'ONN...
...BUT STARRO NEVER LOSES.
SZZZSS
JOIN US. PLEASE.
BAMM
SUPERMAN IS RIGHT ON ONE COUNT...
...THIS IS A FIGHT I CANNOT WIN.
AT LEAST, NOT UNDER THE CURRENT RULES.
THEREFORE I MUST CHANGE THOSE RULES.

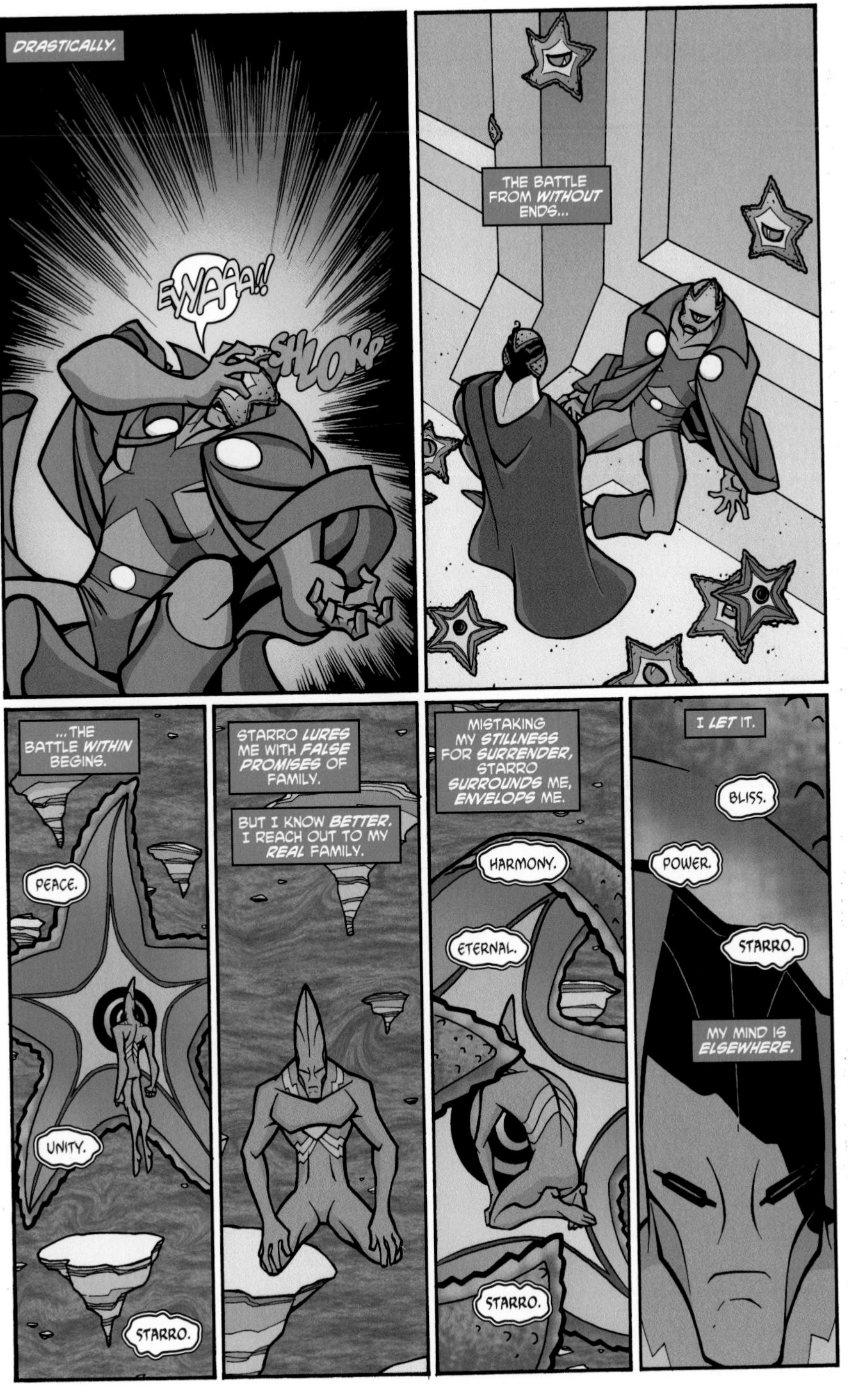
DRASTICALLY.
EYYAAA!!
SHLORP
THE BATTLE FROM WITHOUT ENDS...
...THE BATTLE WITHIN BEGINS.
PEACE.
UNITY.
STARRO.
STARRO LURES ME WITH FALSE PROMISES OF FAMILY.
BUT I KNOW BETTER. I REACH OUT TO MY REAL FAMILY.
MISTAKING MY STILLNESS FOR SURRENDER, STARRO SURROUNDS ME, ENVELOPS ME.
HARMONY.
ETERNAL.
STARRO.
I LET IT.
BLISS.
POWER.
STARRO.
MY MIND IS ELSEWHERE.

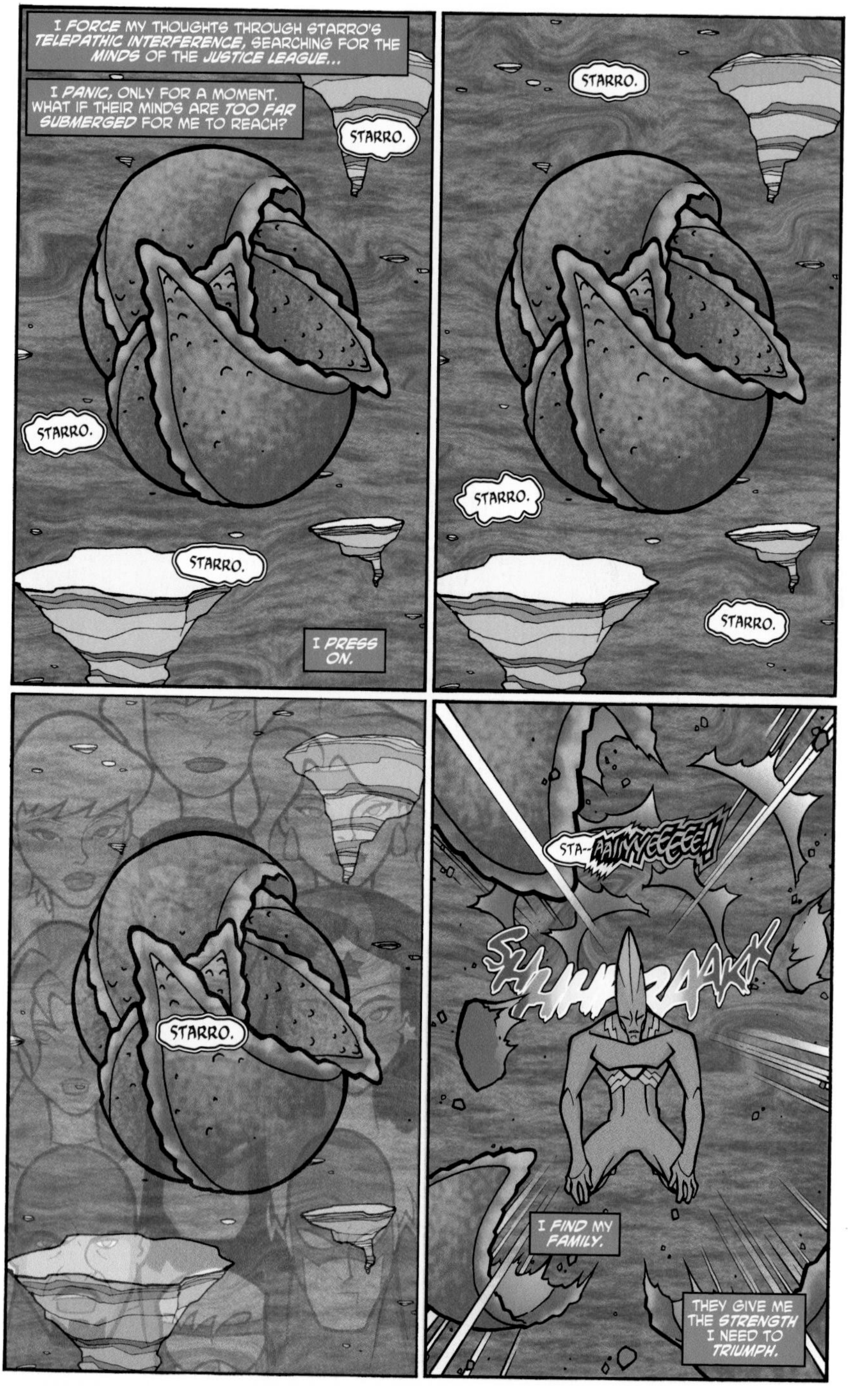
I *FORCE* MY THOUGHTS THROUGH STARRO'S *TELEPATHIC INTERFERENCE*, SEARCHING FOR THE *MINDS* OF THE *JUSTICE LEAGUE*...
I *PANIC*, ONLY FOR A MOMENT. WHAT IF THEIR MINDS ARE *TOO FAR SUBMERGED* FOR ME TO REACH?
STARRO.
STARRO.
STARRO.
I *PRESS ON*.
STARRO.
STARRO.
STARRO.
STARRO.
STA--AAIIYYEEEEE!!
I *FIND* MY *FAMILY*.
THEY GIVE ME THE *STRENGTH* I NEED TO *TRIUMPH*.

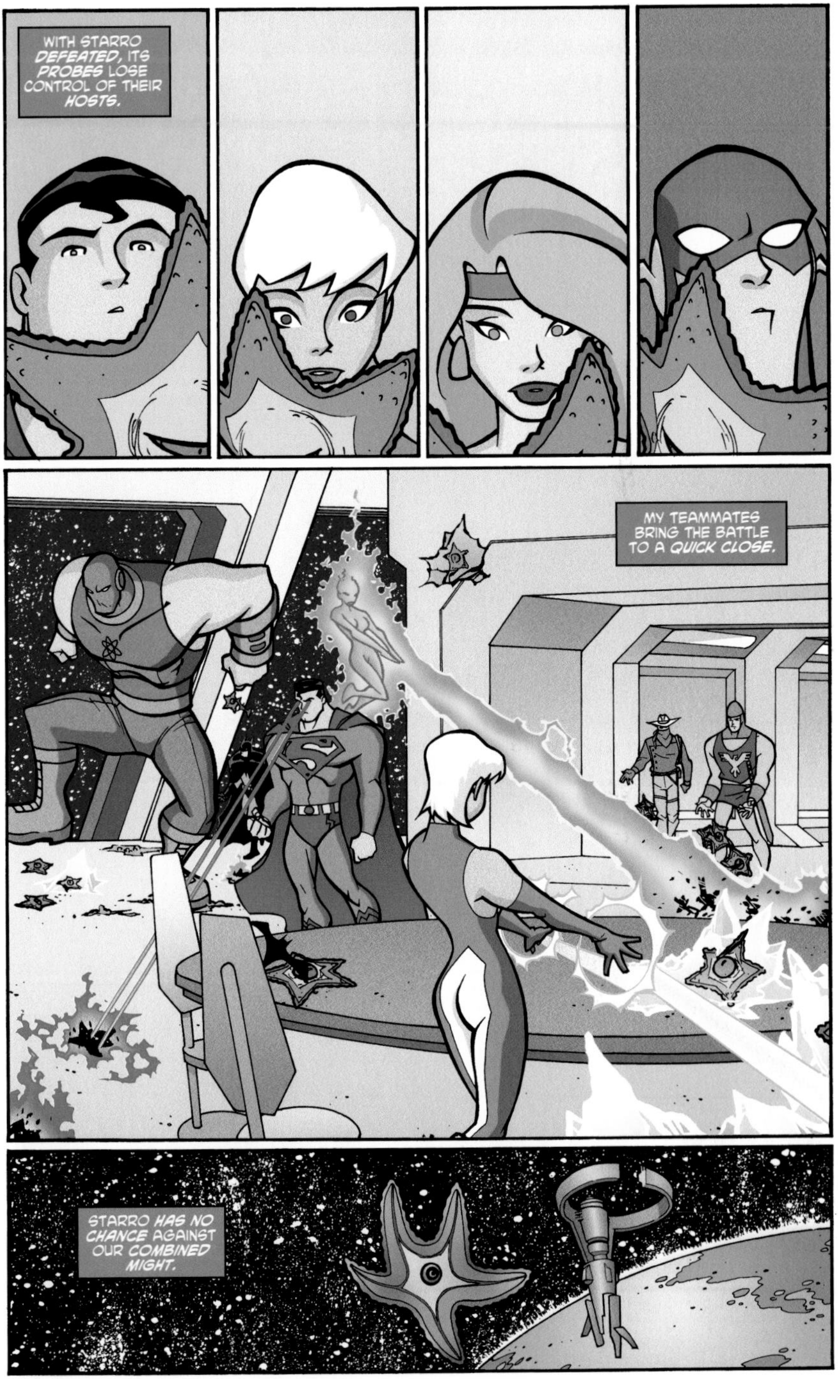
WITH STARRO DEFEATED, ITS PROBES LOSE CONTROL OF THEIR HOSTS.
MY TEAMMATES BRING THE BATTLE TO A QUICK CLOSE.
STARRO HAS NO CHANCE AGAINST OUR COMBINED MIGHT.

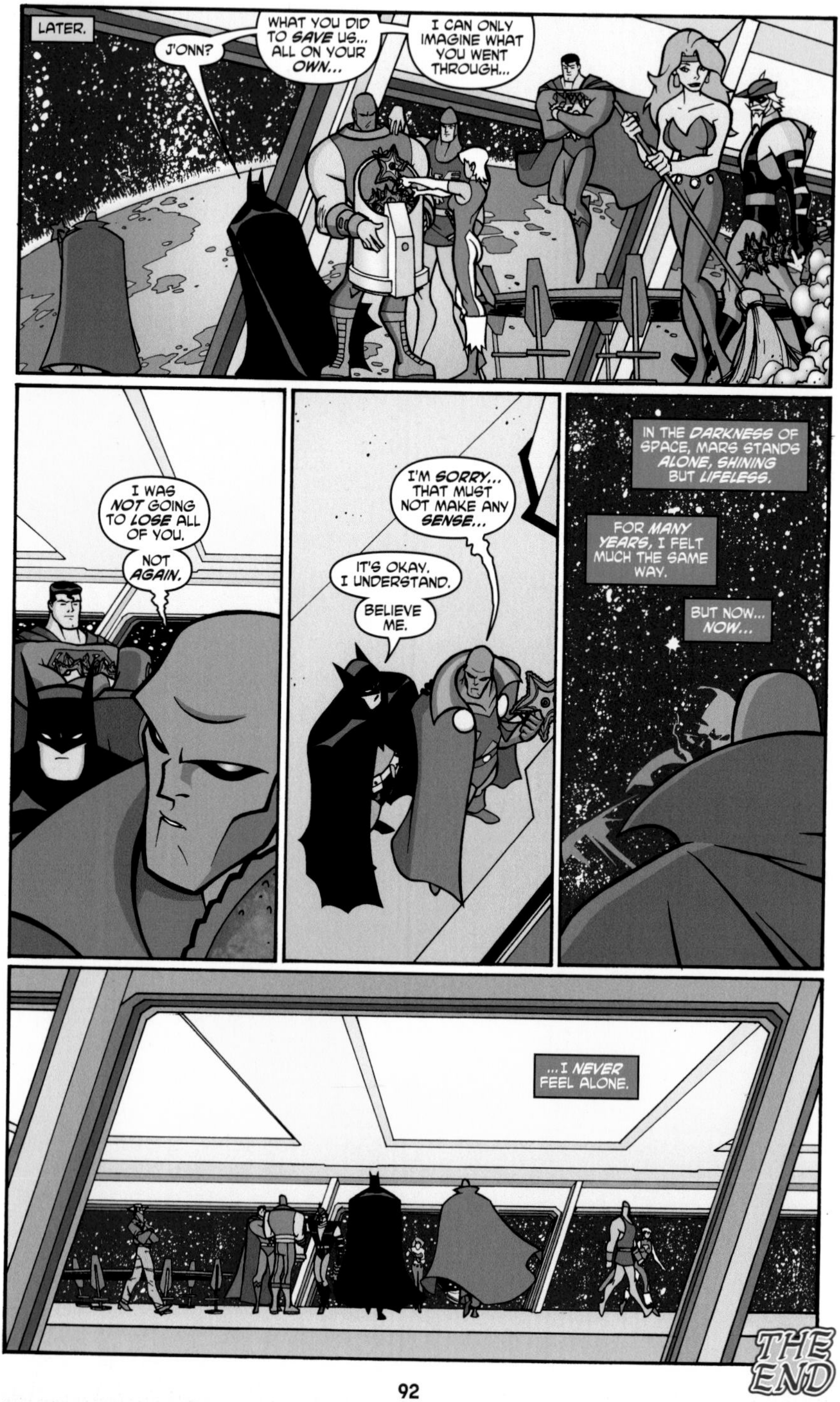
LATER.
J'ONN?
WHAT YOU DID TO SAVE US... ALL ON YOUR OWN...
I CAN ONLY IMAGINE WHAT YOU WENT THROUGH...
I WAS NOT GOING TO LOSE ALL OF YOU.
NOT AGAIN.
I'M SORRY... THAT MUST NOT MAKE ANY SENSE...
IT'S OKAY. I UNDERSTAND.
BELIEVE ME.
IN THE DARKNESS OF SPACE, MARS STANDS ALONE, SHINING BUT LIFELESS.
FOR MANY YEARS, I FELT MUCH THE SAME WAY.
BUT NOW... NOW...
...I NEVER FEEL ALONE.
THE END

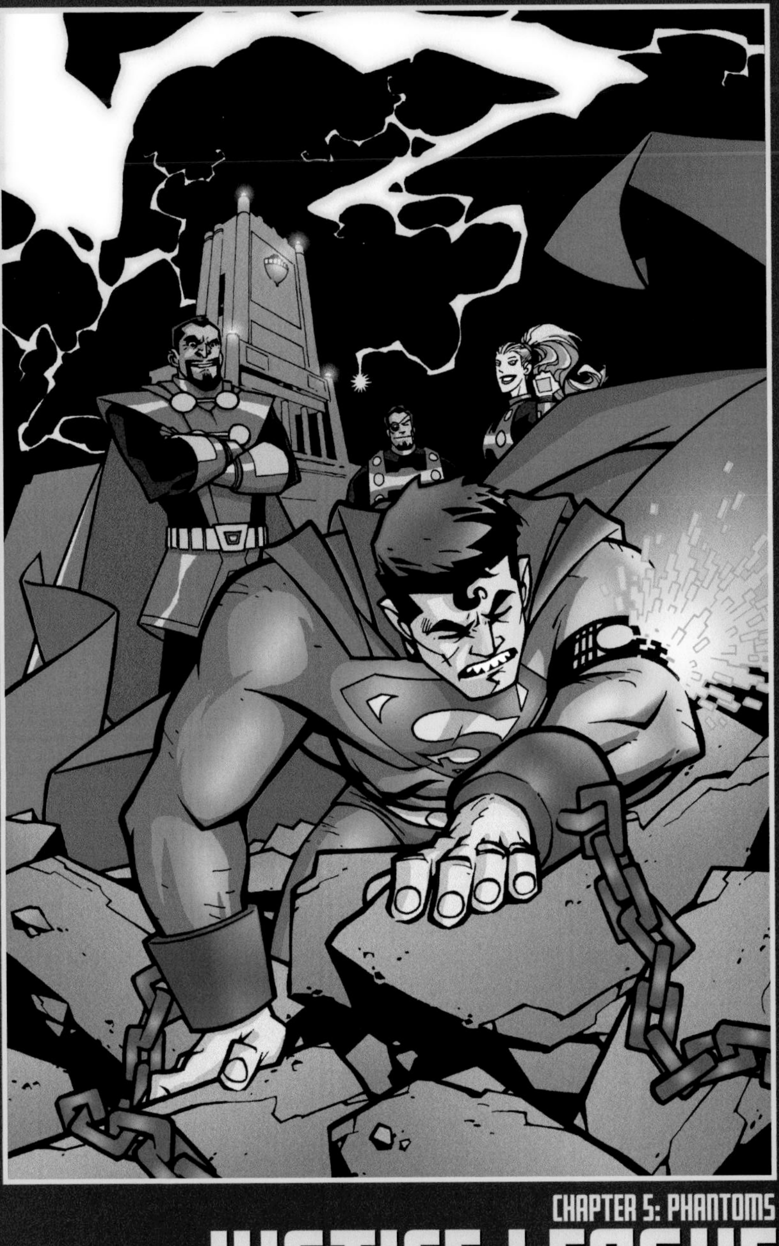

CHAPTER 5: PHANTOMS

JUSTICE LEAGUE UNLIMITED

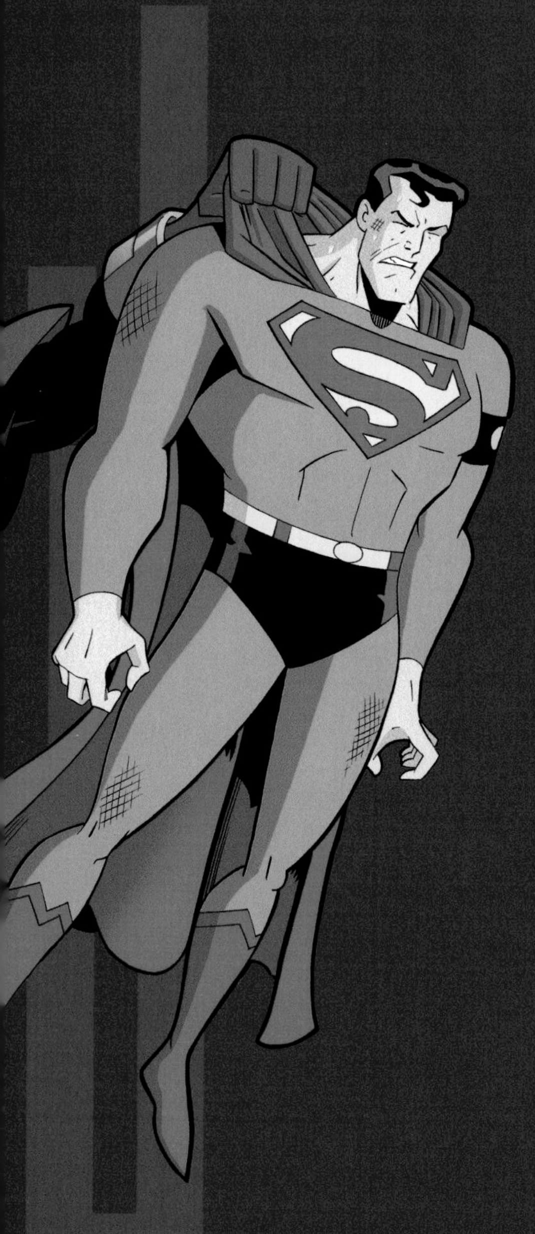

COVER ART BY ZACH HOWARD AND NAWIN TANGUAY

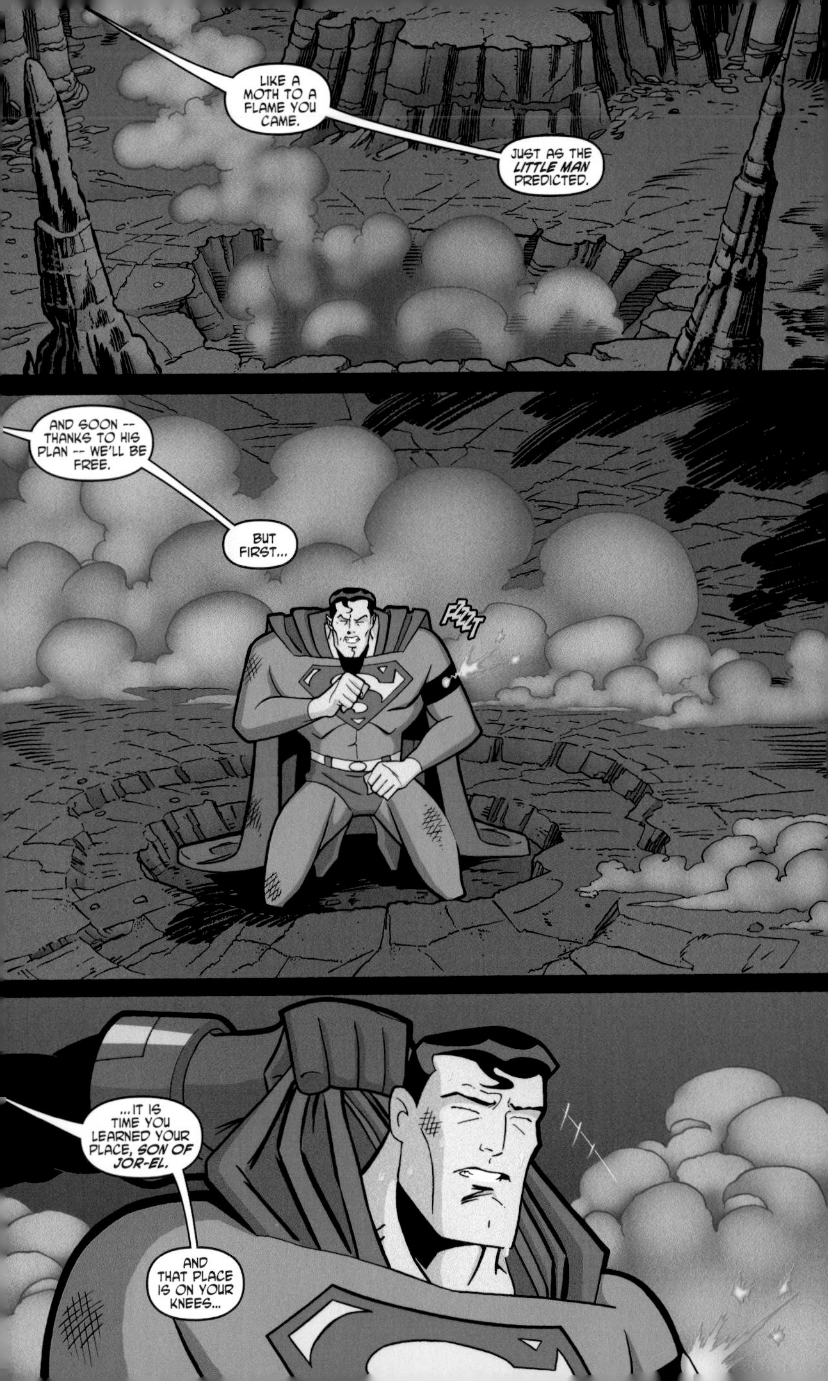
LIKE A MOTH TO A FLAME YOU CAME.
JUST AS THE *LITTLE MAN* PREDICTED.
AND SOON -- THANKS TO HIS PLAN -- WE'LL BE FREE.
BUT FIRST...
FZZZT
...IT IS TIME YOU LEARNED YOUR PLACE, *SON OF JOR-EL.*
AND THAT PLACE IS ON YOUR KNEES...

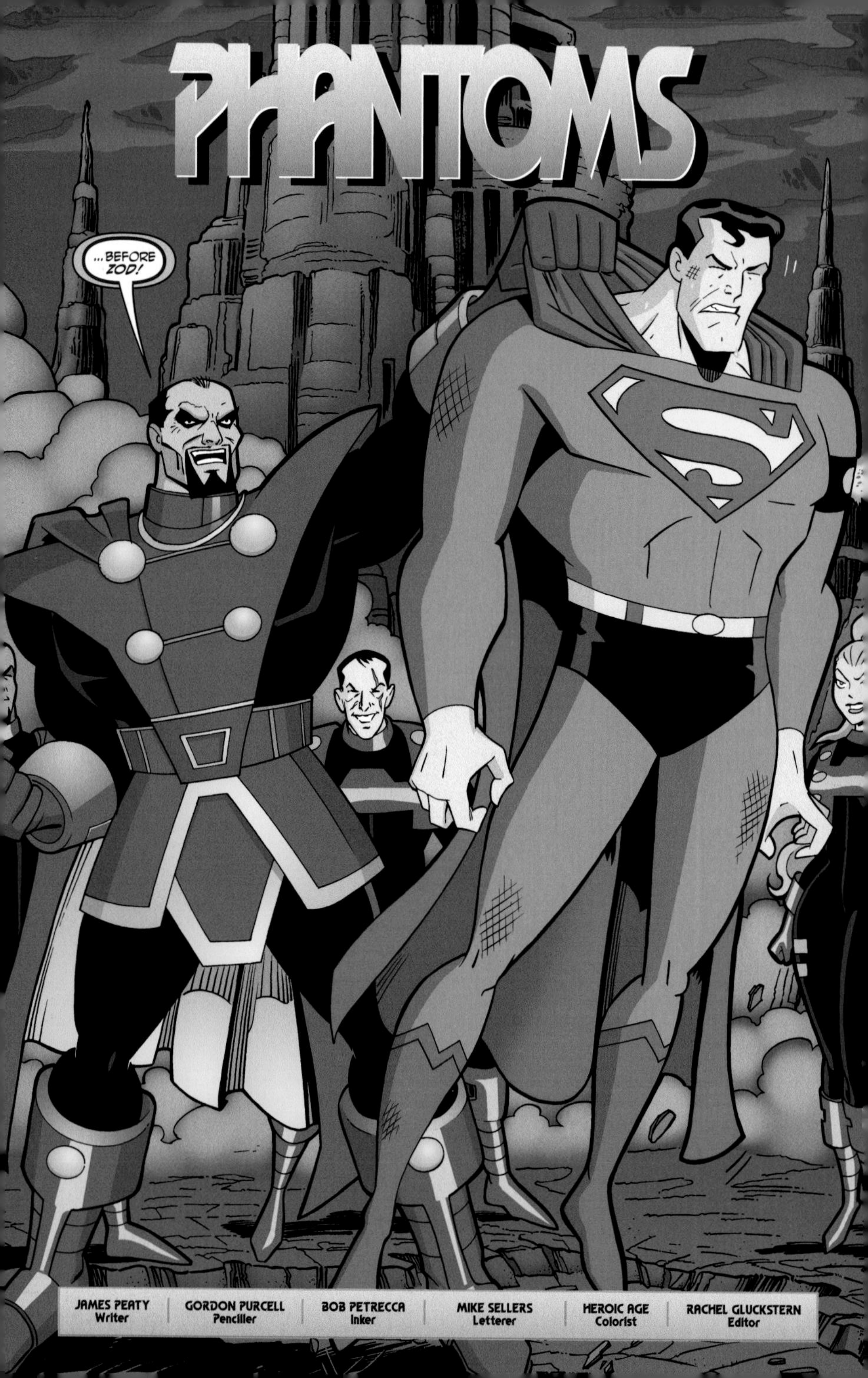
PHANTOMS
...BEFORE ZOD!
JAMES PEATY Writer
GORDON PURCELL Penciller
BOB PETRECCA Inker
MIKE SELLERS Letterer
HEROIC AGE Colorist
RACHEL GLUCKSTERN Editor

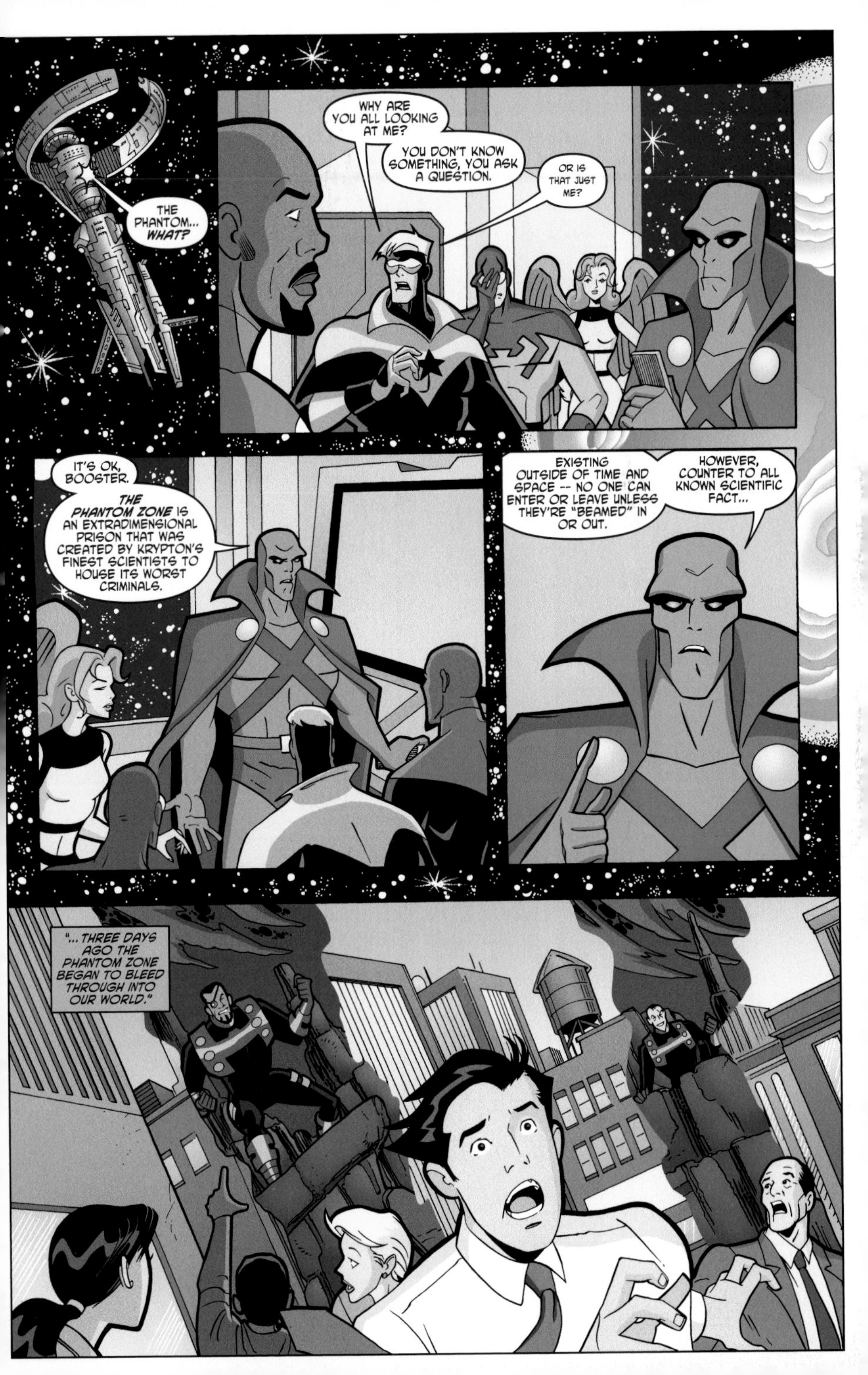
THE PHANTOM... *WHAT?*
WHY ARE YOU ALL LOOKING AT ME?
YOU DON'T KNOW SOMETHING, YOU ASK A QUESTION.
OR IS THAT JUST ME?
IT'S OK, BOOSTER.
THE PHANTOM ZONE IS AN EXTRADIMENSIONAL PRISON THAT WAS CREATED BY KRYPTON'S FINEST SCIENTISTS TO HOUSE ITS WORST CRIMINALS.
EXISTING OUTSIDE OF TIME AND SPACE -- NO ONE CAN ENTER OR LEAVE UNLESS THEY'RE "BEAMED" IN OR OUT.
HOWEVER, COUNTER TO ALL KNOWN SCIENTIFIC FACT...
"...THREE DAYS AGO THE PHANTOM ZONE BEGAN TO BLEED THROUGH INTO OUR WORLD."

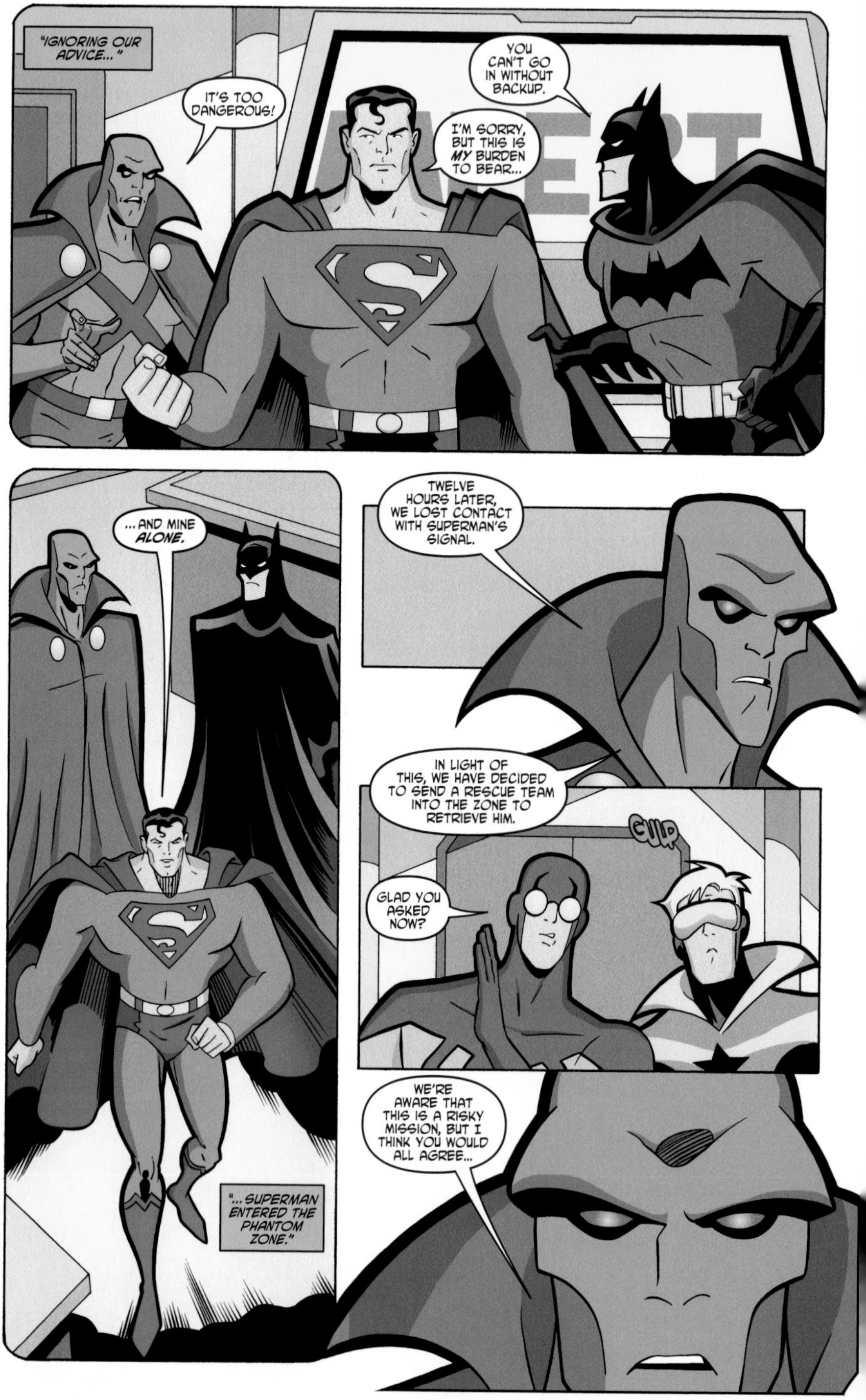
"IGNORING OUR ADVICE..."
IT'S TOO DANGEROUS!
YOU CAN'T GO IN WITHOUT BACKUP.
I'M SORRY, BUT THIS IS *MY* BURDEN TO BEAR...
...AND MINE *ALONE.*
"...SUPERMAN ENTERED THE PHANTOM ZONE."
TWELVE HOURS LATER, WE LOST CONTACT WITH SUPERMAN'S SIGNAL.
IN LIGHT OF THIS, WE HAVE DECIDED TO SEND A RESCUE TEAM INTO THE ZONE TO RETRIEVE HIM.
GULP
GLAD YOU ASKED NOW?
WE'RE AWARE THAT THIS IS A RISKY MISSION, BUT I THINK YOU WOULD ALL AGREE...

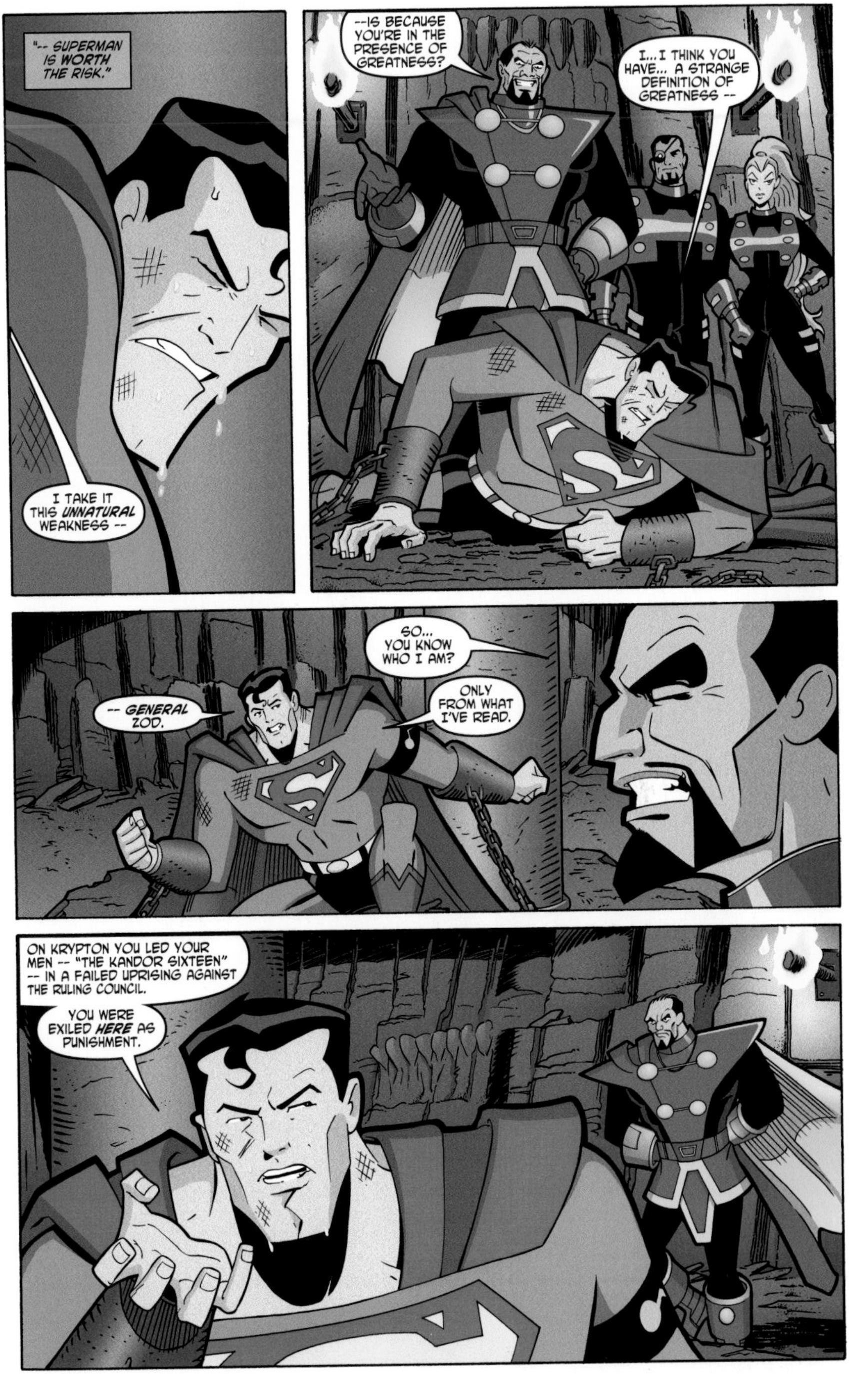
"-- SUPERMAN IS WORTH THE RISK."
I TAKE IT THIS UNNATURAL WEAKNESS --
--IS BECAUSE YOU'RE IN THE PRESENCE OF GREATNESS?
I...I THINK YOU HAVE... A STRANGE DEFINITION OF GREATNESS --
SO... YOU KNOW WHO I AM?
-- GENERAL ZOD.
ONLY FROM WHAT I'VE READ.
ON KRYPTON YOU LED YOUR MEN -- "THE KANDOR SIXTEEN" -- IN A FAILED UPRISING AGAINST THE RULING COUNCIL.
YOU WERE EXILED HERE AS PUNISHMENT.

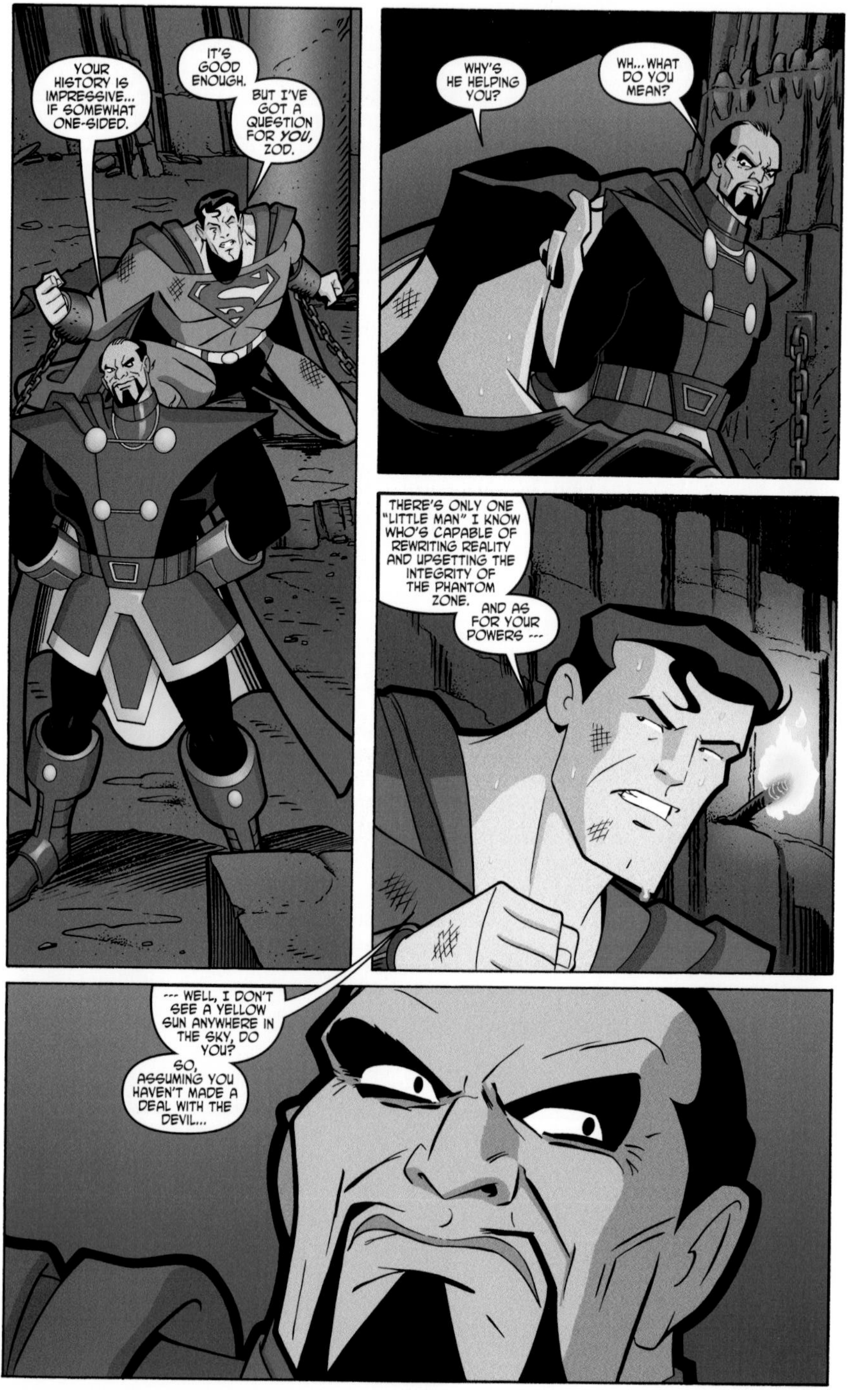
YOUR HISTORY IS IMPRESSIVE... IF SOMEWHAT ONE-SIDED.
IT'S GOOD ENOUGH.
BUT I'VE GOT A QUESTION FOR *YOU*, ZOD.
WHY'S HE HELPING YOU?
WH... WHAT DO YOU MEAN?
THERE'S ONLY ONE "LITTLE MAN" I KNOW WHO'S CAPABLE OF REWRITING REALITY AND UPSETTING THE INTEGRITY OF THE PHANTOM ZONE.
AND AS FOR YOUR POWERS ---
--- WELL, I DON'T SEE A YELLOW SUN ANYWHERE IN THE SKY, DO YOU?
SO, ASSUMING YOU HAVEN'T MADE A DEAL WITH THE DEVIL...

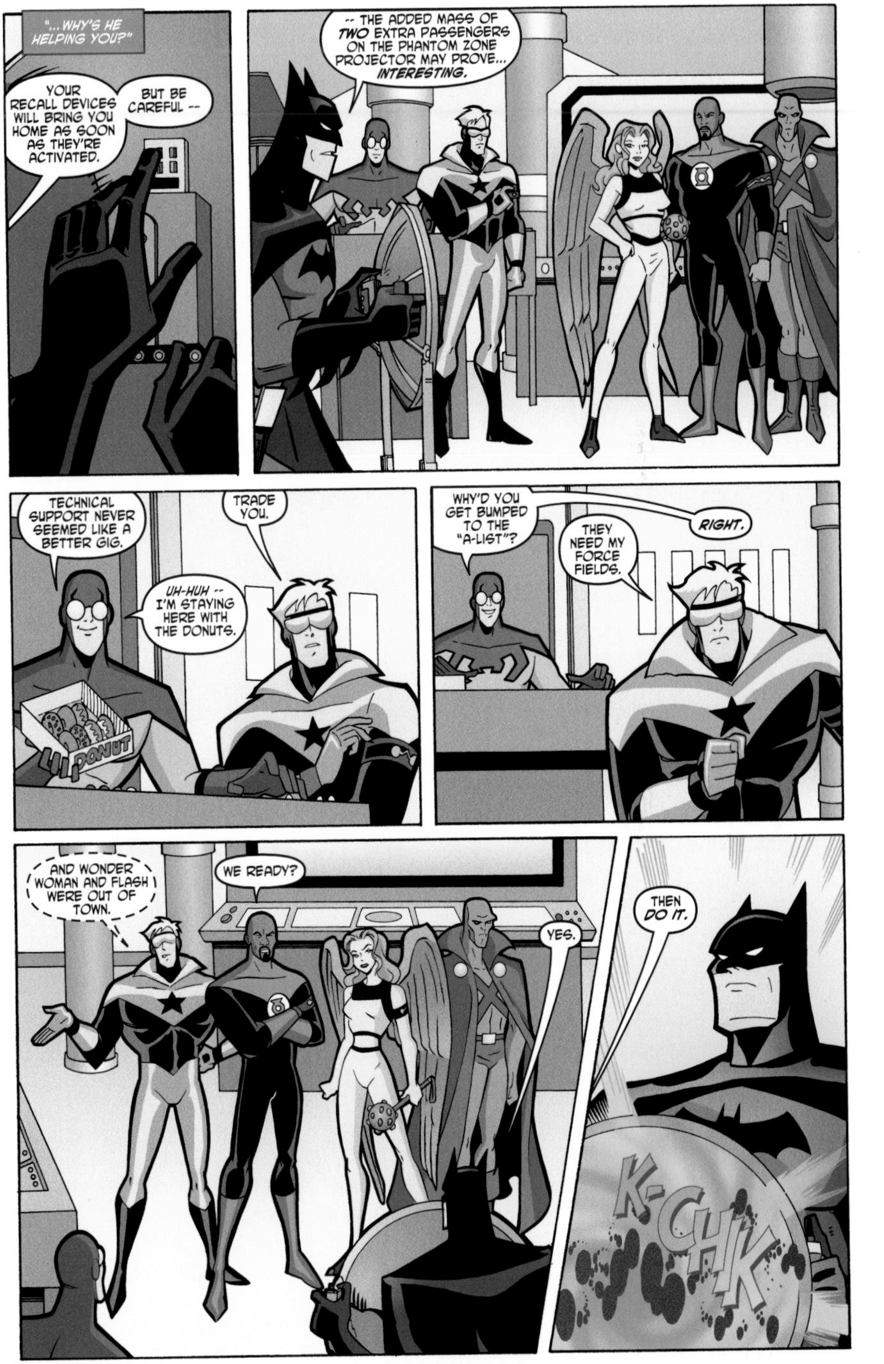
"...WHY'S HE HELPING YOU?"
YOUR RECALL DEVICES WILL BRING YOU HOME AS SOON AS THEY'RE ACTIVATED.
BUT BE CAREFUL --
-- THE ADDED MASS OF TWO EXTRA PASSENGERS ON THE PHANTOM ZONE PROJECTOR MAY PROVE... INTERESTING.
TECHNICAL SUPPORT NEVER SEEMED LIKE A BETTER GIG.
TRADE YOU.
UH-HUH -- I'M STAYING HERE WITH THE DONUTS.
DONUT
WHY'D YOU GET BUMPED TO THE "A-LIST"?
THEY NEED MY FORCE FIELDS.
RIGHT.
AND WONDER WOMAN AND FLASH WERE OUT OF TOWN.
WE READY?
YES.
THEN DO IT.
K-CHK

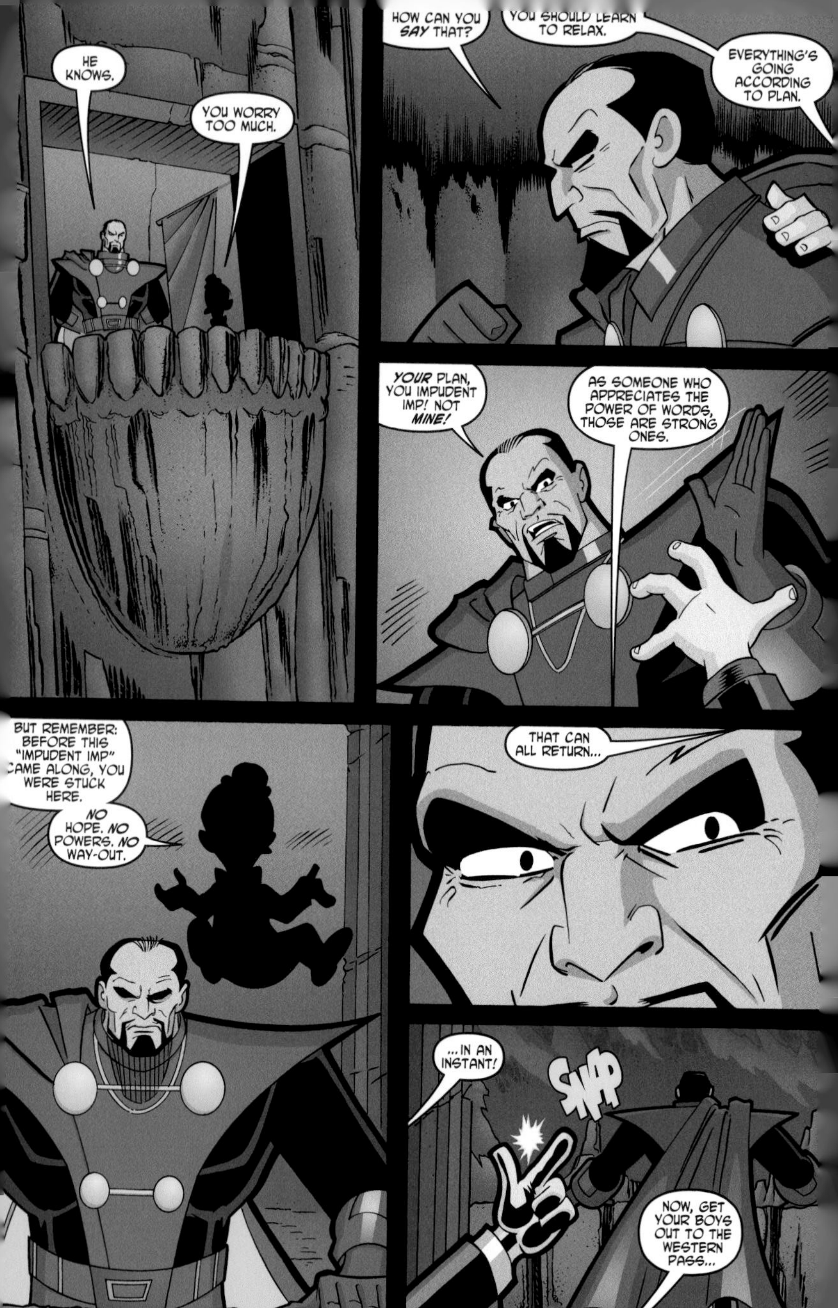
HE KNOWS.
YOU WORRY TOO MUCH.
HOW CAN YOU SAY THAT?
YOU SHOULD LEARN TO RELAX.
EVERYTHING'S GOING ACCORDING TO PLAN.
YOUR PLAN, YOU IMPUDENT IMP! NOT MINE!
AS SOMEONE WHO APPRECIATES THE POWER OF WORDS, THOSE ARE STRONG ONES.
BUT REMEMBER: BEFORE THIS "IMPUDENT IMP" CAME ALONG, YOU WERE STUCK HERE.
NO HOPE. NO POWERS. NO WAY-OUT.
THAT CAN ALL RETURN...
...IN AN INSTANT!
SNAP
NOW, GET YOUR BOYS OUT TO THE WESTERN PASS...

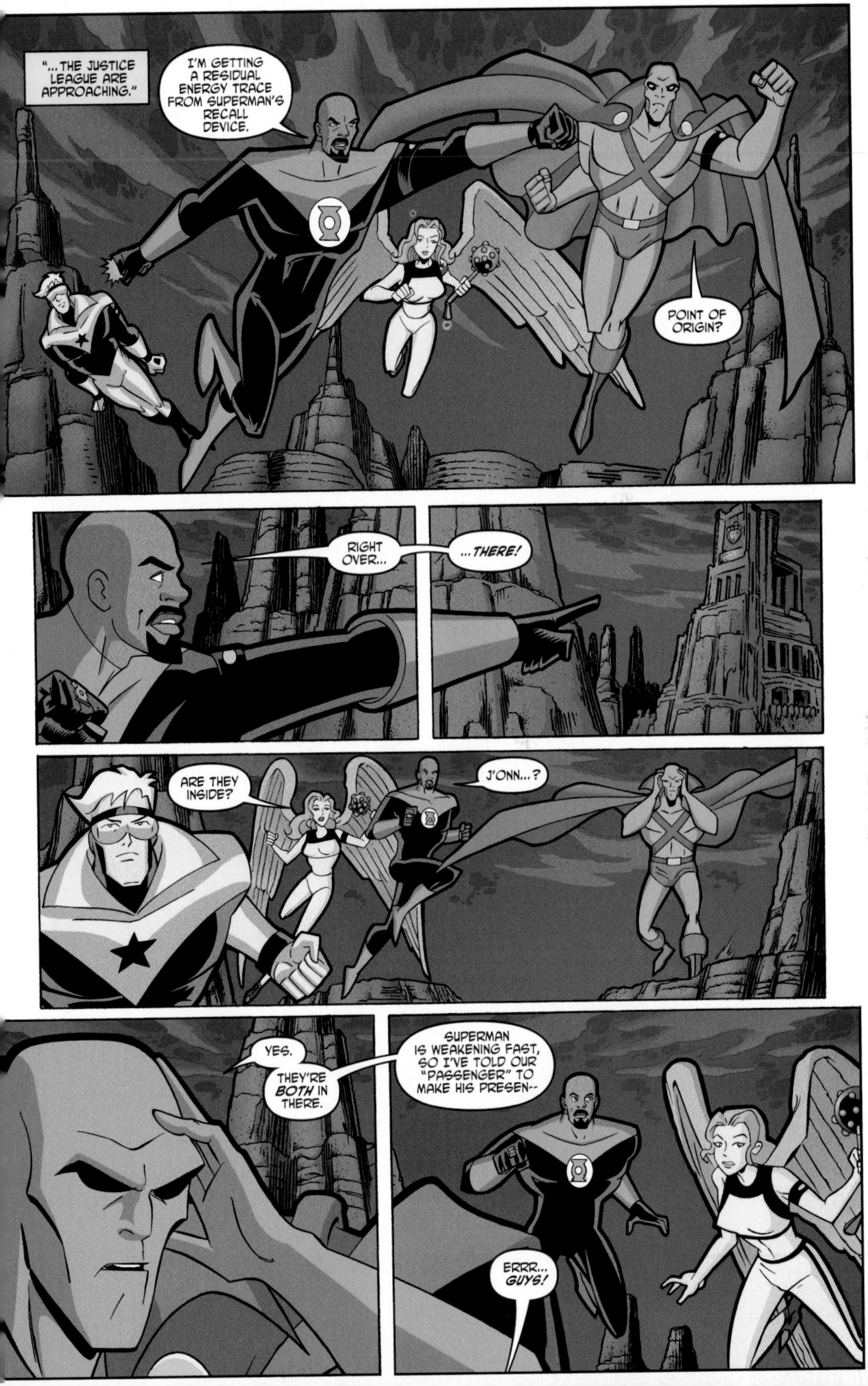
"...THE JUSTICE LEAGUE ARE APPROACHING."
I'M GETTING A RESIDUAL ENERGY TRACE FROM SUPERMAN'S RECALL DEVICE.
POINT OF ORIGIN?
RIGHT OVER...
...THERE!
ARE THEY INSIDE?
J'ONN...?
YES.
THEY'RE BOTH IN THERE.
SUPERMAN IS WEAKENING FAST, SO I'VE TOLD OUR "PASSENGER" TO MAKE HIS PRESEN--
ERRR... GUYS!

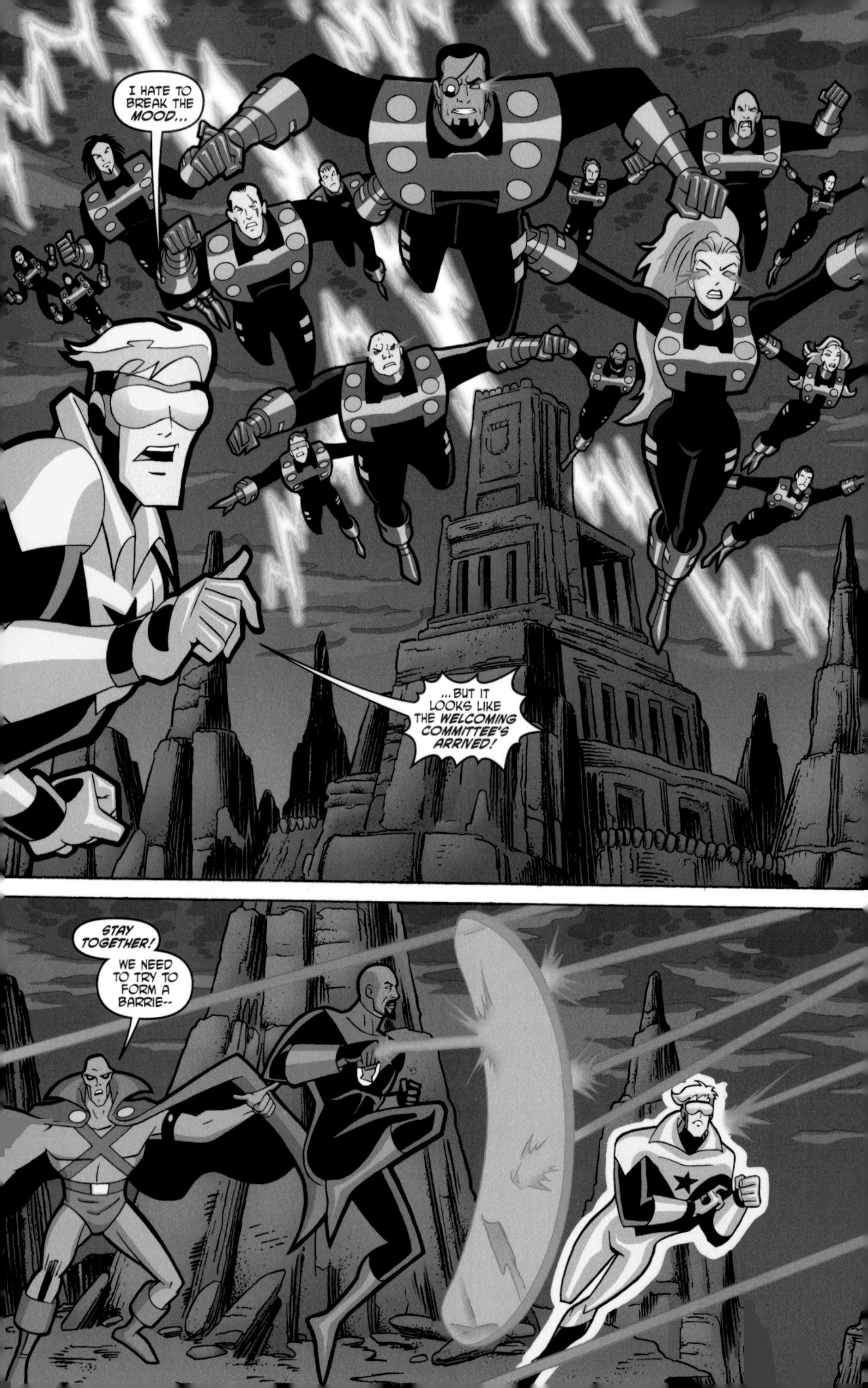
I HATE TO BREAK THE MOOD...
...BUT IT LOOKS LIKE THE WELCOMING COMMITTEE'S ARRIVED!
STAY TOGETHER!
WE NEED TO TRY TO FORM A BARRIE--

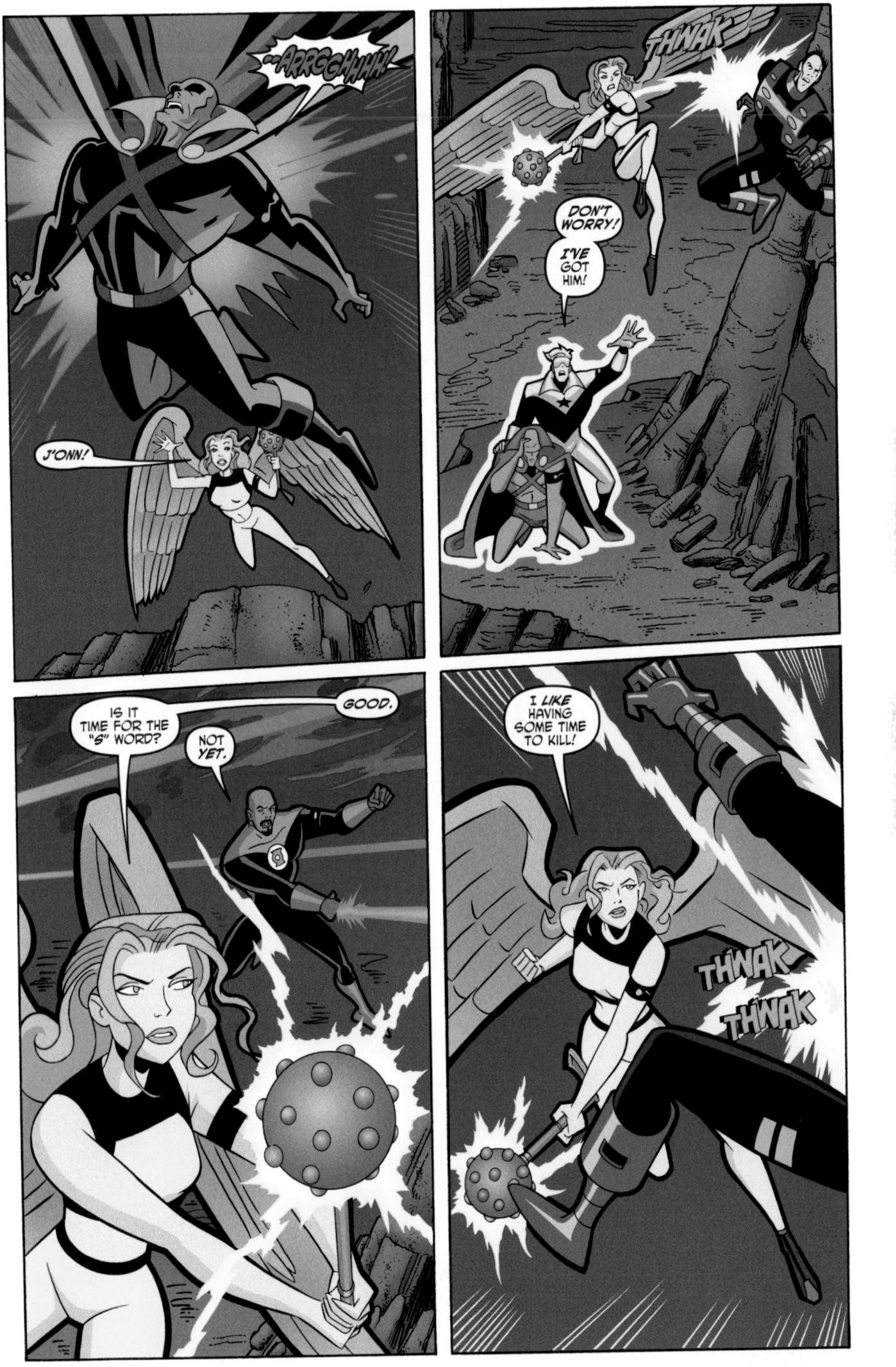
--ARRGGHHH!
J'ONN!
THWAK
DON'T WORRY!
I'VE GOT HIM!
IS IT TIME FOR THE "S" WORD?
GOOD.
NOT YET.
I LIKE HAVING SOME TIME TO KILL!
THWAK
THWAK

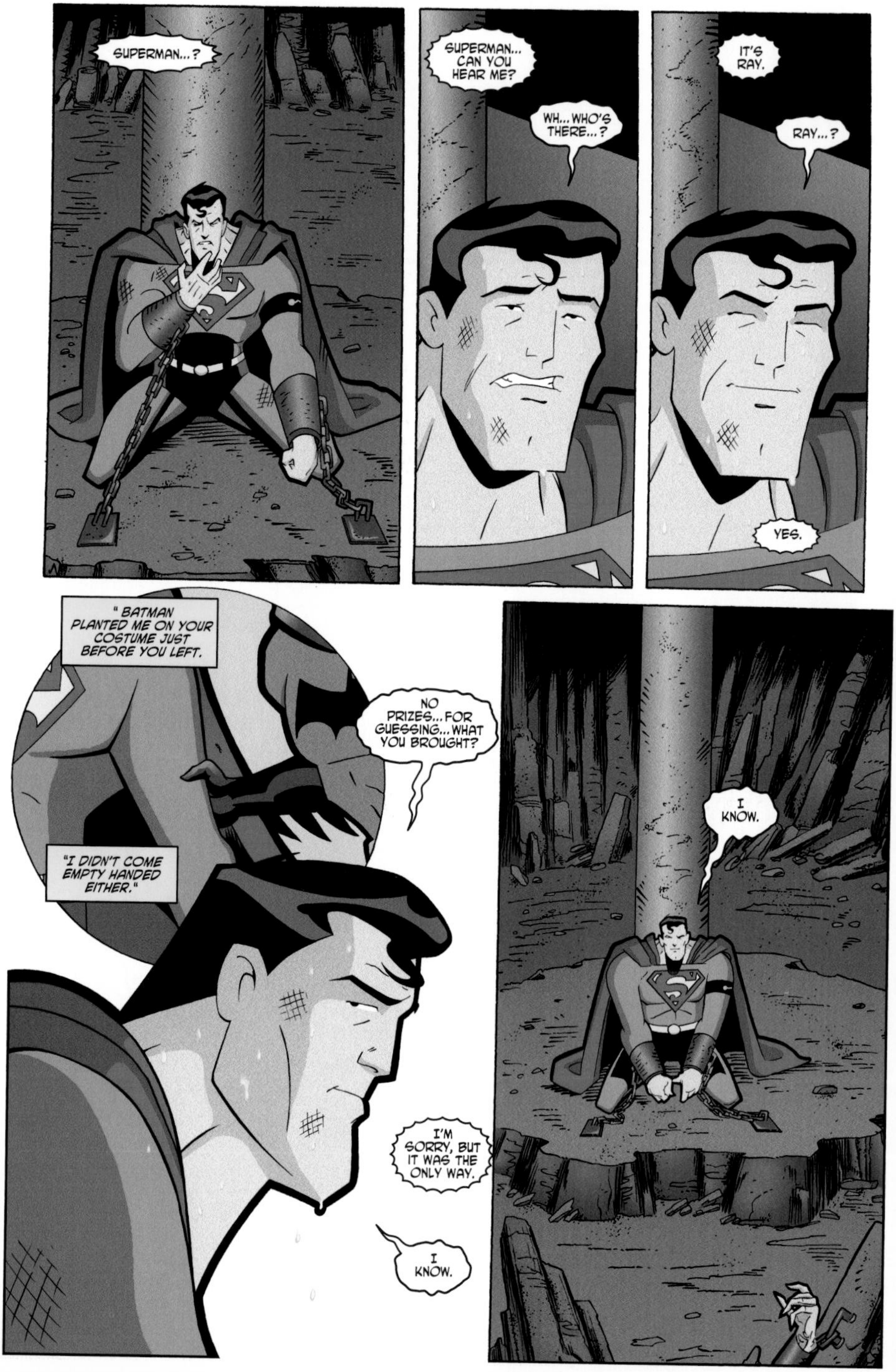
SUPERMAN...?
SUPERMAN... CAN YOU HEAR ME?
WH... WHO'S THERE...?
IT'S RAY.
RAY...?
YES.
" BATMAN PLANTED ME ON YOUR COSTUME JUST BEFORE YOU LEFT.
NO PRIZES... FOR GUESSING... WHAT YOU BROUGHT?
"I DIDN'T COME EMPTY HANDED EITHER."
I'M SORRY, BUT IT WAS THE ONLY WAY.
I KNOW.
I KNOW.

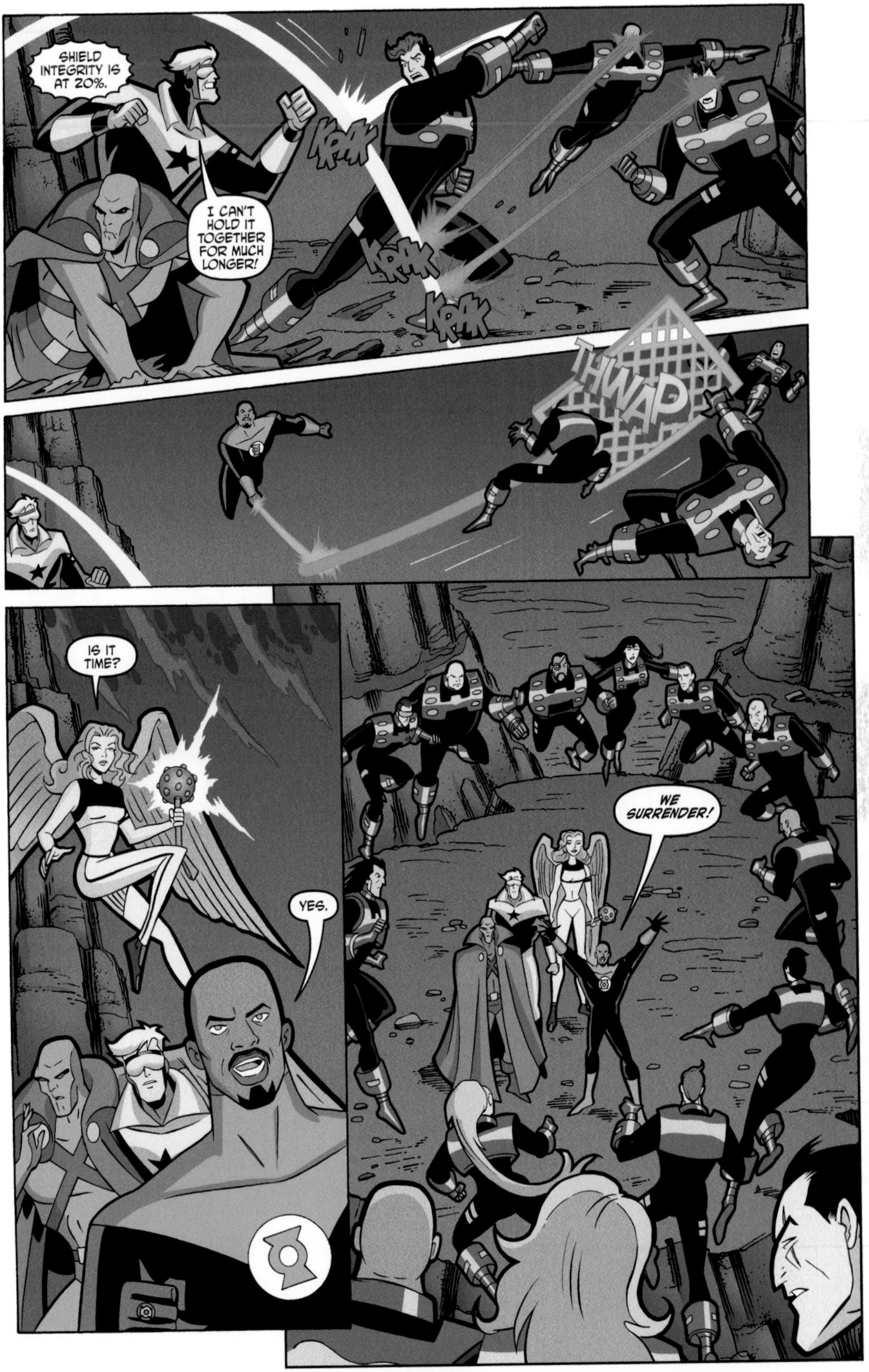
SHIELD INTEGRITY IS AT 20%.
I CAN'T HOLD IT TOGETHER FOR MUCH LONGER!
KRAK
KRAK
KRAK
THWAP
IS IT TIME?
YES.
WE SURRENDER!

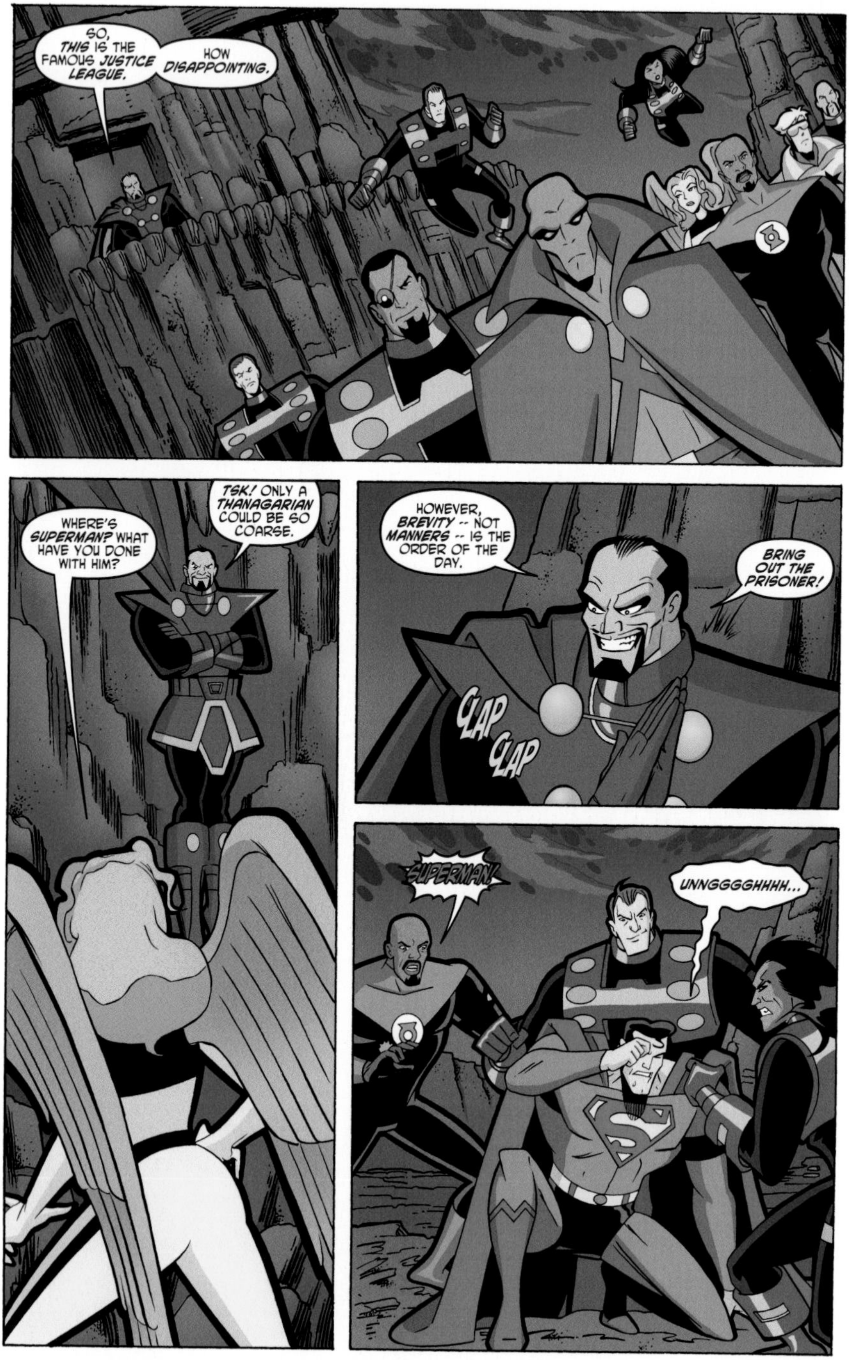

SO, THIS IS THE FAMOUS JUSTICE LEAGUE.
HOW DISAPPOINTING.
WHERE'S SUPERMAN? WHAT HAVE YOU DONE WITH HIM?
TSK! ONLY A THANAGARIAN COULD BE SO COARSE.
HOWEVER, BREVITY -- NOT MANNERS -- IS THE ORDER OF THE DAY.
BRING OUT THE PRISONER!
CLAP CLAP
SUPERMAN!
UNNGGGGHHHH...

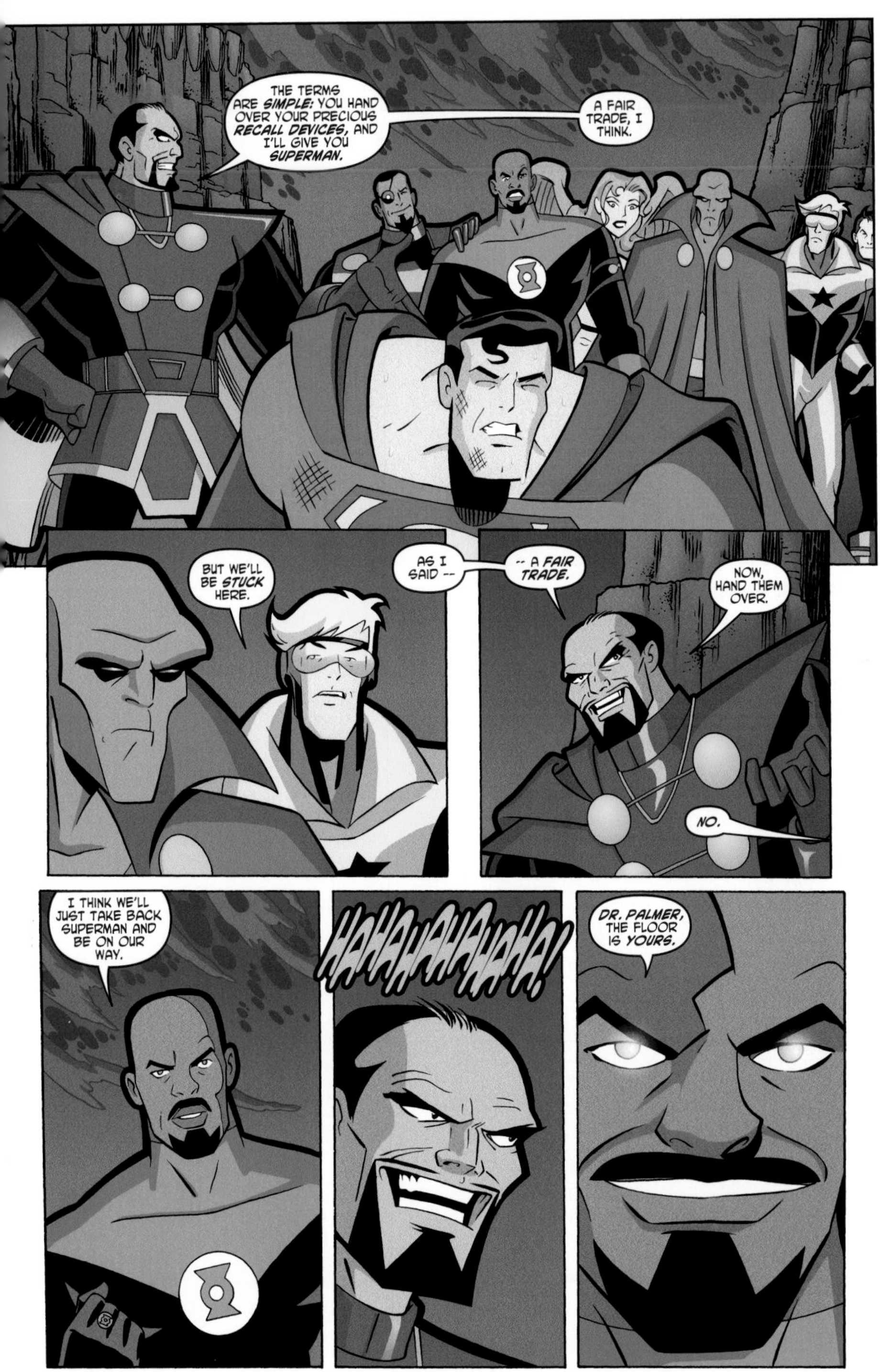
THE TERMS ARE SIMPLE: YOU HAND OVER YOUR PRECIOUS RECALL DEVICES, AND I'LL GIVE YOU SUPERMAN.
A FAIR TRADE, I THINK.
BUT WE'LL BE STUCK HERE.
AS I SAID --
-- A FAIR TRADE.
NOW, HAND THEM OVER.
NO.
I THINK WE'LL JUST TAKE BACK SUPERMAN AND BE ON OUR WAY.
HAHAHAHAHAHA!
DR. PALMER, THE FLOOR IS YOURS.

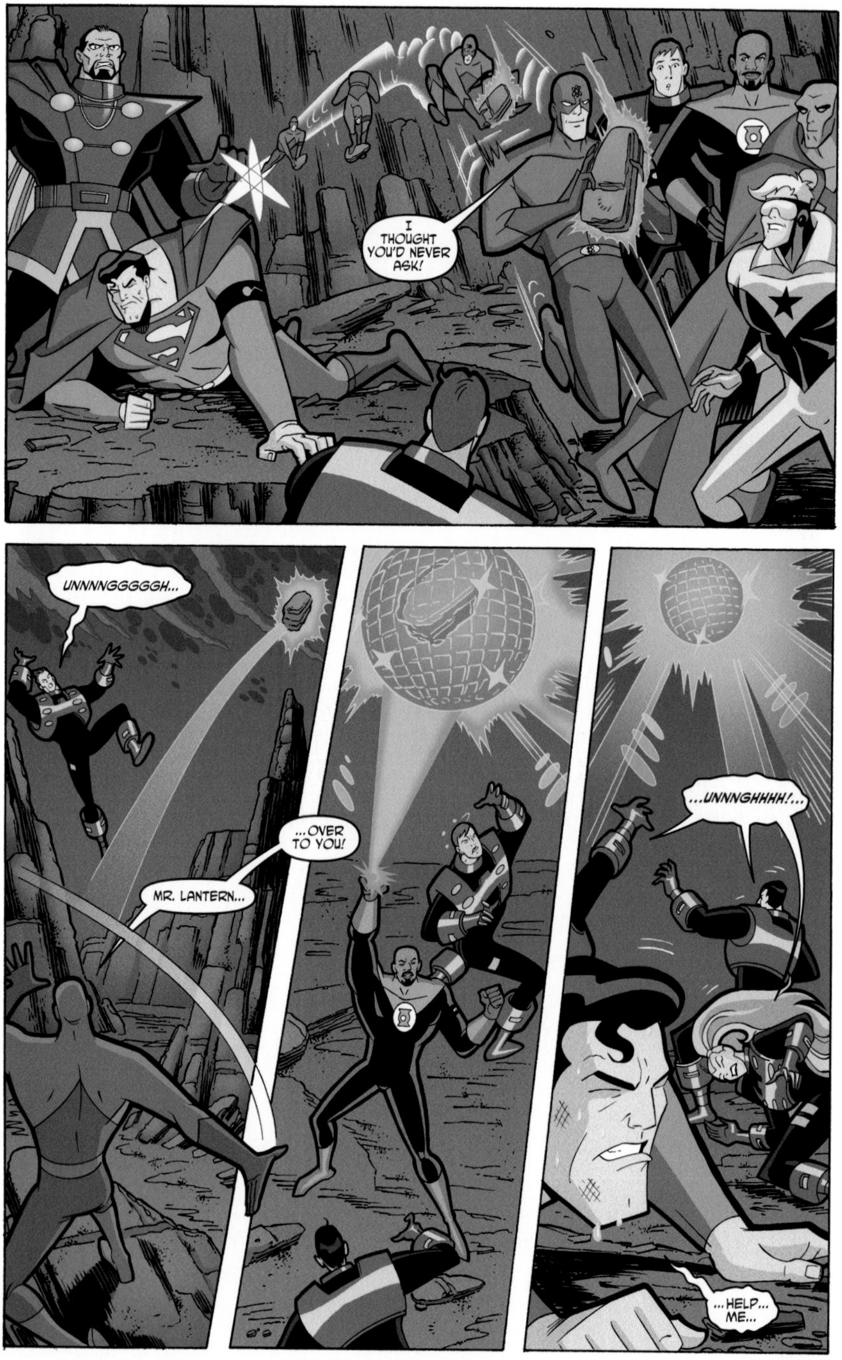
I THOUGHT YOU'D NEVER ASK!
UNNNNGGGGGH...
MR. LANTERN...
...OVER TO YOU!
...UNNNGHHHH!...
...HELP... ME...

I'VE GOT HIM!

WE READY?

GOOD TO GO.

THEN WHAT ARE WE WAITING --

ZZZZZZZZZ

-- FOR?

OH.

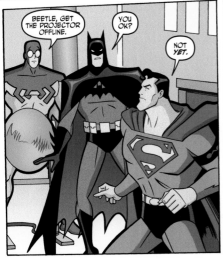

BEETLE, GET THE PROJECTOR OFFLINE.

YOU OK?

NOT YET.

THERE'S NO NEED TO HIDE ANYMORE!

YOU CAN SHOW YOURSELF...

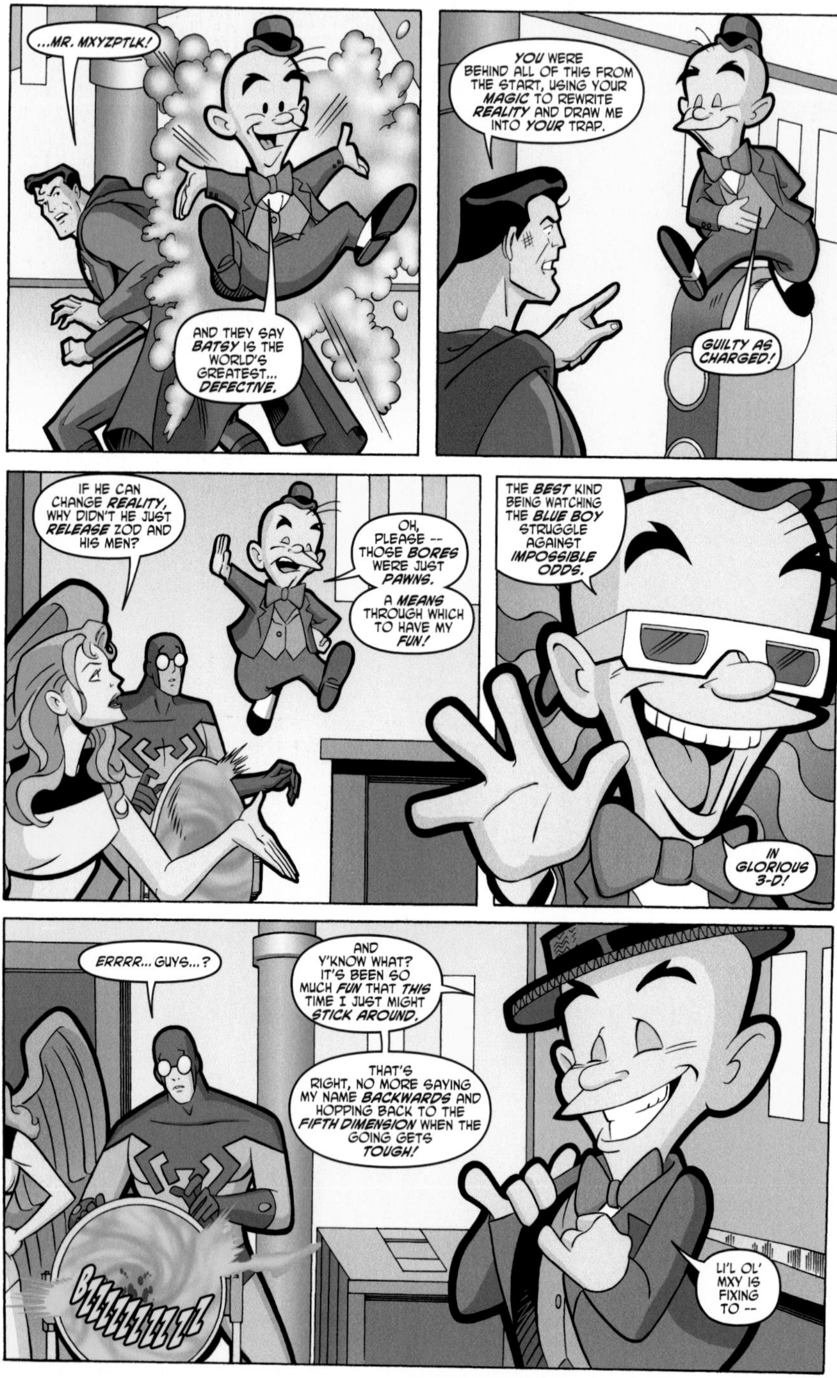
...MR. MXYZPTLK!
AND THEY SAY BATSY IS THE WORLD'S GREATEST... DEFECTIVE.
YOU WERE BEHIND ALL OF THIS FROM THE START, USING YOUR MAGIC TO REWRITE REALITY AND DRAW ME INTO YOUR TRAP.
GUILTY AS CHARGED!
IF HE CAN CHANGE REALITY, WHY DIDN'T HE JUST RELEASE ZOD AND HIS MEN?
OH, PLEASE -- THOSE BORES WERE JUST PAWNS.
A MEANS THROUGH WHICH TO HAVE MY FUN!
THE BEST KIND BEING WATCHING THE BLUE BOY STRUGGLE AGAINST IMPOSSIBLE ODDS.
IN GLORIOUS 3-D!
ERRRR... GUYS...?
AND Y'KNOW WHAT? IT'S BEEN SO MUCH FUN THAT THIS TIME I JUST MIGHT STICK AROUND.
THAT'S RIGHT, NO MORE SAYING MY NAME BACKWARDS AND HOPPING BACK TO THE FIFTH DIMENSION WHEN THE GOING GETS TOUGH!
LI'L OL' MXY IS FIXING TO --
BZZZZZZZZZZ

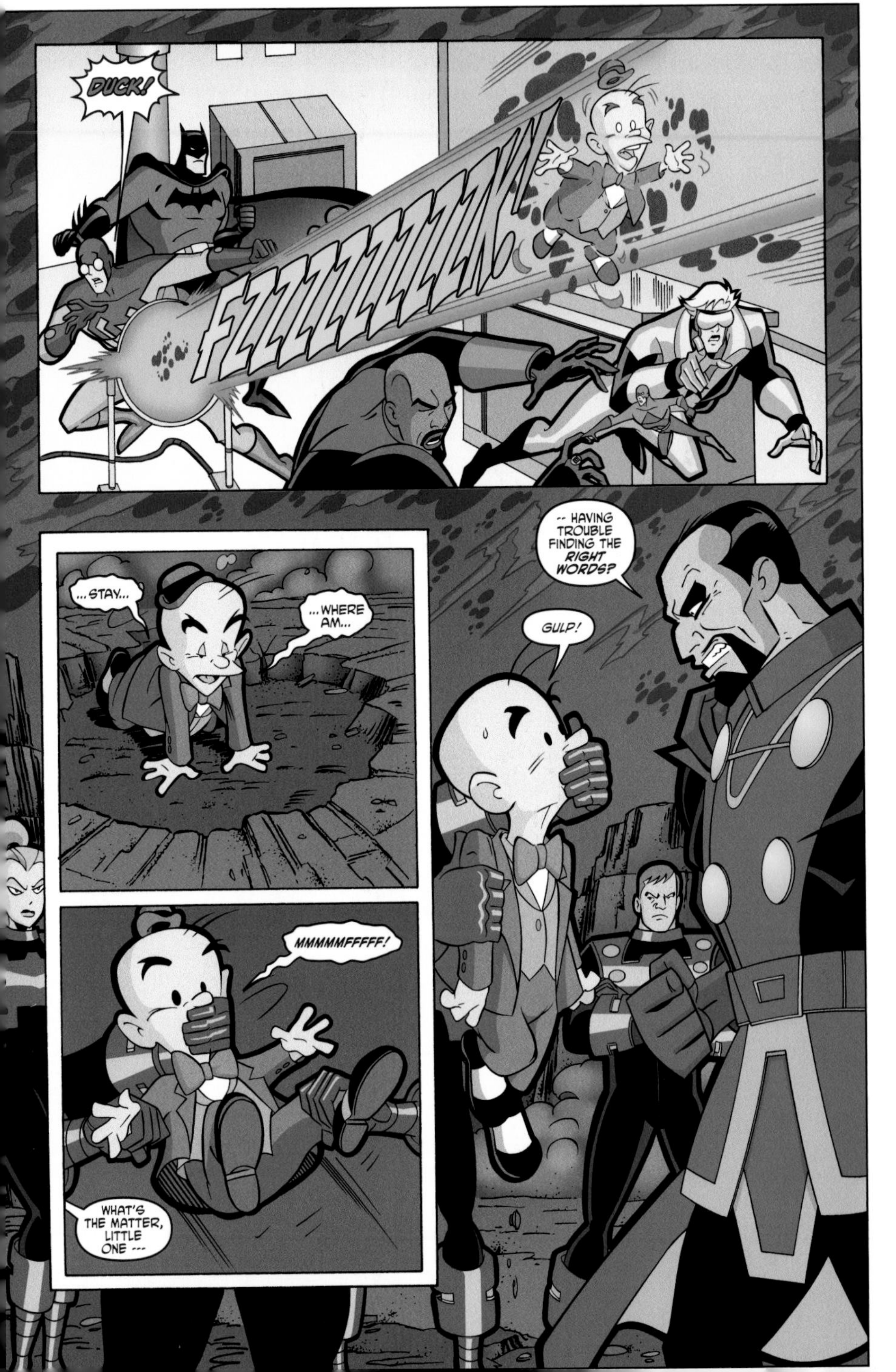
DUCK!
FZZZZZZZZZZZK!
...STAY...
...WHERE AM...
MMMMMFFFFF!
WHAT'S THE MATTER, LITTLE ONE ---
-- HAVING TROUBLE FINDING THE RIGHT WORDS?
GULP!

I WAS A FOOL.

EVERYONE HAS AN ACHILLES HEEL.

YOURS JUST HAPPENS TO BE ANYTHING *KRYPTONIAN*.

PERHAPS. BUT IGNORING YOU LIKE I DID, I *DESERVED* TO BE LEFT IN THE PHANTOM ZONE.

YOU'RE BEING TOO *HARD* ON YOURSELF, KAL-EL.

IT'S OUR *ENEMIES* WHO TRY TO HURT US WHEN WE STUMBLE.

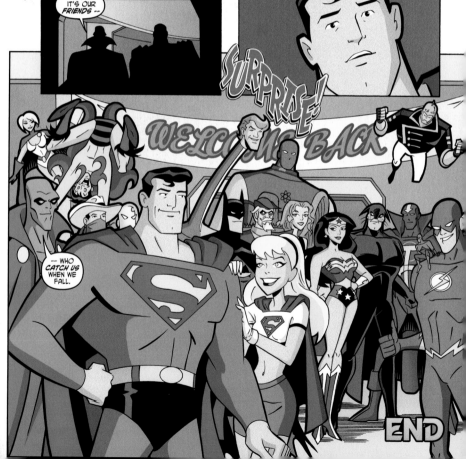

BUT IT'S OUR *FRIENDS* --

SURPRISE!

WELCOME BACK

-- WHO *CATCH US* WHEN WE FALL.

END

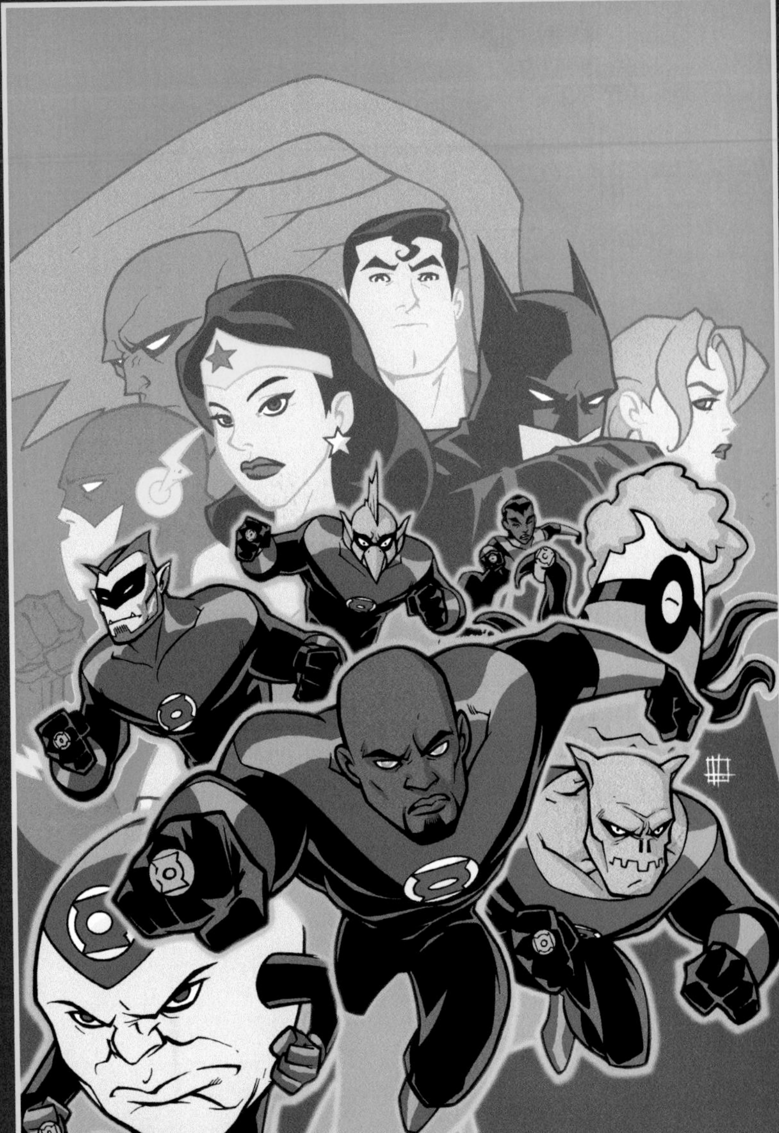

CHAPTER 6: THE DORK, G'NORT, RETURNS

JUSTICE LEAGUE UNLIMITED

COVER ART BY ZACH HOWARD AND DAVID TANGUAY

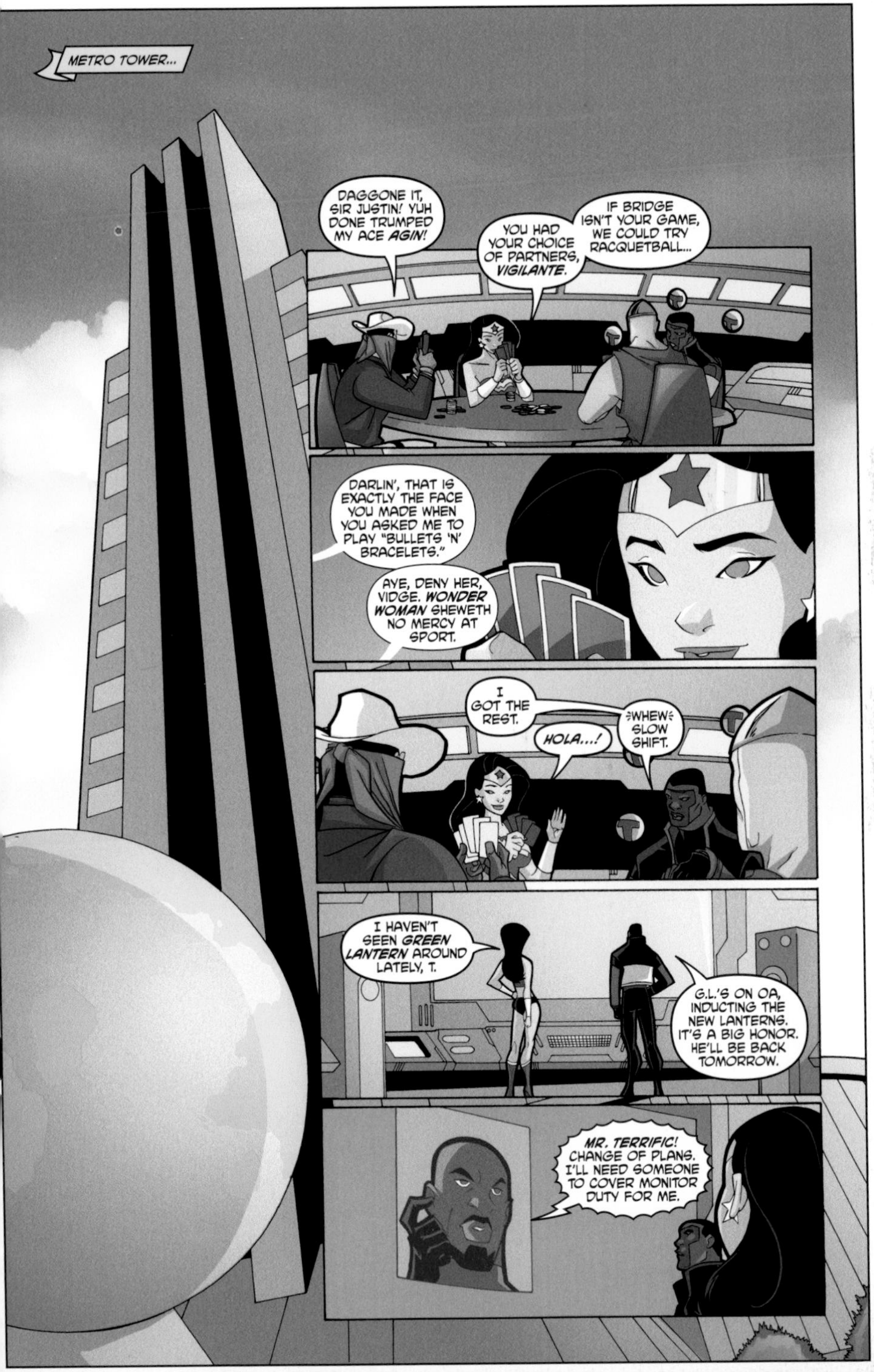

METRO TOWER...
DAGGONE IT, SIR JUSTIN! YUH DONE TRUMPED MY ACE AGIN!
YOU HAD YOUR CHOICE OF PARTNERS, VIGILANTE.
IF BRIDGE ISN'T YOUR GAME, WE COULD TRY RACQUETBALL...
DARLIN', THAT IS EXACTLY THE FACE YOU MADE WHEN YOU ASKED ME TO PLAY "BULLETS 'N' BRACELETS."
AYE, DENY HER, VIDGE. WONDER WOMAN SHEWETH NO MERCY AT SPORT.
I GOT THE REST.
HOLA...!
WHEW SLOW SHIFT.
I HAVEN'T SEEN GREEN LANTERN AROUND LATELY, T.
G.L.'S ON OA, INDUCTING THE NEW LANTERNS. IT'S A BIG HONOR. HE'LL BE BACK TOMORROW.
MR. TERRIFIC! CHANGE OF PLANS. I'LL NEED SOMEONE TO COVER MONITOR DUTY FOR ME.

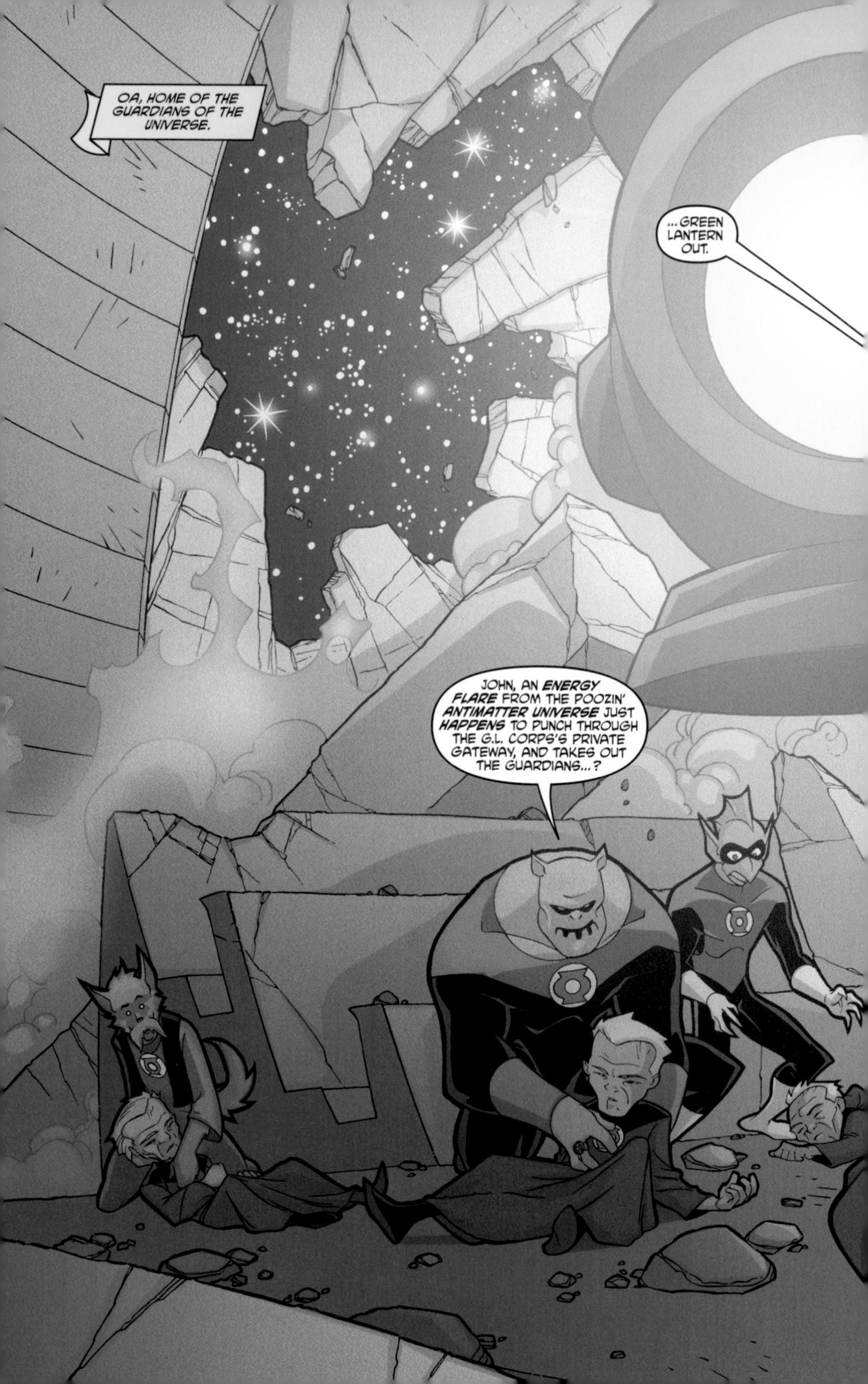
OA, HOME OF THE GUARDIANS OF THE UNIVERSE.
...GREEN LANTERN OUT.
JOHN, AN ENERGY FLARE FROM THE POOZIN' ANTIMATTER UNIVERSE JUST HAPPENS TO PUNCH THROUGH THE G.L. CORPS'S PRIVATE GATEWAY, AND TAKES OUT THE GUARDIANS...?

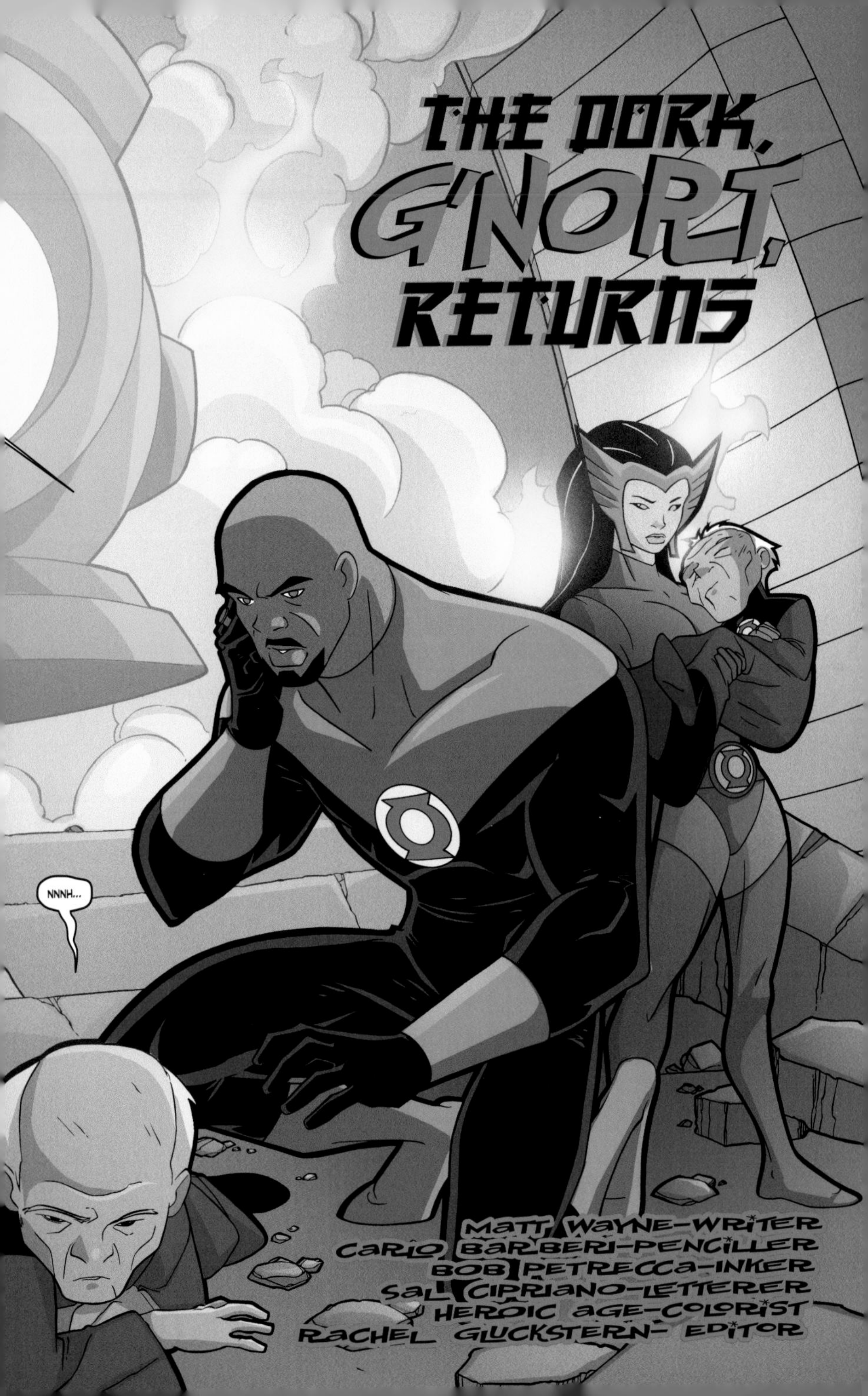
THE DORK, G'NORT, RETURNS
NNNH...
MATT WAYNE-WRITER
CARLO BARBERI-PENCILLER
BOB PETRECCA-INKER
SAL CIPRIANO-LETTERER
HEROIC AGE-COLORIST
RACHEL GLUCKSTERN- EDITOR

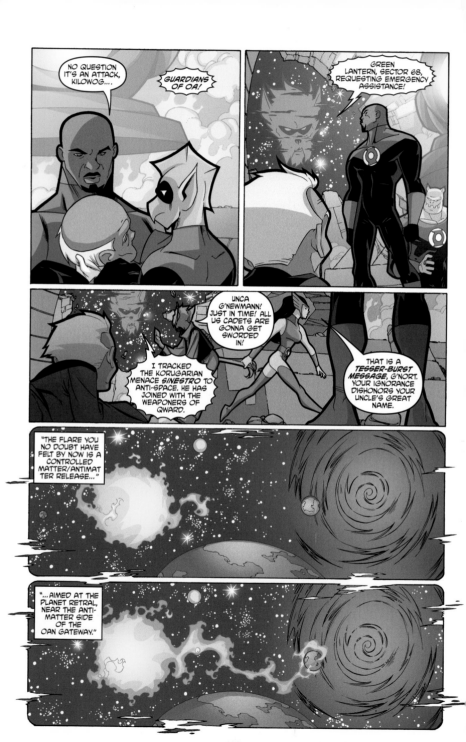

NO QUESTION IT'S AN ATTACK, KILOWOG....

GUARDIANS OF OA!

GREEN LANTERN, SECTOR 68, REQUESTING EMERGENCY ASSISTANCE!

UNCA G'NEWMANN! JUST IN TIME! ALL US CADETS ARE GONNA GET SWORDED IN!

I TRACKED THE KORUGARIAN MENACE *SINESTRO* TO ANTI-SPACE. HE HAS JOINED WITH THE WEAPONERS OF QWARD.

THAT IS A *TESSER-BURST MESSAGE*, G'NORT. YOUR IGNORANCE DISHONORS YOUR UNCLE'S GREAT NAME.

"THE FLARE YOU NO DOUBT HAVE FELT BY NOW IS A CONTROLLED MATTER/ANTIMATTER RELEASE..."

"...AIMED AT THE PLANET RETRAL, NEAR THE ANTI-MATTER SIDE OF THE OAN GATEWAY."

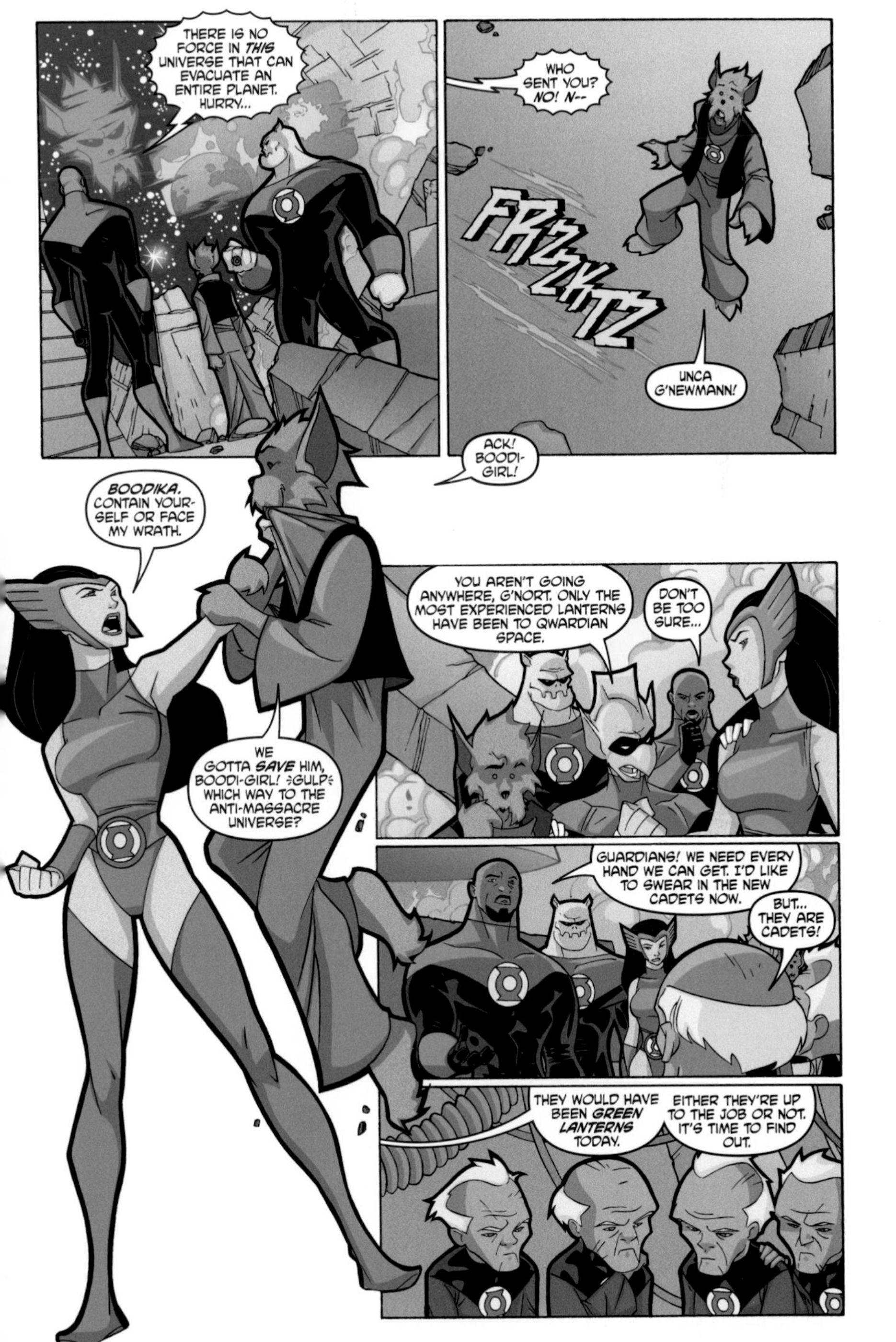
THERE IS NO FORCE IN *THIS* UNIVERSE THAT CAN EVACUATE AN ENTIRE PLANET. HURRY...
WHO SENT YOU? *NO! N--*
FRZZKTZ
UNCA G'NEWMANN!
ACK! BOODI-GIRL!
BOODIKA. CONTAIN YOURSELF OR FACE MY WRATH.
WE GOTTA *SAVE* HIM, BOODI-GIRL! *GULP* WHICH WAY TO THE ANTI-MASSACRE UNIVERSE?
YOU AREN'T GOING ANYWHERE, G'NORT. ONLY THE MOST EXPERIENCED LANTERNS HAVE BEEN TO QWARDIAN SPACE.
DON'T BE TOO SURE...
GUARDIANS! WE NEED EVERY HAND WE CAN GET. I'D LIKE TO SWEAR IN THE NEW CADETS NOW.
BUT... THEY ARE CADETS!
THEY WOULD HAVE BEEN *GREEN LANTERNS* TODAY.
EITHER THEY'RE UP TO THE JOB OR NOT. IT'S TIME TO FIND OUT.

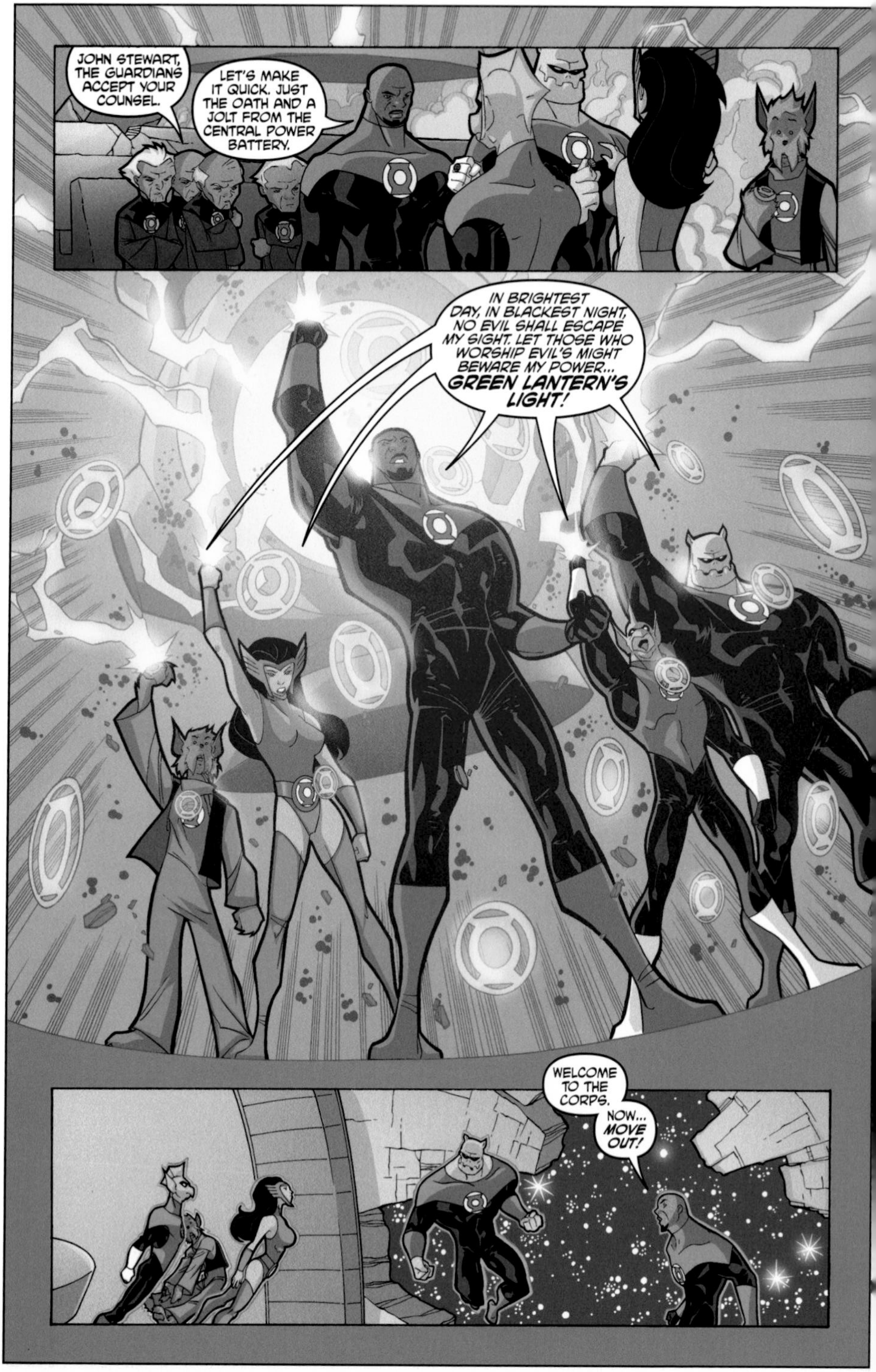
JOHN STEWART, THE GUARDIANS ACCEPT YOUR COUNSEL.
LET'S MAKE IT QUICK. JUST THE OATH AND A JOLT FROM THE CENTRAL POWER BATTERY.
IN BRIGHTEST DAY, IN BLACKEST NIGHT, NO EVIL SHALL ESCAPE MY SIGHT. LET THOSE WHO WORSHIP EVIL'S MIGHT BEWARE MY POWER... GREEN LANTERN'S LIGHT!
WELCOME TO THE CORPS.
NOW... MOVE OUT!

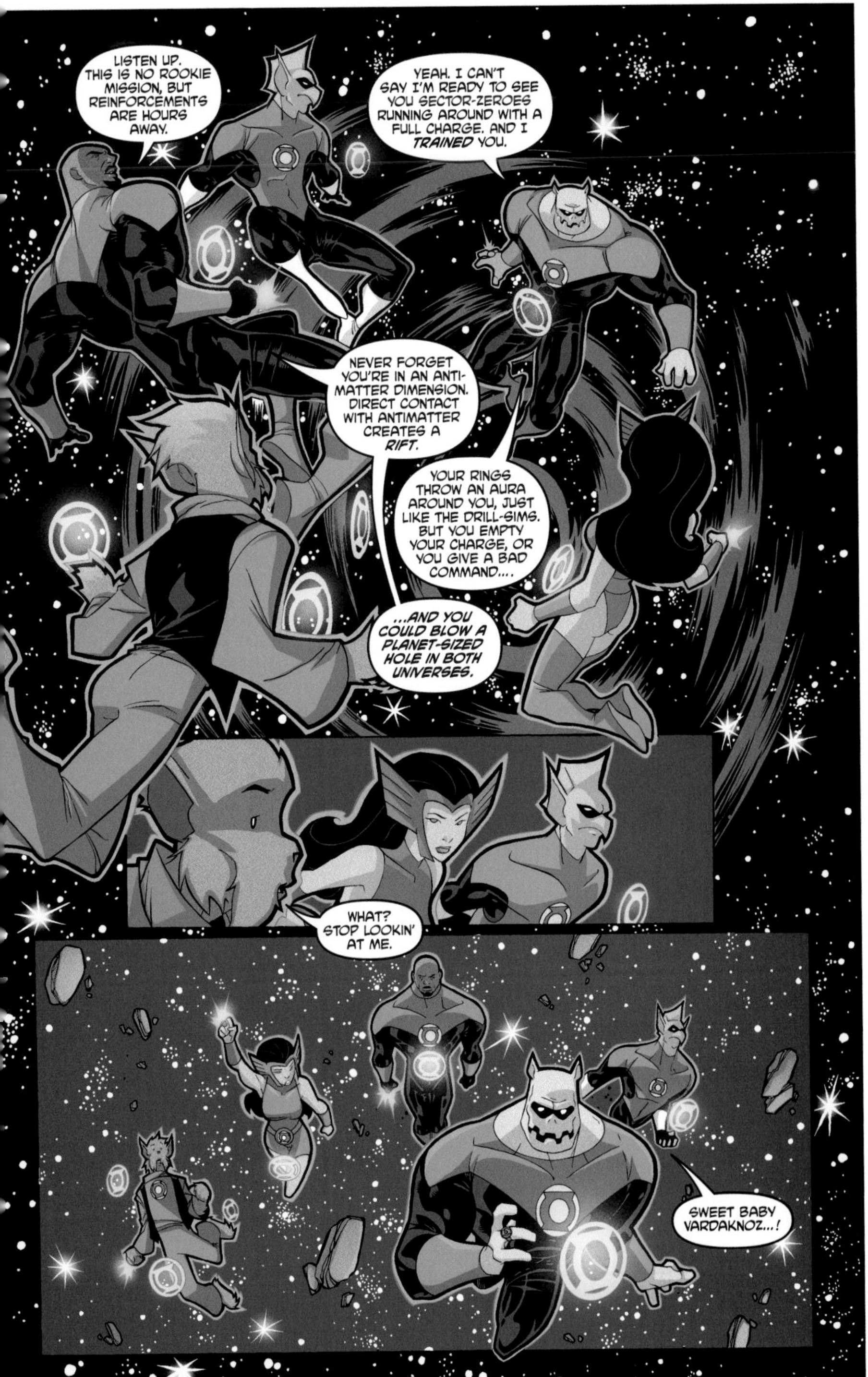
LISTEN UP. THIS IS NO ROOKIE MISSION, BUT REINFORCEMENTS ARE HOURS AWAY.
YEAH. I CAN'T SAY I'M READY TO SEE YOU SECTOR-ZEROES RUNNING AROUND WITH A FULL CHARGE. AND I *TRAINED* YOU.
NEVER FORGET YOU'RE IN AN ANTI-MATTER DIMENSION. DIRECT CONTACT WITH ANTIMATTER CREATES A *RIFT*.
YOUR RINGS THROW AN AURA AROUND YOU, JUST LIKE THE DRILL-SIMS. BUT YOU EMPTY YOUR CHARGE, OR YOU GIVE A BAD COMMAND....
...AND YOU COULD BLOW A PLANET-SIZED HOLE IN BOTH UNIVERSES.
WHAT? STOP LOOKIN' AT ME.
SWEET BABY VARDAKNOZ...!

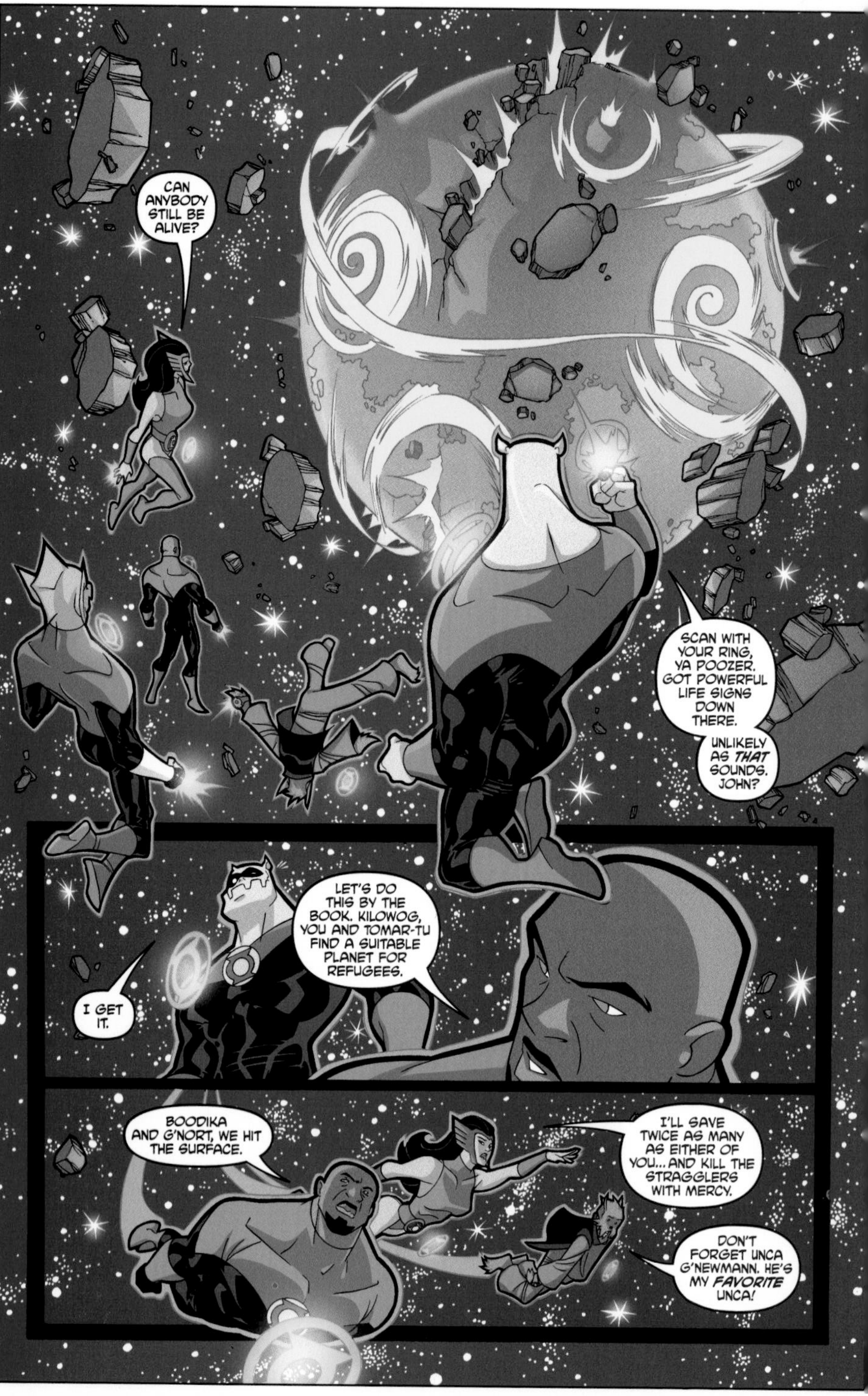
CAN ANYBODY STILL BE ALIVE?
SCAN WITH YOUR RING, YA POOZER. GOT POWERFUL LIFE SIGNS DOWN THERE.
UNLIKELY AS *THAT* SOUNDS, JOHN?
LET'S DO THIS BY THE BOOK. KILOWOG, YOU AND TOMAR-TU FIND A SUITABLE PLANET FOR REFUGEES.
I GET IT.
BOODIKA AND G'NORT, WE HIT THE SURFACE.
I'LL SAVE TWICE AS MANY AS EITHER OF YOU... AND KILL THE STRAGGLERS WITH MERCY.
DON'T FORGET UNCA G'NEWMANN. HE'S MY *FAVORITE* UNCA!

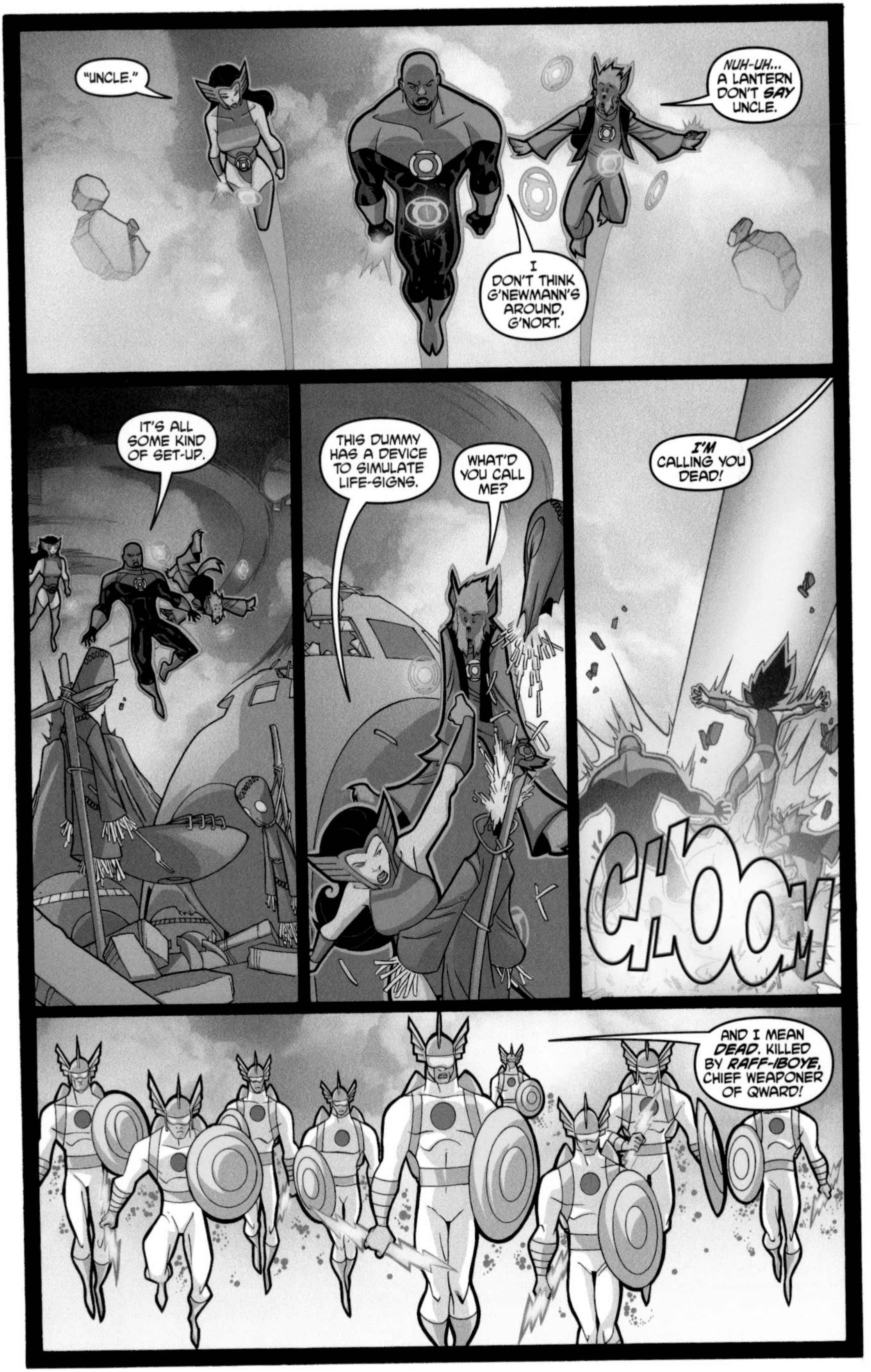
"UNCLE."
NUH-UH... A LANTERN DON'T SAY UNCLE.
I DON'T THINK G'NEWMANN'S AROUND, G'NORT.
IT'S ALL SOME KIND OF SET-UP.
THIS DUMMY HAS A DEVICE TO SIMULATE LIFE-SIGNS.
WHAT'D YOU CALL ME?
I'M CALLING YOU DEAD!
CHOOM
AND I MEAN DEAD. KILLED BY RAFF-IBOYE, CHIEF WEAPONER OF QWARD!

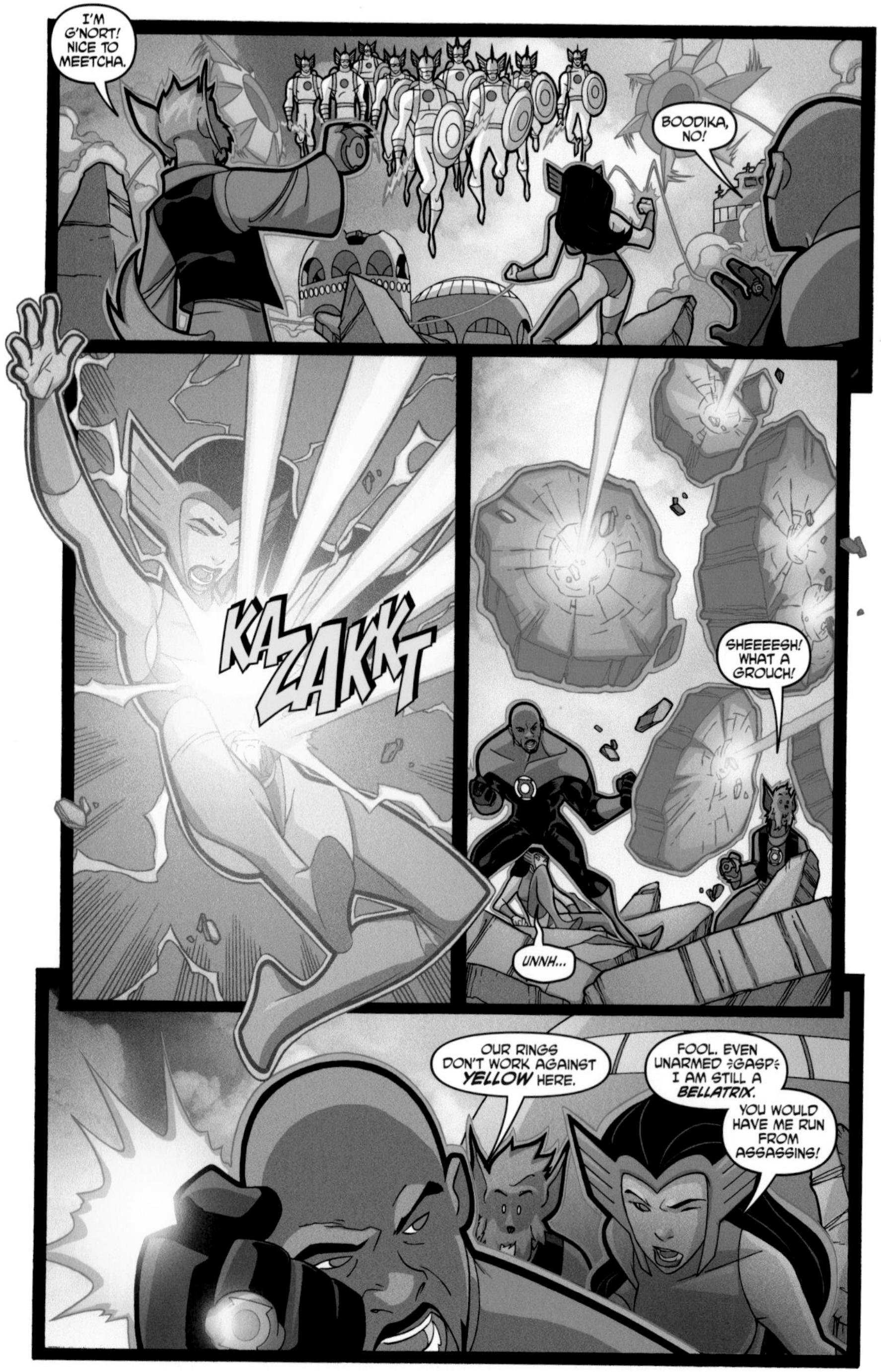
I'M G'NORT! NICE TO MEETCHA.
BOODIKA, NO!
KAZAKKT
SHEEEESH! WHAT A GROUCH!
UNNH...
OUR RINGS DON'T WORK AGAINST YELLOW HERE.
FOOL. EVEN UNARMED ÷GASP÷ I AM STILL A BELLATRIX.
YOU WOULD HAVE ME RUN FROM ASSASSINS!

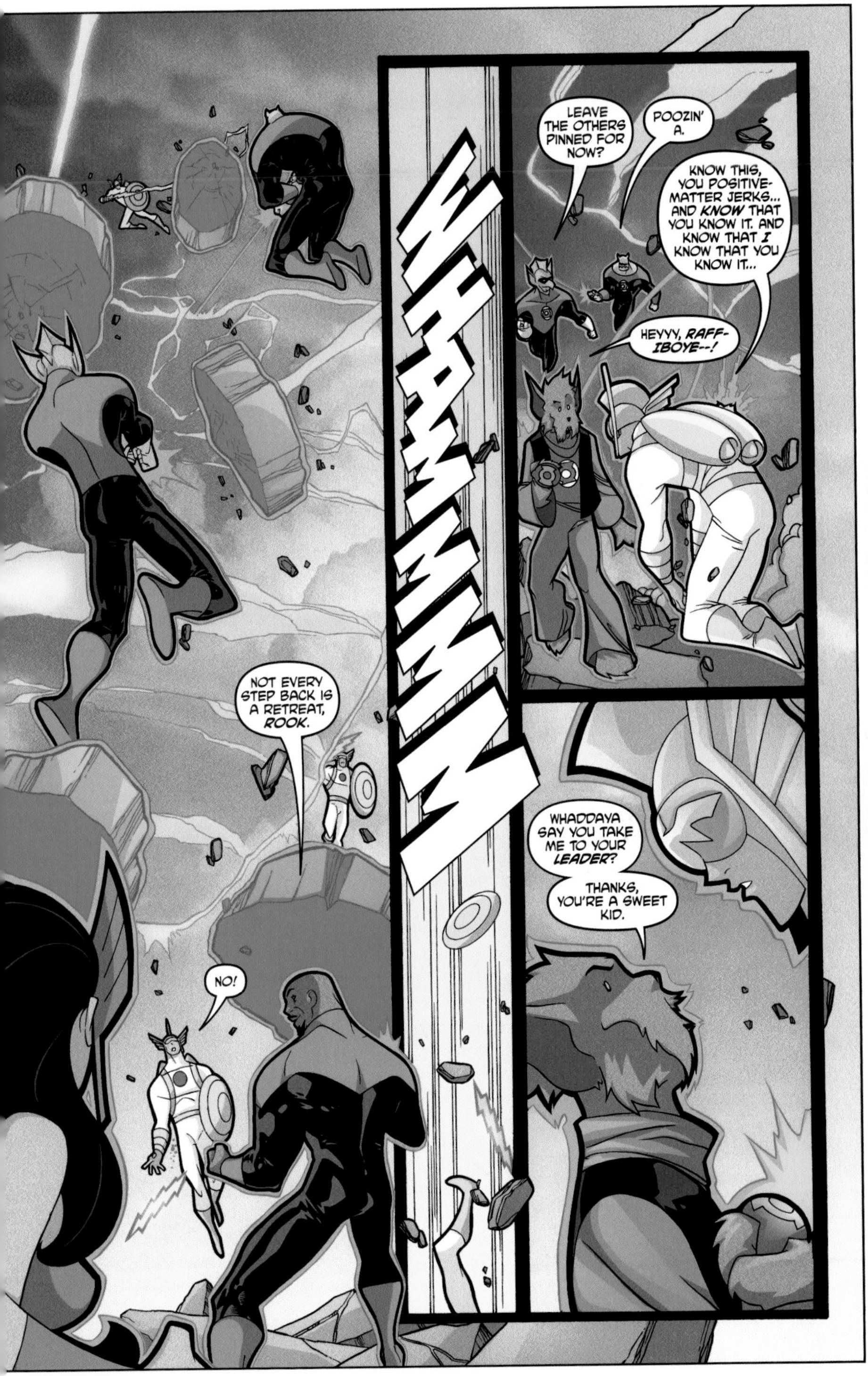
NOT EVERY STEP BACK IS A RETREAT, *ROOK*.
NO!
WHAMMMMMM
LEAVE THE OTHERS PINNED FOR NOW?
POOZIN' A.
KNOW THIS, YOU POSITIVE-MATTER JERKS... AND *KNOW* THAT YOU KNOW IT. AND KNOW THAT *I* KNOW THAT YOU KNOW IT...
HEYYY, *RAFF-IBOYE*--!
WHADDAYA SAY YOU TAKE ME TO YOUR *LEADER*?
THANKS, YOU'RE A SWEET KID.

THE TEMPLE OF THE HIGHLORD, ORBITING THE PLANET QWARD.

ONE'S NEVER APPRECIATED IN ONE'S OWN UNIVERSE, EH, G'NEWMANN?

IS THERE ENOUGH FOOD? WATER? HOW'S THE CHEW TOY?

WHY DON'T *YOU* CHEW IT?

⸮TSK⸮ YOUR RING IS ALL BUT DISCHARGED. OA'S LEFT UNGUARDED. ONCE MY SECOND ENERGY FLARE STRIKES THE *CENTRAL POWER BATTERY...*

"...I'LL BE ABLE TO CAREFULLY *IMPLODE* THE POSITIVE-MATTER UNIVERSE INTO THIS ANTI-MATTER SPACE...

"...DESTROYING THE GREEN LANTERN CORPS, AND THE UNIVERSE THAT DOES *NOT* BOW TO ME!"

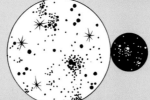

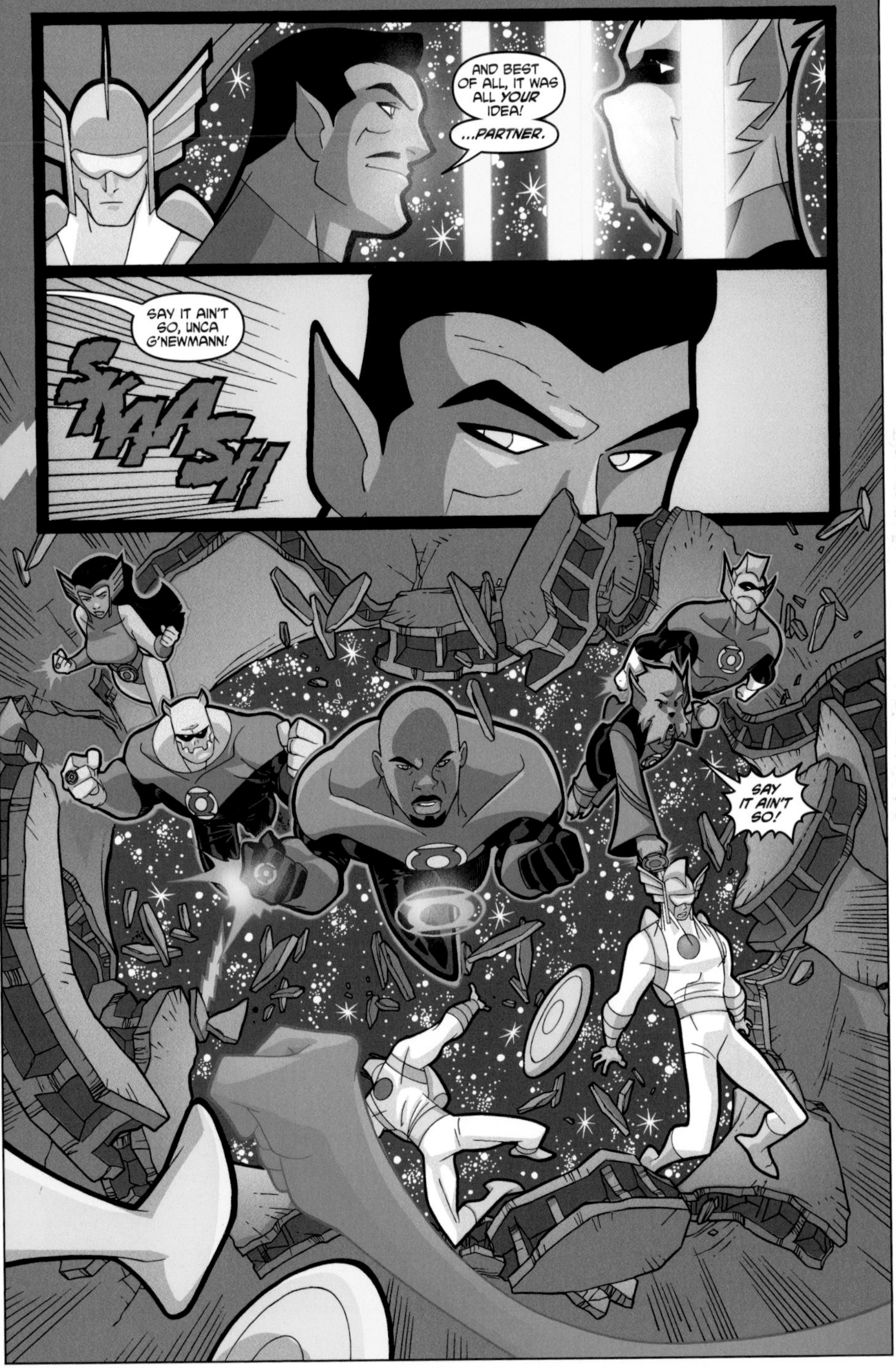
AND BEST OF ALL, IT WAS ALL YOUR IDEA!
...PARTNER.
SAY IT AIN'T SO, UNCA G'NEWMANN!
SKAASH
SAY IT AIN'T SO!

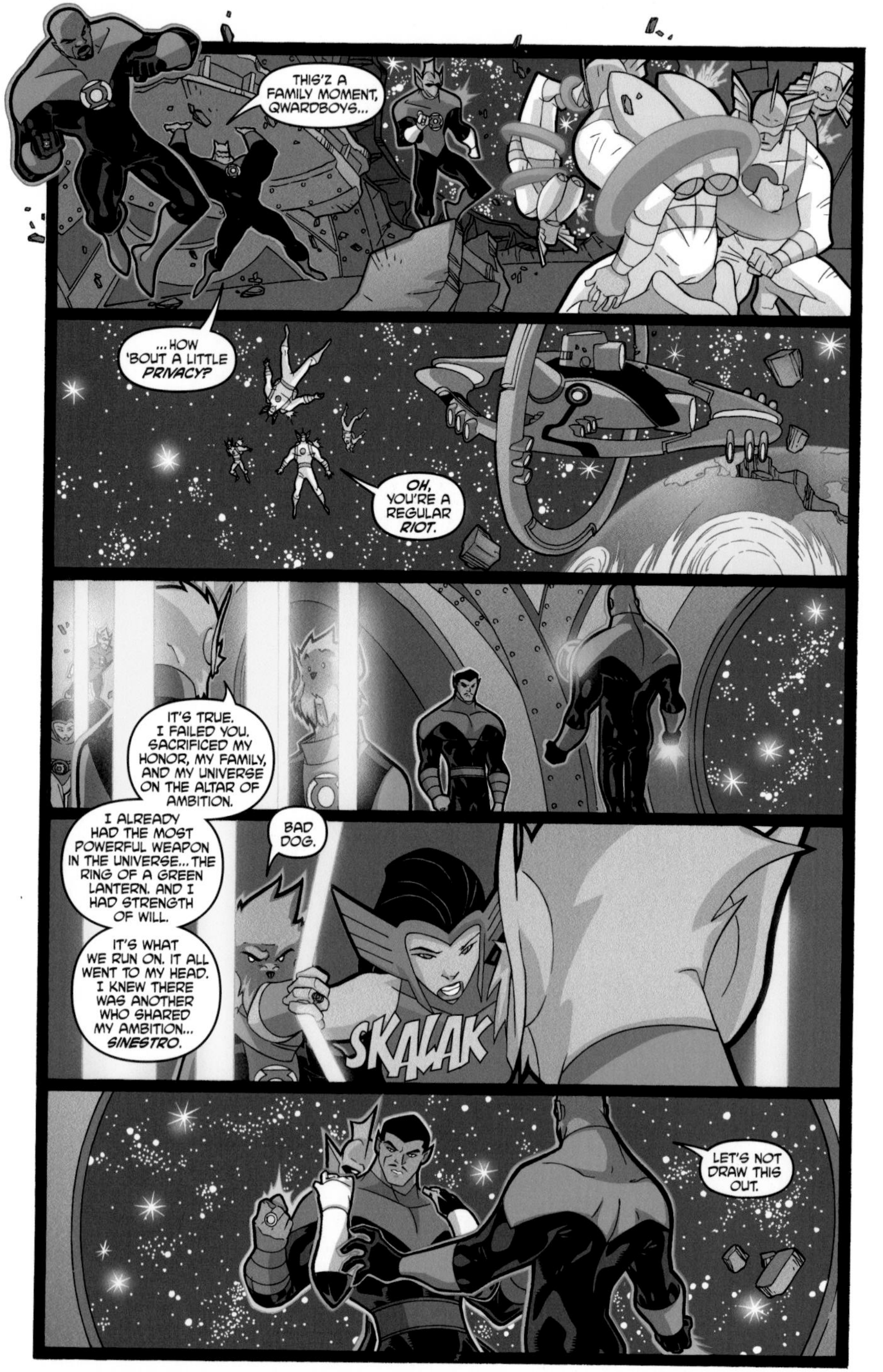
THIS'Z A FAMILY MOMENT, QWARDBOYS...
...HOW 'BOUT A LITTLE PRIVACY?
OH, YOU'RE A REGULAR RIOT.
IT'S TRUE. I FAILED YOU. SACRIFICED MY HONOR, MY FAMILY, AND MY UNIVERSE ON THE ALTAR OF AMBITION.
I ALREADY HAD THE MOST POWERFUL WEAPON IN THE UNIVERSE... THE RING OF A GREEN LANTERN. AND I HAD STRENGTH OF WILL.
BAD DOG.
IT'S WHAT WE RUN ON. IT ALL WENT TO MY HEAD. I KNEW THERE WAS ANOTHER WHO SHARED MY AMBITION... SINESTRO.
SKALAK
LET'S NOT DRAW THIS OUT.

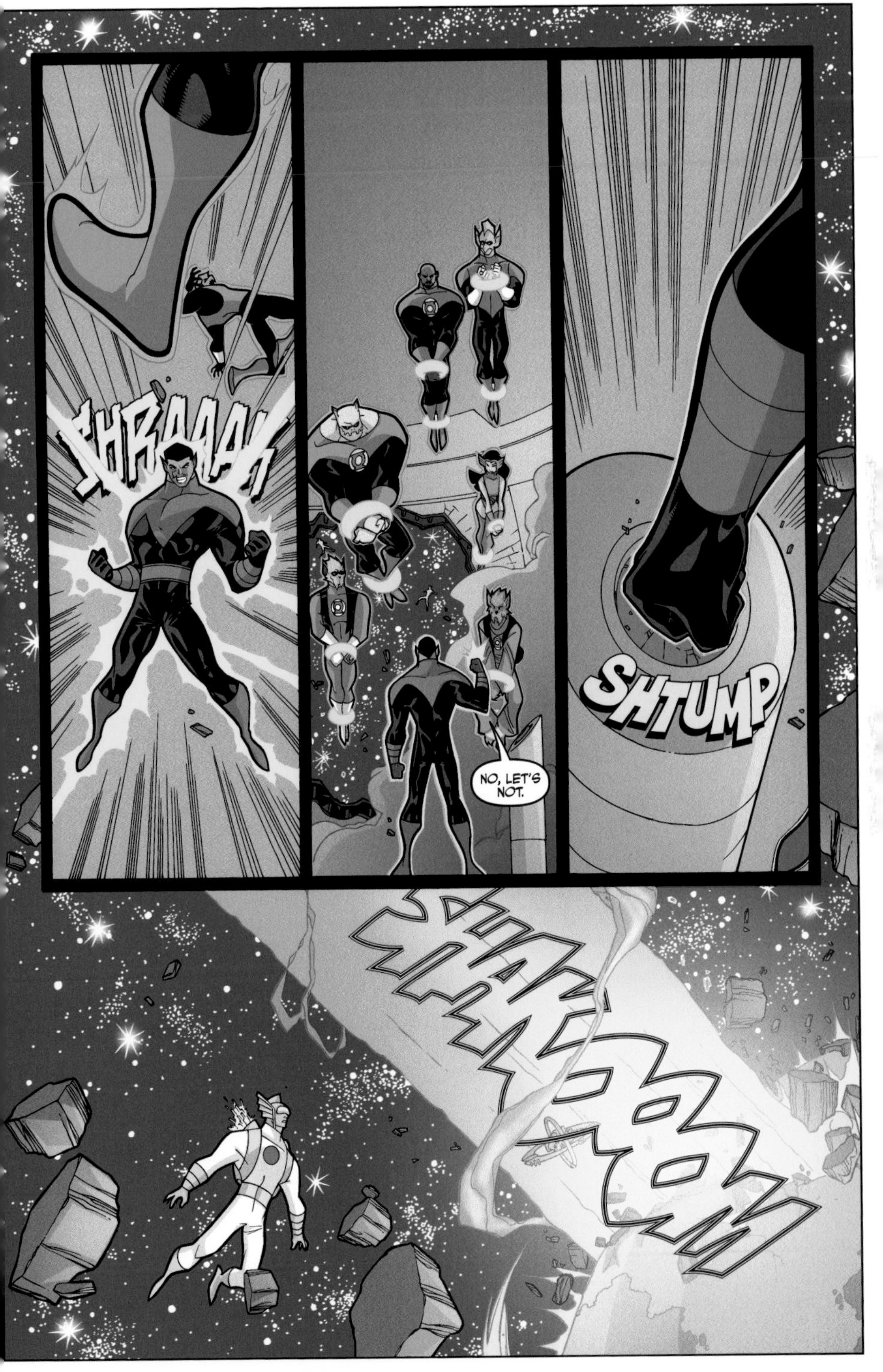
SHRAAAK
NO, LET'S NOT.
SHTUMP

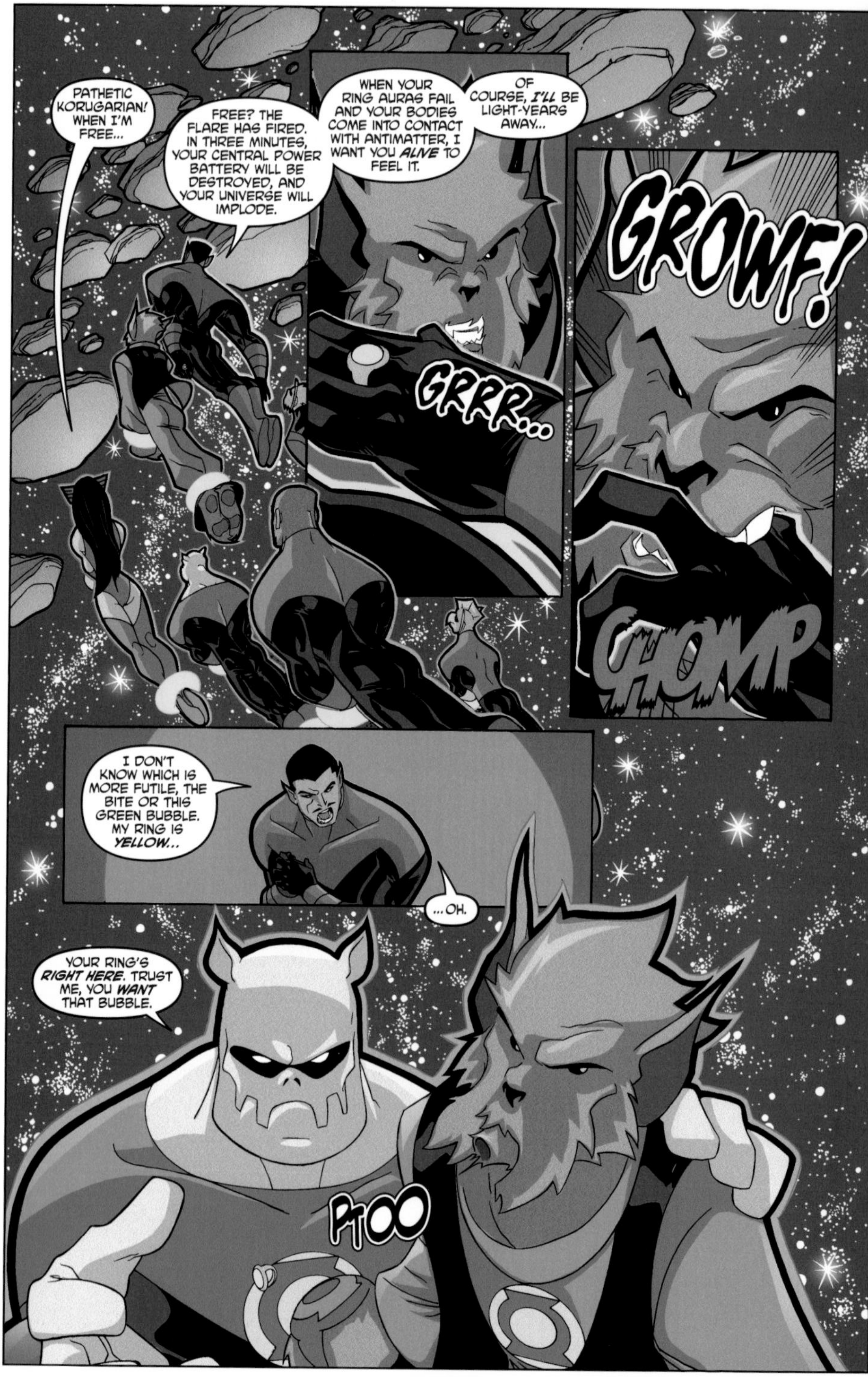
PATHETIC KORUGARIAN! WHEN I'M FREE...
FREE? THE FLARE HAS FIRED. IN THREE MINUTES, YOUR CENTRAL POWER BATTERY WILL BE DESTROYED, AND YOUR UNIVERSE WILL IMPLODE.
WHEN YOUR RING AURAS FAIL AND YOUR BODIES COME INTO CONTACT WITH ANTIMATTER, I WANT YOU *ALIVE* TO FEEL IT.
OF COURSE, *I'LL* BE LIGHT-YEARS AWAY...
GRRR...
GROWF!
CHOMP
I DON'T KNOW WHICH IS MORE FUTILE, THE BITE OR THIS GREEN BUBBLE. MY RING IS *YELLOW...*
...OH.
YOUR RING'S *RIGHT HERE*. TRUST ME, YOU *WANT* THAT BUBBLE.
PTOO

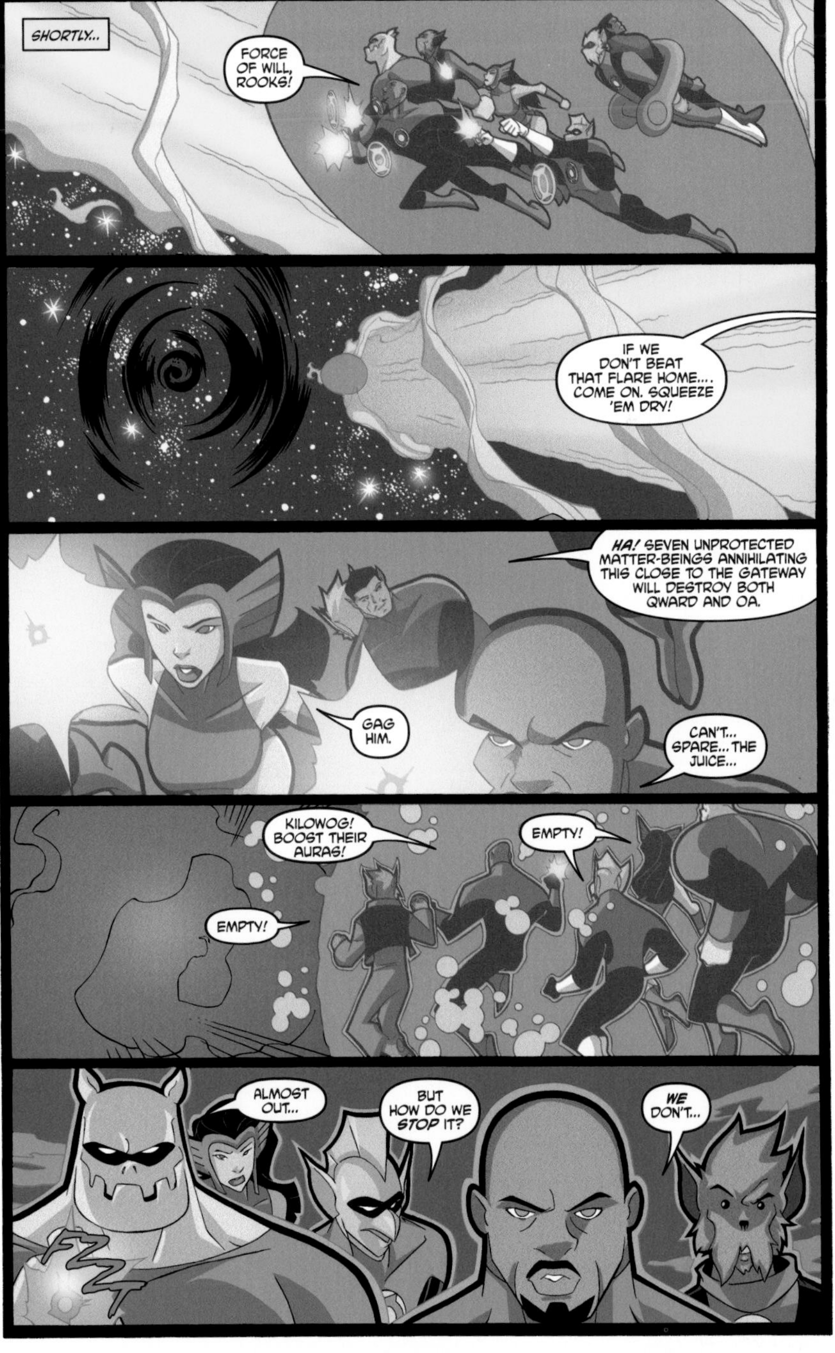
SHORTLY...
FORCE OF WILL, ROOKS!
IF WE DON'T BEAT THAT FLARE HOME.... COME ON. SQUEEZE 'EM DRY!
HA! SEVEN UNPROTECTED MATTER-BEINGS ANNIHILATING THIS CLOSE TO THE GATEWAY WILL DESTROY BOTH QWARD AND OA.
GAG HIM.
CAN'T... SPARE... THE JUICE...
KILOWOG! BOOST THEIR AURAS!
EMPTY!
EMPTY!
ALMOST OUT...
BUT HOW DO WE STOP IT?
WE DON'T...
FZZT

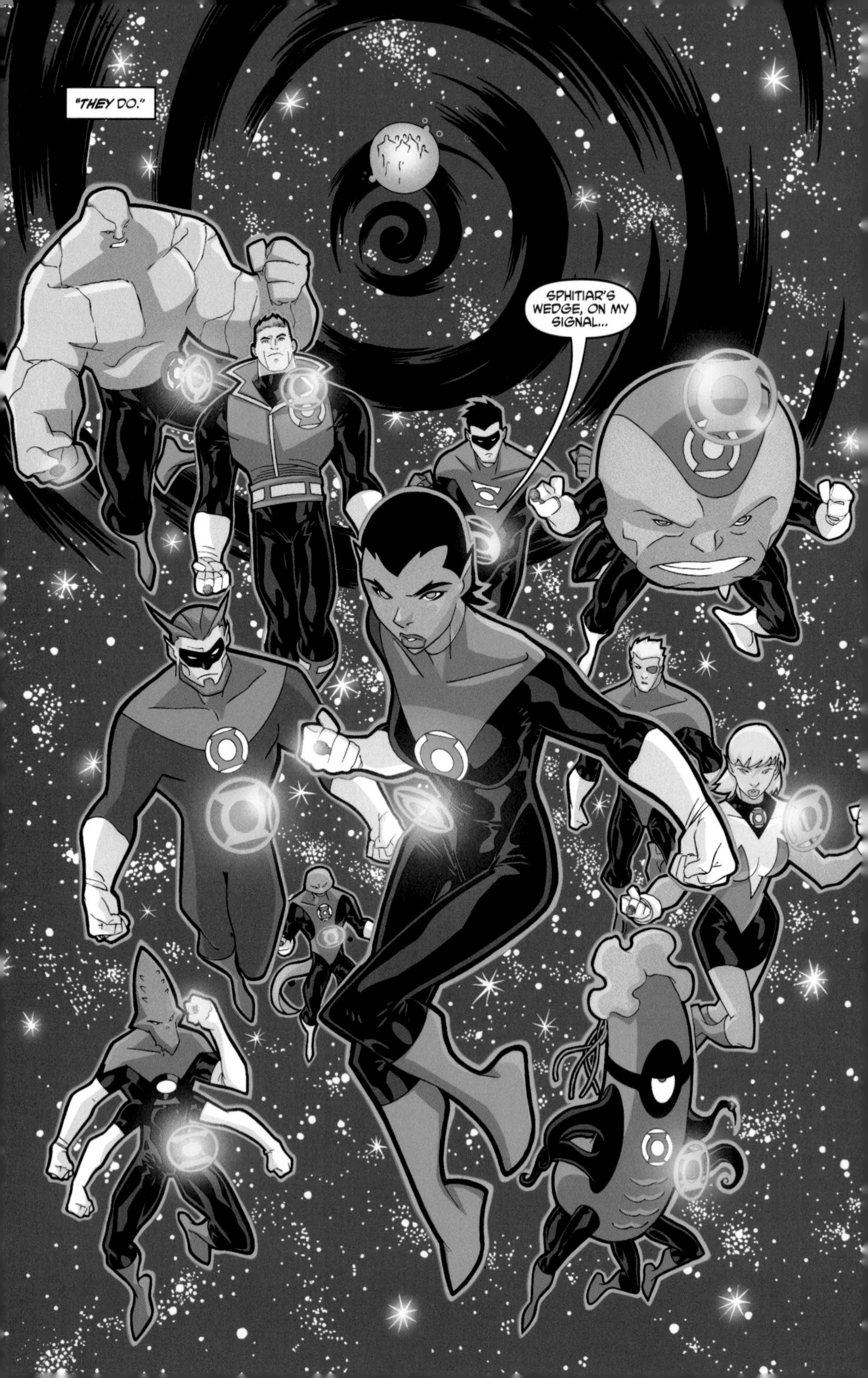
"THEY DO."
SPHITIAR'S WEDGE, ON MY SIGNAL...

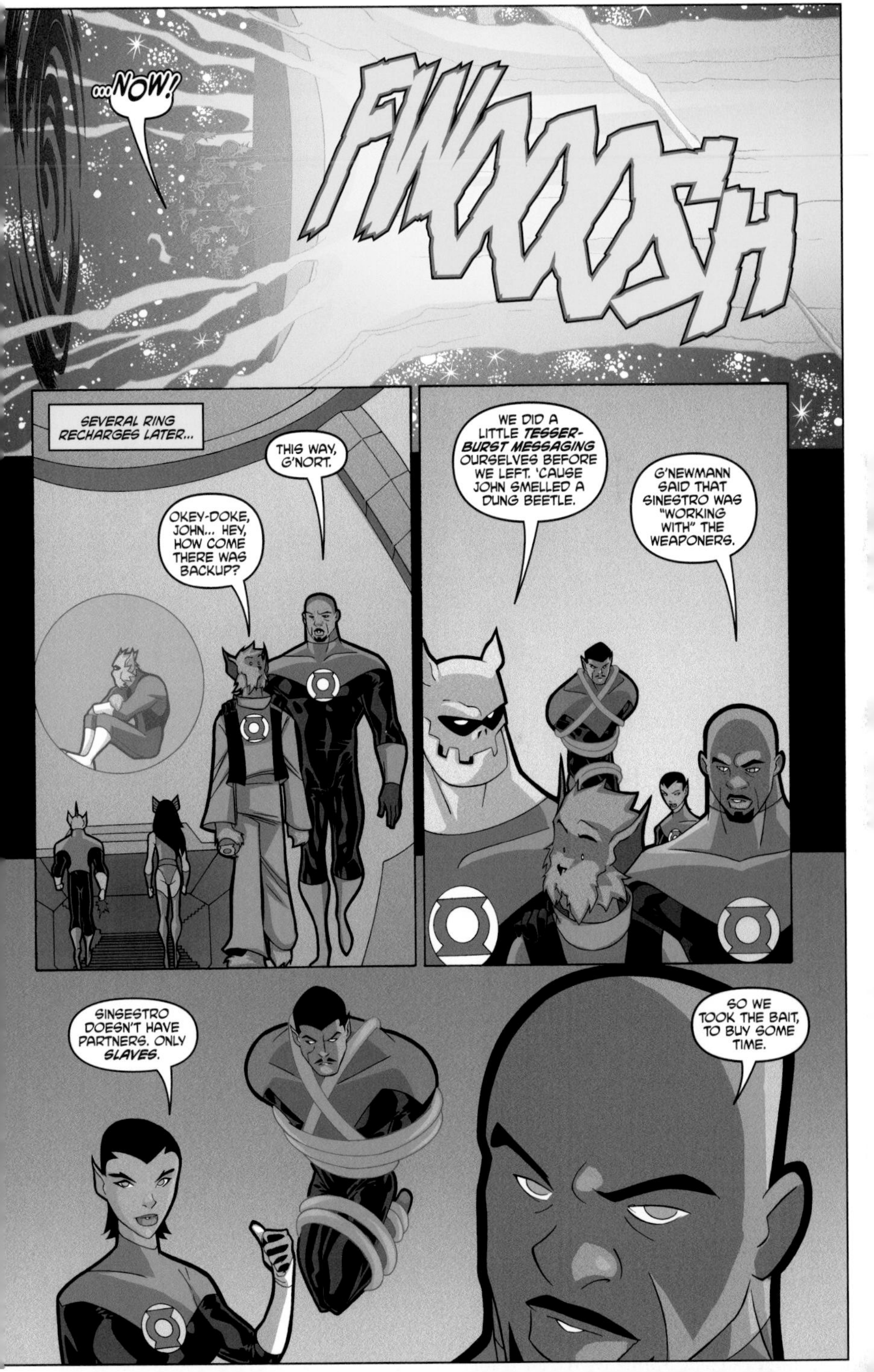
...NOW!
FWOOOSH
SEVERAL RING RECHARGES LATER...
THIS WAY, G'NORT.
OKEY-DOKE, JOHN... HEY, HOW COME THERE WAS BACKUP?
WE DID A LITTLE TESSER-BURST MESSAGING OURSELVES BEFORE WE LEFT. 'CAUSE JOHN SMELLED A DUNG BEETLE.
G'NEWMANN SAID THAT SINESTRO WAS "WORKING WITH" THE WEAPONERS.
SINSESTRO DOESN'T HAVE PARTNERS. ONLY SLAVES.
SO WE TOOK THE BAIT, TO BUY SOME TIME.

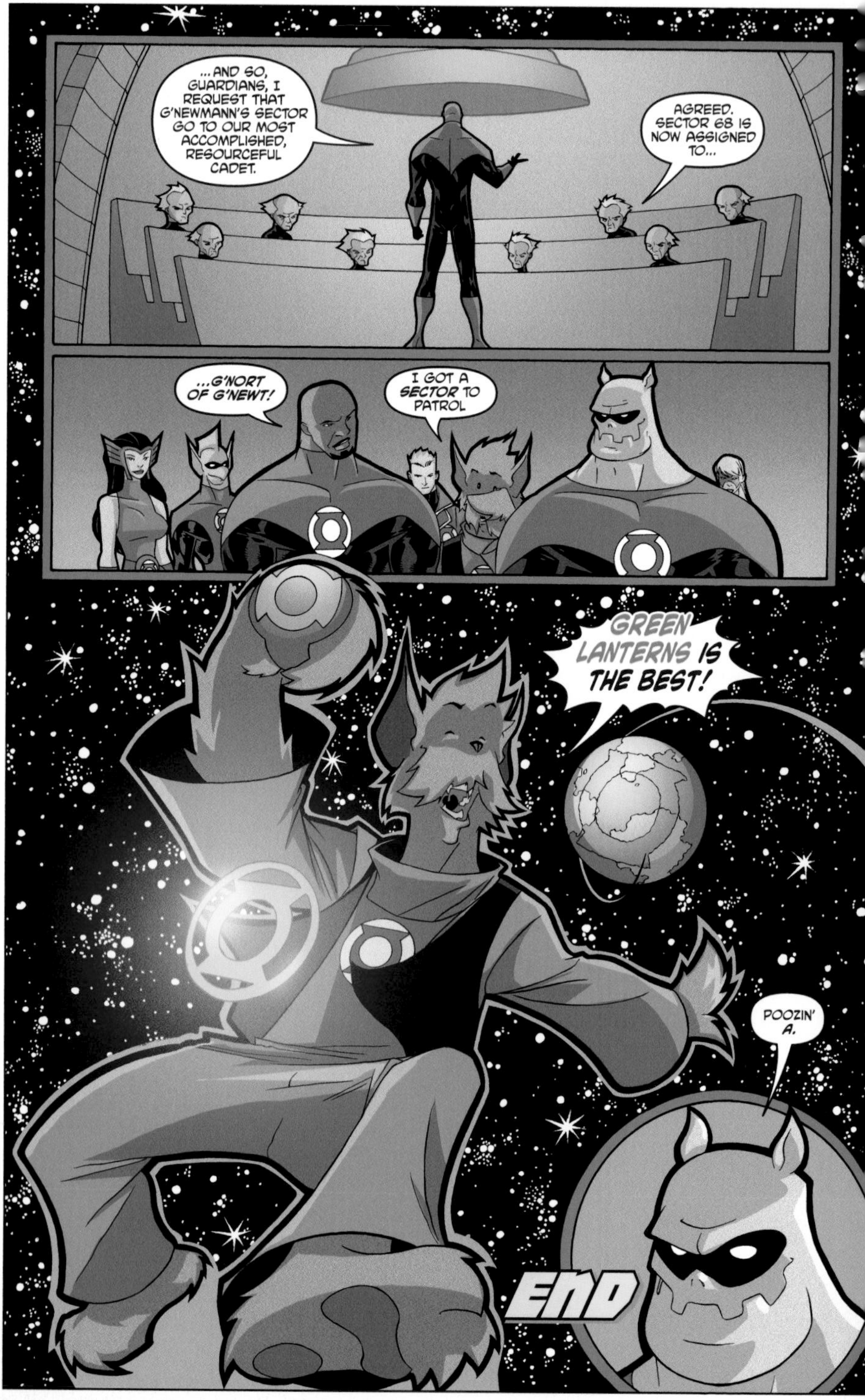
...AND SO, GUARDIANS, I REQUEST THAT G'NEWMANN'S SECTOR GO TO OUR MOST ACCOMPLISHED, RESOURCEFUL CADET.
AGREED. SECTOR 68 IS NOW ASSIGNED TO...
...G'NORT OF G'NEWT!
I GOT A SECTOR TO PATROL
GREEN LANTERNS IS THE BEST!
POOZIN' A.
END

CHAPTER 1

Dear Superman

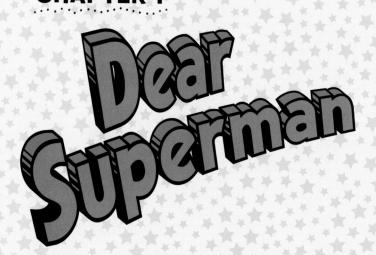

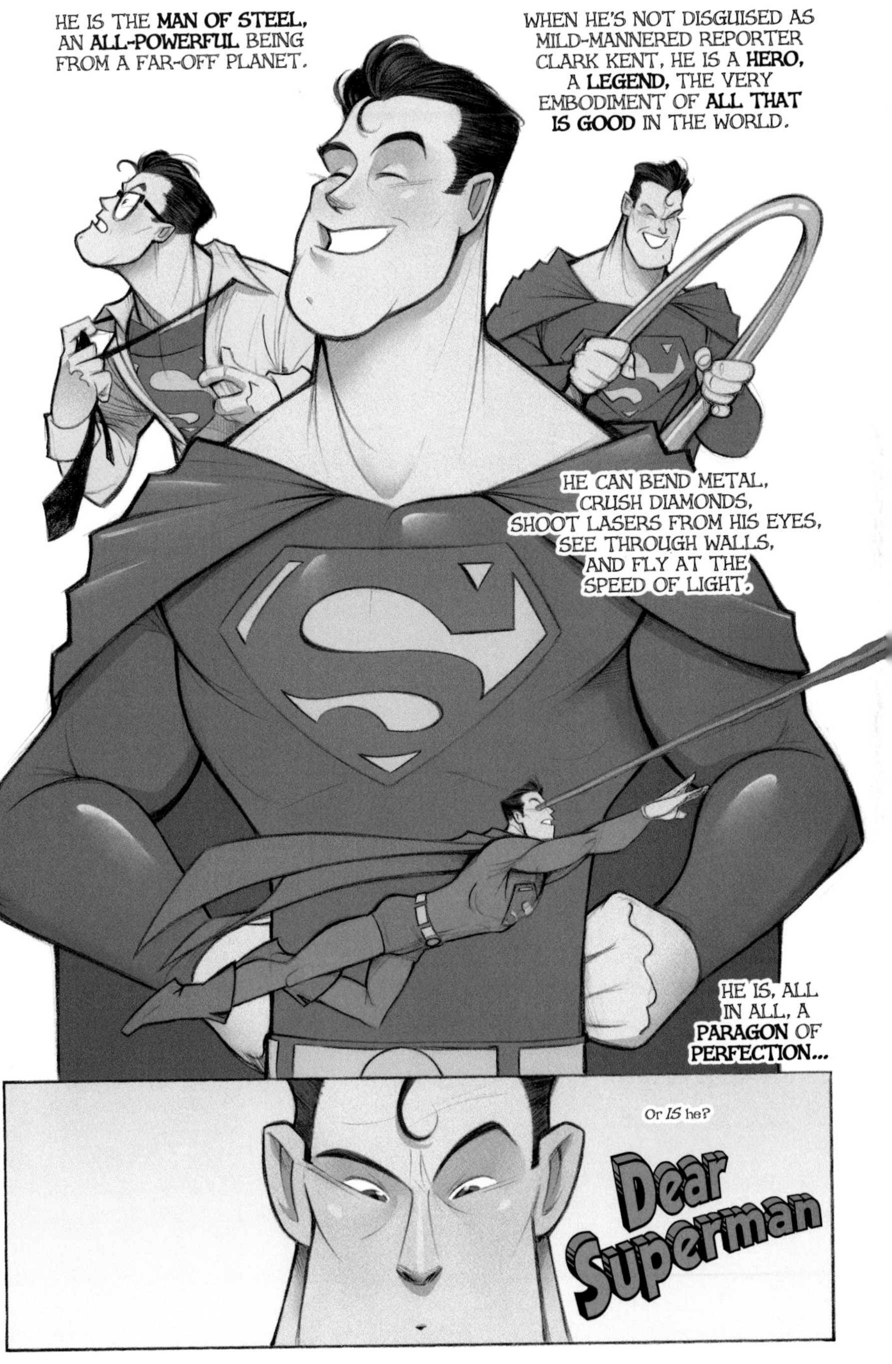
HE IS THE MAN OF STEEL, AN ALL-POWERFUL BEING FROM A FAR-OFF PLANET.
WHEN HE'S NOT DISGUISED AS MILD-MANNERED REPORTER CLARK KENT, HE IS A HERO, A LEGEND, THE VERY EMBODIMENT OF ALL THAT IS GOOD IN THE WORLD.
HE CAN BEND METAL, CRUSH DIAMONDS, SHOOT LASERS FROM HIS EYES, SEE THROUGH WALLS, AND FLY AT THE SPEED OF LIGHT.
HE IS, ALL IN ALL, A PARAGON OF PERFECTION...
Or IS he?
Dear Superman

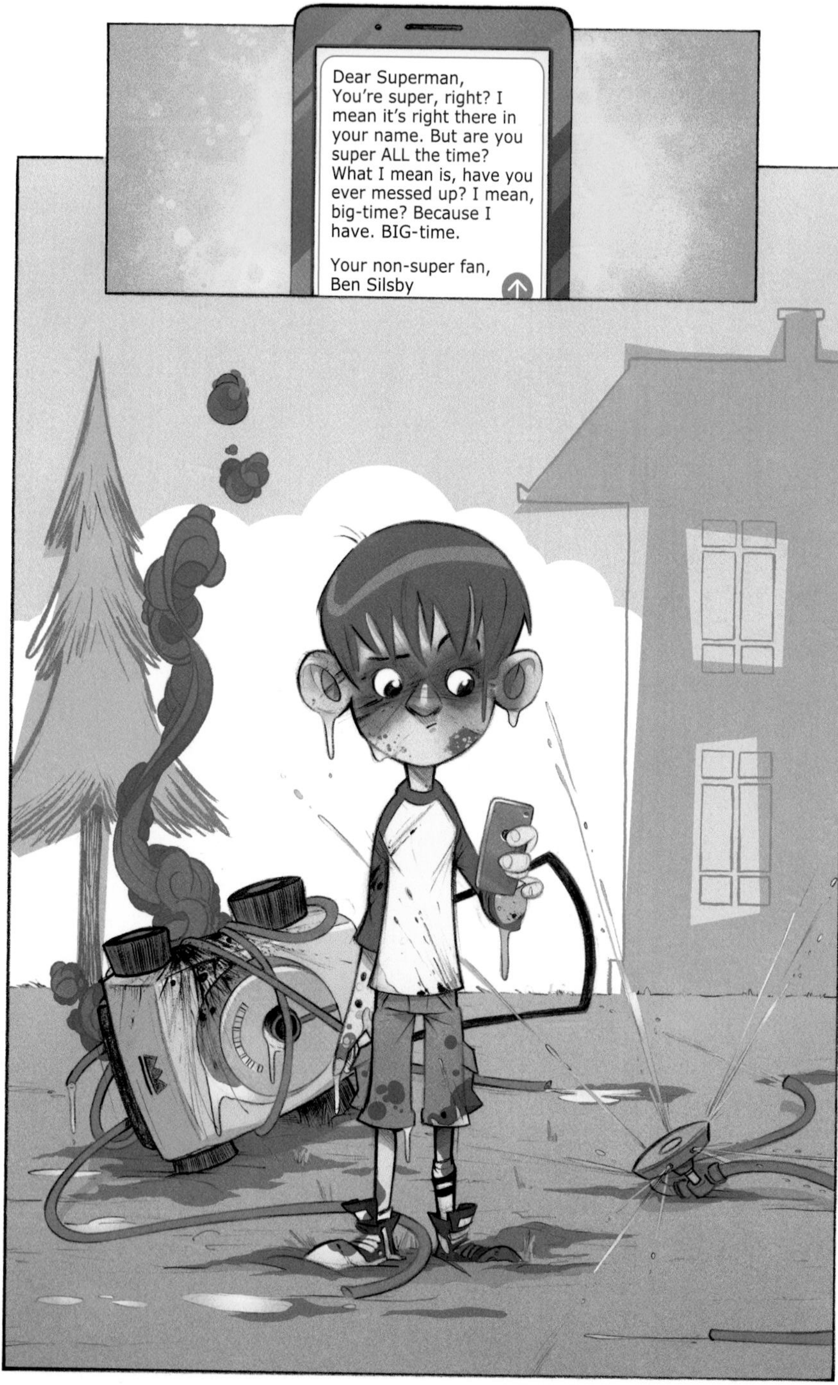
Dear Superman,
You're super, right? I mean it's right there in your name. But are you super ALL the time? What I mean is, have you ever messed up? I mean, big-time? Because I have. BIG-time.
Your non-super fan,
Ben Silsby

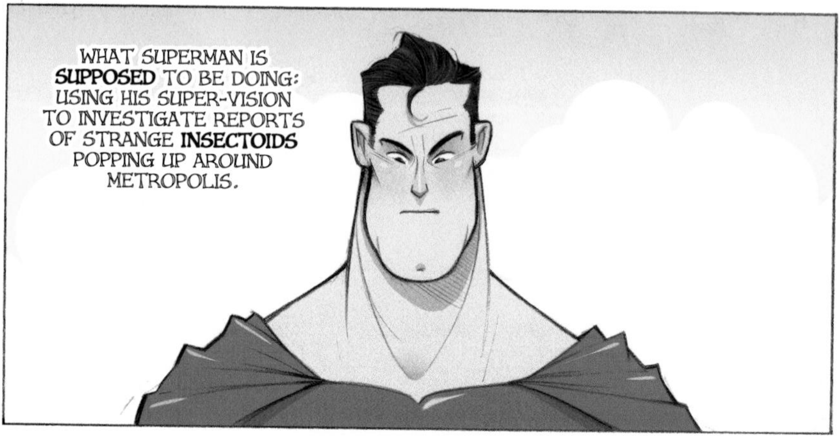
WHAT SUPERMAN IS **SUPPOSED** TO BE DOING: USING HIS SUPER-VISION TO INVESTIGATE REPORTS OF STRANGE **INSECTOIDS** POPPING UP AROUND METROPOLIS.

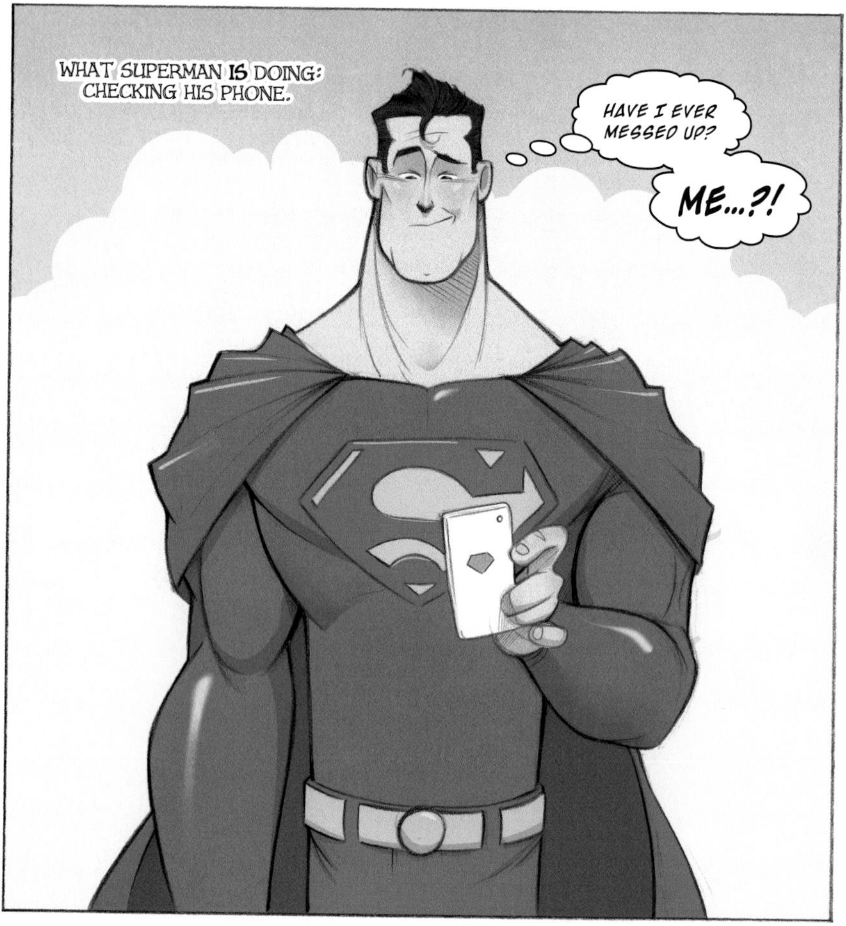
WHAT SUPERMAN **IS** DOING: CHECKING HIS PHONE.
HAVE I EVER MESSED UP?
ME...?!

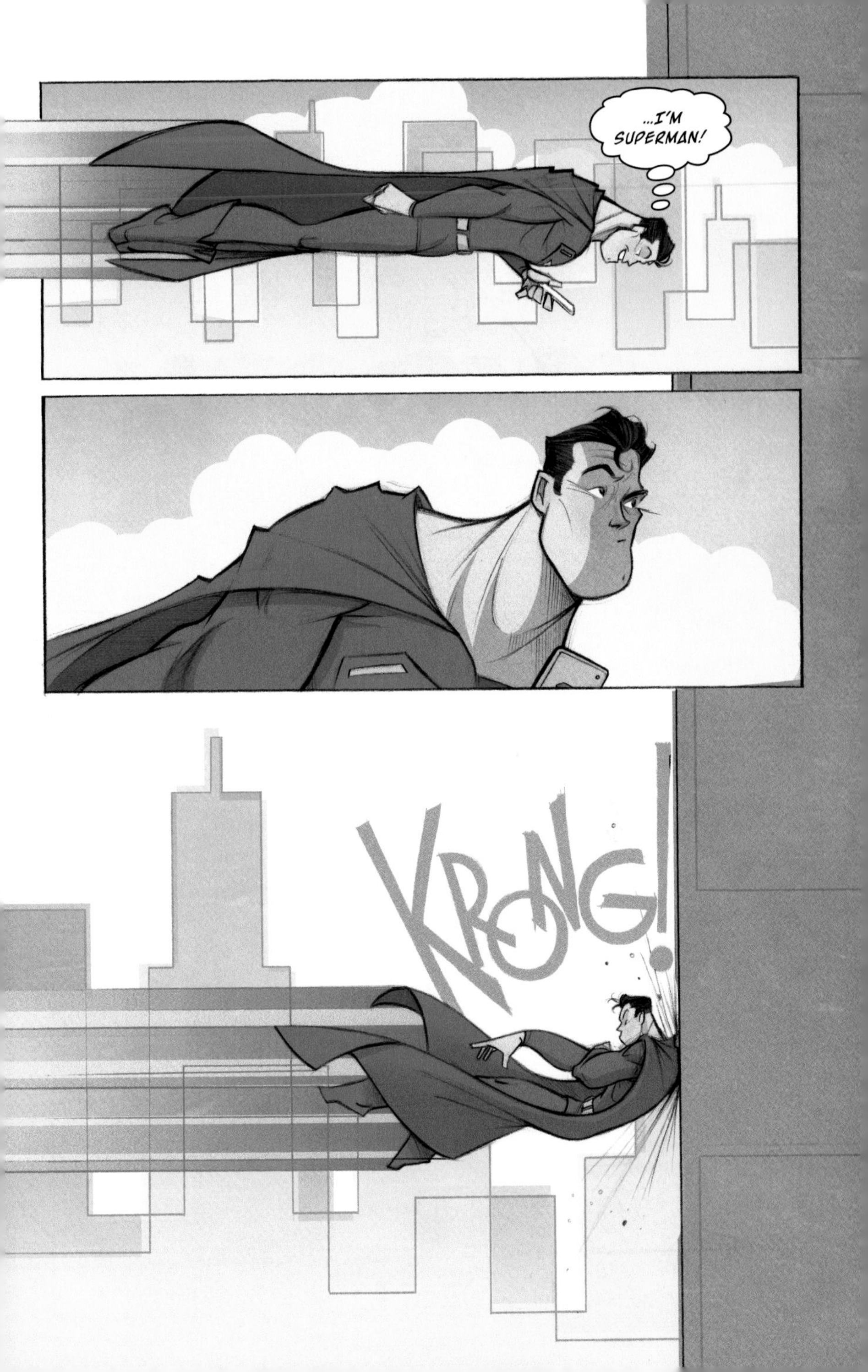
...I'M SUPERMAN!
KRONG!

SHOULD'VE BEEN LOOKING WHERE I WAS GOING— I'M SUPPOSED TO LEAP OVER THESE THINGS!
YEEK!
SPLIK!
GAH!
HELP ME!
GREAT SCOTT!
X-RAY VISION!
WHOOOOOOSH

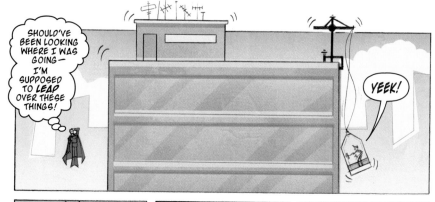

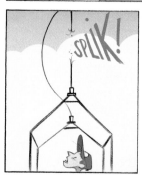

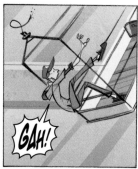

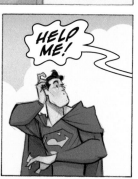

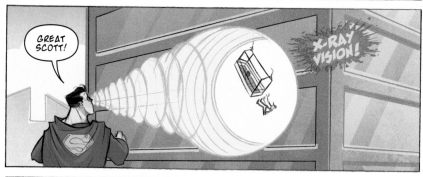

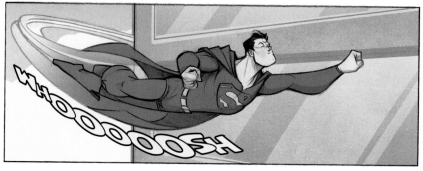

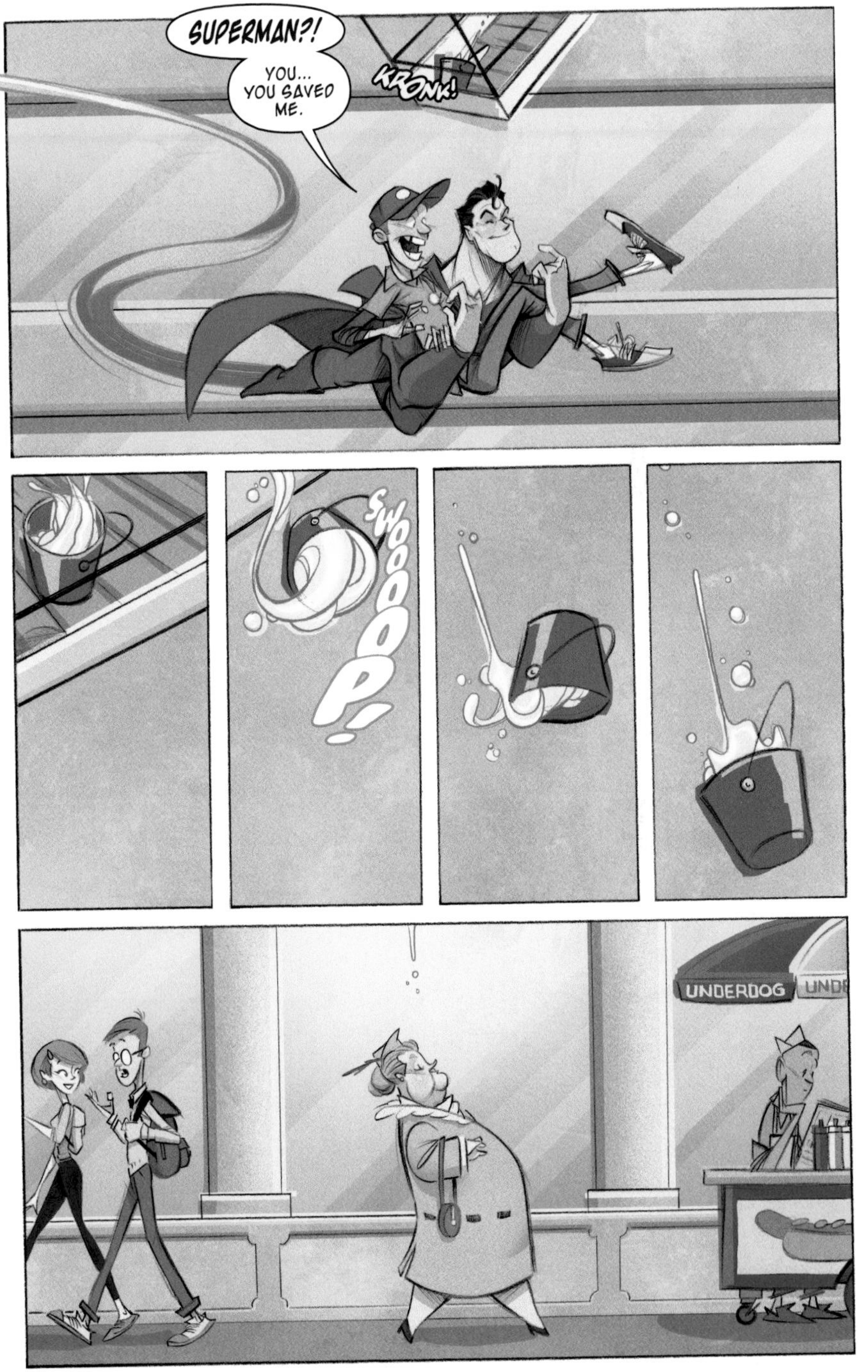
SUPERMAN?!
YOU... YOU SAVED ME.
KRONK!
SWOOOOOP!
UNDERDOG
UNDE

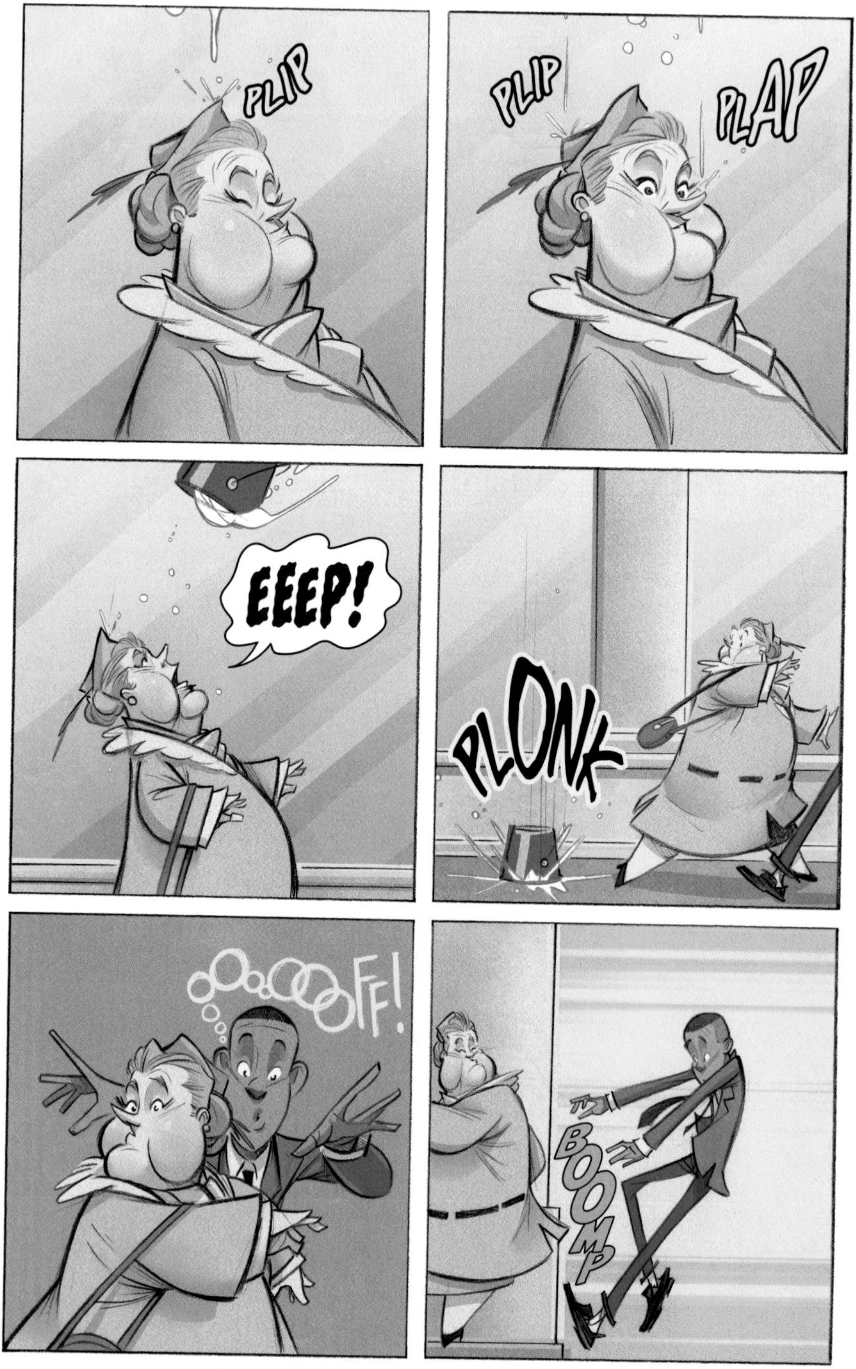
PLIP
PLIP
PLAP
EEEP!
PLONK
OOOOOOOFF!
BOOMP

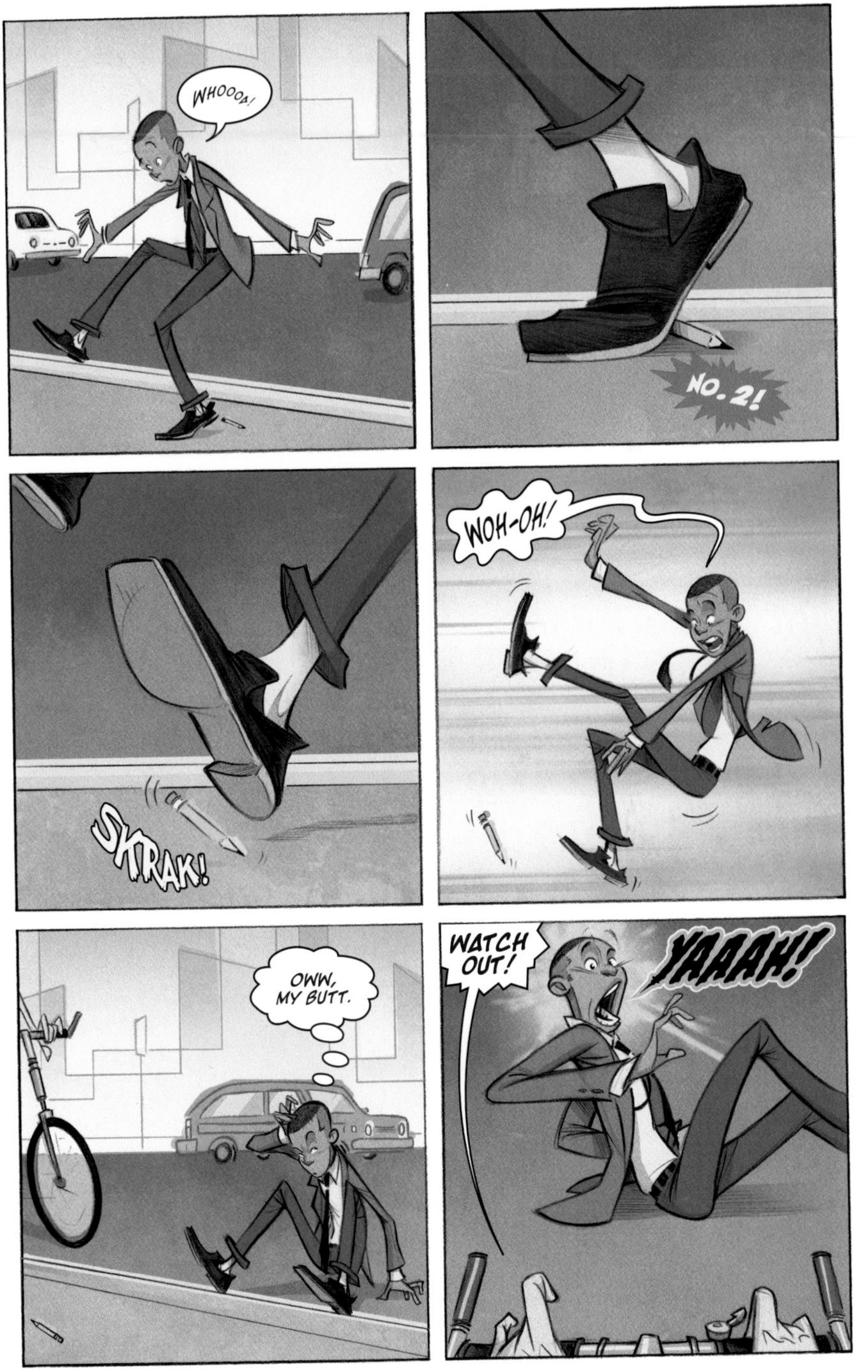
WHOOOA!
NO. 2!
SKRAK!
WOH-OH!
OWW, MY BUTT.
WATCH OUT!
YAAAH!

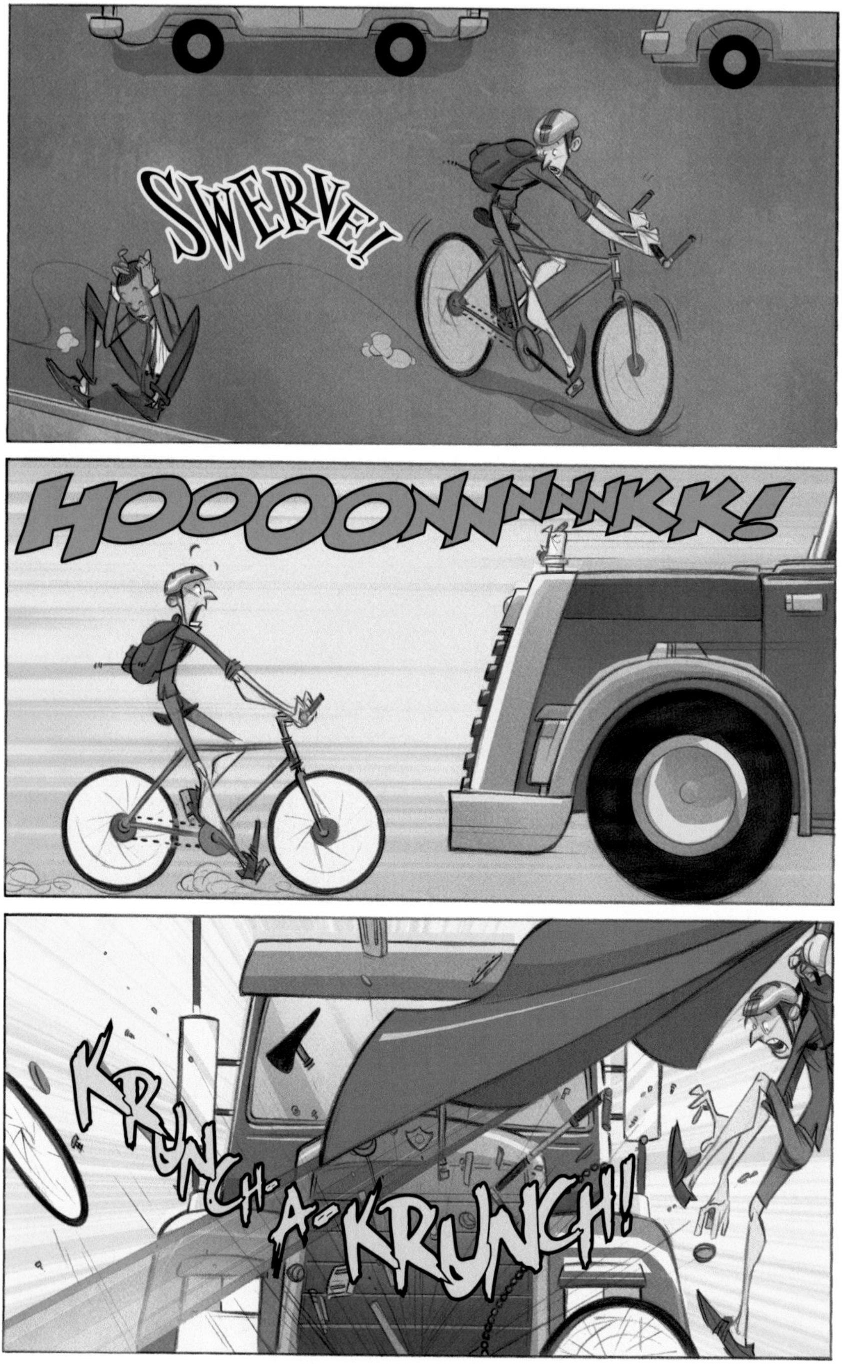
SWERVE!
HOOOONNNNKK!
KRUNCH-A-KRUNCH!

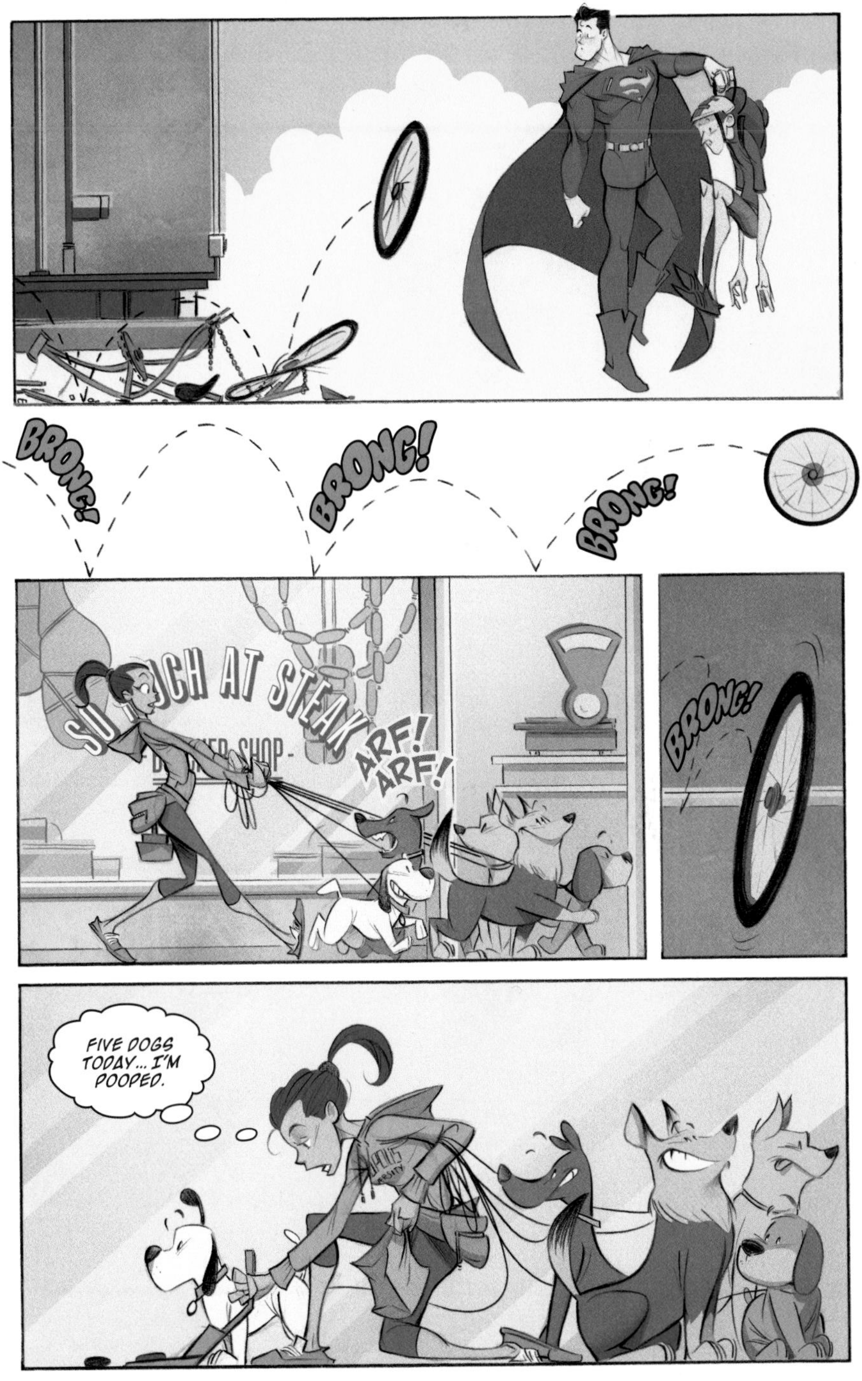
BRONG!
BRONG!
BRONG!
ARF! ARF!
BRONG!
FIVE DOGS TODAY... I'M POOPED.

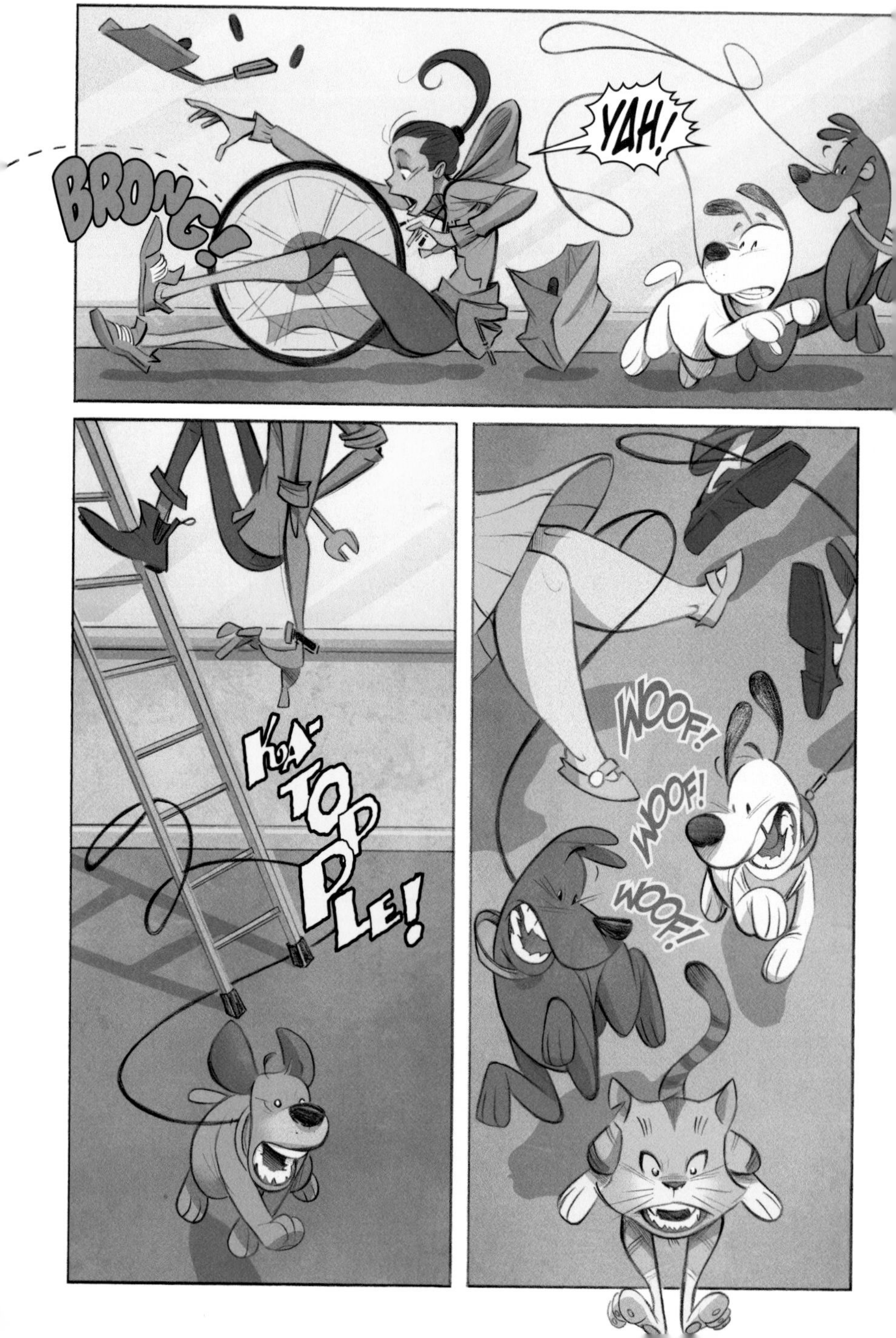
BRONG!
YAH!
KA-TOPPLE!
WOOF!
WOOF!
WOOF!

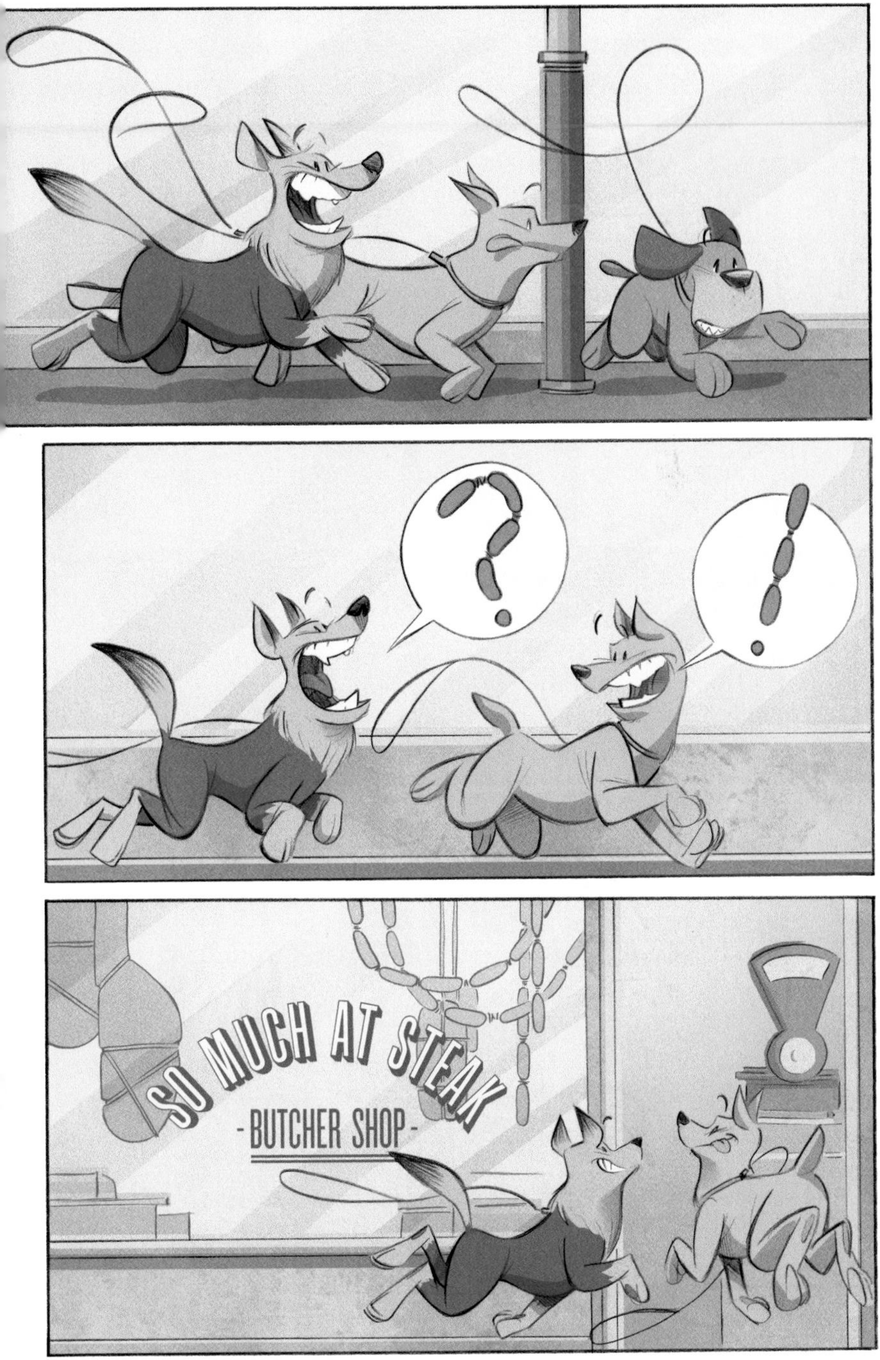
?
!
SO MUCH AT STEAK
-BUTCHER SHOP-

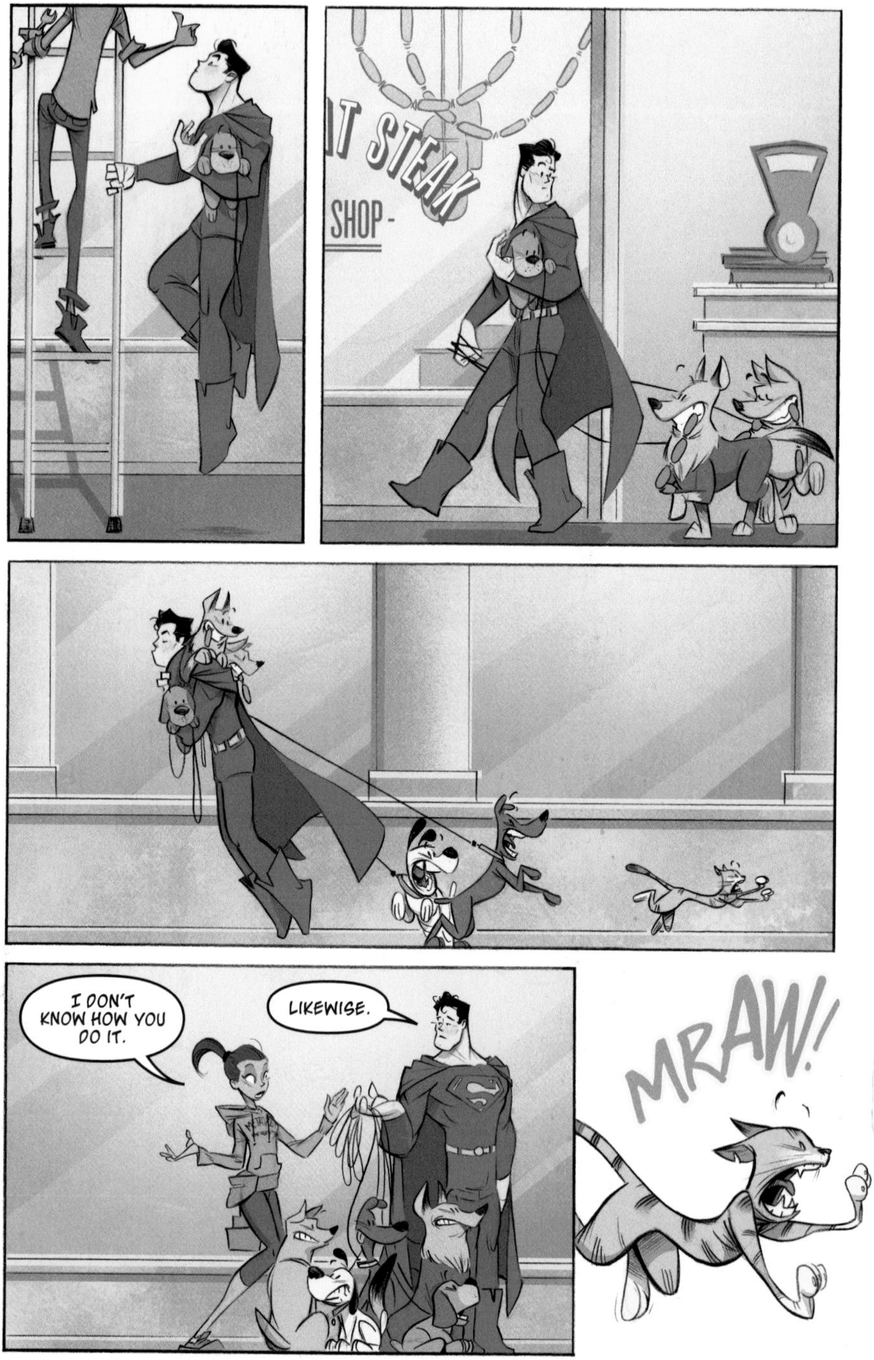
STEAK
SHOP -
I DON'T KNOW HOW YOU DO IT.
LIKEWISE.
MRAW!